# Common Cause

# Common Cause

A Novel of the War in America

SAMUEL HOPKINS ADAMS

*Annotated and with an introduction by*
John Maxwell Hamilton *and* Amy Solomon Whitehead

Potomac Books
*An imprint of the University of Nebraska Press*

Library of Congress Cataloging-in-Publication Data
Names: Adams, Samuel Hopkins, 1871–1958, author. |
Hamilton, John Maxwell, writer of supplementary textual
content, writer of introduction. | Whitehead, Amy
Solomon, writer of supplementary textual content, writer of
introduction.
Title: Common cause: a novel of the war in America / Samuel
Hopkins Adams; annotated and with an introduction by John
Maxwell Hamilton and Amy Solomon Whitehead.
Description: [Lincoln, Nebraska]: Potomac Books, an imprint
of the University of Nebraska Press, [2019] |
Includes bibliographical references.
Identifiers: LCCN 2018053132
ISBN 9781640120020 (paperback: alk. paper)
ISBN 9781640122178 (epub)
ISBN 9781640122185 (mobi)
ISBN 9781640122192 (pdf)
Subjects: LCSH: World War, 1914–1918—United
States—Fiction.
Classification: LCC PS3501.D317 C66 2019 | DDC 813/.52—dc23
LC record available at
https://lccn.loc.gov/2018053132

Set in Bulmer MT by Mikala R. Kolander.

# INTRODUCTION

*"Distinctly a War Story"*

John Maxwell Hamilton and Amy Solomon Whitehead

"HAS THIS CRUEL WAR killed off our book sales entirely?" Samuel Hopkins Adams asked Ferris Greenslet, a director of the Boston publishing house Houghton Mifflin, in an August 1914 letter.[1] Earlier that summer orders for Adams's forthcoming novel, *The Clarion*, had been brisk. There was no reason to think foreign affairs would edge out his tale of a newspaper editor's crusade against patent medicine manufacturers who hoodwinked the public with bogus elixirs. Americans were focused on their country. Progressive writers such as Adams thought in terms of domestic social and political reforms. Europeans themselves were slow to foresee the horrific World War looming even after the assassination of the heir to the Austro-Hungarian throne, Archduke Franz Ferdinand, on a sunny Sunday morning in late June. The first British journalist did not leave London for Vienna until the end of July, a week before Germany marched into Belgium to invade France.

By the time Adams wrote his worried letter to Greenslet, Europe had been transformed into a battleground, with France, Britain, and Russia arrayed against the Central Powers of Germany and Austria-Hungary.[2] Greenslet, who was ill with whooping cough and mumps, struggled to figure out what the war meant for his publishing house. He could not be reassuring about the impact it would have on Adams's strictly American novel. Some of the country's best journalists were headed to Europe to focus the nation on the Great War. With the understatement publishers employ to soften bad news for authors, Greenslet wrote Adams in return, "You will be somewhat hit by it, I am afraid."[3]

Sales for *The Clarion* reached thirty thousand copies, which was a respectable amount attributable to Adams's skill as a popular writer. Nevertheless that was a third of what Greenslet hoped the book would achieve. In 1915, as the conflict raged in Europe and on the pages of American newspapers, the publisher continued to blame poor sales on "the untimely outbreak of the European War."[4]

The United States remained neutral, and so did Adams. Vast numbers of Americans, including progressives like Adams, considered the war a strictly foreign affair. Untroubled by the conflict in Europe, Adams continued to produce light novels and used his newspaper columns to fight false advertising. When Woodrow Wilson campaigned for reelection in 1916 with the slogan "He Has Kept Us Out of War," Adams joined fifty other writers in signing a letter designed to put Wilson's Republican opponent, Charles Evans Hughes, on the spot for his waffling on the possibility of the United States joining the war. It was a brilliant stroke of propaganda by the Democratic National Committee Publicity Bureau, which played a large role in keeping Wilson in the White House.

All the while Greenslet pressed Adams for another "opus." When the writer finally agreed, he was no longer a passive spectator. In April 1917 the United States had entered the conflict, and so presently did Adams. Like many war-reluctant progressives, his enthusiasm was vivified by Wilson's high-minded goal of making the world "safe for democracy." Adams helped sell Liberty Loans, government bonds issued to fund the war, and, at the end of 1917, again joined a number of prominent writers aiming to sway public opinion on Wilson's behalf, this time in service to the Committee on Public Information, the first United States government agency dedicated to propagandizing the public. The committee used every medium available, from newspapers and posters, to speakers and pamphlets, to rally patriotic support for the U.S. war effort.

"From now on," Adams somewhat misleadingly told his publisher in September 1917, "it looks as if I should be putting in most of my time still-hunting pro-German and peace propaganda."[5] Still-hunters stalked their prey noiselessly, and Adams's pursuit of German-American treachery was anything but silent. All the while, he kept up his commercial writing, including the opus for Greenslet. The novel combined his familiar theme of newspaper crusading with his new cause: combating German-American subversion of the war effort. The book, Adams told another executive at Houghton Mifflin, "is more of a story of loyalty vs. German propaganda than anything else, and while the scene will be largely in a newspaper environment, it is distinctly a war story."[6]

• • •

Samuel Hopkins Adams was to writing what Macy's was to selling dry goods. His output encompassed nearly every literary product that existed at the time. It was consumed by the masses.

Born in 1871 in the small town of Dunkirk along Lake Erie in western New York, Adams began his journalism career at the *New York Sun* immediately after graduating from Hamilton College in 1891. While he continued to write for newspapers after the turn of the century, his byline became a staple in *McClure's, Collier's Weekly*, and other leading periodicals. Magazine publishing boomed at the time with reporting and fiction—both of which Adams produced at an astonishing rate.

And Adams wrote books. When he died in 1958, he had written more than fifty. As a sign of his writing vigor, an additional volume was published posthumously. These books ranged from *The Clarion* and other serious novels to romance and light-hearted fiction, history, biography, children's books, science fiction, mysteries, a game book, and a Western. He even penned racy books under the pen name Warner Fabian. These latter novels he did not mention to Greenslet at the staid Houghton Mifflin publishing house.[7]

While on the staff of *McClure's*, Adams wrote advertising copy and edited stories. He scribbled a smattering of poetry, ghostwrote for others, and tried his hand at movie scripts. Many of his works were adapted for the stage and cinema. A short story for *Cosmopolitan* became Frank Capra's *It Happened One Night*, starring Clark Gable and Claudette Colbert. It was the first film to win all five major Academy Awards (Best Picture, Director, Actor, Actress, and Screenplay). Two of his stories were adapted for phonograph records. One served as the basis for a Broadway musical.

Adams wrote for the market, had a natural talent for popularizing, and possessed enormous energy and discipline. He was an avid sportsman, with a hard-driving tennis serve and a passion for fishing that he shared with Greenslet. Adams and his wife, a former actress, were enthusiastic socializers. Nevertheless, he was up each day to work before the sun rose and pushed himself to write a thousand words before lunch.[8] Once, when his home caught on fire, he went next door to finish "his stint," as his wife put it.[9]

These characteristics are common to market writers of all eras. Another Adams trait, though, was rooted in the progressive era in which he thrived. For progressive journalists focused on exposing corruption and injustice, *publicity* did not automatically carry the whiff of "spin" or manipulation that it does today. These muckrakers, as they were called, used the word in the sense of eighteenth-century political thinker Jeremy Bentham, who argued for making government deliberations transparent to ordinary citizens. Progressives broadened the concept to cover all aspects of society, especially those dark recesses most in need of scrutiny.[10] Adams shed the purifying sunlight of publicity on mining companies' treatment of labor, the monopolistic practices of the "Beef Trust" to control the meat packing industry, and government corruption. A pioneer in consumer reporting, he rooted out deceptive advertising in everything from straw hats to "cure-all" drugs.

Adams's journalistic crusades reemerged as themes in his fiction. In a short story published in *McClure's*, "B. Jones, Butcher," the protagonist takes on the Beef Trust.[11] *The Health Master*, a novel for Houghton Mifflin, was based on his medical reporting. *The Clarion* picked up one of his favorite themes: newspapers that kowtow to special interests. In this story, a young journalist buys a failing newspaper with the help of his father, who has prospered selling fraudulent medicine. When the editor decides he has to clean up the community, businesses around town withhold advertising to crush *The Clarion*. In the happy ending the paper prevails, and the father repudiates his trade. The editor's girlfriend, who owns a tenement that fosters a typhoid outbreak, also comes around to see the evil of her ways. After *The Clarion* was published, a flattering profile of Adams noted, "There is not one page of his book that is inactive or freed from the necessity to drive home the evils of journalism."[12]

Adams wanted to affect change as well as earn money. He did not limit himself to exposing bogus advertising exclusively through his books, newspaper articles, and magazine stories. He traveled to Washington to lobby for Pure Food and Drug Laws and served on the executive committee of the National Consumers League.[13] And as a result of his mounting fame as a medical writer, the American Medical Association made him an associate member. It was, thus, an easy leap to volunteer as a government propagandist for a war President Wilson promised would spread democracy around the world. It was an idealistic call to arms that many progressives like Adams could embrace.

•  •  •

Every segment of the nation—farmer and factory worker, Boy Scout and homemaker—was conscripted into the war machine. The writing industries were not exempted.

The war placed restrictions on publishers of newspapers, magazines, and books. Enlistments depleted their staffs. Shortages of paper and other material impeded production. When an author of war poetry insisted her book have a red cover, Greenslet struggled to find the dye, which usually came from Germany. "The Germans, among their other atrocities," he said, "have prevented its exportation."[14] On top of this, Congress passed laws to restrict speech, which the administration aggressively implemented and the courts upheld.

Despite these hardships, complaints among journalists and publishers were remarkably muted. A strong feeling of patriotism prevailed generally. And where that sentiment was not so strong, say, among some German-American newspapers, the instinct for self-preservation was a moderating force. Apart from pacifists and Socialists, who were jailed for speaking against the war, objections to free speech were not chiefly about the principle of suppression—editors and reporters enthusiastically offered suggestions for censorship and propaganda. Their frustrations lay with inefficient, clumsy censorship. Few reporters within establishment news organizations wanted to erode support for the war with stories that called its purposes into question.

The word *Hun*, a derogatory reference to Central Asian barbarians who invaded Europe in the fourth and fifth centuries, became a pejorative shorthand in newspaper headlines for Germans, whose supposed secret plots to subvert the war were rampant throughout America. This was a stark turnaround from only a few years before when German-Americans were esteemed for their hard work and good citizenship. Back then, Americans embraced the Germans' sobriquet for themselves, *das Land der Dichter und Denker*, "the land of poets and thinkers."[15]

When he joined Houghton Mifflin in 1910, Greenslet was sent abroad to obtain an "international point of view."[16] In 1913, he published *Pan Germanism*, by Roland G. Usher, a rare volume that foresaw the Great War. Once war did erupt, Greenslet persuaded his fellow directors at the company that the public's interest in the European conflict would soar and that Houghton Mifflin should prepare to meet this demand. In 1915 Greenslet sailed to England to scout authors and book ideas. He "read up on the German case and felt the force of their need for living room" and, prior to 1917, published books that presented the German point of view. But, as he later admitted, his overriding aim was "to educate America to a full knowledge of the evil ambitions that were loose in the world, even if in the end it would lead us to join in fighting them."[17]

Publishing war books was Greenslet's chief occupation during the conflict. He brought out Ian Hay Beith's best-selling novel, *The First Hundred Thousand*, a comic account of a British military unit's travails, and Mildred Aldrich's *A Hilltop on the Marne*, which recounted the first days of the war and enjoyed sixteen printings.[18] Houghton Mifflin also published manuals for army training camps, patriotic textbooks for colleges, *The Patriotic Reader* for middle school students, and the food-conservation-minded *How to Make the Garden Pay*.[19] Like other publishers, Houghton Mifflin collaborated with the National Board of Historical Service, an organization created by university professors to help promote the war. Greenslet reckoned Houghton Mifflin published more than one hundred war books with sales of nearly 1.5 million.

During this time, literary propaganda flourished in every belligerent country. Writers, journalists, and educators were mobilized to sell their country's side of the war to its own citizens as well as to those in other countries. Efforts in the United States tracked closely with those undertaken in Great Britain, a country which had inspired many American political institutions and with whom Americans shared a common language. Wellington House, the site of the National Insurance Commission in London, served as the British government's propaganda center at the start of the war. Its existence was not officially acknowledged until well after the war ended, whereas the Committee on Public Information in Washington was highly visible from its start. The emphasis on writers, however, was similar.

Publishers in the United States benefited financially by cooperating with the Wilson Administration's censorship apparatus. Concerned that postal censors were holding up export of books for sale in Europe, publishers struck a deal with the Censorship Board, vowing to "go to any lengths provided the flow of books abroad could be restored."[20] These concessions included agreeing to export only "pro-American" books and submitting publication lists and the books themselves for approval to export.

That's not to say the book businesses' patriotism was insincere. George Putnam, of G. P. Putnam's Sons, was a founder and major funder of the National Security League, a super-patriotic organization created in December 1914 to promote military preparedness. It continued its strident pro-war propaganda after April 1917.[21] George's brother, Herbert Putnam, was the Librarian of Congress. As part of *his* war work, Herbert Putnam provided space to the Committee on Public Information to screen books, and he informed the CPI of individuals who checked out volumes deemed suspicious.[22]

The Vigilantes, the leading group of American writers dedicated to promoting the war, also was a source of book material for Greenslet.[23] Hermann Hagedorn, a German-American author and poet, conceived the organization in the home of playwright Porter Emerson Browne in November 1916. "Germany," Browne said, "has unsheathed and brought into play one weapon that the Allies and ourselves didn't even know existed. . . . It is propaganda."[24] The Vigilantes sought to mold public opinion through syndicated articles, poetry, and art. The group sent typeset stories every Friday to newspapers in towns with populations over five thousand inhabitants. It reached ten thousand weeklies through the American Press Association.[25] Many members of the Vigilantes signed on to the CPI staff, which became a virtual government writers' colony.

The formation of the Committee on Public Information was the only instance in United States history when the government had an official information ministry. (Post-war propaganda was, and remains, diffuse throughout the bureaucracy.) George Creel, the chairman of the CPI, was a fiery muckraker who worked on Wilson's reelection campaign and helped orchestrate the embarrassing letter to Charles Evans Hughes that Adams and other writers signed. Every aspect of modern propaganda can be traced to the CPI. Much of it, such as the *Federal Register* (under the CPI it was called *The Official Bulletin*), or public diplomacy to shape foreign public opinion, is positive. But, contrary to Creel's insistence the CPI hew strictly to facts, it went beyond those by appealing to base emotions and endorsing coercion. It also resorted to another standard feature of propaganda: the suppression of inconvenient information and opinion.

At the time, Creel, Adams, and others on the CPI staff did not view their work a perversion of the progressive vision of wholesome "publicity." In public and private they showed no indication they worried about the implications of their actions, let alone admitted they used techniques they claimed to abhor within enemy propaganda. Their fervor to prosecute the war to the fullest trumped any considerations that the CPI's tactics were non-consensual. Adams, who had unflinchingly railed against false advertising, regarded his efforts to advertise the war as righteous; he considered anyone who objected to his messages a traitor. "The fact is that I am in a rather cynical mood as to those untrammeled spirits who tremble lest war methods fix upon us shackles that we never can throw off," Adams told Greenslet. "Wherever I had talked with men of this mind I have found them to be either pro-German or pacifist at bottom; generally the latter."[26]

• • •

Adams referred to himself as a "National Security and Defense Executive."[27] It was difficult to tell when he was on the job directly for the

CPI and when he was independently writing propaganda to earn a living, something he had to do since he came to Washington at his own expense.[28] In "The Dodger Trail," a short story for *Collier's*, a small-town editor helps a "War Intelligence" agent ferret out German agents. Accompanying the story was a vague author's sketch that touched on his working life. "Nowadays," Adams was quoted as saying, when he picked up his pen, "it is mainly in the conscientious endeavor to earn the dollar a year which a recklessly extravagant Government pays me, or to write articles or fiction dealing with the one all-engrossing subject, the war."[29] In a letter to one of Greenslet's associates, he confided, "I'm frightfully busy trying to make a living and at the same time do such war work as its handed to me—and it is being handed at an increasing rate, I assure you."[30]

This blurring of the lines at the CPI was not unusual. The organization was constantly adding units and, occasionally, discarding them. Staff drifted in and out of journalism. Its syndicated features division drew on Mary Roberts Rinehard, Booth Tarkington, and other popular writers for articles it distributed to newspapers and magazines at home and abroad.

Adams's most clearly identified job at the CPI was with its Four Minute Men, an innovation that remains an astounding propaganda feat more than one hundred years later. This unit, created a few days after the United States entered World War I, brought the Wilson Administration's themes into movie theaters. The Four Minute Men spoke to captive audiences during the change in movie reels. A modern analog is the ubiquitous ads that pop up when viewing videos online. The speakers, comprised of community volunteers, were seemingly local expressions of patriotism, but were in fact carefully orchestrated by Washington and managed through statewide and city structures. Speakers were admonished to limit their talks to four minutes and to stick to whatever messages Washington wished to convey. These themes ranged from promoting Liberty Loans to "Unmasking German Propaganda."

Adams was a member of the Four Minute Men National Advisory Council, established in November 1917.[31] He recruited speakers and assisted with the *Four Minute Man Bulletin*, a vehicle for managing speakers. Solomon H. Clark, a fellow council member and head of the University of Chicago's Department of Public Speaking, told one Four Minute Men audience they enjoyed more influence than journalists because they reached the masses with messages "carefully laid out for us by experts in our main office at Washington."[32] By the end of the war, the CPI had a force of seventy-five thousand Four Minute Men across the country. Although the great majority spoke in movie theaters, they could also be found at Grange Halls, at picnics, and under Chautauqua tents. Four Minute Men spoke at five hundred different logging camps and once, when a North Dakota town's lone church was not available, in a village pool hall.[33]

The war work that played most to Adams's strengths was an extension of the "Ad-visor" column exposing dishonest advertising he wrote for the *New York Tribune*.[34] The *Tribune* created an internal Bureau of Investigations to unearth information for Adams's use. At the CPI he had access to information from government agencies whose agents were on constant lookout for evidence of German perfidy.

Adams's first major investigation for the CPI grew out of a stash of papers seized from the New York office of Wolf von Igel in 1916. Von Igel had been involved in German espionage. His papers documented subsidies to journalists, connections to Irish revolutionaries working against the British, and possible sabotage of shipping and war industries. The Justice Department, with the blessing of Secretary of State Robert Lansing, shared the documents with the CPI. Adams prepared "a skillful analysis . . . that showed German intrigue down to the last sordid detail," CPI chief George Creel later wrote.[35] Newspapers across the country hyped the "official exposé," as it was described in the *New York Times*.[36] Although the von Igel papers belonged to a period before the war (von Igel had returned to Germany before he could be tried for conspiring to destroy a canal in Canada), the clear implication was that German treachery skulked in every corner of the United States.

The *New York Tribune* ran the von Igel story, in the form it was distributed by the CPI, on page one, minus Adams's byline. Next to it was the second installment of a three-part series under Adams's byline on "Herr William Randolph Hearst." The series portrayed Hearst as the "leading spirit of German propaganda in the United States today."[37] The maverick newspaper tycoon had deployed his signature style of sensationalism to argue against U.S. involvement in the war. Once Americans were on the European battlefields, Hearst's newspapers adopted a far more patriotic tone, but the publisher remained a major annoyance to President Wilson, who asked his attorney general if legal means existed to bring him to book. The Justice Department's Bureau of Investigation and Military Intelligence, with help from Creel, investigated Hearst in hopes of making a case, all in vain.[38]

Adams also used the *Tribune* to attack the editor of the Yiddish daily *Forward* and Victor L. Berger, editor of the *Milwaukee Leader*, two Socialists not supportive of the war. Adams went after anti-war Senator Robert M. La Follette, of Wisconsin, posing the question, "Is Wisconsin Against America?"[39]

Adams followed up that accusation in a three-part investigative series for *Everybody's* magazine. The series, "Invaded America," took Adams to Wisconsin, a state with a large population of German ancestry, for an investigation purporting to show the surreptitious German poisoning of "the American mind." It was insidious, according to Adams's findings: "Of the precise method employed I can not [*sic*] speak with knowledge," he wrote. "It may be that there is a central and secret bureau, a German official press agency, which plans each separate campaign and issues instructions or even syndicated matter." He cautioned that "perhaps my country is too tolerant of the alien within its gates."[40]

In this same series in *Everybody's*, Adams celebrated the Treasury Department's coercive techniques for selling Liberty bonds. Methods included ostentatiously writing on blue cards the names of those who declined to buy the bonds and forwarding them to higher authorities, who sometimes revisited the reluctant customer. Adams considered this "blue-carding" especially effective with immigrants, calling the blue card "an energizing and regenerating force for nationalism."[41]

In addition to articles in this vein, Adams wrote on military medical preparedness and about organizations that sought to boost soldiers' morale.[42] He reprised war themes in his short fiction. One told the story of a young man so determined to join the army that he bribes his draft board so he can enlist. Another story concerned a speaker on behalf of War Savings Stamps. A third story, also about War Savings Stamps, involved a rich man, a beggar, and a magic wallet.

It seemed as though Adams would affix his name and a few pro-war words whenever asked. In order to oxygenate anti-German sentiment in the United States, the British promoted the work of Dutch artist Louis Raemaekers, whose drawings depicted babies with throats slit by the Germans. When the Century Company published Raemaeker in book form in the United States, Adams joined President Wilson, Creel, and many of his CPI associates in supplying commentary. Alongside a drawing of the Kaiser strung up by his wrists, Adams, anything but a subtle still-hunter, declared:

> To me the deliberate, coldly reckoned murder of the invaded countries' trees and vines so that the children of the slain and enslaved and their children's children may draw no sustenance from the kindly earth— that seems the most perverse, the most detestable, the most typical of all the crimes of Kaiserism. The sterilization of Mother Earth. It took the mind of a Wilhelm to conceive it.[43]

• • •

*Common Cause* began as a short story by the same name in the *Saturday Evening Post* in May 1918.[44] It drew on Adams's investigations for the "Invaded America" series in *Everybody's*. After reading the story, Greenslet wired Adams: "The Common Cause is worth building up. Could you make it fifty or sixty thousand words and introduce a skirt?"[45] Greenslet had found his opus.

*Common Cause* tells the story of Jeremy Robson, publisher of a patriotic newspaper in the fictional Midwestern town of Fenchester. Robson's muckraking has spurred special interests to withhold advertising in order to drive him out of business. When war comes in 1917, his equally passionate exposé of local German-American fealty to their homeland inspires Fenchester's plutocrats to put aside differences with Robson to save the *Guardian*.

Looking to tie the book into war themes, Greenslet recommended the hero's love interest be a "levelheaded" young lady who organizes "the women on the right side."[46] One of Greenslet's colleagues chimed in, "I wish you could double the appeal by mixing up the women's committees which are so active today and which form a part of the Public Safety Committees and the Hoover work all over the country."[47] Adams's heroine, Marcia Aimes, fell in line by mobilizing women and, in fearless suffragette fashion, hardboiled men as well. She helps rally the townspeople to Robson's side.

Adams accelerated his writing speed that summer of 1918 for fear the war would end before he finished. In July he informed Greenslet he was producing nearly twice his normal rate of a thousand words a day.[48] In August he called off a fishing trip, because "the novel is pressing too hard."[49] At the end of the month he sent in his first draft.[50] He mailed a revision in mid-September.[51] Adams was delayed reviewing the page proofs due to a case of influenza, which was sweeping the country, including Houghton Mifflin's offices. "You jangled our sensitive nerves here with apprehension lest you were to pass out before those proofs could come back," Greenslet told him.[52]

Greenslet also worried the ever-changing war would somehow diminish the relevance of *Common Cause*, as it had *The Clarion*. Roger Scaife, his associate, asked for the book's opening pages in late May so he could provide them to the salesforce when it hit the road to promote the autumn book list.[53] Greenslet had the book jackets printed in July, much ahead of the usual schedule.[54] "The best time to publish a war book," he had learned, "is the day you accept it."[55]

Greenslet's fears proved well-founded. Adams mailed the corrected proofs on November 8. Three days later, the Armistice was signed. His war book was ready for printing, but there was no war. "The war, contrary as I recall it . . . to your views, has come incontinently to an end," Greenslet informed Adams, "and things have been at sixes and sevens as to our making publishing plans."

To Adams's annoyance, the publisher saw no reason to now rush the book off the presses before Christmas, as originally planned. The new publication date was January 25, when Houghton Mifflin would launch it "not as a war book, but as a #1 novel of Western newspaper life, with a certain amount of historical interest."[56]

Reviews were good. Sales were not. Only 7,500 copies were purchased, about a quarter of the sales recorded for *The Clarion. Common Cause* was a "darn good book," Scaife told Adams. "There are every now and then passing regrets that the armistice was signed so quickly."[57]

Although Greenslet wanted to market the book as a newspaper novel, many reviewers focused on the public's "historical interest" in the war. "The foundation of fact which underlies this story," *Booklist* observed, "has come to light in an investigation made by Mr. Adams, and the book in its varying moods reflects very accurately the attitude of the people of the United States toward the Germans among them."[58]

*Common Cause* had particular resonance in Wisconsin. Adams sent copies to newspaper editors across the state, noting the book "is based upon the Wisconsin situation as I found it in 1917 and the early part of 1918." The editor of the *Sauk County Democrat* in Baraboo replied to Adams, "The book completely satisfies a feeling that I have had, and one that I am sure has possessed every citizen who has lived close to this situation in Wisconsin, that the struggle through which this state passed in conquering itself should not be forgotten or permitted to go unreviewed by those who failed to see its portent at the time."[59]

The review in the *Sauk County Democrat* noted the similarity between the book's fictitious Governor Embree and the sitting Republican governor, Emanuel L. Philipp, a railroad executive, "except he combined many of the traits of character of Senator La Follette." The review added, "If you are a red-blooded American, you will want to read 'Common Cause' . . . If you are a pacifist you won't like it." The book, it said, held "the mirror up to Wisconsin."[60] Adams mailed the review to Greenslet with a letter written on leftover CPI stationery.[61]

Adams sent an autographed copy of *Common Cause* to the secretary of the Wisconsin Loyalty League, which had been "the right-arm distributing agency of the CPI" in the state.[62] He praised the League "for its inspiring and winning fight . . . in Wisconsin to make and keep the state loyal to American principles."[63] Pleased with "the splendid tribute to militant Americans in Wisconsin," the secretary forwarded Adams's letter to newspapers around the state to promote his organization.

• • •

Samuel Hopkins Adams is not well remembered today. *Common Cause* is all but forgotten. Although they were creatures of their time, Adams's book is worth revisiting both for its value in understanding the past and its relevance in thinking about the present.

As the *Booklist* reviewer and others pointed out when it was first published, *Common Cause* draws the reader into the home front atmosphere that existed during the Great War. While technically fiction, the novel provides a profound history lesson. It draws on events that Adams and his readers knew well, and vividly portrays attitudes and emotions that were widely held at the time. Adams's novel is such a powerful endorsement of these sentiments that modern readers who are appalled by the xenophobic hate-mongering that is currently sweeping over America are nevertheless likely to find themselves identifying with the hero, Jeremy Robson, and his sweetheart, Marcia. To read *Common Cause* today is to recreate the emotional experience of war. The novel is, as Adams maintained, "distinctly a war story."

After the war, many progressives (although not Adams and George Creel) felt betrayed. They regretted their complicity in promoting a war that did not produce the just peace Wilson had promised. Speech had been suppressed. Domestic reforms stalled. Big business grew more powerful. The progressive movement became dispirited and faltered. "We failed to give liberty to Europe. We might have saved America," lamented Frederic Howe, a civic organizer, journalist, and official in the Wilson entourage during the treaty negotiations in Paris.[64]

In postmortems on the war that asked what went wrong, one of the most common complaints was the evils of propaganda—both by foreign countries and the United States. "The whole discussion about the ways and means of controlling public opinion testifies to the collapse of the traditional species of democratic romanticism," wrote Harold Lasswell, whose scholarship contributed to making propaganda a field of study. "That credulous utopianism, which fed the mighty words which exploited the hopes of the mass in war, had in many minds given way to cynicism and disenchantment."[65]

"'Propaganda' is a horrid word that has come to have a horrid meaning," a British propagandist wrote after the war. "If it could be turned out of our language I should rejoice."[66] In a sense it has been: no one admits to disseminating propaganda. Yet, for all the postwar hand-wringing, the practice of government propaganda—never referred to by the pejorative, always recast with some benign designation such as "public information"—has only grown. New social media tools power modern propaganda. Its effectiveness is enhanced by scientific research at the U.S. government's Defense Advanced Research Projects Agency (DARPA), where neurologists study blood flow to the brain to evaluate the effectiveness of "messages."[67]

Propaganda is a tool of modern governing in times of peace as well as in war. But it is most virulent and undemocratic in times of national crisis, when fears are most easily aroused and emotional shortcuts to persuasion are favored over factual debate.

Therein lays the fundamental contemporary lesson that emerges from this book. Even in the hands of well-meaning writers, the zeal to marshal public opinion too easily careens into suppression of thought. *Common Cause: A Novel of the War in America* is a reminder of how easy it is for democracy to lose its way.

## Notes

The "historical interest" Ferris Greenslet recognized in Samuel Hopkins Adams's novel remains just as strong a century later. The storyline and the references to real people and events made it a primer on the United States involvement in the Great War. To enhance the experience for contemporary readers, we have annotated *Common Cause: A Novel of the War in America* in addition to writing this introduction.

1. Samuel Hopkins Adams to Ferris Greenslet, August 12, 1914, Houghton Mifflin Papers (hereafter HMP), Houghton Library, Harvard University. In the original version of this quote, Adams used the archaic form of "cruel": "crewel." The change was made to avoid distracting the reader. For similar reasons, we have modernized other spellings in the text, for instance substituting "today" for "to-day." Otherwise the text remains as it was originally published.

2. Emmet Crozier, *American Reporters on the Western Front: 1914–1918* (New York: Oxford University Press, 1959), 6.

3. Samuel V. Kennedy, *Samuel Hopkins Adams and the Business of Writing* (Syracuse NY: University of Syracuse Press, 1999), 95; Ferris Greenslet, *Under the Bridge: The Autobiography of a Publisher* (London: Collins, 1944), 108. Kennedy's biography is indispensable to anyone writing on Adams, as indeed it was for us in writing this essay.

4. Kennedy, *Samuel Hopkins Adams*, 96, 101.

5. Adams to Greenslet, September 5, 1917, HMP.

6. Adams to Roger L. Scaife, May 24, 1918, HMP.

7. Kennedy, *Samuel Hopkins Adams*, 130–31.

8. Kennedy, *Samuel Hopkins Adams*, 78–79.

9. Kennedy, *Samuel Hopkins Adams*, 194.

10. Jeremy Bentham, "Of Publicity," in *The Works of Jeremy Bentham*, vol. 2 (New York: Russell & Russell, 1962), 310–17.

11. Kennedy, *Samuel Hopkins Adams*, 66.

12. Montrose J. Moses, "Samuel Hopkins Adams," *Book News Monthly* (January 1915): 215.

13. Kennedy, *Samuel Hopkins Adams*, 79, 86.

14. Hazel Hutchison, *The War That Used Up Words* (New Haven CT: Yale University Press, 2015), 134.

15. Ruth H. Sanders, *German: Biography of a Language* (New York: Oxford University Press, 2010), 176.

16. Greenslet, *Under the Bridge*, 81.

17. Greenslet, *Under the Bridge*, 109.

18. Hutchison, *War That Used Up Words*, 119.

19. Franklin S. Hoyt to James T. Shotwell, July 11, 1917, National Board for Historical Service Records, Library of Congress.

20. Minutes of the Censorship Board, September 5, 1918, Entry 1, Records of the Committee on Public Information, National Archives and Records Administration.

21. George H. Putnam to Henry S. Burrage, May 15, 1915, Herbert Putnam Papers, Library of Congress. Herbert Putnam, the Librarian of Congress, and George Putnam were brothers.

22. Wayne A. Wiegand, *"An Active Instrument for Propaganda": The American Public Library during World War I* (Westport CT: Greenwood, 1989), 101.

23. Hutchison, *War That Used Up Words*, 120.

24. Porter Emerson Browne, "The Vigilantes," *Outlook*, May 8, 1918, 67–69.

25. Eugenie M. Fryer, "The Vigilantes," *Book News Monthly* (January 1918): 150.

26. Adams to Greenslet, November 2, 1918, HMP.

27. Kennedy, *Samuel Hopkins Adams*, 116–19.

28. George Creel, *How We Advertised America* (New York: Harper, 1920), 225.

29. Samuel Hopkins Adams, "The Dodger Trail," *Collier's*, October 12, 1918, 30.

30. Adams to Roger L. Scaife, May 24, 1918, HMP.

31. Wayne Alfred Nicholas, "Crossroads Oratory: A Study of the Four Minute Men of World War I" (Ph.D. diss, Columbia University), 111–14.

32. *Four Minute Men News*, Edition B, January 1917.

33. Nicholas, "Crossroads Oratory: A Study of the Four Minute Men of World War I," 117, 119.

34. Kennedy, *Samuel Hopkins Adams*, 103.

35. Creel, *How We Advertised America*, 225.

36. Kennedy, *Samuel Hopkins Adams*, 114; *New York Times*, September 23, 1917.

37. *New York Tribune*, September 16 and 23, 1917.

38. David Nasaw, *The Chief: The Life of William Randolph Hearst* (Boston MA: Houghton Mifflin, 2001), 261.

39. Kennedy, *Samuel Hopkins Adams*, 115.

40. Samuel Hopkins Adams, "Invaded America," *Everybody's Magazine* (December 1917): 10, 13, 86. The series ran monthly through March 1918.

41. Adams, "Invaded America," *Everybody's Magazine* (February 1918): 30.

42. Kennedy, *Samuel Hopkins Adams*, 117.

43. Louis Raemaeker, *America in the War* (New York: Century, 1918), 106.

44. Samuel Hopkins Adams, "Common Cause," *Saturday Evening Post*, July 27, 1918, 5–8ff.

45. Greenslet to Adams, May 15, 1918, HMP.

46. Greenslet to Adams, May 15, 1918, HMP.

47. Scaife to Adams, June 1, 1918, HMP.

48. Adams to Greenslet, July 11, 1918, HMP.

49. Adams to Greenslet, August 20, 1918, HMP.

50. Adams to Greenslet, August 28, 1918, HMP.

51. Adams to Greenslet, September 17, 1918, HMP.

52. Greenslet to Adams, December 2, 1918, HMP.

53. Scaife to Adams, May 27, 1918, HMP.

54. Scaife to Adams, July 31, 1918, HMP.

55. Greenslet, *Under the Bridge*, 107.

56. Greenslet to Adams, November 25 and December 2, 1918, HMP.

57. Scaife to Adams, April 24, 1919, HMP; Kennedy, *Samuel Hopkins Adams*, 120.

58. For this and other reviews, see *Book Review Digest*, February 1920, 5.

59. R. J. Osborne to Adams, January 26, 1919, HMP.

60. *Sauk Country Democrat*, n.d., files of HMP.

61. Adams to Greenslet, February 15, 1918, HMP.

62. Karen Falk, "Public Opinion in Wisconsin in World War I," *Wisconsin Magazine of History*, 25, no. 4 (June 1942): 404.

63. Adams to George Kull, n.d., reproduced in flyer Kull sent out to editors, attachment Kull to Adams, February 3, 1918, HMP.

64. Frederic C. Howe, "Where Are the Pre-War Radicals?," *Survey* (February 1926): 50.

65. Harold Lasswell, *Propaganda Technique in World War I* (Cambridge MA: MIT Press, 1971, originally published 1927), 2–3.

66. Wickham Steed, *The Fifth Arm* (London: Constable, 1940), 1.

67. Sharon Weinberger, "Still in the Lead?," *Nature*, January 2008, 390–93.

# Common Cause

# PART I

"DEUTSCHLAND, DEUTSCHLAND ÜBER ALLES!" Three thousand voices blended and swelled in the powerful harmony. The walls of the Fenchester Auditorium trembled to it. The banners, with their German mottoes of welcome, swayed to the rhythm.

"Über alles in der Welt!"

The thundering descent of the line with its superb resonances was as martial as a cavalry charge. Three thousand flushed, perspiring, commonplace faces above respectable black coats in the one sex and mildly ornate blouses in the other, were caught by the fire and the ferment of it and grew suddenly rapt and ecstatic. Wave after wave of massed harmonies followed in the onset. One could feel, rather than hear, in the impassioned voices a spirit instantly more fanatic, more exotic, a strange and exultant note, as of challenge. It was inspiring. It was startling. It was formidable. It was anything for which young Mr. Jeremy Robson, down in the reporters' seats, might find an adjective, except, perhaps, American.

Yet this was the American city of Fenchester, capital of the sovereign State of Centralia, in the year of grace and peace, nineteen hundred and twelve, half a decade before the United States of America descended into the Valley of the Shadow of Death to face the German guns, thundering out that same chorus of "Germany over all in the world!"

All the Federated German Societies of the State of Centralia in annual convention[1] assembled might sing their federated German heads off for all that Jeremy Robson cared. He mildly approved the music, not so much for the sense as for the sound, under cover of which he was enabled to question his neighbor, Galpin, of The Guardian, concerning the visiting notabilities upon the stage. For young Mr. Robson was still a bit new to his work on The Record, and rather flattered that an assignment of this importance should have fallen to him. The local and political celebrities he already knew—the Governor; the Mayor; Robert Wanser, President of the Fenchester Trust Company; State Senator Martin Embree; Carey Crobin, the "Boss of the Ward"; Emil Bausch, President of the local Deutscher Club; and a dozen of the other leading citizens, all ornamented with conspicuous badges. Galpin obligingly indicated the principal strangers. Gordon Fliess, of Bellair, head of the Fliess Brewing Company; the Reverend Theo Gunst, the militant ecclesiast of a near-by German Theological Seminary; Ernst Bauer, of the Marlittstown Herold und Zeitung; Pastor Klink, the recognized head of the German religious press of the region; Martin Dolge, accredited with being the dictator of the State's educational system; and the Herr Professor Koerner, of the University of Felsingen, special envoy from Germany to the United States for the propagation of that widespread and carefully fostered Teutonic plant, Deutschtum, the spirit of German Kultur in foreign lands.

At the close of the musical exaltation of Germany above all the world, including, of course, the hospitably adoptive nation under whose protection the singers sat, the exercises proceeded with a verbal glorification of the Fatherland. The Governor, in complimentary and carefully memorized German, lauded the Teutons as the prop of the State. The Mayor, in strongly Teutonized English, proclaimed them the hope of the city. Several other speakers, whose accents identified them as more American than their sentiments, acclaimed the upholders of Deutschtum as salt of the earth and pillars of Society. Then a chorus of public school children, in the colors of imperial Germany, rose to sing "Die Wacht am Rhein,"[2] and everybody rose with them, or nearly everybody. They sang it directly in the face of his Imperial Majesty, Kaiser Wilhelm, gazing, bewreathed, down at them from over the stage, with stern and martial approval.

"They do it mighty well," commented young Jeremy Robson.

"Ay-ah. Why wouldn't they!" returned Galpin.

"You mean they've been specially drilled for it?"

"Specially nothing! That's part of their regular school exercises."

"In the German schools?"

"In the *public* schools. Our school. Paid for out of our taxes. 'Come to order.' Tap-tap-tap with Teacher's ruler. 'Der bupils will now rice and zing "Die wacht am Rhein."' But try 'em with 'America,' and they wouldn't know the first verse."

"You seem to feel strongly about it."

"Not in working hours. Haven't got any feelings. I'm a reporter."

From this point the programme was exclusively in German. The next speaker, Pastor Klink, rose and glorified God, a typically if not exclusively German God. Emil Bausch, following, extolled the Kaiser rather more piously than his predecessor had glorified the Kaiser's Creator. Martin Dolge apostrophized the spirit of Deutschtum,[3] which, if one might believe him, was invented by the Creator and improved by the Kaiser. Just here occurred an unfortunate break in the programme. The next speaker on the list had been called out, and an interim must be filled while he was retrieved. The chairman motioned to the band leader for music. Whether in a spirit of perversity or by sheer, unhappy chance, the director led his men in the strains of "The Star-Spangled Banner."

In justice to our citizens of German descent and allegiance, it must be admitted that they are of equable spirit. Nobody openly resented the playing of the national anthem. A glance of disapproval passed between the professorial envoy from Germany and Pastor Klink, and some of the others on the stage frowned momentarily. But their habitual tolerant good nature at once reasserted itself. Of course, no one rose; that gesture was reserved for the German national music. No one, that is, who counted in that assemblage. But from the reporters' seats Jeremy Robson and Galpin dimly made out a figure, long-coated, straw-hatted and slim, in the first row of the balcony's farthest corner, standing stiffly erect.

Around it buzzed a small disturbance. There were sounds of laughter, which spread and mingled with a few calls of disapprobation. A woman beside the erect figure seemed to be making an effort at dissuasion. It was unavailing. On the stage there were curious looks and queries. Presently the whole house was gazing at the slender, lone figure.

"Who's the kid?" asked Jeremy Robson, interested.

"Don't know him," answered Galpin, staring.

"I like his nerve, anyway."

"It's better than his style," commented the other, grinning. "If he's going to stand to attention, why doesn't he take off his hat?"

"Here's another one," said The Guardian reporter, turning toward the lower tier box on their right.

An iron-gray, square-jawed man with shrewd and pleasant eyes, who, in his obviously expensive but easy fitting suit of homespun, gave the impression of physical power, was shouldering his way to the rail. A small American flag occupied a humble position in a group of insignia ornamenting the next box. The man plucked it out and made as if he would raise it above his head, then changed his mind. Holding it stiffly in front of him he turned to face the distant figure, and so stood, grim, awkward, solid, while the chosen voice of the Nation's patriotism sang to unheeding ears below.

"Movie stuff," observed Jeremy Robson with that cynicism which every young reporter considers proper to his profession.

"That's Magnus Laurens," said his mentor. "Nothing theatrical about Magnus. He's a reg'lar feller."

The novice was impressed. For Laurens was a name of prestige throughout Centralia. Its owner controlled the water-power of the State and was a growing political figure.

"What's he doing it for?" he inquired.

"Because he's an American, I suppose. Queer reason, ain't it!"

"There's another, then," returned Robson, as there arose, from a front row seat on the stage, the strong and graceful figure of Martin Embree, State Senator from the Northern Tier, where the Germans make up three fourths of the population.

"Trust Smiling Mart to do the tactful thing," observed Galpin. "He's the guy that invented popularity, and he's held the patent ever since."

The Senator was wearing his famous smile which was both a natural ornament and a political asset. He directed it upon Magnus Laurens who did not see it, turned it toward the slim patriot in the gallery who may or may not have observed it, and then carried it close to the ear of the chairman. Snatches of his eager and low-toned persuasion floated down to the listening Robson.

". . . all up. Can't . . . harm. National . . . after all. If don't want . . .
leave . . . me."

The chairman shook his head glumly, broke loose from the smile,
spoke a word to the erring orchestra leader. The music stopped. The
figure in the balcony sank into the dimness of its background. Magnus Laurens sat down. Senator Embree, smiling and gracious still,
returned to his chair.

"There's my story," said young Jeremy Robson, ever on the lookout for the picturesque. "If I can find that kid," he added.

"Try Magnus Laurens," suggested his elder. "Maybe he knows him."

Throughout the address of the Herr Professor Koerner, young Mr.
Robson sat absently making notes. The notes were wholly irrelevant
to the learned envoy's speech. Yet it was an interesting, even a significant speech, had there been any in those easy days, to appreciate
its significance. The learned representative of German propaganda
impressed upon his hearers the holy purpose of Deutschtum. German
ties must be maintained; German habits and customs of life and above
all the German speech must be piously fostered at whatever distance
from the Fatherland, to the end that, in the inevitable day when Germany's oppressors, jealous of her power and greatness, should force
her to draw the sword in self-defense, every scion of German blood
might rally to her, against the world, if need be. Amidst the "Hochs!"
and "Sehr guts!" which punctuated the oratory, the negligent reporter
for The Record sat sketching the outlines of his word-picture of the
stripling in the gallery and the magnate in the box, standing to honor
their country's anthem, amidst the amused and patronizing wonder-
ment of the Federated German Societies of Centralia.[4] As the session
drew to a close, he left.

Magnus Laurens had already gone. By good fortune, young Jeremy
Robson caught a glimpse of his square and powerful figure, emerging
from the crowd and going down a side street. A girl in a riding-habit
was with him. In the bearing of her slender body, in the poise of the
little head with its tight-packed strands of tawny hair, Jeremy Robson caught a hint of a subtle and innate quality, something gallant and
proud and challenging. He overtook them.

"I beg your pardon, Mr. Laurens. My name is Robson. I'm a reporter for The Record. Could I have a word with you?"

The water-power magnate turned upon him a face of mingled annoyance and amusement.

"This is what I get for making a spectacle of myself, I take it," he grumbled. "What do you want to know? Why I did it?"

"No. That's plain enough. Who was the boy in the balcony?"

"Boy?" repeated Mr. Laurens in surprise.

"Yes. The kid that stood up when they began 'The Star-Spangled Banner.' Do you know him?"

"Let me refer that question to Miss Marcia Ames. She was right at the spot, in the balcony. Miss Ames, Mr. Robson."

Jeremy bowed and found himself looking into two large, young, and extremely self-possessed grayish eyes, frank and happy eyes on the surface, but with inscrutable lights and depths beneath. For the rest, his hasty impression recorded an alert, intelligent, and delicately slanted face, and an almost disconcertingly direct regard. The skin was of that translucent brown-over-pink which the sun god bestows only upon his tried and true acolytes.

"Do you know the boy, Miss Ames?"

"What boy?" Her voice was cool and liquid and endearing, and just a bit lazily indifferent, with a strange hint—never anything more—of accent.

"The boy who stood in the first row of the balcony."

"That was not a boy."

"No?"

"That was I."

"You! You're much too tall."

"If you thought me a boy I would seem much shorter," she returned composedly.

"Do you mind telling me how you came to stand up as you did?"

"I always do when they play my national anthem. Do not you?"

The "do not you" gave the young man the clue to her speech, to the slightly exotic quality of it. It was less the accent than the clear precision of her use of words, without the slur or contraction of common usage. The charm of her soft and rather deep voice saved it from any taint of the pedantic.

"No," said he.

"Ah? But perhaps you are not an American."

"What else should I be?"

She shrugged her shoulders slightly.

"Nor do I," put in Magnus Laurens, "I'm ashamed to say."

"At all events, you did it this time. It was very nice in you. Usually I feel quite lonely. And once they were going to arrest me for it."

"Where was that?" asked Jeremy Robson, stealthily reaching for his folded square of scratch paper.

"In Germany. When I was at school there. Are you going to put all this in the paper?"

"Would you mind?"

"I suppose I ought to mind. It is very forward and unmaidenly, is it not, to permit one's self to be dragged into print?"

"It is," said Magnus Laurens, his shrewd eyes twinkling, "and about one hundred and one maidens out of every hundred just love it, according to my observations."

"I do not think that I should object," said Miss Ames calmly. "In fact I should be curious to see what you would say about me."

That was Jeremy Robson's first intimation of her unique frankness of attitude toward herself as toward all other persons and things.

"We are on our way to the hotel where Mrs. Laurens is waiting for us," explained the water-power dictator. "Why not walk along with us while you conclude the interview?"

"I haven't much more to ask Miss Ames," said the reporter, complying, "except what started her on her patriotic habit."

"My father was an army officer," she explained. "While he was alive we always stood up together. Now I could no more sit through 'The Star-Spangled Banner' than you would wear your hat in church. But I really do not see anything to write about in *that*. There was much, surely, more interesting at the meeting."

"What, for instance?"

"The whole affair," she said vaguely. "It seemed to me strange. What are so many German subjects doing over here?"

"Those aren't German subjects, my dear," said Mr. Laurens. "They're American citizens, mostly."

"Surely not!" exclaimed the girl. "The German flags, and the pictures of the Emperor, and all the talk about the German spirit, and—and 'Deutschland über alles.' From *Americans*?"

"Certainly," said the reporter. "And good ones."

"I should think they would better be called good Germans. One cannot imagine that sort of thing occurring in a German city. I mean if the case were reversed, and Americans wanted to hold such a meeting."

"No? What would happen?"

"Verboten. Lèse-majesté. Anti-imperialismus. Something dreadful of that sort."

"They aren't as broad-minded in such things as we are," observed Mr. Laurens, in a tone which caused young Jeremy Robson to glance at him curiously and then become thoughtful.

"Did you notice that fat and glossy person on the stage, the one who had just made that speech—what was his name? Bausch,[5] I think—did you notice his patronizing grin when you got up, Mr. Laurens? As if he felt a calm superiority to your second-rate patriotism."

"What a malicious young person!" said Laurens. "There's really no harm in Bausch that can't be blown off like froth from beer."

"I suppose there *is* a story in all that," ruminated young Jeremy Robson: "if I had the sense to see it. Maybe it would take a historian's mind instead of a reporter's to see it right. But I think I can get some of it into my 'Star-Spangled Banner' story."

"Good luck to you and it, then," said Magnus Laurens cordially. "I'd like to see someone in this town at this time point out that, after all, America is America."

"Would you?" said the girl. "Walk around to the next block and I will show you what I saw this morning as I passed."

They followed her around the corner and stopped before a tiny shop with a giant's boot swinging in front of it. The legend over the door read:

Boot & Shoe Infirmary
Eli Wade, Surgeon

Across the window was stretched a brand-new American flag, and beneath it a second legend, roughly inked on packing-paper and secured to the glass with cobbler's wax:

The Flag of Our Country. It stands alone.

Two beribboned, bespangled, bebadged German Federates passed near them, and paused.

"That is the man who refused to decorate with *our* colors," said one, in German.

"Pfui!" said the second contemptuously, "'s machts nichts. Matters nodding!"

Jeremy Robson took off his hat and made his adieus. "You've given me something to think about," he said, apportioning his acknowledgement impartially, though his eyes were on the strange and alluring face of Marcia Ames. "Good-bye, and thank you."

"If you're grateful for being made to think," returned Magnus Laurens, good humoredly, "there's hope for you as a reporter yet. That's a good-looking boy," he added to his companion, as the young man turned away.

"Good-looking?" she repeated, with a rising inflection that controverted the opinion.

"Oh, not a young Adonis. But there's something under that thatch of hair of his or I'm no guesser. Grit, and purpose, and, I think, honesty. I hope he doesn't make hash of us in his paper."

Allowing himself an hour and a half, the reporter turned out in that time what he firmly believed to be "a pippin of a story." After delivering the final page to an approving copy-reader he washed up, got his coat and hat and started for the door. In the hallway he came upon Senator Martin Embree, just closing a conversation with Farley, the editor-in-chief.

"No politics in this, you know," the Senator was saying, in his sunny voice.

"I understand," said Farley. "If there were—"

"We'd probably be on opposite sides as usual. This is simply a case of not stirring up useless ill-feeling."

"Quite right. And we're much obliged to you. As long as The Guardian won't touch it, you can rely on us."

"I was sure I could." The Senator turned and came face to face with the reporter. "Hello, Mr. Robson," he said with his enveloping smile, and Jeremy went on feeling that the world was a more friendly place, for having encountered that expression of human good-will.

He descended into Fenchester's main street. For the day, it might have been a foreign city. It was all aflutter with streamers inscribed "Wilkommen" followed by sundry German tags. German speech crossed German speech in the humming air. German faces, moist, heavy-hued, good-humored, were lifted to the insignia of the various Bunds, Vereins, Gesellschafts, and Kranzes, all pledged to the fostering and maintenance of a tenacious and irreconcilable foreign culture in the carelessly hospitable land which they had adopted as their own. Over streets, residences, stores, public buildings waved the banners of imperial Germany.

Far above it all, from the dome of the capitol, floated the Stars and Stripes. The flag represented a formality. It meant nothing in particular to anybody, except that the Legislature was then in session. Weaving in the languid air, it seemed remote, lonely, occluded from the jovial fellowship of the swarming Teuton colors. For the time, at least, it had been put aside from men's minds. It was an alien in the land whose sons had died for it, and would again die for it in a day drawing inevitably nearer.

THE PIPPIN[1] OF A story never ripened into print. Young Mr. Robson's formal report of the meeting, a staid bit of journalism, appeared in full. But not a word of that brilliant pen-picture which he had so affectionately worked out. With a flaccid hope that there might have been a mistake somewhere, its author perused the columns of The Record a second time. Nothing! Perhaps, whispered hope, they had held it over. Being of the "sketch" order, it was good at any time. Daring greatly, he invaded the editorial sanctum where the proof-hooks hang. On the second he found his work of art. Upon the margin was rubber-stamped a single word:

"Killed."

Young Jeremy Robson felt as if that lethal monosyllable had been simultaneously imprinted upon his journalistic ambitions. Like salt to the smart of his professional hurt came another thought. What would Miss Marcia Ames think of him when she opened the paper and found nothing of the promised article there? Would there be disappointment in the depths of those disturbing eyes? Or—more probable and intolerable supposition—laughter at the expense of the young cockerel of a reporter who had crowed so confidently about what he was going to do? Happily for the reporter's immediate future, Mr. Farley had departed. For, were that mild, editorial gentleman still available for the purpose, young Jeremy Robson had straightway bearded him in his lair, demanded an explanation, denounced him as a soggy-souled Philistine, thrown his job in his teeth, and if he had exhibited symptoms of being "snooty" (the word is of young Mr. Robson's off-duty hours, and he must be responsible therefor), bunged him one in the eye.

At which critical point young Mr. Robson came to and laughed at himself, albeit somewhat ruefully. It was his saving grace that already he had learned to laugh at himself. Many an equally high-spirited young-ster has gone to the devil, because he let the devil get in his laugh first.

"Souvenir of a lost masterpiece," observed Jeremy, folding the galley for accommodation to his pocket. He decided to take his medicine; to say no word of the matter to anyone, though he would mightily have liked to know why the story was killed.

His resolution of silence was abandoned as the result of a meeting with Andrew Galpin on the following morning. The Guardian man accosted him:

"Didn't see your 'Star-Spangled' story, Bo."

"No."

"What became of it?"

"Killed. What became of yours?"

"Didn't write any."

"Why not?"

"I'm a reporter; that's why. Why queer your paper by writing Amer-ican stuff on a German day!"

"Think that's why my stuff was killed?" asked Robson, impressed.

"Ay-ah," assented Galpin. "What did *you* think?"

"I thought perhaps it wasn't good enough."

"Bunk!" said the downright Galpin. "You didn't think it at all."

"Well, I didn't," admitted his junior, reddening. "I read it over in proof. I think it's dam' good."

"That's the talk! Got a proof with you?"

"Yes."

"Let's see." Galpin leaned against a convenient railing, and pro-ceeded to absorb, rather than read, the two-thirds column, with the practiced swiftness of his craft. "Ay-ah. You're right," he corroborated. "It *is* dam' good."

"But not good enough for The Record."

"Too good. It's got too much guts."

Jeremy Robson repeated the rugged Saxon word in a tone of uncom-prehending inquiry.

"Too American," expounded the other. "Too much 'This-is-our-country-and-don't-you-forget-it' in it."

"Show me one line where—"

"It's between the lines. You couldn't keep it out with barbed wire. You're no reporter," said Andrew Galpin severely. "What d' you think you're writing for The Record? Poetry?"

"Look here!" said the bewildered Robson. "You just said it was good and now—"

"And now I'm telling you it's rotten. Punk! *As* newspaper work, *for* The Record. Or any other paper hereabouts on this great and glorious German day. Why, it'd spoil the breakfast beer of every good and superior citizen of German birth and extraction that read it."

"Then they aren't any sort of Americans if they can't stand that!"

"'Bah' said Mary's little lamb to Mary," observed Mr. Galpin impolitely. "Who said they were Americans? Did you hear much American at that meeting? Did you catch any loud and frenzied cheering for the red, white, and blue, or get your eyesight overcrowded with photographs of the American eagle? Did you mistake the picture of the gent with the wild-boar whiskerines for a new photo of His Excellency, the President of the United States? Did you—"

"Oh, cut it!" said the exasperated Robson.

"Ay-ay," grunted Galpin, and studied the younger man. "Sore?" he inquired carelessly.

"A little, I guess."

"Like to kick a hole in The Record shop, and walk haughtily out through it?"

"That's the way I felt yesterday."

"Want a job on The Guardian?"

"Could you get me on?"

"I can *take* you on. Beginning Monday, I'm city editor. I could use one guy that can write." He glanced again at the killed proof, before folding it to return to its owner.

A thought struck the reporter. "Will you print this?"

"Lord; no!"

"The Guardian wouldn't be any more independent or any less timid about this than The Record?"

"Not a bit."

"Then why do you advise me to change?"

"I don't."

"But you offered—"

"Stop right there while you're still on the track. I offered. I didn't advise. If you're in this business to write what you want, and to hell with the public, I've got just one piece of advice for you. Turn millionaire and get a paper of your own."

Jeremy flushed. "I may do it yet. Not the millionaire part, but the other."

"Give me a job, then," said the other good-humoredly, "as you won't take one from me. If you should want it, it's twenty a week to start. Not bad for a town of 70,000, Bo."

"The Record's promised me better. I guess I'll stay."

"Ay-ah." Galpin accepted the decision indifferently. "Well, I guess you'll get somewhere sometime if you don't go bucking your head against stone walls. But don't waste your poetic style on patriotic kids who stand nobly up in galleries for the honor of the flag."

"That kid was a girl."

"So I noticed in your story. Think I know her."

"Do you?" cried the other eagerly.

"Only as far as business requires. She's going to make newspaper copy one of these days."

"How's that?"

"Only girl intercollegiate athlete in America," replied Galpin in the manner of a headline. "Trying for the golf team, and from what I hear, liable to make it."

"At Old Central?" asked Robson, using the local name for the State University of Centralia, on the outskirts of Fenchester.

"Ay-ah," assented Galpin. "She's a special. Lives down on Montgomery Street with old Miss Pritchard."

His companion made a mental note of it.

"Weren't you a golf-sharp in Kirk College?"

"Captained the team."

"Well, if you really want to write a story about Miss Marcia Ames, watch out for the team trials next month. The Record 'll print that all right. Ay-ah," he added reflectively. "And there'll be no spiking of the story by Mart Embree, either."

"Senator Embree?" said Robson, surprised. "Where does he come in?"

"Didn't happen to see him around The Record office before you went to press yesterday, did you?"

"Yes, I did."

"Ay-ah. Thought he might 'a' dropped in. He made a call on The Guardian too."

"What for?"

"Dove-o'-peace mission. Wanted to make sure that nothing would get in about the 'Star-Spangled' business to stir up ill-feeling."

There rose in Jeremy Robson's mind the recollection of Farley's assurance to Embree, "You can rely on us;" which he had not before connected with his slain masterpiece. Now he perceived with indignation that it had been slaughtered to save a German holiday, at the hands of the Honorable Martin Embree.

"He's the one that put a crimp in my story, is he!"

"Not necessarily," qualified The Guardian man. "Probably they wouldn't have run it anyway. But he wanted to be sure. That's Smiling Martin's way. You don't catch him missing many tricks."

"What's his interest?"

"Just to smooth things over and keep everything lovely. Rasping up the comfortable Dutchers wouldn't do anybody any good, according to his figuring, and would only make things unpleasant."

"A pussyfooter, eh?"

"Don't you believe it," returned Galpin. "Martin Embree will fight and fight like the devil when he sees good cause for it. How else do you think he could have got where he is?"

"I don't know," retorted the younger man sullenly. "But I don't see where he comes in to interfere with me."

"Ask him."

"I will. Where can I find him?"

"As quick as all that!" commented The Guardian reporter. He noted a hardening of the small muscles at the corner of Robson's mouth. "Scrappy little feller, ain't you!"

"Thanks," said Jeremy Robson, with his sudden, pleasant grin. "I get what you mean. Don't think I'm going to make a fool of myself. Just the same I *will* ask him, if you'll tell me where I can catch him."

"Round at Trask's boarding-house, after dinner, most likely. That's where he lives."

At Trask's that evening Jeremy Robson ascended through a clinging aroma of cookery, to a third-floor room, very tiny, very tidy, very much overcrowded with books, pamphlets, a cot, and the spare squareness of the Honorable Marin Embree. The visitor was somewhat surprised at finding a political leader of such prominence so frugally housed. Embree sat at a small table, making notes from a federal report on railroad earnings. He lifted his head and Robson noted a single splash of gray in the brown hair that waved luxuriantly up from the broad forehead. His meetings with the Northern Tier leader had been casual: so he had been the more flattered at Embree's ready recognition on the previous evening. Now he was struck anew with the soft, almost womanish brilliance of the prominent eyes, and the sense of power in the upper part of the face, sharpening down into shrewdness, in the mouth and chin. A thoroughly attractive face, and more than that, a winning as well as an impressive personality. Embree smiled as he greeted his caller by name, and the reporter suddenly felt all the animus ooze from his purpose. He still wanted to know the why and wherefore of Embree's action. But his interest in knowing was equally apportioned between himself and his adversary. Characteristically, Jeremy went straight to the point.

"I came to find out why you got The Record to kill my story."

"Sit down." The Senator relinquished his chair, motioned his visitor to it and seated himself on the edge of the cot. "Your story? What story was that?"

"Why, about the band playing 'The Star-Spangled Banner' and Miss —— and just two people standing up for it."

"Was it your story? I'm sorry if it was killed." Embree's tone was of the simplest sincerity. "But it really wasn't my doing. I only suggested to Mr. Farley that a mishandling of the episode might create an unfortunate impression and incidentally reflect upon The Record. You know how sensitive our German-Americans are."

"It'd be better for us if we American-Americans were a little more sensitive," blurted Robson.

"You're wholly right, Mr. Robson. I wish more of us had the spirit of that young lady in the gallery. What a gallant little figure she was; something knightly and valorous about her! And she, all alone."

"There was Mr. Laurens," suggested Robson.

"Quite another matter. For political effect only, and not in the best of taste, I thought. If the chairman hadn't been a numskull he would have called the whole audience to its feet, and the matter would have been a graceful and pleasant and patriotic incident. But Felder is a blunder head. He stopped the music. I would have got the people up, myself, in another two seconds."

"Senator, you understand the Germans," said the reporter, reverting to his central interest. "I'd like you to read this and tell me if it would have given offense to any decently loyal German-American."

Marin Embree took the proofs, and leaned forward under the lamp to read them. What Andrew Galpin had absorbed, almost in a glance, the politician plodded through with exasperating slowness. Impatience gave way to interest in the reporter's mind, however, when he perceived that his reader was perusing the galley a second time over.

"Well?" he inquired, as Embree raised his head.

The senator's fine smile enveloped him. "Frankly, it wouldn't do."

"What's wrong?"

"Too much fervor."

"It's American fervor."

"True. But it's exclusively American. 'All the rest of you not born Americans, be damned!' It's—well—uncharitable."

The writer's color deepened. "You mean it's unfair."

"Not intentionally. But there are phrases in there that sneer."

"They could be edited out."

"Not so easily. I don't think your writing would be easy to edit, Mr. Robson. It hangs together pretty tight. But, so far as this is concerned, I can plead 'Not guilty' to being an accomplice. I'm sure Mr. Farley would never have let it get into print."

"It was all set up."

"But not OK'd, I assume. You see, Mr. Robson, one must live among our Germans to understand them. They're the best people in the world and the highest-minded citizens. Germany isn't a nation to them. It's a sentiment. It's El Dorado. It's music and poetry and art and literature—and a fairy-land. Lay a profane hand on it, and they're as sensitive as children, and as sulky. But at heart they're just as sound Americans as you or I, and in politics they're always for the right and clean and progressive thing. All they need is to be humored in their harmless and rather silly sentimentalism. You see, I'm talking to you quite frankly."

"And I appreciate it, Senator."

"Well, I appreciate having seen this." Embree tapped the proof with the back of his finger. "Apart from the substance of it, I'm interested. I'm mightily interested."

Jeremy Robson met his direct intent gaze and waited.

"If I know anything about writing, you can write. There's stuff in this. It's a real picture. Perhaps there was a touch of inspiration, too." His face became sunny again with its conquering smile. "Did you know Miss Ames?"

"Not before the interview with her." To his annoyance Jeremy Robson felt his face grow hot. Had he written *that* between the lines, too?

"No? A gallant figure. Young America; the imperishable spirit. Do you think you could write like that—without special inspiration?" he demanded abruptly.

"It's the best story I've done yet. But I can beat it, when I've had more experience."

"Then this town is going to be too small for you." There was no tone of patronage or flattery in the rich, even voice. "Were you thinking of staying here?"

"Until I learn the ropes. I want to own a pa—"

Jeremy Robson stopped short. Why should he be confiding his ambitions to this stranger, to whom he owed nothing, unless an injury?

"A paper of your own," concluded Embree. He fell thoughtful. "Ever write any editorials?" he asked presently.

"No."

"Why don't you try it?"

"I don't know. I never thought of it."

"Think of it now."

"Reporters aren't supposed to go outside their own department."

"Pshaw! A newspaper is like any other business; it needs all the ability it can command. Now, I believe you could write editorials. And if you care to try, I'll be glad to speak a word to Mr. Farley."

"That's mighty good of you, Senator."

"Not at all. Gives me a chance to set myself right in your mind," smiled the other, "for appearing to interfere with your activities. We need a new paper, a new kind of paper here in the capital," he added after another of his pauses.

Jeremy Robson became uncomfortable. "I guess I've been talking through my hat," he confessed. "It must take a lot of capital to buy a newspaper."

"Not so much, for a small-city plant."

"More than I'll ever see, though."

"If the right man came to light and proved himself, he might find backing. That's why I take an interest in the local newspaper situation. It's only a question of the right man. We're looking for him."

"I'd like to be that man," blurted the caller.

"But *are* you? That's the question." The Senator's fine eyes twinkled. But his tone was serious enough.

"How should I know, myself? I've only had a few months' experience. Unless you count college journalism."

"I do," answered the other unexpectedly. "A client of mine is a trustee at Kirk College. I had the occasion to follow the Kirk-Bell's attacks on the Board in the intercollegiate football mix-up. You were editing The Bell, I believe."

"Yes," admitted Robson. "I guess we were a pretty brash lot."

"All of that. And you were quite wrong. But you were fighting for what you thought a principle, and I liked the way you fought." He put up a large, well-kempt hand and pushed a wave of hair back from his forehead. "I'm fighting for a principle here."

"Political?" said Jeremy Robson.

"Do politics interest you?"

"They make me sick," returned the reporter vigorously.

"That's bad. Why?"

"Because of the cheap skates and drumheads I run into whenever I get a legislative job."

"On behalf of myself and my colleagues, I thank you."

Jeremy Robson blushed. "Well, you know I don't mean you, Senator."

"Possibly some of my associates are shrewder than you give them credit for being. But the State Legislature isn't politics. It's only the sieve through which politics pass. If you're not interested in politics, the newspaper business isn't your line."

"I didn't say I wasn't interested in politics."

"True enough. You didn't." Embree shot one of his reckoning glances at the young fellow. "Well, if you can prove yourself—if you can fight as well as you write and write as hard as you fight—you're going to be worth keeping an eye on. And I'm going to keep an eye on you for my own reasons."

"I'll remember that," said the reporter, rising, "when I come to try my hand at editorial writing."

"Sit down. Unless you've got some engagement." Jeremy shook his head. "I want to talk to you a little more." Another of those pauses, which gave the effect of being filled with considered thinking. "About myself," finished the Honorable Martin Embree.

The visitor resumed his seat.

"Do you read your own paper?"

"Every word of it, every day."

"Then you see an occasional editorial about your humble servant."

"Yes," Jeremy began to feel uncomfortable. The Record's editorial attitude toward the Honorable Marin Embree was, to put it mildly, unsympathetic. "I was surprised to see you in the office," he added bluntly.

"Did you think I was as thin-skinned as that?" Embree's smile was good-humor itself. "Politically, Farley is my enemy. Personally, we get along pleasantly. In his heart he knows I'm right," announced the Senator from the Northern Tier, with calm assurance.

"Then why doesn't he say so?"

"He's only a hired man."

"He's editor-in-chief."

"By title. The real boss is Clarence Ensign."

Jeremy stared. "How's that? I thought Mr. Ensign was nothing but a traveling millionaire."

"So he is, mostly. But he owns the controlling interest in The Record. Absentee landlordism. It's worse in a newspaper than in a mill, because a newspaper is supposed to be representative of its public. Ensign's newspaper represents only the investments which let him sport around the fashionable seaside places in his yacht. Because I'm after some of the big interests that pay his graft-money, The Record is after me. It's all part of the game."

As the politician proceeded to amplify on his theme, Jeremy Robson became thoughtful. "See here, Senator," he said at length, "suppose I should 'prove up,' as you say, and should get backing for a paper, I'd be just a hired man for my backers, wouldn't I?"

"Not if you were strong enough to make yourself the necessary part of the paper. But you'd have to believe in the policies of your backers."

"I don't believe I could believe in anything I had to believe in," returned Jeremy quaintly.

"Correct answer," approved Embree with emphasis. "No fellow could that's worth his salt. Anyway, it doesn't so much matter, provided you believe in something and stick to your belief instead of singing whatever tune you're paid or ordered to sing." Again, one of his frequent pauses. "Like The Record and The Guardian."

"The Guardian, too?"

"Oh, that's worse. The Record at least represents its own interests, even if they are pretty sordid. The Guardian is anybody's hired man. Do you know Wymett, the editor?"

"No."

"He's a crook."

"That's a short and ugly word, Senator."

"Wymett's a short and ugly animile. Short on payment of his obligations, and ugly in a fight because you never know who he's sold to last. Though, at that"–and here the considering pause came in the middle of the statement–"you can be pretty sure that Montrose Clark will have the deciding word."

"Is that the President of the Public Utilities Corporation?"

"That's the man. Know him?"

"I've reported him at meetings, twice. He didn't say anything much."

"He never does, in public or for the public. What did you think of him?"

"I thought he was a pompous little stuffed shirt," was the reporter's irreverent opinion.

"He's pompous enough. But there's brains behind those piggy eyes of his. We were talking of politics. Well, Montrose Clark *is* politics. He's politics, big."

"I would have thought he was finance, and bluff."

"Finance, of course. That is politics. Let me give you a one-minute synopsis of the politics of this State. I told you the Legislature was a sieve. Well, the men that feed and shake the sieve are the financial and public utility interests; Montrose Clark representing the traction crowd, Magnus Laurens representing the water-power grabbers, Robert Wanser representing the banks, Sam Corliess representing the lake shipping, Selden Dana representing the railroads, and so on. And our newspapers are mostly just their little yellow dogs, useful to help put over their deals and to fool the people. What we need, and we need it right here in the capital, is a newspaper that will tell the people, not fool them."

"Who's 'we'?"

The Senator's earnest gaze flickered for a moment. "I," he said, at length. "I'm making this fight pretty near alone so far."

"What fight is that?"

"The fight to get the control of the State away from the grafters and exploiters and turn it over to the people. And I'm beginning to get the support I need now."

"From the German crowd?"

The Senator smiled at his caller with an expression almost affectionate. "You wouldn't take to politics much worse than a duck to water. Yes; from the Germans largely. I'm a reformer, and I'm not ashamed of the name. The German-Americans are solid for reform and clean government. Government by corporations is never clean. It can't be. It uses the kind of tools that Wymett is."

"The Guardian has offered me a job," observed Jeremy.

"Don't touch it," advised the other earnestly. "They're on the ragged edge. As I told you, Wymett is a crook. One of these days I'm going to tell the State that."

"Maybe I'll be there to report it," said the caller, smiling.

"Maybe you'll be there (you should work into the legislative end, by the way, for the experience); but you won't report it. Your paper would print any attack by Wymett on me that suited its purposes. But if I proved Wymett to be a crook and a grafter—not a word in The Record. That's the way the papers hang together."

"Well, that's all right," returned Jeremy stoutly. "Why shouldn't newspaper men stand together? Politicians do."

"You feel that way about it?" The Senator's tone was colder. "It's a question of fair play. However"—the sunny smile returned to his face—"we've had a pretty straight talk, and I hope I've given you something to carry away with you. I'll admit my object is largely selfish. I'm looking everywhere for the man who can eventually make a newspaper for the public. It won't come tomorrow, or next day. But it'll come someday. It's got to. And don't forget that editorial writing. Make it mild, at first."

Before he went to bed that night, Jeremy Robson had sketched out three editorials. For a week he re-wrote and re-cast and polished them. To his keen satisfaction, two of them were accepted. The third, which touched upon the "Star-Spangled Banner" episode, most tactfully and in what the writer deemed to be the broadest and most charitable spirit, was turned down. Farley encouraged him.

"Keep it up, Robson. As soon as you've learned our ways you'll fit into the page."

## 3

"Oh, happier he who gains not
The Love some seem to gain:
The joy that custom stains not
Shall still with him remain.
The loveliness that wanes not,
The Love that ne'er can wane."

THE SOFT, YOUNG CONTRALTO voice floating out from the old house
on Montgomery Street, mingled with the breath of roses that spread
possessively over the veranda. A ripple of sparkling chords, like wind
passing over water, died away in a delicate and plaintive minor cadence.
A light footstep moved within the house. The voice, now not more than
a clear murmur, hummed in the hallway. Something told the listener
and lurker on the sidewalk that it were advisable he should be on his
way. To be caught staring, gawking and explanation-less, before the
Wondrous Maiden's domicile is not the happiest method of producing a favorable impression upon the Wondrous Maiden, which latter
was become the immediate and predominant purpose of young Mr.
Jeremy Robson's existence.

He passed on. After a score or more of paces he began to lag and
waver. Yet an undue hesitancy of spirit had never been reckonable as
among young Mr. Robson's major failings. He had come along Montgomery Street, which is a free public thoroughfare wherein any and
all may pass, without let or hindrance, upon their lawful occasions, a
youth upright and secure of himself. Nothing more formidable had
marked his itinerary than a singularly sweet young voice, singing to
an unknown measure the words of Mr. Andrew Lang's haunting and
wistful lyric. Yet young Mr. Robson became instantly aware of strange

symptoms within himself. His pulse was markedly uneven. His eyes were affected by a spasmodic inclination which all but twisted his neck about in the opposite direction to that of his reluctant steps. His mind was a kingdom divided against itself.

Arrived at the corner he found himself racked by conflicting muscular intentions and inhibitions. He turned into Nicklin Avenue, leading downtown to his proper occupation, and almost immediately executed a right-about-face. He returned to the corner, and rebounded from the impact of an unreasoning and unmanning fear. Again he retraced his steps and halted. His feet gave him the painful impression of a divided allegiance, and he recognized and resented the invalidity of the poet's praise of those supposedly useful members:

"I only have to steer 'em, and
They ride me everywheres."

In the midst of his confusion he became hotly aware of the surprised scrutiny of a small boy with a dog.

"Lost somethin'?" inquired the small boy, scornfully.

Jeremy Robson started. Was the urchin possessed of the spirit of divination? Certainly young Mr. Robson had lost his nerve. That much he confessed to himself. The small boy's dog divined the fact also. He made a charge upon the wavering youth with the evident intention of chasing him up a tree. To be flouted in the open day by a cur of highly impeachable antecedents was a little too much!

"Get out!" commanded Jeremy Robson, in a tone which left no room for doubt.

The small boy and his dog retired hastily. Their intended victim, somewhat reconstituted in soul by the victory, clinched his final decision, not indeed without a sinking of the breath, and with a firm tread and an unwavering eye (as he had once written of an unfortunate going to his execution) again plunged into the imminent, deadly breach of Montgomery Street, and headed for the old house amid the roses. He reckoned that she would be just about on the porch now. If she weren't, he would go on past and make for the office, and try again on the morrow. If she were—well, he had recovered command of at least three matured and plausible lies to explain his presence. Then he saw her, and the lies forsook and left him stranded with nothing better than the truth to tell, if the issue rose.

She was standing at the top of the five veranda steps. An errant wind weaving among the roses above her, let through swift glints of sunlight, which played upon her face and hair with fairy touches. There was a dreamy and wistful smile, as in lingering memory of the music she had sung, upon her lips. Her face, broad at the temples and narrowing down to a small, self-willed chin, was modeled nearer upon the sensitive and changeful lines of the triangle than upon the cold and classic oval. Above it the splendid mass of tawny hair was hardly kept respectably within bounds by the prisoning devices of net and band. She was slender, and firm-set, and straight with the soft and strong lines of young, untainted health and vigor. By the warm hues, and the lithe poise of her, she was a creature bred in the happy usages of sunlight and free winds and the open spaces. Again he felt in her that subtle, disturbing, starry quality that makes for dreams.

In her hand she swung a broad sun-hat. Reluctantly she lifted her arms to set it on her head. The pulses of Jeremy Robson made a bound of hopefulness. Evidently she was coming out upon the street. Her eyes were lifted and he wondered that he could ever have thought them gray, so flooded were they with hazel lights as they met the radiance, sifting down through the trees. She turned them upon him and a slow recognition grew in them. Opening the gate, she stood waiting. He lifted his hat as he approached.

"Good-morning," she greeted him in that voice which, with its indefinable distinction of accent, had thrilled in his memory, since he had first heard her speak.

He returned her greeting, calling her by name.

"It is The Record you write for, is it not?" she asked.

"Yes. But they don't print all I write."

"So I infer," she returned with grave and intent eyes.

"Were you disappointed?"

"A little."

"I'm sorry."

"I supposed that you had made up your mind that it was not worth writing after all."

"It was worth writing."

"But not worth printing?"

"Worth printing, too. But the editors were afraid of offending the Germans. So they killed it."

"Did you write it in that way?"

"What way?"

"To offend the Germans."

"No. I wrote it to show that there was a place for Americanism even in a German meeting."

"I am glad you did that," she said quietly.

"You've a right to be. You're responsible. For the way I wrote it, I mean. You gave me the notion."

"I am glad of that, too. But I am sorrier than ever that I did not see your article."

"Perhaps I'll show it to you some day."

She nodded, without asking him how or where. Marcia Ames was one of those individuals who wait unquestioningly and accept generously. "It is quite a coincidence my meeting you here," she said. "For I wished to ask you about the article."

Behold the path now made plain for the lurker and retracer of steps! No need even for those well-formulated lies; he could simply accept the theory of coincidence. And, most unaccountably, he found that he couldn't. Perhaps he could have, had he not looked into her eyes just then. That steady, limpid, candid, confident regard of hers forbade even a petty and harmless deceit of convenience. Once for all Jeremy Robson knew that whatever might be between them in future, there would at least be truth. And with a sharp pang, felt the foreboding that the truth might yet hurt him to the limit of his capacity for pain.

"No," he denied. "No coincidence."

"Not?" she asked, surprised.

"I've passed here every day for the last ten days."

"Do you live on this block?"

"No. In the other end of town, up near the University."

"Then you would not pass here to go to The Record office."

"Your geography is unimpeachable."

"Is it a riddle? I am not at all clever at them."

"It's a confession. I've been coming this way day after day for a particular purpose."

"What was it?"

"To see you again."

"What did you wish to see me about?"

"Nothing. Nothing in particular."

"Just to see me? That is very nice of you." She studied him with her direct and serene regard. But a small and willful dimple materialized on the brown curve of her cheek, and a little one-sided smile went up to meet it. "Not as a reporter this time?"

"Not in the least. A reporter may be just an ordinary human being, off duty, you know."

"Are you just an ordinary human being?"

"Very much so. Don't I strike you that way?" His tone was one of exaggerated anxiety.

The girl studied him with impersonal interest, quite free from embarrassment. Magnus Laurens has credited him with good looks. In the usual sense, Miss Ames decided, confirming her first opinion, he was not entitled to this credit. He was rather rugged of build and face, with mobile lips, boyish and pleasant eyes, an obstinate jaw which looked as if it might set to courage and endurance or perhaps to sullenness, and the expression and bearing of one vividly and intelligently curious about the life-scheme of which he was a part. The girl noted, with approval, his dress: quietly harmonious in every detail yet without suggesting the finicky habit; a style which would have been unremarkable in New York or London, but which stood out with a pleasant distinction among the more casual and careless garb of the Middle West.

"I really had not given it much thought," she answered, having completed her scrutiny. "Your methods seem rather out of the ordinary."

"Are you a million years old?" he asked abruptly.

If his intention was to startle her, it failed signally. "Surely that is a very personal question. I am not—quite. Why do you ask?"

"Because you look so like a kid and yet you've got the nerve—no, not nerve—the confidence and manner of your own great-grandmother. It's very confusing," complained young Mr. Robson, leaning dejectedly upon the gate.

"Perhaps it arrives from my having been brought up abroad and much among older people," she surmised, with one of her slightly un-English turns of phrase. "One reason for my coming here to the University is to accustom myself to your American ways."

"'*Your*' American ways?"

"Our American ways," she amended sweetly. "Oh, I am all American in my heart!" The gay and willful little dimple again materialized on her cheek. "Still, one cannot remain indefinitely leaning over a gate in conversation, however thrilling, with a young man whose name one does not even know, can one?" she pointed out.

"You don't know my name?" Young Mr. Robson looked distinctly annoyed. "Mr. Laurens presented me. Don't you remember?"

"But you were only a reporter who was going to write something about me, then." With an emphasis on the final word, slight, indeed, yet amply sufficient to make amends.

Her caller brightened perceptibly. "Surname Robson. Given name, Jeremy. Jem, when you get to know me better."

She opened her eyes very wide to take in this idea.

"You expect that we are going to know each other so well as that?"

"We certainly are if I can bring it about. Don't you think I've made a good start?"

"At least a quick one. What is your next step?"

"That's what's worrying me a little."

"But so progressing a young man as you, with so much perseverance," she taunted, "surely if you planned to see me once, you would plan how to see me again. Perhaps, though, you do not wish to see me again soon," she added, with an adorable mock-melancholy droop of the alluring lips.

"You'll never win any guessing contests on that form, Miss Ames," he assured her, shaking his head solemnly. "But you're right enough about my having a plan. The question is, will it work."

"Try it."

"Here goes. You're trying for the Varsity golf team, aren't you?"

"I intend to, if I improve enough."

"Are you pretty good?"

"I am steady. Only twice I have been as high as one hundred. But my short approaches are bad."

"I can help 'em."

"Can you? Are you a good player?"

"Fair. But I'll tell you what I am. I'm a good coach. We never lost an intercollegiate at Kirk in the three years I captained the team."

"And you offer to coach me? It is very kind of you."

"Wait. It may not be so simple as all that."

"Shall you exact terms?" she smiled.

"This depends on how much you are in earnest about making the team."

"Very much."

"Enough to get up at five in the morning and play a round?"

"Why such an unearthly hour?"

"It's about the only time I can be sure of. Don't forget I'm a hard-working reporter."

"I thought you wished me to forget it, only a moment ago," she teased.

"I want you to remember that I'm a man," he retorted, "besides being a reporter. And that you and I are going to be friends." He looked her fairly in the eyes. "At least," he added quietly.

The baffling lights in her eyes deepened as she met his gaze, unwaveringly. "I believe that we are—at least," she said. "When shall we begin?"

"We *have* begun."

"The golf, I mean."

"Tomorrow."

She laughed outright. "You lose no time."

"I don't know that I have any to lose. I don't know how long you're to be here."

"Nor do I," she answered with a sudden gravity. "Very well; tomorrow. I will meet you at the club house as 5.45. Oh! I forgot. My golf shoes are at Eli Wade's. You remember; the 'Boot & Shoe Surgeon'?"

"I'll get them this afternoon, and bring them with me."

"'Lo, Miss Marcy!"

The interruption, in a cheerful sing-song, came behind Jeremy. He turned to face the small boy and the dog of his earlier encounter.

"Good-morning, Buddy," returned the girl.

"I've come to weed the sparr'grass."

"Yes: we have been expecting you."

"I stopped by home to get you these." He brought out a fistful of deep-hearted pansies, bound in a pink string.

The girl took them, gave him a little, quick pat of the hand which he accepted with a flush of mingled adoration and embarrassment, and pinned them at her throat.

"This is Mr. Burton Higman," she said. "Mr. Jeremy Robson. To his friends, Jem, and Mr. Higman to his friends, Buddy."

Mr. Higman regarded Mr. Robson with a consideration in which there was more of suspicion than friendliness.

"Where 'dje gittim?" he demanded of Miss Ames.

"I did not get him. He came," explained the girl.

"Yep. I seen him before he got here. He was down on the corner, actin' queer."

"Hold on, now, Buddy," protested the other, looking pained. "Don't take away a man's character."

Miss Ames motioned him to silence, and turned an eye of lively anticipation upon the urchin.

"What was he doing?"

"Snake-turns. Walk down Nicklin Avenya; turn. Walk up to the corner; turn again. Stop at the corner; talk to a tree. Walk down Nicklin Avenya again; turn oncet more. Stand still. I watcht him."

"What did he do then?" asked the girl, enjoying the discomfiture of her caller.

The narrator rubbed one foot over the other and considered. "Sweat," he stated conscientiously. "Look at his collar."

Mr. Robson's involuntary hand and Miss Ames' involuntary gaze met upon the article of apparel indicated. It melted under the double pressure.

"Walked back up to Montgomery Street," continued the conscientious chronicler enjoyably. "Stopped. Cussed the tree. Sweat some more. Turned down Bank—"

"That will do, Buddy. You should be a detective." Mr. Burton Higman blushed in glory. The girl turned to the accused. "Is all this true?"

"Guilty as charged."

"Any mitigating circumstances?"

"I was screwing up my courage to face an ordeal."

"What's an ordeal?" demanded the watchful Mr. Higman.

"I am," replied Miss Ames.

"Yep: I'm on," observed her youthful admirer, enlightened. "Mr. Wade on the School Board made us a talk Sat'day, about ordeals. Said each of us should adopt a high ordeal and stick to it. If you're one, and I got to do it, I choose to adopt you."

"Buddy," said his rival.

"Yep?"

"Will you sell out your claim for a dime?"

"No, *sir!*"

"For a quarter?"

"Nope."

"For a dol—"

"Quit! No fair!" protested Mr. Higman in a voice of poignant agony.

"You're right. It isn't fair. Shake, old boy." Young Mr. Robson gravely shook young Burton Higman by the hand. "Between you and me, only honorable and knightly rivalry. We'll go fishing someday and talk over high ordeals and other matters close to the heart."

"And at present Buddy and I will map out the attack upon the asparagus," said the girl.

She turned away, with a smile of dismissal for her informal caller.

As he took himself off, Marcia Ames turned to her other admirer. "Well, Buddy. What do you think of him?"

"He's a nut," was the prompt and uncompromising decision.

"So bad? If it is bad. What is a nut?"

"Plumb crazy."

"You think so? Perhaps, a little."

"Plumb!" persisted the other jealously. But the innate and responsive fair-mindedness of youth prompted him to add: "But say! When he kinda smiles that way at ye, it's all off. There's nothin' to it. It gets you. Ain't it true?" inquired Buddy earnestly.

The unanalytical Buddy was flattered, thrilled, and faintly puzzled by the instant response to this speech when, laughing, his goddess caught him in a quick, warm little hug. He didn't wholly understand why she did it.

For that matter, neither did she.

## 4

"GOLF BOOTS?" SAID ELI WADE, Boot & Shoe Surgeon. "Fer the young lady at Miss Pritchard's? Right here." He held them up to his own admiration. "A foot that's *right*," said the Boot & Shoe surgeon. "Right *and* light. Honest wear on them boots. Even as a die. No sloppy, slovenly running down at one side of the heel. The wearer of them boots carries her weight square an' level, she does. She stands straight, an' looks you straight in the eye. Why didn't she come for 'em herself, same as she brung 'em? Not ailin', is she?"

"I was going by this way so I stopped in to save time," said Jeremy Robson.

"You're welcome. But I'd ruther she'd come, herself. We had a good talk, her an' me, when she brung in the boots." He wrapped them up clumsily but carefully. "An *extry* good operation. But no extry charge."

A figure stirred in a long canvas chair in the corner. From it came a mutter in which the words "Scab-work" in a contemptuous tone were alone comprehensible. The figure reared a white-thatched head, and a keen, lined face, above a sinewy neck set upon a spare frame. "Rich, ain't she?" said the figure. "Let her pay extry, then, for extry work."

"Rich she may or may not be," replied the Boot & Shoe surgeon. "Proud she ain't. Comes in here as free as fresh air an' as pleasant. 'Mr. Wade?' s' she. 'Doctor Wade, when I'm in the Surgery, Miss,' s' I. 'Doctor Wade, you get my trade,' s' she, and laughed a little, for she hadn't meant to say it that way. 'That's as purty a rhyme as ever I heard in my life, Miss,' s' I. I looked at the boots. 'Furrin?' s' I. 'No,' s' she. 'American,' s' she. 'As American as you are.' 'Glad to hear it,' s' I. 'You must be an American from 'way-back,' s' I, 'fer the wades f'm Wal-*tham*,' s' I, 'have fit in every war f'm the Revolution sence, all an' inclusive, an' I reckon to live to fight in the comin' one, ef they take 'em over sixty years of age,' s' I. 'What is the comin' one, Doctor Wade?' s' she. 'Why, the war when us Americans has got to get together and fight for Americar against all these durn furiners that think they own the earth,' s' I. 'That's the comin' war as I reckon it, an' I guess it's comin' right here in Centralia an' through the Middle West purty soon unless we figger to let ourselves get shevved plum off the map,' s' I. Then she told me about noticin' the flag an' the motter in my winder, an' says that's why she brung me her trade, an' she hopes the flag'll stay there, fer trade follers the flag, s' she, or ought to in sech a good cause. An' she laughs that laugh of hern, like music, an' we settled down an' had a real good palaver. So," said the Boot & Shoe Surgeon, "she gets a low-priced, extry-good operation. Though I'm bound to say, she'd 'a' got somethin' extry jest on the straight way she wears shoeleather."

"You read character from shoes, then," commented Jeremy Robson, mildly amused.

"What'd I be if I couldn't? A cobbler! A leather-patcher! Not a genuwyne Boot & Shoe Surgeon. Character in shoes? Of course there is. Lemme see yours." He lifted up first one, then the other foot of his visitor, as if he were a horse, and shook his head soberly over them.

"You stumble," he said. "You ain't struck your gait, yet. Bump up against things when there's no sense in it. Foolish. Obstinit, too, I wouldn't wonder. Lazy? M-m-m! I dunno. I guess you like the easy way an' a clear path pretty good. If you're sensible an' saving, better leave them shoes with me for a little toning-up."

"Will you undertake to improve my character with the improvement to my shoes?"

"Laugh at me if you like. You don't laugh at folks that believes in palmistry. What's a man's palm to read! He can change every line in it with a hoe, or an awl, or a golf-stick. But his shoes! Ah! As a man walks, so he is. An' his shoes tell the tale. Take these, young man." The Boot & Shoe Surgeon laid an affectionate hand upon Miss Marcia Ames' boots. "Study 'em. They'll repay you. There's courage an' clean pride an' a warm heart that travels the path she walks. Yes; an' a touch of vanity—Why not? An' a temper of their own, them boots. Hot an' quick an' generous. You've got to travel some to keep pace with them boots. I dunno when I've had a pair to match 'em. Here's another pair'll go far." He lifted them into view. "Hand-made, stout-made, and serviceable. They're climbers, they are! They'll reach the high places—if they don't slip."

"Who owns them?"

"The Honorable Martin Embree."

"A faker," grunted the white-haired figure.

"A climber. A hustler. A fighter. No faker. Yet—they may slip," said the diagnostician, studying the sole of the left boot. "They *may* slip. Gave me some advice, when he saw my winder. 'Leave the flag, but take out the motter,' s' he. 'There's no sense in that "It stands alone." The country is big enough an' broad enough for all nationalities, an' welcome,' s' he."

"Sensible enough," growled the figure in the chair. "But he's a faker. A half-heart. All for the people in words. But put it up to him in deeds—he ain't there."

"He's a Socialist,"[1] explained the Boot & Shoe Surgeon, pointing his awl at the chair. "Nicholas Milliken. Make you acquainted. What did you say your name was?"

"Jeremy Robson," said its owner, who hadn't yet said anything of the sort.

The figure in the chair for the first time honored him with its attention.

"On The Record?" he asked.

"Yes."

"Reporter?"

"Yes."

"Then you've got the soul of a louse."

"Soft words, Nick," prescribed Eli Wade.

"Soft words? Hard facts! The soul of a louse!"

"Who the devil are you?" demanded Jeremy.

"A Socialist," repeated the Boot & Shoe Surgeon. "Don't mind him."

Milliken rose and stood before the subject of his contemptuous phrase; long, lean, dry, and bitter. "Me?" said he. "I'm a man. I'm no hired pen. I write for The Free-Thinker, when I write."

"Rest of the time he sets type on The Record," explained Wade.

"That's it. Many a time I've run the stick over your stuff."

"It seems to have made an unfavorable impression on you," remarked Jeremy.

"Oh, you can write." The other flung the concession to him condescendingly. "I grant you that. What good does that do you? You've got to trim your facts to your owner's orders, haven't you?"

"Not facts," denied the reporter with some heat. "Facts are facts. I don't trim them for anybody."

"Nobody trims them after they're written, either, I suppose."

The tone was not to Jeremy's liking. "The copydesk—" he began.

"Oh, cut the guff! The copy-desk is a hired blue pencil, just like you're a hired pen. You know what I mean. Why didn't they print your story on the girl at the Federated German Societies meeting? Wasn't it facts? Wasn't it good enough?"

Jeremy was silent.

"I'll tell you," resumed the implacable Socialist. "They were afraid. Afraid of the German crowd. Call their souls their own? Not any more than you can."

"What about yourself, Nick?" put in the proprietor of the place. "You take The Record's money, the same as this gentleman, only maybe not so much of it."

"Do I sell myself for it? Would I write for The Record? Or any other of the capitalistic press? Eli Wade, you're honest, you are. A fool, but honest. You don't know what a reporter's go to do to hold his job. Why, if you was to get into some mix-up over a pair of shoes with the owner of his paper tomorrow, he'd be sent down here to write you wrong, whether you were right or wrong, and he'd do it. He'd have to do it. That's what comes of a privately owned press, under our capitalistic system."

Through the gross exaggeration Jeremy felt the point of a half-truth and resented it. "No decent reporter would do it," he asserted.

"Who said anything about 'decent' reporters?" countered the other.

Jeremy's face changed; his weight shifted slightly upon his feet. Not so slightly but that the pedal diagnostician noticed the movement.

"Want to get your eye punched?" he inquired, of Milliken. "You're going the right way for it."

The Socialist grinned wickedly and relishingly. "Don't like that, huh? All right. Come to me a year from now and tell me I'm wrong, and I'll apologize. That's fair. Ain't it?

"That's fair," corroborated the Boot & Shoe Surgeon.

"Mind you," continued the Socialist, pursuing his favorite path of self-explication; "I wouldn't ha' printed your story either. It was a fool story. Ain't the Germans just as good as we are? Better'n a lot of us. They believe in the rights o' men, they do. None of your dirty aristocratic notions about them. Look at Germany! Most Socialistic country in the world today. Most civilized, too."

"Let 'em stay I their own country, then," said Eli Wade. "We don't want 'em."

"Ah, but we do! We need 'em to help on the Social Revolution."

"My folks fit in one American Revolution," said the Doctor stoutly. "I don't reckon none of us is going to fight in another led by Germans and crazy folks."

"You'll come around," laughed Milliken. "You'll live to be ashamed of that silly motto in your window. Take it out! Take it out, Eli Wade, and put the Red Flag of World-Brotherhood in its place."

"Above the American flag, mebbe?"

"Along with it. My stock's as good Yankee as yours, Eli. But I'm ready to fight again for libutty, and you ain't. You read too much in the capitalistic press. Someday you'll be reading this young feller's editorials, all about the rights o' capital and what the laboring man owes to his employer."

"You will not," said Jeremy.

"Trying your pen at editorials, ain't you?"

"Have you been setting those up, too?"

"Exactly. You'll land. You've got the knack. The slick, smooth, oily trick of making the thing seem what it ain't. So pretty soon I'll have to take that back about your having the soul of a louse. You'll be worse than that. I'll tell you what you'll be." And he told, naming a very ancient and much blown-upon profession.

"That'll be enough an' some-to-carry from you," said the Boot & Shoe Surgeon indignantly. "Get out of my place an' don't come back until you've cleaned your dirty tongue."

Resentment of his brusque dismissal was far remote from Mr. Nicholas Milliken's philosophic mind, if one were to judge by the cheerful smile with which he rose. "All right, old moozle-head!" he returned affectionately. "He fires me about once a week," he explained to Jeremy. "That's when he can't stand any more good, plain facts. They boil over on him and out I go, with the steam. Don't you mind me, either, young feller. You'll see I'm right, one day. We're all bound upon the Wheel of Things,[2] as the old Lammy said to Kim. Sup-prised, are you, that I know Roodyerd Kipling?" He preened himself with a childish vanity. "I read everything! The old Lammy was a bit of a Socialist himself. All bound upon the Wheel of Things. And if I see a little clearer than you, it's only because I happen to be bound a turn or two higher up."

The ineffable patronage of this amused Jeremy into good humor. "I'll call on you for that apology, though, one of these days," he said to the parting guest.

Eli Wade looked after Milliken with a frown. "Them shoes of his have got a gallows gait," he declared. "Lawless paths! Lawless paths! Why do I stand his bitter tongue? I guess it's because he makes me think. I wish I had his education," sighed the old man.

"Where did he get it?"

"Picked it up. Libraries, night schools, and the like. He was a New England mill-hand, always in hot water. Stirrin' up labor troubles and all that. Picked up typography an' drifted out here. A quirky mind an' a restless one, an' a bad course it sets for his feet to follow," said the gentle, one-ideaed old philosopher of foot-gear. "But not a bad heart, Nick hasn't. Come in again, young gentleman," he added. "Not in the way of trade. Come in an' talk with the old man. One of you newspaper gentlemen drops in for a chat, often. Mr. Galpin of The Guardian. You'll know him, I guess?"

"Very well."

"Them are his spare shoes, yonder. Rough, ordinary, plain articles. Plodders. But good wearing stuff in 'em an' right solid on the ground, every inch. Slow-moving," he nodded thoughtfully. "Yes; they'll move slow, but they won't never wobble. An' don't think to trip up the man that walks in 'em. It ain't to be done."

"I believe you're right, there."

"Right? Cert'nly I'm right. Leather never lies. Not good leather. An' poor leather's a dead give-away. My museum of soles." He waved a showman's hand toward the rows of shoes suspended neatly in brackets of his own devising against the walls. "Look at them Congress gaiters. Wouldn't you know they was a banker's belongings? Robert Wanser, President of the Trust Company. Full and easy and comfortable and mebbe a little sly in the gait. But there's weight in 'em. Don't get in their way. There's Rappelje's next 'em; Professor Rappelje, of the University. Queer neighbors. Straight and thin and fine finished, his gear. Mebbe a little pinchy. But a man to swear by. And Bausch: them high-button calfs. He's a buster. Busts his buttons off. One of them big, puffin'-up Germans. Always marching. Tramp-tramp-tramp: the goose-step. Nothin' o' that in that lot on the end. Judge Dana. See the ball of the soles? Worn down. Creeps, he does. Guess he can jump too, after he's crept near enough. An' that pair below, on the right. That's a shuffler. Mr. Wymett. Owns The Guardian and runs it. Now here's a mincer. Dainty an' soft he goes an' daity an' soft he lives: the Rev. Mr. Merserole, rector of our rich folks' church. For all that, there's stuff an' weight in his shoes." His hand hovered and touched a pair of elegantly made, low, laced Oxfords, of almost feminine delicacy. "Style there, eh? Know what they want, those shoes. Got to be jest so. Spick an' span. They say Montrose Clark never has to pay to have 'em cleaned."

"Why is that?" asked Jeremy, responsive to the look of invitation in the old man's eye.

"Got so many boot-lickers around him, chuckled the philosopher. "Kick you as soon as look at you, those would, for all they look so finicky."

"I'll come in to see you when I need pointers about people," said Jeremy, smiling.

The Boot & Shoe Surgeon handed him the repaired golf-boots. "I'm an ignorant old man," he said, "but I know folks's feet and sometimes I can guess what path they'll take. I've been talking pretty free to you, Mr. Robson, for a stranger. But I reckon you're trustable, 'spite of what Nick Milliken says."

"I reckon I am, Doctor Wade," returned Jeremy, and believed himself as he said it.

"Yes: the old man likes to talk," confessed Eli Wade; "an' about people. Gossip, some call it. That's a silly word. What's history but gossip about folks that are dead? But, of course, a man like me has to be careful who he talks to, being in public life."

"Certainly," acquiesced the amused Jeremy. "But I didn't know you were in public life. What office do you hold?"

"I'm on the Fenchester Public School Board," said Eli Wade with simple but profound pride.

## 5

BOBOLINK ON A GRASS-TUFT piped ecstatic welcome to a long-lost friend, the sun. Five gray and weary days had passed since that amiable orb had bestowed so much as one uncloaked beam upon birds and men, and on each of those rain-soaked days, Jeremy Robson had racked his overstrained vocabulary for new objurgations against the malign fates which had spread a watery barrier between himself and Marcia Ames. Now the sun was an hour above the eastern horizon with a flawless sky outspread like a luxurious carpet for its day's journey. Secure at that hour in the undisputed possession of the earth, bobolink swayed and sang, when to its wrath and amaze a shining missile descended from the sky and bounded with sprightly twists toward its chosen choir-loft.

"Sliced into the rough again," said a voice of despair from the hollow below, and two figures appeared, headed toward the singer, who moved on with an indignant and expostulatory chirp, but found another perch still within ear-shot.

"Because you will *not* keep your head down," reprehended the deeper tones of the young man.

Bobolink stretched his liquid throat in a love-song. He sang the warm sweetness of the earth, and the conquering glory of the sun; the breeze's kiss and the welcome of the flower for the bees, and youth which is made up of all these and comes but once. Out of a full heart he sent forth his missioning call to young hearts; then, as the girl turned an exquisite face toward him, he waited for her response.

"That is four," said she, "and I am not out yet." And she hewed away a whole clump of innocent daisies, with one ferocious chop.

"You should have used a niblick the first time," observed the young man.

Perceiving that romance had forever departed from the human race when, on such a May morning, such a maid and such a youth could satisfy their soul with such conversation as this, bobolink flew away to a tussock in an adjacent field where his own private romance was safe hidden.

To versatile human kind, it is given to make love in many and diverse manners uncomprehended of the bird species. Not the least ingenious of his species, Mr. Jeremy Robson had marked out as his first step the establishment of a systematic association with Miss Marcia Ames, through golf; and until that association could be trusted to walk alone, as it were, he purposed to confine his attention strictly to the matter in hand. Her desire to make the college team was a very genuine one, and he guessed her to be a young lady of no small determination. Therefore, he was well satisfied to observe that, on this their first experiment as teacher and pupil, she was playing rather poorly. This meant longer and more arduous practice. At the end of the first round, during which he had devoted close attention but scant suggestion to her performance, he was four up and her card showed a painful total.

"Fifty-twos will never land you anywhere," was the conclusion which he derived from the addition.

"What is to be done?" she asked in her precise English. "I grow worse."

"Do you read Ibsen?" he inquired.

"I have read him a great deal. But not upon golf," said Miss Ames with raised eyebrows.

"Does your playing suggest any particular character of his?"

"You are being absurd. Or is it one of your riddles, at which I am not clever?"

"I'm giving you a test in self-analysis. The Ibsen character whom you suggest, particularly when you play your iron shots, is Little Eyolf. The *l* silent, as in 'Hades.'"

"I do not think that a very funny joke," she said scornfully.

"It's been turned down by three comic papers, though," he defended.

"Then why must I bear it?"

"To make the point stick in your memory. Once, quite early in the morning, I came around the corner of a barn on a Philadelphia golf course, and there was a nice-looking elderly lady whom I had seen the day before taking her two small grandchildren out walking, addressing a ball with a brassie and saying, 'Eye on the ball; slow back; carry through. Eye on the ball; slow back; carry though' over and over again. Brassie shots were her weakness. The next day that persevering old grandma went out and made low score in the National Women's Championship. Now, if you'll just think of yourself as Little Eyolf until you're good and man, it'll help do the trick."

"What were you doing in Philadelphia?" inquired the girl irrelevantly.

"Not golfing," he returned. "So, if you don't mind, we'll postpone that. This is a golf lesson, and right here the serious business of the day begins. The first consideration is to cure you of star-gazing. You appreciate that that's your main trouble?"

"Raising my head, you mean?"

"That's it. Star-gazing, we call it."

"It occurs because I forget myself."

"And mostly on your irons. You get your wooden shots off clean. Now, let's drive."

Two straight shots flew down the course, his the longer by fifteen yards. A ninety-yard approach lay before her.

"Beginneth here the first lesson," said Jeremy. "It's a sure cure, on the homeopathic principle. Invented it myself for a fellow on our college team who was a stargazer, and he showed his gratitude by eliminating me from the individual championship, that fall." He took a cardboard box from his pocket, and extracted from it one of a number of small, gilt stars such as stationers carry in stock. This he pressed down upon the grass so close behind his pupil's ball as almost to touch its lower arc. "Behold the star of your hopes."

"What am I to do with it?"

"Keep your eye on it—if you can."

"Until after I have struck the ball?"

"Longer than that. After you've played, step forward and plant the sole of your foot on the star. But you won't be able to do it. Not the first time."

"I shall," said the girl with quiet conviction.

Taking her stance, she measured the distance with a careful eye, and sent the ball off with a clean click. Her head remained bent with an almost devotional intentness. She stepped forward and covered the star with that boot which Eli Wade had so warmly praised.

"Good!" approved the instructor. "You've got willpower."

"I have needed to have," replied the girl. Her tone was curiously musing and confidential. "May I look up now?"

"Surely. You'll like the view."

The ball, rising high, had landed upon the edge of the green and rolled to within ten feet of the cup.

"Oh!" she cried. "Do you suppose I could do it again?"

"Any number of times, if you'll keep your eye on the star."

"But one could not carry about a box of stars in a match, could one?"

"One could. But it won't be necessary. Two weeks' practice at that will get you clean out of the Little Eyolf habit."

"Will it, indeed? But why do you look so intently at the spot?"

"I beg your pardon," said Jeremy hastily. "It was your boot—I mean, I was thinking what that queer old codger Eli Wade said when I went after your boots."

"And was *that* golf?" inquired Miss Ames with a demure and candid air. "No? Then, if you do not mind, we will postpone it, shall we not?"

"Stung!" confessed Jeremy. "We shall."

The bestarred second round cut no less than five strokes from the score of the gratified pupil and her even more highly pleased instructor. This in spite of the fact that she had once lifted her head and perpetrated a lamentable foozle, whereupon Jeremy gravely pasted one of the stars on the toe of her left boot: "To keep you reminded," he explained.

"But," he added, "you've got to clip at least three more strokes off to be safe. That'll take you all your time."

It took a disproportionate amount of Jeremy Robson's, too, which, to do him justice, he did not begrudge. As a corollary to the morning lessons he took to dropping in at the Pritchard mansion of an evening to discuss some of the more abstruse points of the game, where he found himself in active competition with the picked youth of the University and the town, for Miss Marcia gathered a court as irresistibly as a flower gathers bees. Quite unjustifiably Jeremy was inclined to sulk a bit over this, unmindful of the favor of the gods in affording him her undivided companionship in those early morning hours. Whereupon the gods, as is their custom, withdrew their unappreciated bestowals. Buddy Higman discovered the golf practice and straightway volunteered as caddy. Jealousy as well as desire to be of service to the liege lady prompted his offer, which was straightway accepted. So the morning practice continued while bobolink from his daisied choir-loft (no longer invaded by balls wandering from the straight and narrow path which leads to the House of Bogie) alternately cheered and jeered at this chaperoned companionship.

One stroke, two strokes, and finally five strokes were subtracted from the aspirant's nine-hole score. Her master gave her his blessing and told her to go in and win. In the Varsity competition, she qualified with a highly respectable round, and in the play-off for the team, won her place. The team captain posted the choice for the yearly match against Kirk College on the athletic bulletin, one line of which read:

No. 4–M. Ames.

In special celebration of the event, the pupil accepted an invitation to dine at the Country Club that evening with the instructor.

"Will you make an agreement?" she asked, as they faced each other across the little table, pleasantly remote in a far corner of the veranda.

"Unsight-unseen?" he smiled. "All right. I'll swap."

"That is quite too American for me. But you agree. Then let us not speak the word 'golf' all this evening. I am tired of it."

"Stale," commented the expert. "You must lay off for a week. Well, let's forget it. What shall we talk about?"

"What are you doing here in Fenchester?"

He smiled at the directness of the question. "Plain and fancy reporting."

"You do not seem to belong here."

"What makes you think that?"

She considered him meditatively. "I suppose it was your clothes, first. You dress differently from the others. More like the men I have known over there."

"Remnants of past glory," he assured her lightly. "I haven't always lived here, you know."

"Where then? Do you mind my asking?"

"Not a bit. I've drifted about doing worthless things for several years. Philadelphia mainly, New York a little. Getting myself mis-educated. You see, I'm something of a failure."

"You should not say that even in fun. I do not like to hear it."

"It isn't in fun. Ask my aged and highly respectable great-aunt, Miss Greer, in Philadelphia, and you'll learn something to my disadvantage."

"I shall," said the girl gravely, "if I ever go back there. Did you live with her?"

"For a time. After my college course she sent me on a year's tour and then made me take one of those ornamental post-graduate courses that lead into the lily-fingered occupations that are neither professions nor business. She had a fond hope that I'd take to diplomacy."

"No!" said the girl with unflattering surprise. "I know many diplomats. I do not think you would be successful there."

"I'm about as diplomatic as a punch in the eye," admitted her companion. "The old lady considered it plumb disgusting of me not to take to refined international mendacity. But then I didn't take to much of anything else that she laid out for me. I had vulgar tastes. I wanted to go into the newspaper business, and when I'd learnt it, have Great-Aunt kindly buy me a paper to play with. Great-Aunt didn't see it that way. She cut me off with a small amount of hard cash and a large amount of hard talk, and I took a School of Journalism[1] course and eventually drifted out here because I liked what I remembered of the town and wanted to bore in where I wasn't hampered by friends and acquaintances. Does that strike you as a record of glowing success? Considering that I'm nearly twenty-seven years old, and haven't made a scratch on the face of the world yet?"

"But you began late," condoned his companion. "And you are still learning. But I cannot see why your aunt should object to your wishing to own a newspaper. One would say, a harmless ambition."

"One that I'm quite unlikely to realize, now. As for its being harmless, why, my dear child—excuse the freedom of an aged golf-professor—there's a charge of dynamite in every font of type."

"Then you have a penchant for high explosives?"

"Have I? I don't think I'd put it that way," mused Jeremy. "I've a taste for adventure. And running a newspaper of your own has always seemed to me about the liveliest and most adventurous job going. But I don't want to blow things up."

"What do you want to do?"

"Oh, just to have a hand in things, in a real, live American community like this, where the soil is good and new ideas sprout. I'd like to get into the political fight, too. A really good one, I mean, with something worth aiming at."

"That I can understand. But I still fail to make you fit into this environment."

"What about yourself?" he countered. "Haven't you rather the air of coming out of the great world and condescending to this raw and rural town?"

"Have I? Have I been condescending to you?"

"If you had, it would be more than I deserve," he said contritely. "I'd no business to say that. And I didn't mean it, anyway. But this is a queer place for you to be, isn't it?"

"Not for my purposes?"

"Are you specializing at Old Central?"

"One might call it that. I made inquiries for the most typically American college, and a list was made up for me. I chose the University of Centralia to be with my mother's cousin, Miss Pritchard."

"Just like that? All yourself?"

"All myself," she assented gravely.

"You came here to get Americanized?"

"Yes. My mother married again. A German. A man of great scientific attainments and high position. He is very gentle and vague and absent-minded, and good to me. And when I told them that I would like to take my own money and come here to my own country for a year before"—she hesitated almost imperceptibly—"before anything was settled for me, he consented. Think what a wrench it must have been for his old-world prejudices against emancipated women and all that!"

"Yet I don't think you need Americanizing. You're a real American type if there ever was one."

She flushed a little. "I like to hear that. My father would have liked it. What makes you say it?"

"It's—it's your honesty, I think. There's a quality of frankness about you that could be—well, almost brutal, I think. Do you know what I mean?"

"I suppose I am a crank. That is American enough, is it not?" she laughed. "A crank about the truth. I hate anything that even suggests a lie, or a dodging, or an evasion. So perhaps I should not like your newspaper profession."

"But that's just it!" he cried eagerly. "If one had a paper of one's own, he could make his own rules for the game."

"If he were big enough—and brave enough."

"Brave enough," he repeated. "Eli Wade said that about you, too. Reading your character from your shoes, you know. That you had courage and honesty. I think he thought it a rare thing in a woman."

"It is not," she flashed. "But if I have, it is no credit to me. I have wholly loved and trusted only one person on earth. That was my father, and he was the soul of truth. So, some of my friends laugh at me a little and think me a crank, because I have—what do you Americans—*we* Americans say?—no use for any one whom I cannot wholly trust."

"And you would be hard, too," he said.

"Perhaps. If I were, it would be because I could not help it. I think that I do things because something inside makes me before I have even time to consider, sometimes."

"Like your standing up alone at the Federated German meeting. By the way, I brought my story of it for you to read."

She held out her hand for the proofs. "I am glad," she said.

She read it, slowly and studiously, and as she read an expression, new to Jeremy in the changeful charm of her face, puzzled his watchful eyes.

"It is very vivid," she said, "and enthusiastic."

She rose. On their way back to the Pritchard house she plied him with questions bearing on the technique of journalism. As he stood, bareheaded under the porch light looking up at her, she asked:

"May I keep the proof of the article?"

"Yes. You like it, then?"

"I love it. But I am glad that it was not published."

"Why?"

"There is too much Me in it." She paused. "Did I seem to you like that—then?"

"Yes. And more."

She shook her head. "I am glad that it was not published," she repeated. "It would have said to too many people—" She hesitated.

"What?" he asked.

For the first time her eyes faltered before his. They were hesitant, and deep-shadowed and troubled.

"What?" he repeated.

"What should have been said to only one."

"Marcia!" he cried.

But the door had closed on her and he barely heard her soft-toned "Good-night" from beyond its jealous interception.

## 6

ABSTENTION FROM THE ART and practice of golf for one week had been Professor Robson's ukase. Had he foreseen the course of more personal events he would never have issued it. For he now had no opportunity of seeing his pupil alone. Nothing so direct as avoidance could be charged against her. But since that parting on the Pritchard porch, he had never been able to achieve so much as two minutes of her undivided time. Her eyes, when they met his only to be swiftly withdrawn, were sweetly troubled. The Eternal Feminine within her was, for the time at least, in flight. And along those paths of delicate elusiveness, the clumsy and pursuing feet of man stumble and trip. Jeremy's soul was sorely tried and not less sorely puzzled.

If he found difficulties in Marcia's attitude, his own future course with regard to her was dubious. What could he, in his position and with his resources, ask of her? To wait? Certainly nothing more than that. And was even that much fair to her? His own feeling was simplicity itself. Life had, in these few short weeks of association, summed and compressed itself into his love for Marcia Ames. Until that abrupt change in the tone of their relations brought about by her half-acceptance of his devotion, she had never evinced anything more than a frank and confident comradeship. Now he felt that he might speak—if he could find opportunity. That he could not, almost caused him to accuse Marcia of unfairness. Yet could he honorably ask her to marry him and tie herself to a meager and as yet unpromising career? Within himself Jeremy had begun to assume that confidence of future success which comes with the assured sense of workmanship. He would cheerfully gamble his own future on it. But how could he ask her to risk hers? Even supposing that she cared for him! There was the thought that ached; the uncertainty of it. In any case he had to know how it stood with him in her heart.

Upon her inviolable truthfulness he could depend for a full and fair answer, if he were able to state his case. He knew that all her frank and unevasive courage would answer to his demand; that she would look that fate, or any other, steadily in the eyes. But not before her own good time. And that the time was not yet, became sufficiently apparent, one week before the match when the lessons were resumed, for with the resumption Buddy Higman was quietly established at once as caddy, chaperon, and dragon with the added qualities of the modestly adhesive burdock. The skill and technique of "No. 4.—M. Ames" prospered and improved mightily, which is more than can be said of the disposition of her instructor.

Some men's work would have suffered. Not Jeremy's. He was of that fortunate temperament which, keeping its troubles to itself, boils them out into steam and transforms the steam into energy. Besides, he had now "the grip of his pen." He derived a glowing satisfaction from the expert performance of his craft. The editorial page was hospitable to him, especially for contributions in lighter vein. Many special assignments for work out of the ordinary, calling for a knack of description or characterization, came to him. His writings were beginning to earn the knighthood conferred by the clipping shears and the paste-pot. Newspapers in larger cities than Fenchester copied and privately asked questions about them. But what made it all so worthwhile, what gave a touch of exaltation to the dogged purpose for success, was the conviction that all this forwarded him upon the road which led to Marcia.

The tournament with Kirk College, on the Fenchester Country Club grounds, was now two days away. Jeremy had asked for and obtained the assignment to cover it. He had long before applied for and received the job of caddying for No. 4 of the team opposing his own college, which was regarded by the visiting Kirks as an ignoble instance of loyalty corrupted by the baser passions. However, Jeremy was perfectly willing that Kirk should win; rather hoped it would, in fact, provided only the No. 4 of Old Central beat her man. He believed her capable of doing it, unless her nerve faltered, which he deemed improbable. On her most recent performances she was from two to four strokes lower than anyone but himself and Buddy Higman appreciated.

Important though the event was to Jeremy Robson, the authorities on The Record considered it rather a waste of their brilliant youngster's time. However, they were appeased by the cropping out meantime of a story so much in the Robson line that it might have been made to order for him. Wackley, the managing editor, outlined it to him, when he arrived in the morning.

"Robson, do you know a queer old bat up on Banks Street who runs a shoe surgery?"

"Eli Wade? Yes; quite well."

"He's a nut of the old Know-Nothing kind, isn't he? Hates all foreigners and all that?"

"He's a pretty hard-shelled Yankee."

"Well; he's done it this time. Made a fine young riot for himself last night. It seems he's been pasting cartoons and mottoes in his show window; and some of the younger fellows from the Deutscher Club, who pass there on their way home, naturally got sore. Last night with a few beers aboard, they stopped and gave him a raree serenade. Out comes the old boy in his nighty and makes 'em a red-hot speech. They give him the whoop, and he begins to damn 'em all back to Germany."

"Yes; he's got fighting stuff in him," agreed Jeremy.

"Too much for his own good. Somebody ups with a rock, and down comes the big boot over the door. Well, the old boy goes dippy over that. Dives inside and grabs up a hammer and right into them. First thing you know, they have him on a rail—a scantling from that new building on the corner—and are yelling for tar. It might have been serious for the old boy, but just then along comes Andy Galpin of The Guardian. You know him; he's some young husky. Guard on the O. C. team for three years. Well, he bucks the center and lays out a couple of the merry villagers and there's a pretty mix-up, and I understand Galpin got one in the eye that didn't improve his make-up. But the boys were sick of the fun anyway, and they let Galpin get away with it and take old Wade home. Instead of doing the sensible thing and sleeping it off, Wade gets all het up, and swears out warrants and they're going to thrash it out in police court this noon, in time for the edition. Probably Wade 'll make a speech. Anyhow, there'll be a circus when he goes on the stand. We want a rattling good story on it; and put in your best touches on the old boy. He'll do for a local character to hang all sorts of stories on, later."

"But look here, Mr. Wackley: I know Eli Wade pretty well. He's—he's a sort of friend of mine."

"What if he is? You can have fun with him, can't you? He won't know the difference. And if he does, he won't care. Those fanatical guys are crazy for publicity. He'll eat it up."

It was Jeremy's settled intention, so he told himself, as he set out for court, to write an account which, while lively, should fairly set forth his friend's side. When he saw Eli Wade at court his heart misgave him, the Boot & Shoe Surgeon looked so whitely wrathful. The proceedings dwindled into nothing. The "life" was out of the story, quite to one reporter's relief, when his evil genius inspired Eli Wade to address the court. At the outset he was simple and dignified. But counsel for the serenaders interpolated some well-timed taunts which roused him to indignation. He had not slept that night, for shame of the treatment to which he had been subjected; and his self-control was in abeyance. Indignation, as he answered the taunts, waxed to fury. He burst into a savage and absurd invective, aimed at "German interlopers," "foreign clubs that run our city," and the like; his voice shrilling louder and louder until he was drowned out by the uncontrollable laughter of the court-room. It was all quite absurd and pitiable. Instinctively Jeremy's pencil took it down. Here was his story, ready to hand.

As he sat in the office, the grip of characterization settled upon him. Oddments and gleams of past conversations in the "Infirmary" came back to him, and he embodied them. Stroke by stroke there grew up under his hand a portrait, crude from haste but vivid, telling, and a stimulant to mirth, not always of the kindliest. It was not intentionally unfair; it was never malicious in purpose. But it was the more deadly in effect. By the magic transformation of print it made out of an unpolished, simple, generous, fervent, and thoughtful artisan, a laughable homunculus. Yet there was in it no element of "fake." Jeremy could have defended it at all points. Any newspaper judgment would have credited it with due fidelity to facts. The sum-total was a subtle and gross misrepresentation. Had the writer read it over he would perhaps have seen this for himself. But there was no time. He barely caught the edition. Wackley's: "Great stuff, my boy! You'll hear of this," happily distracted him from the stirrings of a conscience which faintly wished to know how Eli Wade would take it.

"You're doing golf tomorrow," continued the managing editor. "Don't bother to come to the office first."

Profiting by this, Jeremy, an hour before match time, called at Miss Pritchard's for Marcia. He was informed that she had left on an errand, but would meet him at the Country Club. When, just before the first pair teed up, she appeared, her mentor was startled, she looked so wan and languid.

"Good Heavens!" said Jeremy in a whisper. "You haven't let this thing get on your nerves?"

She shook her head. Her eyes did not avoid his now; but the changeful lights seemed to have dwindled to the merest flicker in inscrutable depths.

"Let me get you a cup of coffee. That'll brace you up."

"I shall be all right," she said with an effort.

At the call for the fourth pair she stepped to the tee and hit a ball straight down the center for 160-odd yards. It was the virtue of her game that she was straight on the pin, nine shots out of ten, thereby overcoming the handicap of greater distance sure to be against her in college competition. Great and grinful was the satisfaction of her trainer at observing the demeanor of her opponent. When he was presented to her, that gentleman, a sightly and powerful youth notable for his long drives, took one extended, admiring, and astounded survey of "M. Ames"—he hadn't known what the bewildering fates held in store for him inquired privately but passionately of high Heaven and his team-mates how a fellow was going to keep his eye on the ball with a vision like *that* to look at, and entered upon a disastrous career by nearly slaying, with his first drive, a squirrel in a tree a good hundred yards off the course. He recovered in time to record an unparalleled ten for the first hole. M. Ames, dead on the pin, scored a correct five. Everson (the Kirk boy) contributed three putts on the second green, and M. Ames won it in a sound four. But as his pupil took her stance for a brassie, after a respectable tee-shot from the third, Jeremy perceived with dismay that her hands were shaking. Up went her head, as she swung, and the ball darted from the toe of her club into the rough. She was out in three, but again she succumbed to star-gazing on her mashie shot, and her opponent still triangulating the course like a care-free surveyor, was able to halve it. From then on, Jeremy the mentor was in agony. Except off the tees, where she clung to her beautiful, free-limbed, lissome swing, as it were by instinct, No. 4 for Old Central topped, sliced, pulled, and scarified the helpless turf. The gallant foeman was so distressed at her obviously unusual ineptitudes, that his own game went glimmering down the grassy bypaths that lead to traps and bunkers. Only this involuntary gallantry saved M. Ames from practical extinction. As it was, she was two down at the end of the first nine, with a dismal fifty-four. As they left the ninth green she turned to Jeremy:

"Would you mind not caddying for me the rest of the match?"

"But Marcia!" he cried, aghast. "What's wrong?"

"You have got on my nerves."

"I haven't said a word except to steady you."

"I am sorry," she said inflexibly.

An angry gleam flashed in Jeremy's eyes. "Of course, if you feel that way about it—"

"I do. I am sorry," she repeated.

"Do you mind my following you?" he asked with semi-sardonic intent.

"I should rather you did not."

"Well, good Heavens! Something has happened to spoil your nerve."

"No."

"Then what—"

"Come for me after the match. We can talk then."

With this Jeremy had to be content. Relieved of his presence, M. Ames summoned all her force to the rescue of her nerves, and astonished her opponent with a forty-four, steadily and carefully played. The match, which had originally been counted upon by a careful captain as a probable win for Old Central, was a tie, under the scoring system agreed upon.

Dismal misgivings, meanwhile, had beset Jeremy Robson, the promising young reporter of The Record. Already he was, in his heart, on the defensive when, as he and Marcia turned out at the gate, she said:

"Did you write the article about Eli Wade?"

"Yes."

"I thought it must have been yours," said her lips. The tone said, "I hoped it was not."

"That's a good sign, for people to recognize my style. What did you think of it?"

"It was clever."

There was no warmth in the tone. Rather a reluctant relinquishment of disbelief.

"I'm glad you liked it."

"I did not like it. I hated it."

"Oh, that's the personal view," he said indulgently.

"Perhaps."

"The Bellair Journal has offered me a job on the strength of it."

"Were you obliged to take that—what is the term—that assignment?"

"A reporter takes what is handed out to him."

"I suppose so. That would be the danger. I should fear that."

"Fear what? I can't imagine you fearing anything."

"I should fear getting into that habit of mind. Complaisant. Servile."

"That's an ugly word, Marcia," he said, flushing.

"I am sorry. Perhaps there is a side to it that I do not understand. But surely, oh, surely, you need not have written it in that way!"

"My dear girl! Personal feeling has no relation to newspaper work. I can't juggle with facts because the man happens to be my friend. That isn't honest."

"Is *this* honest?" She held up the clipping which she took from her pocket.

Jeremy quailed before the hurtness of her eyes, which was wonder more than reproach.

"There isn't a word in it," he began, "that—"

"There is not a thought in it that is not a cruel injustice."

"You've no right to say that."

"That is true. You remind me."

"Oh, Marcia," he cried miserably. "Don't take it that way. I'd have thrown up my job sooner than write it if I'd known that you'd feel it so."

"It does not matter about me. But you! How could you have done it! How could you have used his gentle, sweet, simple philosophy—his talks between friends in the shop—to make a mock of him?"

"I didn't. I swear I didn't."

She put the clipping into his hand. Re-read, now, the words were self-damnatory. Jeremy groaned.

"It has hurt him so terribly," she said.

"You've seen him?"

"Yes. He has resigned his place on the School Board. Mr. Dolge advised him to get off before he was laughed off."

Jeremy stared at the words of his facile portraiture as if they had suddenly been informed with venom. "And he was so proud of it!" he muttered.

"It was a large thing in his little life," said the girl. "He feels disgraced."

Wackley's easy and cynical assumption that the subject of the sketch would be "crazy for publicity" recalled itself to Jeremy. He swore beneath his breath. "When did you see Eli?

"This morning. At the hospital."

"The hospital! Is he injured that badly?"

"No. You had not heard? It is Mr. Galpin, a friend of Eli's—who stood by him."

"Andy Galpin! How bad is it?"

"Much worse than they supposed. He will be nearly blind in one eye."

"Good Lord!"

"And is he a friend of yours, also; Mr. Galpin?"

"Andy? Yes; of course he is."

"But you made no inquiry about him."

"I didn't know."

Her eyes, steady and deep-lighted, still did not judge him, still pathetically wondered at him.

"Marcia!" he broke out. "I haven't been able to think of anything but you. I haven't had anything in my heart—"

"Please!"

He stopped, appealing to her with his look.

"I think you have to think of Eli Wade."

Jeremy winced and was silent. Their car pulled up at the Pritchard gate. She got out, but did not ask him to come in.

"The worst of it is that it's hurt you," he muttered. "I didn't know that you cared so much about him."

"It was not he that I cared so much about," returned Marcia steadily. "It was you."

She turned and passed into the house. Try as he might, on his way to the hospital to see Andrew Galpin, Jeremy could derive from that low-toned avowal neither hope nor comfort for a sick heart and a grilling conscience.

The doctors would not let him see Galpin.

As by tradition bound, his "story" of the golf match focused on the one and unique girl-player on the team. She was the "human interest" center. So skillfully did he skirt the edge of her bad play that only an analysis of the score would apprise the reader of the partial failure. Her good shots were described in glowing terms. To her, the casual reader would have supposed, belonged the chief credit on Old Central's side; and the copy-reader, who was no golfer, in good faith headed it "Miss Ames Gains Tie for O. C."; the final team score having also been all even, though it should have been Old Central's victory had No. 4 played up to her standard. The writing of the article cheered up the writer notably. Here was no wounding word or acid-bitten phrase. There was only the clear purpose to please. Again Jeremy had been caught and carried in the whirl of his semi-creative enthusiasm.

The quality was still there when he read it over on the following day. Intent upon his sunshine-scattering he sent an early proof to "M. Ames." He felt, on the whole, that he had been, if not unjustly, at least untenderly treated. Overnight he had been able to persuade himself that the Wade sketch represented a fine type of loyalty to profession rising triumphant above personal feelings. All that was needed to reestablish

him firmly in the conviction of righteousness, was Marcia's appreciation of his golf-story. He went to the Pritchard house to receive it.
Marcia was not there. She had gone for a few days' visit at the Magnus
Laurens' country place. Jeremy sent a hasty, reproachful and alarmed
note after her. Why had she left without a word? What did it all mean?
When was she coming back? When could he see her and explain? As
a composition it was distinctly below standard for the rising young
star of The Record. But at least it could boast the highly-prized quality of heart-interest.

Jeremy called again at the hospital to see Andrew Galpin. That battered warrior received him with immitigable cheerfulness.

"Ay-ah," he explained. "Something busted inside the eye. It ain't
as bad as they thought. They're going to save quite a glimmer of sight
in it, and 'my right eye is a good little eye,'" he chanted. "Back on the
job in a week or so."

Jeremy, craving solace, asked whether his friend had seen the Eli
Wade story; then, remembering his disability, corrected himself hastily.

"Sure I saw it. Or had it seen for me. I made 'em read me both papers
from end to end. That was a crackajack story. You keep on like this,
young fellow, and Fenchester'll be too small to hold you."

"I'm afraid it hurt Eli Wade's feelings," said the visitor hesitantly.
"Did he say anything to you about it?"

"Ay-ah. He spoke of it."

"What did he say?"

"We-ell; he said—Sure you want to know?" Jeremy nodded. "He
said, 'I'd never have believed it from the way he wears his shoes.' Like
the poor old nut, ain't it?"

"Andy, was the story so rotten?"

"I just told you it was a crackajack piece of work."

"I'm not talking about that. I'm talking about my doing it at all."

"It was your assignment, wasn't it?"

"Certainly, it was," assented Jeremy, comforted and justified. "I had
to take it or quit my job, didn't I?"

"Oh, I guess you're stronger than that on The Record."

"What would you have done in my place?"

"Me? Oh, I'm a reporter. I reckon I'd have done the story." But there was no conviction in Galpin's tone. Jeremy wished he could have seen the bandaged eyes. He mistrusted that they would have avoided his.

"That's part of the business," he declared, self-defensively.

"That's the hell of the business," said Andrew Galpin.

Jeremy left the hospital feeling that Marcia Ames and Andrew Galpin had said much the same thing to him about his article, in widely different terms.

Marcia's reply to his note came several days later. Its brevity did not conceal an indefinable and disturbing reserve. She would see him, she wrote, when she returned. With the note was inclosed the proof of the golf report. Its margin carried a penciled note.

"Can you not see that this only makes it worse?"

Jeremy read his cherished report once more, and saw.

It was a lie.

## 7

LAKE SKOHOTA[1] THRUSTS A long and slender arm past Fenchester to throw it cherishingly about a tiny island, cut off from the University campus and made part of it again by an arched bridge overhanging dappled waters. Willows bending from the islet's bank weave their thousand-fingered enchantments above the dreaming shallows. The subtle spice of sedge and marsh-bloom blows from it to disperse its spell upon the air that whispers a never-finished tale of secrecy and sorcery to the trees. It is a place of witchery.

The sheen of countless stars glowed above the bridge and wavered below it, as two figures emerged from the pathway and paused at the summit of the arch to lean and look down through the darkness at the blackly opalescent gleam of the waters. A canoe stole around the bend and slipped beneath them, the stroke of its paddles accentuated in cool, delicious plashes of sound as it entered the arch.

"Another two," said the soft and happy voice of a girl, rising to them; and a boyish voice answered:

"The night is full of them."

The canoe merged with the darkness. The two figures on the bridge, silent, followed it with their blind speculations into an unknown world. From far across the open spaces of the lake came the music of women's voices blended, which the night breeze hushed to hear; a modulation of wistful, minor strains:

"In dreams she grows not older
The lands of Dream among,
Though all the world wax colder
Though all the songs be sung."

The latter couplet was repeated, a haunting, yearning, falling melody, that suddenly swelled and rose into the splendid, fulfilling major:

"In dreams doth he behold her
Still fair and kind and young."

The taller figure on the bridge stirred from a dream. "That is your song, Marcia."

"Yes," said the girl, a little away from him in the darkness. "I arranged it for them, to be sung so; in parts."

"You sang it the first day we really began to know each other."

"Very long ago," she assented, with her serene gravity. "Two months, is it not?"

"Or years. Or centuries. It doesn't seem to matter."

"I am glad they sang that tonight. For us," she concluded, after the briefest of pauses.

He put his hand over hers, which rested on the stone coping of the bridge. She did not stir nor speak. But it was his hand, not hers, that trembled. A heavy rowboat came lumbering down the reach, two students at the oars.

"Politics for me," said one confidently. "We're going to run the country from this end now. I'm for Mart Embree's band-wagon."

"Too dull," said another. "Gimme a touch of Nuh York."

"It's a rough world for poor, lost lambs like us to be spilled into, anyway," boomed a resonant bass from the stern seat, and their laughter died away around the bend of the island.

Marcia Ames freed her fingers from her companion's clasp.

"Jem," she said.

"I love you," he said.

Her figure, dim-white in the darkness, neither withdrew from nor swayed toward him. But he thought that he saw her head half turn with a sorrowful intent.

"Jem," she said again, "I came here to—"

"I love you, Marcia," he repeated with a still insistence.

"Wait. I am going away."

"When?"

"Very soon. This week. Perhaps sooner."

"For how long?"

"Will you not understand, Jem? I am going away."

The quiet repetition fell, chill and deadening, upon his heart.

"From me?"

"From everything here."

"Why?"

"I must."

"Then you don't care!"

She was silent.

"You're going back?" He made an obvious effort to gather his force for the determinative word. "Abroad?"

"Yes."

"I'll follow you," he declared grimly.

"Now you are angry with me, are you not?" She spoke with a sorrowful, disappointed intonation.

"Haven't I a right to be?"

"Have you?"

"Tell me, if you can, that you haven't cared for me a bit; not at any time. You see," he added with conviction but without triumph, "you can't!"

"If I had ever cried—in my life—since I was a child—I think—I should cry now," she said, in little, uneven sections of speech.

"Marcia!" All the anger passed away from Jem, leaving him shaken. "Don't feel that way. What has happened? What have I done to change you toward me?"

"I cannot tell you—more than I have told you."

"Try," he urged. "Let's have it out!"

"I am not clever at explaining. Not—not such things as this. There is something that rises up inside and—and forbids. Oh, Jem! You must know, without my putting it into words."

"It's that cursed Wade story, of course. But that's because you don't understand. Surely, between you and me a—a petty little matter such as that—"

"Petty!"

"Why, Marcia, it's just part of the day's work. Ask any newspaper man. Ask Andrew Galpin."

"Who has perhaps half-spoiled his life by defending his friend."

"That's different—I'd have done that."

"Would you?"

"Can't you believe that of me, Marcia? Do you think I'm a coward?"

"Falsehood is always cowardly," she said very low. "Perhaps I am abnormal about it. I cannot help it. I was bred that way."

"But try to be fair to me," he pleaded.

"Fair to you? I was more than that. I could not believe that you had written it. When I went into Eli Wade's shop that morning there was a strange, violent white-haired little man there with him—"

"Nick Milliken."

"Yes. He said what—what you have said; that it was all part of the day's work; that you were no worse than any other reporter. He said that you had boasted to him that nobody could control your pen."

Jeremy groaned. "It's true."

"And then he laughed, and said things about you that I would not endure to hear—as I told him."

"You defended me against Milliken!"

"I tried to."

"Can't you defend me against yourself, Marcia?"

He could hear her long, slow-drawn breath before she answered. "I could defend you against *yourself*, in my own heart. But I cannot defend the ideal of you that I had built up, against what you have done to it."

"Couldn't you have told me?"

"Told you what, Jem?"

"That I did represent an ideal to you. Think what it would have meant to me to—to know that."

Something told him that she was smiling in the darkness and that there was pain and pity as well as a sweet mockery in the smile. "Could I tell you that before you told me—what you have told me tonight?"

"That I love you? You can't pretend that you didn't know it. But

I'd no business to tell you then: I've no business to tell you now," he added gloomily. "What have I got to offer a girl like you!"

"That would not matter," she answered him proudly. "It is the other that matters."

"Wade, again! I can't see that it matters so much, even to him. How was I to guess that it would hurt a simple-minded old dreamer of that sort?"

"Have you been to see him since?"

"No."

"Why not?"

The direct query had the stunning force of accusation. "You're right," he said dully. "I knew all the time it was a rotten thing to do, only I wouldn't face it. And I've kept away from the Boot & Shoe Infirmary because I was afraid to go there. It's curious," he added, in a flat, detached manner of speech, "how the little things of life—the things you think are little—wreck the whole business for you, when it's too late to do anything."

"Jem!" gasped the girl. "I cannot bear to hear you talk so. It—it is unlike you. It hurts me."

"I don't want to hurt you, dear, Heaven knows. I only want to get this clear. You—you think I'm unfit to be—that I'm untrustworthy. Is that it?"

"Am I being very cruel?" she whispered.

"You've answered. It's the truth that's cruel, not you."

"I must trust. Absolutely. Or—there is nothing."

"I see. When do you go?"

Of a sudden her strong young arms were about his shoulders; her hot, sweet face was pressed against his. He felt the quick throbbing of the vein in her temple, and was shaken to the foundations of his being with the dear and bewildering shock of it.

"Oh, Jem!" Her whisper fluttered close to his ear. "Why do you *let* me go! Never let me go. It breaks my heart to go. To leave you. Never to see you again. Why must I go!"

"You mustn't. You shan't. Marcia, darling! After this you can't leave me."

He lifted her head to press his lips upon her eyes. They were hot and dry. But when he sought her mouth, her quick hand interposed. As abruptly as she had come into his arms she escaped their jealous clasp and stood back from him.

"How could I!" she panted. "It was unfair of me. I never meant it."

"You can't tell me that—now," he answered, with a new note of joy and triumph.

"It was wrong—so wrong," she mourned. "It did not mean what— what you hoped. For I must go."

"Go?" he repeated incredulously. "And not come back?"

"Oh, *want* me to come back, Jem!" she pleaded. "Keep wanting me to come back. If anything could ever bring me, that would. But it will not. Nothing can. I know it. I am holding to a dream."

"I've lost mine," said Jem. "And everything in life with it—if you go, now."

"Forgive me. And believe that I never meant to hurt you. If I have, it was my ignorance."

"Ignorance? You? I wish I could see your face now, to see how wise it is!"

"You are smiling at me again," she said. "But I am not wise. I am very foolish. And I am very young. Jem, do you know how old I am?"

"Sometimes I've thought you must be at least a hundred."

"I am not eighteen yet, Jem. Indeed, I am not. I once told you that I was old, as a child. So you must forgive me and believe me."

"I'll do anything but give you up."

"That, too," she said very low. She set her hand trustfully within his arm. "Come. You must take me home."

It was a silent walk; the girl full of musings; the man of a grim, dogged determination. At the rose-bowered steps he took her hand.

"Tomorrow," he said. "I'll be here directly I finish my work. No; I've got one errand I must do first."

"What is that?" she asked wanly.

"I'm going to see Eli Wade."

"Yes. I am glad," said she.

He stopped for a moment at the gate, hoping for another sight of her. She had turned up the hall light and now stood in the doorway, beneath the roses. Her face was inexpressibly wistful, inexpressibly lovely, inexpressibly lonely. The subtle and changeful eyes stared widely into the darkness. Suddenly she threw her arm across them with a desolate, renunciatory gesture and turned away.

The shoes which Eli Wade had repaired for Jeremy Robson were leaden-soled to carry home a leaden and foreboding heart, that night.

With the new day came new courage to the lover. Marcia cared for him, by her own tacit confession. After all, his fault had been a minor one; there was sound defense for it: he could convince her of that, and overbear her intention of leaving him. What he failed to perceive was this: that the girl was concerned, not with a fault, but with a flaw of character divined by her subtle and powerful intuition. But a world without Marcia Ames was unthinkable to young Jeremy Robson, considering the prospect calmly in the light of day; and being unthinkable, there remained only to devise the best means of combating her illogical and even—he would go thus far—unfair judgment of himself. Growing more assured and comfortable in his mind, as the day wore on, he contrived to finish up his work early, and left the office at a jubilant skip, intent on getting to Montgomery Street with the least possible delay. He wasn't even going by way of the Boot & Shoe Infirmary. Eli Wade could wait.

On the sidewalk he was accosted by young Burton Higman, who glanced sidelong at him out of ashamed-looking, swollen eyes.

"Cut it short, Buddy," said the hasting Jem.

"She's gone," said the small boy.

Jem stopped dead in his tracks. "Who's gone?"

"Miss Marcy."

"Where? When?" demanded Jem wildly.

"Chicago. Three-thirty-seven," returned the precise Buddy.

A pall of dimness settled down over the glaring street; hot, stark, sterile dimness through which the figures of trivial folk moved lifelessly on futile errands.

"Did she leave any message?" inquired Jem, presently, in a voice which would have been life-like from a phonograph.

"Told me to tell you."

"Why did she go—so soon?" The query was put, not to young Mr. Higman but to a blind and juggernaut providence.

It was young Mr. Higman, however, who responded. "Afraid," he stated.

"Afraid? What of?"

"Herself. She told me so when she k-k-kissed me goodbye." Buddy's eyes winked rapidly. "But she didn't tell me to tell you that," he reflected.

"Did she give you any other message?"

"Not exac'ly a message."

"Go on! Out with it."

"You needn't *bite* a feller," expostulated young Mr. Higman. "She told me if ever you got what you was after, to go to you an' ast for a job, when I needed it, for the sake of a mut—mut—some kind of friend."

Jem registered a silent and pious vow. "Is that all?"

"Yes. Do I get the job?"

"If I can give it to you."

"Say, Mr. Robson. I guess she meant you was that kind of friend. Are you a friend of hern?"

Jem got it out at last: "Yes."

Young Mr. Higman's eyes became suddenly more strained and ashamed-looking. "I'm goin' to miss her somethin' awful, Mr. Robson," he said. "Ain't you?"

But Mr. Robson had passed on. Buddy wondered whether he had suffered a touch of the sun. He seemed uncertain in his walk.

## 8

IN THE COURSE OF a long and varied life, Miss Editha Greer had been consistently eccentric. In the close of it she was not less so. Witness the following telegram received by her great-nephew, Jeremy Robson:

Philadelphia, July 30, 1912

I am dead. Do not come to funeral. Letter follows.

E. Greer.

To say that the recipient of this posthumous message was overcome with grief, would be excessive. His feeling for his aged relative had been one of mild and remote piety, relieved by an intermittent sense of amusement, and impregnated with a vague dread of what she might do next. No more next now for E. Greer. Jeremy was honestly sorry; not on his own account, but for the old lady herself. She had so enjoyed life! Doubtless she had relinquished it with courage; but, also, he felt certain, with profound dissent from the verdict. But, having duly dismissed him from consideration in her lifetime, what should she be writing him about now that she was dead?

Like the telegram, the letter, when it arrived, proved to be an anticipatory document. It dealt, in a frank and unflattering style, with Jeremy's expectations upon her property which, she observed characteristically, was much less than most fools supposed.

I have long considered you a bit of a ninny [continued this pleasing document]. Nor have I valid cause to alter my opinion. But I recently met at a country house a young woman who knows you. [Jeremy's heart performed a porpoise-roll within his breast.] She tells me that I am an old fool. I interpret her expression and bearing, not her words, which are that I do not understand you. Apparently she believes that she does. If I left you all my money, she would perhaps marry you for it. On the whole, however, I believe not. She has neglected much more brilliant opportunities here. Moreover, when I put the question to her, she said not. She added that I was impertinent, and that impertinence was no more tolerable from the old to the young than from the young to the old. I like your Miss Marcia Ames.

The point of importance is that she considers the modest, in fact I may say nominal and complimentary, sum set apart for you in my will, quite insufficient. We discussed it at length. She is possessed of a devil of frankness. She maintains that I should leave you a modest competency. She thinks that it might save your immortal soul, if I correctly interpret her attitude. She thinks your immortal soul is worth saving. She assumes that you have an immortal soul. She even appeared to think that I have an immortal soul. Upon that moot point I shall be better able to judge by the time this letter goes forward to you; but it is improbable that I shall communicate any further or more authoritative information.

She is a strange creature. You should have married her, though she is far too old for you. A hundred years at least. I judge you might have married her but lost your chance. [Here the reader groaned.] She might have made a success of you. I gravely doubt whether my money can.

Do not hastily assume that the money is within your grasp. There is a condition to be fulfilled. I believe that you will not fulfill it. She believes that you will, even though she does not know what it is. Nor shall you. Whether you receive a small pittance or a roundly comfortable sum, depends now entirely upon yourself. I am still malicious enough—I forget that I am now, as you read this, dead and safely buried—I was still malicious enough to wish that I might see your struggles of mind upon receiving this, the last communication wherewith you will ever be troubled from

Your dutiful great-aunt,

E. Greer.

Perturbation over the prospect of comparative enrichment was quite subordinated, as Jeremy read this curious epistle, to the turbulence of emotion excited by the knowledge that Marcia had been interesting herself so intimately in his affairs. So far, the joke turned against Great-Aunt Greer. But she was more than avenged by the sting in her surmise that Jem had forfeited his chance with Marcia. Where was Marcia? If he got the money, or the assurance of it, why should he not set out to find her, even though it took him across the world, and try once more? Would she have the force to escape from him again? Was not her flight the initial confession, upon which her queer relations with E. Greer set the seal? Only as an afterthought came the consideration of the condition upon which he was to secure the larger legacy. He could not seem to get excited or disturbed over it. Nothing mattered much in the bleak soul of Jeremy Robson but Marcia Ames. Great-Aunt Greer would have been sorely disgusted! Or, perhaps she wouldn't.

Three days thereafter a caller came to see Jeremy at The Record office. His card indicated that he was Mr. Arthur Welton, representing the firm of Hunt & Hunt, Attorneys, Philadelphia. His appearance indicated that he was about Jeremy's age. His bearing indicated that he was older than Pharaoh's uncle, and charged with world-destinies. Jeremy had a shrewd guess that this was his first mission away from home.

Mr. Welton looked Jeremy over minutely and shook hands. The firm of Hunt & Hunt, which he had the honor to represent, had charge of the affairs of Miss Editha Greer, deceased, he informed Mr. Robson. Would Mr. Robson kindly put on his coat?

"Do you want me to go out with you?" asked Jeremy.

"As you prefer."

"What's the matter with this? Nobody will interrupt us here."

"Very well." The age-old youth wrapped himself in an air of superior expectancy.

"Go ahead," said the reporter.

"The coat," reminded Mr. Welton.

Jeremy was annoyed. "Why the devil should I put on a coat with the mercury ramping around 90?"

"A mere formality," murmured his visitor.

"Oh, very well!" growled Jeremy. He departed and presently returned, fully and uncomfortably garmented.

Again Mr. Arthur Welton inspected him carefully. "You do not wear mourning, I observe."

"I do not."

"Why not, may I ask?"

"Don't believe in it. It's a pagan custom and usually hypocritical."

"I cannot agree with you," retorted the other weightily. "On principle, I cannot agree with you. In the present instance, would it be an evidence of hypocrisy to have shown a formal mark of sorrow for the loss of your great-aunt?"

"It would."

"You felt, then, no affection or esteem for the late Miss Editha Greer?"

"What business is that of yours?"

"It is so much the business of my firm that I have traveled a thousand miles to ascertain your attitude."

"The condition!" cried Jeremy, aloud. "I beg your pardon," he added. "If you had told me that this was a legal cross-examination—"

"Not precisely that, Mr. Robson. I should have thought that you would appreciate its purport," returned the other in a tone of grave rebuke.

"I do." There was a grim set to the other's lips. "I know Aunt Edie well enough to appreciate her practical jokes."

"Really, Mr. Robson! I am bound to protest against the assumption that our late client—"

"All right! All right! I withdraw it. Fire ahead."

Mr. Arthur Weston looked delicately but impressively pained. "You felt no affection or esteem for the deceased?" he inquired through pursed lips.

"I liked the old lady, in a way," confessed Jeremy reminiscently. "She had such a cheery spice of the devil in her. And her tongue! And her pen! Oh, Lord! What an editorial writer she'd have made, if she could have kept out of jail."

"I need hardly tell you, Mr. Robson, that she gravely disapproved of your journalistic predilections."[1]

"Nobody need tell me after she got through. Nobody need tell anybody anything that my Great-Aunt Greer had told 'em first."

"In order that the record may be clear, let me put this to you. It is admitted that you disapprove of symbolical mourning; that you do not practice it. If you did practice it, would you have worn mourning for the deceased Miss Greer?"

"If the dog hadn't stopped to scratch the flea would he have caught the rabbit?" retorted the irreverent Mr. Robson.

"I must insist upon a reply."

"No; I certainly shouldn't. Why should I? I'm not grieving over Aunt Edie's death. She's no real loss to me. Nor gain, either, now," he added with a rueful grin. "I'm not going to pretend. So, you see, there's not even a mitigating circumstance."

"Mitigating circ—"

"Good legal phrase, isn't it? Oh, I understand your errand perfectly. Aunt Edie wrote me that there was a 'condition' to the legacy that I wouldn't fulfill. If you'd come out here and found me all swathed up in black like a mummy, and with a funereal gulp in my voice when I spoke of my dear old Auntie, and the general manners of an undertaker right on the job, I expect it might have been worth twenty or twenty-five thousand dollars to me. Even a mourning band on my coat and a few appropriate sighs in the right place might have got me five or ten thousand. Maybe if I'd stopped to figure it out, I'd have dressed the part. A fellow will do a good deal for money. Then again, maybe I wouldn't." The memory of Marcia's frank and lustrous eyes checked him. Could he have met their challenge, with the black badge of hypocrisy on him? "No! I'm damned if I would!" he declared with profound sincerity. "So there you have it. I know where I get off, and I don't much care, to tell the truth. I lose."

The overweighted legal victim of responsibilities almost too heavy to be borne slowly and accurately gathered up his hat, his gloves, his cane, his portfolio, and his eye-glasses in the absorbed manner of one taking an inventory. He bowed a solemn and professional farewell to Mr. Robson. At the door he paused. A gleam as of some faint, inward flickering of the eternal human which must at times assert itself even through the cerements of legal procedure, appeared upon his pink and careworn features.

"No," he pronounced profoundly. "You win."

## 9

"What's the matter with you, Robson?"

Young Jeremy Robson turned a lack-luster eye upon Wackley, his managing editor. "Nothing," he said listlessly.

"You're not looking well."

"Oh, I'm all right," said the reporter, dully wishing his solicitous superior at the devil.

"Want a few days off to go fishin'?"

"No, thanks."

"What do you want?" inquired Wackley, dreading to hear that a raise of pay was the requisite. Cheered by the valuable reporter's negative declaration of content with his lot as it was, the editor continued: "A sick owl is a merry wag to what you've been for the last ten days. All the ginger has gone out of your stuff. Can't you dig us up something more as good as your Eli Wade story?"

In that moment Jeremy Robson savored the sensations of the chicken-killing puppy when, awaking from blessedly forgetful reverie, it finds the dismal and penal relic of its crime still fast about its neck.

"Look here," pursued Wackley. "This isn't going to do. You quit for the day, and go home. Tomorrow there's going to be doings in the Senate. Martin Embree is going to spring something. You cover it. We'll want a good story, if the stuff comes through. Beat it for home, now!"

Home? Young Jeremy Robson felt a loathly distaste for his quiet room up off the campus. But so he felt a loathly distaste for the whole of that hollow and lifeless shell about him, which had so lately been the world of his crowded, vigorous interests. Man delighted him not; no, nor woman, either; not even the pride of his work and his satisfaction in having become something of a figure, though in a minor degree, locally. He hungered, with the intensity of a self-willed and rather lonely nature, for the sight and sound and essence of Marcia Ames who was some weeks and Heaven only knew how many miles away from him. Young Jeremy Robson had suffered as severe a hurt as youth can suffer and still continue to be youth.

He wandered idly up the Nicklin Avenue hill and turned into the shaded sweetness of Montgomery Street. Miss Letitia Pritchard was at her hedge-row, cutting roses. She was a placid and vigorous mite of a woman, unfaded at fifty, sweet and hardy and fresh-hued and rugged like a late, frost-resisting apple.

"How hot and tired you look!" was her greeting across the barrier of bloom and fragrance. "Come in and I'll give you some iced ginger-and-lemon." She led the way to a dwarfish table in a fairy grotto of rocks and climbing flowers. "Are you never coming to see me anymore?"

"I didn't know you'd care to have me," he replied, exactly like a forlorn small boy.

"Your rival, Buddy Higman, comes every day. Though that's partly business. But he always starts in by asking, 'Heard from Her, again, Miss Letty?'"

Her visitor gave her a grateful look. "What do you hear, Miss Pritchard?"

"My young and dangerous cousin is dashing about New York at a great rate," she informed him, "enjoying life to the utmost."

"Then she hasn't sailed yet."

"She sails in a fortnight."

"Does she say anything about coming back?"

The rosy spinster shook her head. "Not a word. But then, Marcia doesn't say things. She does 'em."

"Do you think she will come back—some time?"

"Probably not. I think she will—well, do what is best for her. Without being at all a selfish person, Marcia has a singular instinct for doing what is best for herself. In the real sense, I mean."

Undoubtedly! reflected young Mr. Jeremy Robson. She had done the best thing for herself in judging him and finding him lacking. Acceptance of which fact gave to his face an expression which caused Miss Pritchard to look the other way. Presently she went to a shelf in the nook and brought out an envelope which she placed in her caller's hand.

"Aren't they good!" said she.

He smoothed out the curving paper, and Marcia's own face smiled forth its quaint and inscrutable witchery at him.

"I took it the day before she went away. There's one to spare," she suggested.

"Do you think she'd want me to have it?" he asked, his hungry gaze set upon the little print.

"You're a nice boy," said Miss Letitia Pritchard. ("And all the nicer," she thought to herself, "for being so much a boy.") "Yes; she'd be glad to have you have it, I think."

"She didn't say so?"

Sympathy for the eagerness of his tone softened the old maid's smile. "No. She didn't say so. She didn't say anything about you, except that you'd come to see me. For a time I thought her prophecy was wrong."

"I'd like to come again."

"As often as you like," she said kindly. "You're one of three people she talked to me about, the night before she left. The others were Buddy—she is going to help him get an education when the time comes—and Eli Wade."

From day to day Jeremy had postponed the dreaded confessional visit to the Boot & Shoe Surgeon. "You've reminded me of an errand, Miss Pritchard," he said.

Bidding her good-bye, he went direct to the Infirmary. The old practitioner sat hunched over a pair of white buckskins. He lifted a mild, but questioning face to Jeremy.

"Come in, Mr. Robson," said he. "It's quite some time sence you was here."

"I was ashamed to come," blurted Jeremy.

"Shucks! Don't say that. You can't be responsible for what they order you to write. That's a reporter's job."

"Who says so?"

"Nick Milliken. He says any reporter'd have to do the same."

This was a bitter flavoring to the dose. "That isn't so," replied Jeremy quietly. "I needn't have written it; not that way. I needn't have written it at all."

The Boot & Shoe Surgeon set down the subject upon which he was operating. "I don't understand," he said, puzzled and despondent. "Did you want to do it?"

"That isn't the question. I didn't have to do it. If necessary I could have resigned."

The old man's face cleared up. "Quit your job? That'd 'a' been foolish. There wasn't any call for you to do that."

"Anyhow I'm mighty sorry I ever touched the story. And if I'd known what it was going to do to you"—The old man flinched involuntarily at this reference to the dead glories of his School Board incumbency—"I'd never have touched it in the world."

"Sure you would! You'd do it again. Tomorrow if the orders came."

Jem whirled to meet the malevolent smile of Nicholas Milliken, the Socialist, standing in the doorway.

"I told you not to blame this young feller," the newcomer bade Eli Wade. "He can't help it. He's only a louse-souled ratchet in the machinery of the capitalistic press." Obviously much pleased with this rich metaphor, Mr. Milliken entered and seated himself.

"Well, I knew he wouldn't do it to me a-purpose," said Eli Wade.

Jeremy Robson felt sick; too sick even to be incensed at Milliken who proceeded:

"Didn't even know the little game they were playing, did you, young feller? Well, you see, Eli, here, he's a radical as far as his intelligence will carry him. That's my influence on him. The bosses don't want radicals on the School Board. They don't want 'em anywhere. Anyhow the Schools belong to the Germans: that's their specialty. So, Eli being against the cultural-extension-of-German plan, they stir up the Germans against him, and then sick the newspapers onto him, and when they sick, *you* do the yapping. That's all there is to *that*. Except that Smiling Mart, the damned hypocrite, steps up and eases Eli out to help put in another German and clinch his hold on a few more German votes. Not that it ain't all right, at that; if they'll put in a good radical. The cultural extension's good enough, like anything else that'll help people *think*. Oh, these fools! They can't see education is what's going to dish 'em all and bring on the Social Revolution."

"Don't you talk against Martin Embree, Nick," admonished the proprietor. "There ain't a straighter set pair o' feet in the State of Centralia."

"All right. Then I'm a goat; look at my hoofs!" grinned the Socialist. "But be patient with our helpless young hired-man writer here."

Jeremy liked Milliken's contemptuous excusals less than Wade's blame, and said so.

"Oh, you ain't reached the bottom of your ditch yet," jeered the Socialist. "How's the editorial end? Still writing 'em?"

"Yes," said Jeremy shortly.

"Pot of ink; pot o' glue; pot o' soft soap and a pair of blinders; there's your editorial-writer's outfit. Done any slush-bucketing for Montrose Clark yet?"

"No."

"Say it as though you didn't expect to. But you will. Oh, yes; you'll come to it."

"Let him be, Nick," said the gentle old philosopher of foot-garb.

"Did he let you be? Let him listen. One day old Judge Slippery Selden Dana will come puttering into The Record office—"

"On the ball of his sole," put in the Boot & Shoe Surgeon.

"Pussyfooting. *Of* course. He'll suggest to Mr. Farley; that some recognition of Mr. Montrose Clark's eminent services as a citizen would be timely. Know what that means? Means that Puffy Clark and the P.-U. Co. are getting ready to grab another franchise. Does Mr. Farley see it that way? He does! He remembers a little slice of P.-U. stock in the strong-box. And if Young Feller, here, is good enough with his pen, he wins the job of puffery for the puffiest little public-utility-grafting puff-adder that ever stung a city. And will *he* see it that way? He will. He'll remember his little pay envelope at the end of the week, and he'll come through. It's a grand little system."

"Nothing wrong with a system that lets a man get from his employees what he pays for," defended Jeremy.

"Nothing wrong with your cutting Eli Wade's throat to order, either. Eh?"

To this Jeremy found no reply.

"Remember that apology I was going to make on demand? Do I hear any demand? I guess the apology's the other way around."

"I've made it. Not to you, though. I'm going on. Eli! Once more I'm sorry and I'm ashamed."

"Until next time," added the irrepressible malice of the white-haired Socialist.

Not trusting himself to reply, the reporter walked out. Within a few strides Milliken was at his side.

"He's bad hurt, the old boy," he confided in a wholly altered and wholly sincere tone.

"I'm sorry—"

"'Oh, your story is only part of it. Clever! Vur-ree clever. But they'd have got his place on the Board anyway. They needed it."

"What can I do?"

"Nothing. Unless," added the other on reflection, "you could slip something pleasant about him over some time. That'd please him. He's like a child, about print."

At home Jem took out the picture of Marcia Ames and studied it. Tiny though it was, it was instinct with her very poise and spiritual efflu-ence. As so often with herself, he felt the something unsaid behind the serene self-possession of the face; the something vital for which he must grope. What was the message, the demand which the face was making upon him, which she was making upon him through this dear memento? Ranging back, he recalled in a flash that first impression of her in the meeting, while she was still so completely unknown that he had mistaken even the fundamental matter of sex; the impression of an untouched, untainted valorousness. Again he saw it, reflected from the tiny delicacy of the picture. Plain enough now what she demanded of him.

It was courage.

## 10

THE SENATE PROCEEDINGS DID not open until ten o'clock. Meantime Montrose Clark, President of the Fenchester Public Utilities Corporation,[1] and in some part godling of local affairs, had telephoned his commands to The Record that a representative be sent to his office that morning to take a statement for the paper. Jeremy, incautiously dropping in at the office early, got the job to do before going to the Capitol. He was admitted to an outer office by the hand-perfected private secretary, cross-questioned briefly, and passed in to the Presence.

Mr. Montrose Clark was telephoning. He was revealed to Jeremy's inquiring eye as a plump, glossy, red-faced little man with a fussily assured manner, an autocratic voice and a keen and greedy eye. Few indeed were the local pies of promise or flavor in which Mr. Clark did not have a pudgy and profit-taking finger; and his bearing suggested the man comfortably sure of taking care of himself. He snapped "G'-bye" into the telephone and turned to Jeremy.

"You're the rippawtah from The Record?"

The accent of the word stirred Jeremy's bile. He did not know that it was merely a sub-conscious stock trick of Mr. Clark's; that there were certain words, such as "rippawtah," "culchah," "legislaychuh," and the like, whereby he asserted his superiority of intellectual status, reverting to the comfortable speech of the Middle West for the communication of other thoughts.

"I'm from The Record," he said.

"Take this." The public-utilitarian began to dictate . . .

"Got that? Be sure to be accurate. This is important." To the reporter it seemed neither important nor interesting. It was a statement concerning a projected change, petty, administrative, and technical, in the conduct of the trolley system. Had it been of the most vital significance, the "rippawtah" would still have grilled at the impersonal arrogance of the other's attitude.

"Got that?" repeated Mr. Clark, after another passage. "Read it over."

Jeremy laid down his pencil. "Don't you think you'd better send for one of your stenographers?"

"What for?" demanded the other. "A rippawtah ought to be able to take dictation, if he's competent."

"A 'rippawtah,' as you call him, is accustomed to a certain degree of courtesy."

Mr. Montrose Clark pressed a button and his hand-perfected private secretary popped in.

"Garson! Call The Record. Tell Farley to instruct his rippawtah to follow directions and not be insolent."

Red to his cheek-bones, Jeremy tore up the sheet of paper on which he had been writing, dropped the pieces upon the immaculate rug of the outraged Mr. Montrose Clark, and marched out. Straight to The Record office he went and sought Wackley.

"You can have my job. I'm through."

"What's the matter?" asked the astonished and alarmed managing editor.

Jeremy told him. Wackley laughed. He had no intention of losing so valuable a man as Robson.

"Between us, Montrose Clark is an ass," he said. "Don't let him bother you. We'll keep you away from his jobs after this. Anyway, we're going to work you into editorials and specials more, from now on. Trot along now to the Capitol, and keep your eye on Mart Embree."

Anticipation was in the air of the Senate Chamber when Jeremy arrived. Something special was expected from Senator Embree. As always, when he was on the programme, the galleries were full. There was reason and precedent for this, for the two local newspapers were wont to report the leader of the Northern Tier in a cautious, not to say niggardly manner. People who wished to savor the full acidity of the young radical's utterances, would best get seats for themselves, or be dependent upon more provident friends for word-of-mouth synopsis of the proceedings, since the unfortunate instance of the famous "Piracy and the P.-U." speech on the Special Condemnation Bill, in which Senator Embree had held up that civic godling, Mr. Montrose Clark, to the scorn and reprehension of the impious rabble, and the local press had published the whole matter. Politicians had confidently declared that the speech would terminate the public life of Smiling Mart, who, by the way, had smiled only twice in the whole course of his effort, once at the beginning and again at the end. Montrose Clark, they said, would be too strong for him. It did not so appear. When the tumult and the shouting had died and the captains of industry and the kings of local politics had departed and laid their plans for the elimination of the upstart, it transpired that the upstart had by that one speech crystallized a somewhat indefinite policy of progressive radicalism into a campaign for the rescue of the State from the control of the financial and public utility magnates who had quietly taken it over from an older and far more corrupt purely political management. The man in the street rallied to Martin Embree, as well where the street was a country town thoroughfare as where it was a city's artery of trade, and the farmers of the north followed almost in a body and without much respect to party. These were unassimilated Americans; Scandinavians, a few Dutch and Italians, but mostly Germans. Martin Embree had the unbounded confidence of these elements, particularly the Germans. He had cultivated it assiduously, and by legitimate political methods. In and out of season he impressed them with their responsibility for the cleansing of politics, and for reform. Now, to your German-American, uplifted in the conviction of racial righteousness, reform is a word sanctified for his own uses. Reform means compelling other people to think as he thinks. Therefore he solemnly adopts it. Reform, to these Northern Tier farmers, meant Martin Embree. By this support alone, if he had enjoyed no other, he was too strong for the powers that were completely to dislodge. He was clean, honest, earnest, fervent, laborious, and the possessor of a direct and winning address. Too late, the "old gang" perceived that he had developed from a "cheap spellbinder" into a "dangerous demagogue"; and largely because they had so ill-advisedly permitted such part of the press as they controlled, to disseminate that telling speech of his. At least, they wouldn't make that mistake again! Martin Embree was now too considerable a figure to be ignored in print. But no other man in the public life of Centralia was so rigorously "edited."

Today, Jeremy Robson foresaw, his own job would be one of reporting orally, rather than writing. This acting as political lookout he quite enjoyed; it gave him a flattering sense of being on the inside of things. Then, too, there was opportunity for finesse. If the speaker of the day got upon slippery ground, Jeremy would have his chance to trip him up editorially, perhaps. He knew that Embree would not resent this in him. It was part of the game, in which they were, for the present, opponents. The Senator's good-humor and broad-minded acceptance of the matter was one of the qualities which Jeremy most ardently admired in him. And politically he was so right and decent and clear of vision! What would not Jeremy have given for a chance as political expert on a paper supporting Embree's main policies, a progressive and independent paper such as the Bellair Journal, for example! Perhaps that would come in time; already The Journal had offered him a reporter's job. Meanwhile he must, in fairness, be loyal to his employers. Embree himself would admit that. Anyone would admit it, except a hare-brained Socialist like Milliken. Jeremy clung to that justification of loyalty.

Routine business was still in progress on the floor when Galpin of The Guardian came in and seated himself next to Jeremy. There was still a patch over his left eye. His broad and bony face wore an expression of concerned expectation.

"What's Embree after this time?" Jeremy whispered to him.

"Us," said Galpin.

"Editorial 'we'? The Guardian? How?"

"Don't know. Can't pick up much. Martin don't ever say much beforehand. Pulls his gun and shoots."

"And Lord help the bull's-eye!"

"Ay-ah," assented Galpin. "I asked him this morning what's what, and all he said was; 'Better get ready to duck in the Press Gallery,' with that smile of his that may mean fun and may mean murder. Look! There's Slippery Selden Dana on the floor."

"That means the P.-U. is in it."

"Not necessarily. But it means something out of the ordinary. He isn't spending Montrose Clark's time on any picayune stuff."

"You can't blame Embree if he goes after the newspapers," said The Record reflectively.

"Fool trick, though. They always get in the last wallop."

"Look what a raw deal he gets, here in Fenchester. The best he gets from The Record is silent contempt, and The Guardian—well, I don't know why he hasn't sued The Guardian for libel long ago."

"What'd be the use?"

"You mean The Guardian is right in practically saying he's a crook?"

"No. I guess he's the nearest decent thing we've got in this rotten mess of politics," said Galpin with the experienced political reporter's cynical view of public men, "unless it's Magnus Laurens."

"Then why won't they give him a fair shake? I don't mind their going after him editorially. That's opinion. But to cut him out of the news, that gets my goat a little."

"Ay-ah? Well, you see, he's gumming our game."

"What ga—"

"The whole, dam', slick, polite graft that makes the machine run so smooth and nice and turns out the pretty little dividends for the banks and the railroads and the big companies generally. Haven't you seen into that millstone yet?"

"You talk as if you were really on Embree's side."

"Ay-ah. Why not?"

"But The Guard—"

"I'm a hired man," said Galpin impassively.

"If you had a paper of your own—"

"Be a hired man just the same."

"Who could boss you then?" asked Jeremy in surprise.

"Same bunch that bosses The Record and The Guardian."

"Couldn't a paper be run independent of them?"

"Never has been in this town."

"But couldn't it?" persisted the other. "Wouldn't it be fun to work on a paper like that!"

"Gee!" murmured Galpin. They were like two urchins savoring a golden and imaginative treat.

"Mr. President."

The resonant tones[2] of Martin Embree's rich and effortless voice roused the reporters from their boyish vision. He stood tall, handsome, easy, confident, but his usually sunny face was grave, and he held in his hand a document, contrary to his custom. Before he had spoken five minutes to the hushed attention of floor and galleries, it became evident that his talk was centering and converging upon that document. His subject was the "cheese check" scandal which had roused the dairy farmers of his region to fury. He traced the steps whereby the commission men's combine had sought legislation which would have rendered the producer almost helpless in their hands, touched upon alleged bribery in the lower House, referred to the part which two of the Fenchester banking institutions had played ("That's why Dana was here; Montrose Clark's in the banking game on the side," whispered Galpin), and continued:

"For my own conscientious and repeated attempts to block this nefarious deal, I have been consistently derided as a silly reformer by one of the local newspapers, and denounced by the other in terms which, were circumstances otherwise, I should reply to by a suit for criminal libel. I am enabled to deal with The Fenchester Guardian, in a more effective, swifter, and more relevant manner. Will the clerk of the Senate kindly read this letter, which fell into my hands by a happy accident, and the authenticity of which will not be denied by its author?"

The clerk of the Senate received the document with a look of interest unusual in his stolid official bearing. He began to read:

"Editor's Office of The Fenchester Evening Guardian: Undated. My dear Mr. Dorlon:—"

"The date is established as of last month by the envelope," said Senator Embree.

Profiting by the interruption, the clerk ran his eye swiftly through the one-page letter; but, instead of resuming his reading, left his place and carried it to the presiding officer. Their heads bent over it close together. A whisper passed between them. Its sibilance, though not its purport, could be heard through the silenced chamber. The clerk of the Senate turned away, not toward his desk, but toward the curtained exit.

"Mr. Clerk!" Martin Embree's voice was not raised by the iota of a tone; yet it stopped the man in his tracks. "Not one step out of my sight with that document."

"The Senator will come to order. The Senator will address himself to the chair," rebuked the President.

Embree's arm rose, rigid as iron, until his stiffened hand pointed with all the menace of a weapon straight into the face of the discomposed presiding officer.

"Mr. President, I hold you responsible for the safety and integrity of that document. I ask you to direct the clerk to read it."

"Read," said the President after a moment of hesitation.

"'My dear Mr. Dorlon,'" repeated the clerk: "'I have yours of the 19th with directions for claiming the last payment from the Trust Co. Glad you approve the paper's course and are satisfied with what we have done on the Cheese Commission Bill. Locker and Mayne are O.K. I turned over their balance to them. We can whip Smith into line; Cary, Sellers, and Gunderson, too, in time. In the Senate we owe a great deal to'" (the clerk's voice faltered) "'Bellows'" (the clerk's name was Bellows). "'Better look after him. Let me know when you come to the Capitol.

"'Yours very truly, (Signed) A. M. Wymett.'"

Dead silence followed, in which the footsteps of the messenger returning the document to Senator Embree, sounded loud and hollow. Then a voice (unidentified) pronounced from the gallery in accents of intensest conviction: "Well, I *am* damned!" Which inspired another voice (also unidentified) to adjure solemnly, "Burn this letter." The Senate found relief in nervous, shrill, tittering laughter. "Will the papers print *that*?" shouted somebody, and the presiding officer recovering, hammered vehemently for order.

"Gentlemen," concluded Martin Embree, the damnatory letter raised to the level of his head, "I leave to this honorable body the determination as between the Honorable A. M. Wymett, editor and proprietor of The Fenchester Guardian, and myself."

He sat down.

Jeremy turned to his fellow reporter, with questioning eyes.

"Knock-out," said Galpin.

"Criminal charge, isn't it?"

"Guess so. Anyhow, it's good-bye Guardian. So far as Wymett's concerned, anyway. The crooked hound!"

"Didn't you know he was doing their dirty work?"

"I knew he took orders. I didn't know he took money. We all take orders. You'll take orders when you suppress this story."

"Can it be suppressed?"

"It's got to be. Honor of the profession and all that sort of thing. Let's get out. I want some air."

Outside they walked along for a block, before either spoke. Jeremy said: "Andy, how's this going to affect you?"

"Don't know. Shut up about it, can't you! Talk about something else."

"All right," agreed the other cheerfully. "I'll talk about myself. I've got a chance to make a change. What do you think of editorial writing?"

"Nice, soft job. If you can do it. I couldn't."

"I can."

"Go to it, then. Only I wouldn't stick to it."

"Why not?"

Galpin rubbed his shaggy head. "Oh, I dunno. Too much preaching of the other fellow's doctrine, I guess."

Jeremy's mind reverted to Milliken's view and he wondered how nearly the two agreed. Certainly between preaching and the profession to which the Socialist had bitterly likened editorializing, yawned the widest of gulfs. He stated Milliken's characterization.

"Rough stuff," commented Galpin. "I guess there's something in it, though. Ay-ah. I get his point."

"Then you wouldn't take the job?"

"You might try it on for a while. But as a permanency—well, it seems to me a fellow that's settled down to write editorials for another man all his life has sort of given up."

"Given up? What?"

"Everything. He's licked. Ay-ah. He's a beaten man. He's under contract to think another man's thoughts and make other folks think 'em if he can."

"Aren't we doing that as reporters?"

"Not so much. Facts ain't thoughts. You can report and keep your mind independent. That's why I climb off the desk whenever I can, like today. Whew! I came near having Mr. Wymett go along with me. He was held up at the last minute."

Galpin turned into his office. Jeremy went to The Record to report to Wackley and was turned over to Mr. Farley.

"Nothing about The Guardian can be published, of course," prescribed that diplomat, who had already been in communication with the local leaders. "Give us half a column of the rest. And go light. It's ticklish ground."

After finishing, Jeremy went out for a long and thoughtful walk. On his return home he found a letter with the letterhead of Messrs. Hunt & Hunt, Attorneys, of Philadelphia. The firm begged to inform him that, with due allowance for taxes and fees, he was heir, under his great-aunt's will, to the sum of $86,730.18.

AFTER LISTENING TO ANDREW GALPIN'S verbal report upon Senator Martin Embree's painful and convincing characterization of The Guardian's editorial page as for sale to the highest bidder, backed up by discouraging details regarding himself, A. M. Wymett retired to his house to commune with a bottle and a time-table of the trains to Canada. As a man's house is his castle and as castles are not connected with a troublous and uncharitable world by wires of communication, he further fortified his position by cutting off the telephone. He then profoundly considered his prospects and as profoundly misliked them.

As befitted the owner of a pliable daily, Mr. Wymett was thoroughly conversant with the law bearing upon publications. It seemed unpleasantly probable to him that his ill-fated letter laid him open to indictment on any one of three counts. That smiling Mart Embree would push for criminal action, he had little doubt. The Guardian unhappily had nothing on the Senator; he couldn't be blackmailed. If the financial and political powers in control would stand by, The Guardian could weather the storm, albeit severely battered in reputation. But would they? Could they afford to in view of the definite nature of the exposure? Mr. Wymett supped gloomily and alone with this question and afterward took it into his study with him for the evening's speculation. His long, grave, immobile, ascetic face grew longer, graver, more immobile, and more ascetic as the facts in their bearing upon him massed a formidable array of cons against a scraggly and wavering handful of pros.

Upon him thus absorbed, and steadily absorbing (for the bottle was still his counselor), intruded young Robson of The Record.

"Nothing to say for publication," snapped Wymett, professionally shocked at the idea of his rival's making capital of his misfortunes.

"We're not printing anything," pleasantly replied his visitor.

"What do you want, then?"

"Will you sell The Guardian?"

"To whom?"

"To me."

Mr. Wymett leaned back from his desk and studied his caller from beneath heavy eyelids. His posture lent to his face a furtively benevolent look as of one meditating the performance of a good deed on the sly. Such was not his precise intent, as regarded young Robson. He didn't trust young Robson. He didn't trust The Record. For that matter he was not in a mood to trust anybody or anything in a calumnious world. He opened a small cabinet at his elbow which he had hastily closed upon young Robson's entrance.

"May I offer you a drink?" he said.

"No; thank you."

"Good! Nothing mixes so badly with printer's ink," approved the older man patronizingly. "I seldom touch it, otherwise than as a digestant." He poured himself a liberal allowance and set the glass on his desk. "Whom do you represent?"

"Myself."

Mr. Wymett smiled tolerantly.

"Of course. But whose capital?"

"My own."

"A secret deal, eh? What reason have you to suppose that the paper is for sale?"

"I was in the Senate."

Thus unpleasantly recalled to his thorny situation, Mr. Wymett gulped down his whiskey and hastily poured another.

"A bare-faced forgery," he asserted with an effect of judicial severity; "as will be proved at the proper time."

"Let us assume it to be, for the sake of courtesy. It got a quick endorsement," replied young Robson smoothly.

Mr. Wymett hastily set down the re-filled glass which he was voluptuously raising, and rather wished that he hadn't taken that other one. Young Robson was not, perhaps, as young as his years.

"Endorsement?" he inquired.

"Locker and Mayne have skipped out. The forgery impressed them to that extent."

"Yellow," commented the severe Mr. Wymett. His hand crept toward the stimulant which possesses the mystic power of changing timorous yellow into fighting red—up to a point—and was retracted again before attaining the goal. The caller's quick eye noted the movement. "They own no part of The Guardian," added its proprietor, "and their action has nothing to do with the matter of its sale."

"No," commented young Robson in a tone disturbingly indeterminate between confirmation and incredulity.

"I've been offered a hundred thousand for the paper," remarked Mr. Wymett casually.

"Coal-oil Johnny must have been out this way."

"My dear young sir," said Mr. Wymett in a tone intended to be crushing; "I am talking business. May I trouble you to do the same?"

"Then The Guardian *is* for sale."

"Everything in this world is for sale, at its price," returned the editor-owner, thereby unconsciously voicing his philosophy of life.

"I assume that the price of The Guardian has not been increased by the events of today."

"Assume nothing of the sort."

Young Mr. Robson leaned forward over the desk. "Shall I talk plain talk?"

"If you please."

"There'll be an indictment if you stay here."

"There will. For forgery. Against the author of that faked letter."

"Against you. Nothing can stop it."

"Did Embree promise you that?"

"There's no question of promise. I don't even get your idea."

"Indeed! Suppose you give me credit for a gleam of intelligence. Nothing more is required to see your game. Yours and Embree's. He wants to get his hands on a paper here. He fakes up this attack on me and The Guardian to bulldoze me into selling the paper. You are his tool. The pair of you think you can run me off my own property with an unloaded gun. Not A. M. Wymett!"

"Very ingenious. But Senator Embree doesn't happen to enter into this in any way, shape, or manner."

"Then who is backing you? Is it Phipps and the brewery crowd? Or the banking trust? I don't suppose you've saved the money out of your twenty-five a week from The Record."

"That's beside the question. The money is there. Seventy thousand dollars flat."

Into Mr. Wymett's parched-looking eyes shot a swift gleam, only to be as swiftly veiled. He lifted and slowly drank the liquor before him. He shook his head.

"Not to be considered. Absurd."

"It is what I figure The Guardian to be worth; to have been worth up to two-fifteen this afternoon."

"It is worth just as much now as it was yesterday."

"Seventy thousand dollars," pursued young Robson as if the other had not spoken. "I'd like your answer."

"Indeed! And when would you like it?"

The visitor glanced at the clock.

"Say, an hour."

"Come, now! You aren't so innocent of business as to suppose that deals of this importance are put through on any such hair-trigger basis."

"Not ordinarily. This is rather special, isn't it?" insinuated the other.

"Frankly, I don't like your attitude, Mr. Robson."

"Consider your own." Jeremy's eyes hardened. "You're fiddling and faddling within a step of the penitentiary. They'll get you if you try to hang to The Guardian. Public sentiment will demand it. Do you know that the Bellair papers are carrying the story?"

"Damn 'em!" said Mr. Wymett and visited the decanter again.

"So, you see how far it's gone. Now, if it is known that you're out of the paper, they'll let up on you, won't they? That looks to me like the politics of it."

"Probably," agreed Mr. Wymett.

"Well, what do you say?"

"Let me talk to my lawyer."

The Honorable Selden Dana was summoned, and came after a short delay, in the course of which Mr. Wymett had two more whiskies to his own good luck, for the price offered was better than he could have reasonably hoped. On Judge Dana's arrival he and Mr. Wymett retired for a conference. It was brief. Three words comprised the lawyer's advice: "Sell and git!"

"You've bought, Mr. Robson," he said, returning with his client for a drink, and departed thoughtfully, leaving the old and the new owner of The Guardian with duly signed preliminary agreements in their pockets. Jeremy was to take over control the first of the succeeding month.

"So you won't say where the money comes from?" said the now relaxed and smiling Mr. Wymett.

"For publication?"

"Oh, no. To satisfy personal curiosity."

"For that I wouldn't. Public curiosity, though; that's different. I suppose people will be interested to know who's back of the paper."

"Certainly."

"Then I'll look to you to tell them. In tomorrow's Guardian. These are the facts, which you can verify by wire if you wish." And he related to the surprised Mr. Wymett the main circumstances of the Greer will. "When that is published," he concluded, "people will understand that it's my own money, that The Guardian is my own paper, and that there are no strings on it or me."

Mr. Wymett had another drink—"just one more"—to the success of The Guardian under its new management, and became expansive for once in his cautious life.

"You've bought into a sporting proposition, young man." The retiring editor rested his lined and puckered face on his hand, and regarded his vis-à-vis thoughtfully. "A sporting proposition. Oh, God; I'm glad to be out of it—and sorry! It's a hell of a life, and I've loved it. But in the end it gets you. Like a drug."

He sat staring in a brief silence at the young, sanguine, keen face before him; a sad, humorous-eyed, ageing, slovenly, dishonest, tolerant philosopher.

"You're young," he broke forth. "Young enough, probably, to believe that you can run a newspaper and still be—and still keep your ideals. Oh, I had 'em, when I started in, just as you've got 'em. Of course you've got 'em! They go with youth. Perhaps they'd stay with youth if youth would stay with us. But you grow old so damnably fast in this game. Look at me! Or perhaps you'd better *not* look at me. You might see yourself as you'll be at my age."

"Not me," returned Jeremy Robson with unflattering conviction.

"Not? Well, perhaps not. I'm an old babbler. So you want Fenchester to know that it's your own money that's behind the paper?"

"Yes; so they'll understand that it's a strictly one-man proposition."

"And you think it's going to be. Oh, well; for a little while, maybe. Then—" His voice was as that of one who regretfully deprives a child of a sweetmeat—"you'll forego that happy and infantile dream. You're not going to run your newspaper just because you've bought it. The politicians are going to run it for you. The banks are going to run it for you. The railroads and trolley lines and water-power companies and public-utility people are going to run it for you. And always the advertisers—the advertisers—the advertisers. You're going to be just a little, careful, polite Recording Secretary for them all. You'll print what they tell you to and you'll kill what they forbid you to print. Otherwise you can't live. Don't I know! I've tried it—both ways."

He dreamed with somnolent eyes back over the happy, troubled, iniquitous, exciting years of The Guardian. "And so you think you'll change all that! Not much to be left of the old Guardian, eh? Perhaps not even his figurehead, blowing his trumpet over the paper's title. I hope you'll leave that, though. It's been there a long time. Fifty-odd years. Almost as long as I've lived. For old times' sake I'd like to see him stay, the old Guardian. We newspaper men are all sentimentalists and conservatives at heart."

"Not me," denied Jeremy. "Not the conservative part, anyway. But I'll leave The Guardian his trumpet."

"That trumpet! I was going to rock the walls of Jericho with it! They still stand; you may have noticed that. There's a lot of solidity about our modern Jericho. As for us poor Joshuas of the newspapers, our trumpet isn't a trumpet any more. It's the horn of a talking-machine. We're just damned phonographs playing the records that bigger men thrust into our mechanical insides. Am I boring you?"

"Go on," said Jeremy Robson. "I took a course in journalism at college. There was nothing in it like this."

"There wouldn't be. *I'd* like to lecture to 'em on the Voice of the Press. The Voice from the Horn! Nickel-in-the-slot and you get your tune. The politician drops his coin in and gets his favorite selection, in consideration of a job on a board. The city authorities drop their coin in—that's the official printing—and you sing their little song. The railroads drop in a few favors, passes and the like, and the horn grinds out their pet record. And always the advertiser, big, small, and medium; he owns your paper, news and editorials, and you'll do as he says or— where do you get off!

"And then there's the silencers," continued the remorseless lecturer. "Don't forget the silencers. The Dutch and the Swedes and the Norwegians and the Irish, all with tender toes. The Jews and the Methodists and the Catholics and the Lutherans, all touchy as wasps. You can't afford to play any tune they don't like. And always there's Deutschtum. Know what 'Deutschtum' is? No, you wouldn't. Well, it means that German-Americans are organized for German purposes all through the Middle West, and nowhere more strongly than in this State. When Germany declares war on Europe, which will be within ten years—yes, I've been grinned at before by people who considered this just a crazy hobby of mine—all our Bunds and Vereins and Gesellschafts are going to see to it that the United States either stays out or goes in on the 'right' side. Why, they're making a Little Germany of us right here in this State and city by slow, methodical, Teuton education,[1] managed by our school boards which are run by Germans, trained to it in the public schools—"

"That's a thing I'd like to tackle," said Robson thoughtfully.

"Hands off, young David! The Dutch Goliath is too big for your sling. No, sir! Stand in with them. You'll find them reasonable and easy enough to deal with so long as you don't interfere with their programme. Play the German tune and they'll play yours. Study 'em, flatter 'em a little, and watch 'em. Theirs is the winning game.

"To trail along with the successful element," continued the cynical oracle: "That's the great secret. It's the only way for a newspaper. There lies your profit."

"In other words, selling out to the highest bidder," translated his disenchanted listener.

The volunteer professor of journalism took one more drink and gazed with surprise and reproach at the empty bottle.

"Oh, I don't say you'll sell out, all at once. It's a gradual process. Step by step, finding a nice soft excuse to plant your foot on each time, until you hit the bottom. Don't I know! What you won't do for fear, you'll do for friendship—and then for favor—and then for preferment." His voice dropped, and his eyes sought the empty liquor glass. "And then—for cash."

The younger man stirred, uneasy under that intimate and betraying confidence.

"Oh, it's a rotten game, and Lord! how I hate to be quitting it!" pursued the philosopher. "How I'd love to be you, just getting really into it! Perhaps I'd do different. Make a better job of it. Keep to my ideals. Perhaps not. Too heavy odds." His eyes lifted again with a bleary, dreamy wistfulness. "So you're going to run an honest newspaper in Fenchester, are you, son?"

The visitor rose. "You bet I am!" he said jubilantly.

[Often in the vivid years to follow, the young owner of The Guardian had cause to reflect that the shrewdest professional advice which he had ever disregarded came from one who had just "stuck" him with an all-but-ruinous bargain.]

Late as was the interview, he couldn't go to bed without telling Andrew Galpin. Much depended on that astute youth. Jeremy routed him out of bed, at his boarding-house.

"Come out and get a rarebit and a stein of beer, Andy."

"Ay-a-a-ah!" yawned Galpin. "Watsamatter with you? What time is it?"

"Quarter to one."

"You're crazy, young fellow."

"I'm worse than that. I've just bought The Guardian."

"*What!*"

"That's what."

"Where'd you get the money?"

"Left to me."

"How much did you pay?"

"Seventy thousand."

"Seventy! You fat-wit!"

"What's the matter with that?" asked Jeremy, crestfallen.

"Twenty thousand nice, fat, round, cool dollars is what's the matter with it. Why didn't you tell me?"

"Didn't have the time. I caught Wymett when he was scared."

"He caught you when you were easy," retorted Galpin in disgust. "How did you happen to get stuck for seventy?"

Jeremy looked sulky. "I figured it out on a basis of advertising and circulation."

"Oh, hell! You poor innocent!" These unpalatable observations he left his caller to digest while he retired to wash his face. In the act of lacing up his left boot he remarked: "You could have got it for fifty. Fifty-five at the outside."

"It ought to make eight thousand a year."

"On paper," was Galpin's laconic comment. He looked up from his right boot. "Its advertising rate card is all bunk. Rotten with rebates."

"Oh!" said Jeremy blankly. "Anyway, it can be made to make money," he added, recovering.

"Maybe. How much reserve have you got?"

"Oh, about fifteen thousand."

"It'll eat that in the first year," observed Galpin, slipping into his suspenders.

A dismayed silence fell between the friends. "Well, come on," said Jeremy finally.

"I'm afraid I'll spoil your appetite."

"You haven't improved it," admitted Jeremy. "So you think I've made a fool of myself."

"I think you've bought a dog, and an old dog."

"It can be taught new tricks."

"A yellow dog."

"It hasn't always been yellow. It needn't keep on being."

"I don't think you'll be comfortable in its hide."

"Andy, I'd counted on you."

Galpin stopped buttoning his waistcoat and looked up. "For what?"

"To help me make a real newspaper."

"As how?"

"General manager."

"Is that why you're asking me out to beer up, young fellow?"

"Yes."

Galpin removed his waistcoat and hung it neatly on a chair back. He then proceeded to unlace his right boot. "What are you doing?" demanded Jeremy.

"Going back to bed."

"Not interested?"

"Worse than that. I'm excited."

"Want time to—"

"Want nothin'!"

"Well, but—"

"No beer for me. No midnight racketings. I go on the water wagon right here. Also the sleep wagon." He folded his trousers lengthwise upon his trunk, and reached for his pajamas. "I advise you the same," he added. "We've got a job, you and I, training a yellow dog to jump in and fight for its life."

"You're on for the job, then, Andy?" cried Jeremy.

"Boss," said Andrew Galpin, rolling over into his dishevelled bed, "you've hired a hand."

# PART II

## 12

MOTIVES NOT FULLY FORMULATED had impelled Jeremy Robson to the purchase of The Fenchester Guardian. Now that he was face to face with the multiform problem of what he was to do with his new responsibility, he sought to determine why he had possessed himself of it, hoping to discover in that Why a clue to his future course.

Several figures at once stepped to the front of his mind and imperiously claimed credit for inspiring his action. There was Montrose Clark who had capped his impersonal insolences by the shibboleth, "rippawtah." Nobody was ever going to give Jeremy Robson curt orders as a "rippawtah" again. (But he had the saving sense to grin at himself for the triviality of it!) There was Andrew Galpin, who had said of the pleasant pursuit of editorial writing that the practitioner of it "was licked—a beaten man," thus taking all the gloss from that phase. There was Milliken, crude, coarse, malicious, with his inept but biting epithets, and his blatant jibes at the necessities of hired-man (or worse-than-hired-woman) journalism. There was Eli Wade, whom he had written down to order—though herein Jeremy was still dallying with self-delusions, since it was the lure of his own facile pen that had betrayed him there—and to whom he owed a reparation which he could perhaps now make. There was his old purpose of someday owning a paper; quite a different paper, however, from the feeble and dubious Guardian. More potent was the influence, never wholly abated, of that talk with Senator Martin Embree wherein the shrewd judge of men and agencies had suggested the power to be exerted for good by a fair-minded, independent daily. But the real motivating power was Marcia Ames. Withdrawing herself from him, she had left him a legacy of influence which was, at the same time, a debt. He owed it to himself to prove to her that he could be as honorable as she had deemed him dishonorable; as trustworthy as she had deemed him unfit to be trusted; and he must do this through this same medium of print whereby he had offended. Something dogged in him prescribed that he should work out his salvation there on the spot. She might never return to see it. She might never even know of it. But it would be her work. By so much, at least, Jeremy would hold her. And in doing what she would have him do, he would fill that bleak and arid void, which, lacking hope, can be appeased only by activity.

It was no easy task which Jeremy Robson had set himself, that of making his new property a vehicle for ideals. He was content that it should not be easy. He craved hard, exacting, stimulant work. The Guardian offered it in more generous measure than a better paper could have done. Jeremy purposed to save The Guardian's soul. Perhaps he had some underlying notion that he might save his own, in the process.

That bad name which, given to a dog, is proverbially alleged to bring down upon him a peculiarly un-canine fate at the hangman's hands, had long attached to The Fenchester Guardian. But the paper's ill-repute was no man's gift. It had been justly earned. Once the stiffly high-minded personal organ of a stilted and honorable old-school statesman, it had fallen, under A. M. Wymett, to become a mongrel of journalism, a forlorn and servile whiner, fawning for petty favors, kicked about by the financial and political interests of the State, and not infrequently ornamented with a tin can of scandal to its tail in the form of dirty work performed for some temporary subsidizer in the background. Thanks to shrewd legal advice and his own editorial adroitness, its guiding spirit had contrived to escape the law, and, up to the episode of the disastrously imprudent "cheese-check" letter, open and public contumely. Further, he had, by dint of sheer ability of a low ethical order but high technical grade, maintained a fair circulation for his paper.

Its only competitor in the bustling, growing State capital, with its seventy thousand inhabitants, was The Record. There was no morning newspaper. Several plans to start one had come to naught, because of the secret opposition of the local leaders of politics and industry, who were well content with the two mild and amenable specimens of journalism already in the field. The Record represented stolid, stodgy, profitable, and unprogressive respectability in a community now astir with new and uneasy fermentations. The Guardian had always represented what it was bidden to represent. What attitude it might adopt under the new control was a question not assumed to be troublesome by those whom a change might conceivably trouble in no small degree. It was comfortably taken for granted that The Guardian would "be good" when the time and test came. For the corruptible to put on incorruptibility, in the newspaper world, is a phenomenon so rare as to be practically negligible.

Soon or late these questions would come to an issue between the new owner of The Guardian and those who had quietly controlled it for their own ends. So much Jeremy Robson apprehended. What he had not foreseen was a more immediate and imperative consideration. He had vaguely believed that he was taking possession of a semipublic agency of enlightenment. He found that he had bought a Struggle for Existence. Quite a number of shrewd and active citizens whose existence had not hitherto impressed him as important, loomed as figures and probably antagonists in the struggle. Jeremy found himself in the way of learning some new and important things about the newspaper business, with his local advertisers in the pedagogic chair.

Newspapers do not live by the bread of circulation alone, but chiefly by the strong and sustaining meat of advertising patronage. This important fact had duly entered into Jeremy Robson's calculations. On paper he had figured a clear profit for The Guardian, before purchasing. After taking over the property he found his estimates borne out by the formal accounts. But he also found, to his discomfiture, that The Guardian's books had been kept by a sunny optimist with a taste for fiction. This gentleman had plugged up the discrepancies in the papers finances with ingenious figures, as a boat-jerry might doctor a leaky seam with putty and paint—for sale only.

The book figures showed but one scale of advertising rates, with the normal discounts to heavy users of space. While the new toy was still agleam in the eyes of its proud possessor with all the glamour of novelty, he began to discover that instead of a standard price to advertisers, The Guardian had more scales than even so fishy a proposition was entitled to; that, in fact, A. M. Wymett had peddled about his precious advertising space like a man with stolen diamonds to sell, and covered the shady transactions by a system of ingenious and destructive rebates. Thus, the columns which young Mr. Robson had confidingly calculated at four to nine cents per line, were actually fetching from five cents downward.

"That's the first thing to be set right," announced Jeremy after a profoundly unsatisfactory study of his property's earning capacity as contrasted with its paper profits. "We'll have a one-price-to-all system hereafter."

"Ay-ah," drawled Andrew Galpin, to whom the decision was communicated. "Your advertisers'll just love that!"

"They ought to be satisfied. It's the only square way."

"Oh, they'll be satisfied if you put the scale low enough. But if you put the scale low enough you'll go broke."

"Wymett didn't go broke."

"The Guardian had other sources of revenue under Wymett."

"Such as the Cheese Bill fund?"

"Occasionally. Also the steady, reliable revenue from the advertising matter that doesn't bear the a-d-v sign."

"You mean store 'readers' and that sort of thing? I'm going to cut those out."

"Are you? They're semi-legitimate. Compared with some of the stuff we've carried they're so high-principled they're almost holy."

"Well, what, for instance?"

"Paid editorials. Paid political articles. Paid puffs and roasts. Brewery checks. Railroad checks. P.-U. checks. Paving and other contractors' checks. You can read it all in the back files, if you're newspaper man enough to read between the lines."

"I never saw any of that on The Record."

"It ain't there. The Record don't do it that way; a little more decent. The Record's a kept-lady. We're on the street—or were."

"'Were' is right." Jeremy ran his hands through his hair and regarded his companion anxiously. "Andy?" he said.

"Ay-ah?"

"Were you—Did you—Never mind. It doesn't matter."

"Ay-ah; it matters all right. You were going to ask me whether I had to write any of that bought-and-paid-for stuff. And you were afraid to. Is that right?"

Jeremy turned red.

"It's right," confirmed the other. "Well, I never did. I wouldn't. I gave 'em notice that I was fired the noon of the morning I got one of those jobs. They were decent about it. But I had to do the next worse thing. I had to let myself be called off a story so that some other guy could write it, and write it crooked."

"Have we had any—any offers since we took hold of the paper?"

"Give 'em time, Boss. It's only a month, and in the slack period at that. But I'll tell you one thing. If you're going to change the entire advertising policy, you'll have to change your advertising manager, for Perley don't know anything different from the news-selling and rebate game."

"Perley's fired."

"So far, so good. Who've you got to take his place?"

"Nobody, yet. Could you manage it, Andy?"

"Temporarily, I might. But I'm going to have my hands too full remaking the old sheet on the news side to give much time to advertising, in the next year or so."

"Temporarily will do. I'm going to get the principal merchants together and talk it out with them. And I want to show 'em a change in the advertising managership that'll convince 'em the change of policy is real."

"Ay-ah," assented Galpin. "It sounds like the rumble of distant thunder to me."

"Not at all. All I want is a decent, living rate for the paper. Every merchant expects a living profit on his merchandise. Why shouldn't a newspaper get the same?"

"Logical. Perfectly logical. But can you get 'em to see it that way?" Andrew Galpin paused and then delivered himself of a characteristic bit of shrewdness. "The average storekeeper regards advertising outlay as a sort of accepted blackmail which he pays under protest; he don't know exactly why, and he don't know exactly for what. If you made him reason it out, he'd probably say that he don't believe it pays, but everybody does it. Of course, he don't know whether it pays or not. Nobody does, really."

"Then why does he do it?"

"Because his competitors do. He's afraid not to. He has some dim sort of fear that the papers will soak him if he don't. That's where the blackmail comes in, if he had sense enough to figure it."

"There won't be any blackmail with us."

"But the merchants won't know it. They'll advertise, and because they advertise they'll think they're entitled to a say in the paper. They'll try to run it for you, too."

"Will they?" muttered Jeremy in a tone which suggested that there might be difficulties attending the fulfillment of the ambition.

"Ay-ah. In good faith, too. There's something in their theory—I guess—from their point of view."

"Well, I'll give them a chance to explain it," said the new owner. "My plan is to round 'em up at a lunch, and then have it out with 'em. What do you think?"

"Fine! Feed 'em. Then kick 'em in the stomach."

"No, sir! pat 'em on the back and talk reason to them. That's where *you* come in. They know you're a real newspaper man. They've got to find it out yet, about me."

Out of thirty of the principal local advertisers in The Guardian, twenty-one accepted Jeremy Robson's invitation to lunch with him at the Fenchester Club, with a "business conference" to follow. Their attitude toward the gustatory part of the proceedings was that of wary fish toward food which might conceal a hook. Very nice luncheon, but—what was behind it? They had never had confidence in The Guardian under A. M. Wymett. Why should they have more in an unknown quantity like young Robson?

Sensing plainly this feeling, Jeremy perceived that here was the time and place for finesse. Unfortunately he lacked that particular quality. What was the next best thing to having it at call, he appreciated his want of it, and instead of blundering strategically around the point he went straight to it in the briefest of speeches.

"Gentlemen: I've brought you here to state the new policy of The Guardian. The advertising rate will be that of the rate card. The same system of discounts to all. No rebates. I'd be glad to hear your views."

He sat down. A hum of surprise went about the table. Someone started applause: the effort was abortive. It was no occasion for empty courtesies. This was business!

"Talks straight," remarked Betts, of Kelter & Betts, dry goods, in a loud whisper, to his neighbor Arthur Turnbull, of the Emporium.

"Bluff," opined Turnbull.

"Get up and call it," suggested A. Friedland, proprietor of the Big Shop who had overheard.

"Let Ellison do the talking," returned Turnbull. "He's president of our association."

Obedient to several suggestions, Matthew Ellison, head of Ellison Brothers' department store[1] and president of the Retailers' Association, reared his ample form, and smiled his conscientious smile, from above a graying chin whisker, upon the assembled feasters. In a long and rambling talk which Andrew Galpin would have fairly slaughtered with an editorial blue pencil, Mr. Ellison referred to Jeremy something more than two dozen times as "our esteemed young friend" and at least a dozen as "my dear young friend"; both of which were equally accurate and sincere. The gist of his speech, so far as any one present could grasp it, seemed to indicate a guarded agnosticism concerning the announced policy of the paper. Upon the heels of the windy compliment with which he closed, Adolph Ahrens, junior partner and advertising manager of the Great Northwestern Stores, popped up. Mr. Ahrens was a young, blackish, combative-jawed man with twitchy eyes.

"This don't go," he said belligerently. "I've got a letter in my files, stipulating a rebate, that's as good as a contract."

"Signed by?" queried Jeremy suggestively.

"Signed by The Guardian, per A. M. Wymett."

"So have I," declared Turnbull, and was echoed by Lehn, of Stormont & Lehn, Betts, and half a dozen more.

"It seems to have been a habit," remarked Jeremy. "But, gentlemen,

A. M. Wymett is no longer The Guardian. His secret rebates do not bind us indefinitely."

"The courts'll have a word to say on that," declared the combative Ahrens.

"Easy, gentlemen! Let's be friendly," purred Matthew Ellison.

"We needn't go to the courts," put in Andrew Galpin. "In the cases where rebates were offered, the rate will be raised to a point where it covers the rebates."

"Where do *you* come in?" demanded Ahrens.

"As acting advertising manager of The Guardian."

"What becomes of your 'one-rate-for-all' claim?" Turnbull turned upon Jeremy.

"Discarded," said the owner, promptly accepting Galpin's strategy.

"Why ain'd I neffer gud any discound?" inquired Bernard Stockmuller, the leading jeweler of the town, in a powerful and plaintive voice.

"Because you never had the sense to stick out for it, Barney," retorted Betts. "You were easy."

"There you have the unfairness of the system," Jeremy pointed out. "Mr. Stockmuller is as frequent a user of space as some of you who have taken rebates. Gentlemen, it doesn't go anymore."

"Well, this is a hell of a note!" murmured a discontented voice which seemed to emanate from the depths of the abdominal curve of the senior partner of Arndt & Niebuhr, furniture dealers.

"Did any of these private letters from Mr. Wymett mention reading notices as an extra inducement?" asked the host of the occasion.

"There was no need," stated Ellison. "'Readers' are a recognized courtesy to advertisers."

"They take up space," Jeremy pointed out. "They cost money, for ink, paper, and setting up. From the newspaper's viewpoint, they're a dead loss."

"We pay for 'em in our advertising bills," said Friedland, of the Big Shop.

"Then you regard them as advertising?"

"Certainly."

"But they don't appear as advertising. They are in regular news type, made up to look like news items, and they carry no a-d-v mark."

Matthew Ellison took it upon his kindly self to enlighten this innocent young adventurer in untried fields. "If they appeared as advertising, the public would be less likely to read them."

"Then they're a fraud on the public."

"Fraud? Oh, really, Mr. Robson," deprecated the merchant. "A—a harmless—er—subterfuge."

"The Guardian cuts them out," announced The Guardian's revolutionary proprietor. "No more 'readers' except with the a-d-v sign, and paid for at full rates."

"What are you trying to do—insult us?" growled the saturnine Mr. Ahrens.

"You would have to be mighty thin-skinned to find an insult in that."

"Well, drive us out of the paper, then?"

"That would be pretty foolish of me, wouldn't it?"

"Would be? It *is*. First you violate an agreement—"

"To which I was not a party."

"—and then you try to raise rates on us; and now you cut out the best advertising the department store gets."

"As for raising rates, I haven't suggested it except as an offset to rebates."

"Comes to the same thing," said several voices.

"Gentlemen," said Jeremy with an accession of positiveness, "you're getting the best advertising rate in the State of Centralia today. With practically ten thousand circulation—"

"Bunk!" interjected Turnbull.

"Upwards of nine thousand, seven hundred."

"A good third of it pads and graft copies," put in Betts.

For the first time Jeremy was at a disadvantage. He glanced quickly at Galpin.

"Nothing of the sort," declared that gentleman readily.

"How much is your list padded?" challenged Vogt the florist, in his slightly thickened accent. "Come on, now! On the level."

"Tell them, Mr. Galpin," directed Jeremy. "Our cards are on the table."

"I don't know. But it's padded all right," confessed the general manager. "Not a third. Not a quarter. But—well, enough."

For the second time that day Jeremy Robson took a snap resolution. "Appoint a committee to go over the books, Mr. Ellison," said he. "Make your estimate of *bona fide* circulation, and I'll adjust my rate to make it as low per thousand as any daily in the State of equal size. Is that fair?"

"Yes. I guess that's fair enough," answered the Retailers' Association president, hesitantly.

"That don't satisfy me," asserted Ahrens.

"What will, Mr. Ahrens?" asked Jeremy politely.

"'Readers,' like the Great Northwestern's always had."

"The next time I come to your store to buy a necktie, will you throw in a box of collars?"

"It ain't the same thing."

"Pardon me; it's precisely the same, considered as a deal. You don't give people more than they pay for. Why should you expect to get it? All I ask for The Guardian is a living profit on the plant and product."

"Wymett made a living out of it."

"What Mr. Wymett did is not under discussion."

"I'll say this for it, though," interjected Galpin. "We're not going to make the kind of living in the kind of way that Mr. Wymett made his. Get that, you men?"

The stir that this roused was sufficient evidence of general knowledge concerning The Guardian's former management.

"Now, you're talking!" said Betts.

"Dot's goot. I like dot," added Stockmuller.

It was the first evidence of approval that the new policy had elicited.

"So much having been said," proceeded Jeremy: "I'll tell you gentlemen this. The Guardian is going to be run straight. If you ever see any evidence that it isn't, I want to know it."

"That's fine, Mr. Robson," said Ellison warmly. "That's the kind of thing we want to hear. We're all for that and will wish you the success you deserve. And now there's one more matter I think ought to be taken up here. We considered it at the last meeting of the association, and this is as good a time and place as any to thrash it out. Speaking for myself and associates, Mr. Robson, we'd like to know what consideration an advertiser in The Guardian may expect at its hands."

"Consideration?" Jeremy said, puzzled.

"In the matter of news."

Another side-glance at Galpin apprised Jeremy that this was at least as important as anything that had gone before.

"I'm afraid that I shall have to ask you to explain," said Jeremy.

"I will give you an example: the case which we had up for discussion at our last meeting. It concerns one of our members, Mr. Barclay, of Barclay & Bull, shoe dealers. Barclay & Bull are liberal advertisers in The Guardian, Mr. Robson."

"Yes."

"Last Tuesday The Guardian published a report of the Blair Street Methodist Church meeting, which put Mr. Barclay in a quite unfortunate light."

"Wasn't our report accurate?"

"I am not saying whether it was accurate or inaccurate," returned Ellison conservatively. "The point is that it was unfortunate. It subjected Mr. Barclay to criticism. How could Mr. Barclay foresee that The Guardian, which his firm had always patronized, would catch up a hasty and somewhat violent expression used in the heat of debate, and publish it?"

"The meeting was a public meeting. Why shouldn't we report it?"

"My dear young friend, I am endeavoring to tell you. Do you not owe something to Mr. Barclay, as an advertiser?"

"Does Mr. Barclay owe anything to me because I buy my shoes at his store?"

Mr. Ellison's face shone with the prognostication of argumentative triumph. "Pree-cisely the point! He does. He owes you courtesy as a patron. You owe him courtesy as a patron. That article should, if I may express an opinion, have omitted his name."

"I see. Because Mr. Barclay is an advertiser in The Guardian."

"Quite so," beamed Ellison.

"But I'm selling Mr. Barclay advertising, not news."

"The courtesy due to an—"

"Pardon me. It's no question of courtesy. The Guardian sells its news to its readers. It sells its advertising to its advertisers. You've got two different things badly mixed."

Mr. Ellison looked crestfallen, but rallied to another and more direct argument. "Barclay & Bull intend withdrawing their advertising from The Guardian."

"That's their affair," said Jeremy shortly.

"But, surely, my dear young friend, it is equally the affair of your paper."

"If it's a question of Barclay & Bull withdrawing their advertising or The Guardian withdrawing its news policy, we'll have to hump along without the advertising."

"Look here!" The twitchy eyes of Adolph Ahrens focused themselves angrily on the host. "S'pose I go motoring up to Bellair. S'pose I get pinched by a joy constable. S'pose I send around word I want it kept out of the paper. Don't I get a show?"

"Not a show," declared Jeremy good-humoredly. "You're too prominent a character, Mr. Ahrens, not to make good reading."

From the ventriloqual depths of Mr. Arndt there again emanated that gentleman's conviction concerning the infernal quality of the note of Mr. Robson's conversation.

Engel the grocer saw The Guardian's finish, and made no secret of his prophetic vision.

Aaron Levy, pursuing his trade under the ambitious title of "The Fashion," expressed the opinion that no man's business was safe in a town where such practices were permitted.

"Und you maig funny-nesses aboud the Chermans, too," accused Bernard Stockmuller, the jeweler, unexpectedly.

Vogt came to his support. "That reporter ought to be fired," he proclaimed. "The one that wrote the police court article about the brewery driver."

"'Why, there was no malice in that," defended Jeremy. "It was all good-natured fun."

"It wass fun at the Chermans," declared Stockmuller. "Cherman accents. Cherman ignorances. What you wan ta pigk on the Chermans for, always?"

"We don't, Mr. Stockmuller. That's absurd. We'd print an Irish dialect story just as quickly. In fact we do, frequently."

"You should understand," said Blasius the hatter, heavily, "that we Germans are as good citizens as anybody else."

"Granted, but—"

"And priddy heavy advertisers in The Guardian." This was Vogt's contribution.

Jeremy began to lose his temper. "Gentlemen," said he sharply, "if you take over the job of running The Guardian as you seem to wish to do, where do I come in?"

"Easy! Friendly!" pacified Ellison. "No use in getting excited."

"Thinks he can run the town," growled Ahrens.

"There is much in Mr. Robson's point of view," continued the pourer of oil. "And I am sure that he will concede the force of much that has been said upon the other side. In any case I am sure we have all come to a better understanding, and that we thank Mr. Robson most appreciatively for his bounteous hospitality. And, now, gentlemen, I propose that we—er—adjourn."

Ahrens and two of the others forgot to bid Jeremy good-bye. When all had left, the giver of the feast turned to his lieutenant.

"Well, they know where we stand. How many advertisers will it lose us?"

"I don't know that it'll lose us any, right away."

"Ahrens, surely."

"Don't believe it. He'll be afraid to drop out. He don't understand your go-to-hell attitude."

"Was I as bad as that, Andy?"

"I'm taking his point of view. He don't understand it, and probably he don't believe it. Thinks it's bluff. But he's scared and he's cautious. So he'll stay in—for a while, anyway. What we've got to do in the long run, is to keep 'em all scared."

"Going in for blackmail, Andy?" smiled his boss.

"Keep 'em scared, by making the paper so strong that they dassent do without it."

"That means more circulation."

"It means more circulation, a lot of it, and pretty darn quick. That's my job."

Arrived at the office, Jeremy got his final glimpse of the day into the ramifications of advertising. In his editorial sanctum waited a mild, self-possessed, and profoundly laconic Chinaman.

"Take ad?" inquired he.

"Your ad? What is it?"

"Laundry." He proffered a neat and competently prepared two-inch single column "card," announcing that Wong Kee stood ready to perform high-class laundering for the discerning public at reasonable prices.

"All right. Take it to the Advertising window."

"No good."

"Why not?"

"Turn down."

"Nonsense!"

"Chinese laundry. Turn down," asseverated Wong Kee evenly.

"When did you try?"

"Nineteen-eight. Nineteen-nine. Nineteen-ten. Nineteen-eleven."

"Every year? Nineteen-twelve wins."

Jeremy marked "Must J. R." on the copy and sent the satisfied Celestial downstairs.

On the following morning, eight local professional apostles of cleanliness, comprising the Laundry Association of Fenchester, indignantly notified The Guardian of the withdrawal of their patronage.

"Even the laundrymen want to edit the paper for us," the disgusted Jeremy observed to Galpin. "Well, they can stay out till hell breaks loose under the State of Centralia."

As a matter of fact, that is exactly what they did.

## 13

No ADVERTISING PATRONAGE WAS lost to The Guardian as the result of the luncheon-conference. But Jeremy Robson's offer to let a committee investigate his circulation was costly. More than fifteen per cent of The Guardian's list proved either "phony" or dubious. Jeremy reconstituted his rate card in accordance with the actual figures, and cut recklessly into his free list. Appeased by this practical and to them profitable concession, the Retailers' Association abandoned the issue of rebates. For the time, at least, they accepted the new proprietor's distasteful decision as to "readers." The matter of "courtesies" extended to advertisers was left in abeyance. That was sure to come up in the inevitable course of events. The general status was that of a truce, with one side wary and the other disgruntled.

Unsatisfactory though this might be to the mercantile element, it was more so to the newspaper. For The Guardian simply could not make a living at the reduced rates. There was but one thing to be done: increase circulation, thereby giving the paper augmented advertising value, and raise the advertising rates proportionately. It had been agreed between the Retailers' Association committee and Jeremy that in view of his reduction of tariff, there would be no opposition to an increase when the circulation should warrant it. Ellison and the other committeemen did not believe that The Guardian could add to its circulation materially. Jeremy and his general manager did. They didn't know just how. They only knew that it had to, or pass ignominiously out of existence!

So they took the customary business-man's gamble. In the hope of making money they spent money. The paper began to swell out and look lively and prosperous. But Jeremy's bank account evidenced the ravages of a galloping consumption. And though the public talked about The Guardian and speculated interestedly upon its future, it did not fall over itself to subscribe. It waited to see and be convinced. The public has that habit.

Meanwhile two able gentlemen with no ostensible interest in journalism were quietly watching and estimating the course of The Guardian. President Montrose Clark, of the Fenchester Public Utilities Corporation, and his legal aide-de-camp Judge Selden Dana, a pair far more potent in Fenchester's political affairs than Fenchester's undiscerning citizenry ever dreamed, were concerned with the newspapers as affecting their own plans, and were specially concerned with Jeremy Robson's newspaper because they possessed no reliable data on young Mr. Robson.

"Do you know him?" asked Judge Dana.

"No," replied Montrose Clark, whose interview with the "rippawtah" of The Record had failed to leave any memory of the young man's name. "What do you think of The Guardian since he got it?"

"It's silly," pronounced Mr. Clark loftily.

"Silly? Would you call it silly?"

"I *have* called it silly. It is beginning to show leanings toward a half-baked radicalism."

"Robson is very young."

"Even socialistic tendencies," pursued the other.

"Socialism is anything that holds up our programme," grinned the lawyer, who occasionally permitted himself the private luxury of frankness.

The public utilitarian frowned. "Have you been reading the articles on tax-dodgers?"

"I have."

"What is the purpose of them, if not to stir up socialistic unrest?"

"Sensation, I should say. The series has been popular. When Mr. Average Citizen reads in his paper that he is being taxed twice as heavily as Mr. Rich Man next door, he's interested. He begins to think the paper is a devil of a paper. He talks about it. That helps."

"Suppose The Guardian should attack Us on the tax issue?"

"That also would be interesting," remarked Dana. "But they won't. Our trail is too well covered. It would take them a year to get at the facts."

"But what's the young fool driving at, anyway, Dana?" The lawyer rubbed his long angular jaw, and the somnolent look of his eyes deepened into musing. "I figure he's making a bid for the radical support. The radicals have never had a show here, and he may be able to rally them to him."

"What do they amount to, the radicals! A newspaper has got to have the support of people with money."

"That's the accepted theory," admitted the lawyer.

"What do you know of young Robson's financial status!"

"Quite a bit. I handled the sale for Wymett."

"Yes; yes. A good bargain for Wymett. Eh?"

"A stroke of fortune."

"How much has Robson got behind him?"

"Not much. Twenty thousand. Perhaps twenty-five."

Mr. Clark looked relieved. "I think we need have no misgivings."

"I'm not so sure. A paper with radical leanings might find material in that transfer ordinance of ours when it comes up again. Even some of our good friends balk at that as pretty raw."

"An essential step to our expansion, Dana," said the public utilitarian blandly.

"Exactly. But an uncharitable mind mightn't see it that way. Which reminds me: Embree is threatening a legislative investigation if the ordinance goes through."

"Local matters are no affair of Embree's," declared the other angrily. "Fortunately he has no newspaper backing."

"Hasn't he? I wish I were sure."

"You don't think that young Robson has sold out to Embree already?"

"No."

"Very well, then—"

"Not sold out. It isn't a question of cash. This boy isn't A. M. Wymett."

"Nevertheless a newspaper is a business proposition," opined Montrose Clark dryly.

"It ought to be. Much simpler if it were. But this boy is a bit of a sentimentalist. I'm afraid he's in the way of being influenced by Smiling Mart's line of clap-trap."

"Then we must act promptly." The public utilitarian sat, thoughtful. "We'll start a campaign of public education on the transfer question, through the newspapers," he decided. "Including, of course, The Guardian."

"Straight-out, a-d-v kind of advertising?"

"Hardly. The usual thing. Well-prepared articles. Perhaps a careful editorial or two. Do you think it too early?"

"Not too early. Too late for The Guardian. It won't take 'em."

"Oh, I think it will," returned the other comfortably. "At our special rate."

"Not at any price, the editorials. The 'readers,' yes. But they'll have the 'a-d-v' sign at the bottom. Maybe the 'P.-U.' trade-mark also."

Montrose Clark's face puffed red. "Where do you get your information?"

"From inside," answered Dana, whose special virtue and value was to be "inside" on all available sources of information. "Those are the new orders."

"Robson's?"

"I suppose so. Andrew Galpin may have a hand in it. He's in general charge."

"I think I can persuade those young gentlemen," remarked Montrose Clark sardonically, "that it is not to their interest to impose troublesome restrictions upon the corporation."

He pressed a button. There arrived upon the scene, with an effect of automatic response, that smooth, flawless, noiseless, expressionless piece of human mechanism, Edward Garson, the hand-perfected private secretary who, besides his immediate duties about the great man's person, acted as go-between in minor matters, press-agent, and advertising manager for the Fenchester Public Utilities Corporation. Concerning him, Judge Dana had once remarked that the queerest thing about it was that it also had brains.

"Garson," barked Montrose Clark, in the tone which he deemed appropriate.

The hand-perfected secretary bowed.

"Bring in The Guardian advertising account."

The secretary bowed again and disappeared. Almost immediately he was back, bowing once more over a neatly typed single sheet of paper.

"What is our total expenditure in The Guardian for the current year, up to date?"

"For display advertising, eleven hundred and forty-seven dollars, sixty cents. For reading matter, two hundred and seventy-five."

"That includes editorial matter?"

"Yes, sir."

"And in The Record?"

"Seventeen hundred and twenty, sir. All display. They make no charge for editorials or readers, you recall, sir."

"True. We pay them a higher rate for display, and the editorial support is—er—"

"By way of gratitude," suggested Dana.

"Exactly. Do you think, Dana, that either paper is in a position to discard the P.-U.'s support?"

"Just a moment," said the lawyer. "That display advertising bill of The Guardian's; what was the bill as rendered?"

Looking to Montrose Clark for permission and receiving it in a nod, the hand-perfected secretary replied, "Sixteen hundred dollars."

"Scaled down to a net of about eleven hundred and fifty."

"Yes. With discounts and rebates."

"Wymett fooled Robson worse than I had supposed. The young fool bought on the basis of the book rates. Discounts and rebates are going to be an unpleasant surprise to him."

"All of which will make him the easier to handle."

"Maybe. With gloves."

"It is not my habit," said the local potentate austerely, "to concern myself deeply with other people's over-sensitiveness, when it is a matter of business."

"Go easy with him," insisted the other. "He's got a temper. There's a kind of a you-be-damned-ness about him. He's a little puffed up with his new sense of power, and we've got to allow for that."

"Sense of power?" The magnate looked puzzled for the moment. "Oh, you mean his paper!" He laughed. "All right, Dana. I'll be tactful with him. But of course I shan't tolerate any nonsense."

The retort, "I doubt if he will, either," was on the tip of the lawyer's tongue. He suppressed it. It would only have irritated Montrose Clark's vanity which, under friction, was prone to develop prickly heat.

Let him find out for himself how to handle human nettles if he couldn't take cannier men's advice!

## 14

JUDGE DANA'S SURMISE AS to Senator Embree and The Guardian partook of the genius of prophecy. "Smiling Mart" had been waiting to assure himself about the new control of the paper. Conviction grew within him that Jeremy Robson was the man he was looking for: that the seed planted with forethought in the mind of the unimportant Record reporter was now bringing forth harvest in The Guardian. Embree decided upon open measures.

Returning from a hasty luncheon one day, Jeremy found his den irradiated by the famous Embree smile. He was glad to see it. At the points of intersection where politics and newspaper work cross, he had encountered the leader from the Northern Tier perhaps half a dozen times since their first interview, and had liked him better each time, though their talks had been on the professional and impersonal order. No conversation with Martin Embree, however, was ever wholly impersonal. He was too intense a humanist for that. As the Legislature had adjourned for the summer, Jeremy was surprised to see Embree at the capital.

"Hello, Senator," he said, shaking hands. "What brings you down here in all this heat and dust?"

"You," smiled his visitor.

"Well, I apologize. I didn't do it purposely. But I'm glad to see you."

"So here you are, a real newspaper owner. Congratulations, by the way." Jeremy nodded. "Do you remember a little talk we had in my room, one night?"

"Very well."

"This is the next stage in the fairy-tale. Well, I talked pretty openly that evening. As a rule I don't give myself away in chance conversation."

Harking back, Jeremy failed to recall that the rising politician had given himself away, in any sense. He leaned back in his chair and waited.

"I've been watching your course with The Guardian," continued the Senator earnestly. "I wanted to see which way you were going. Now I know."

"What convinced you?"

"Your editorial on the tax-dodging railroads. That," said Senator Embree, his brilliant smile playing again, "was a soaker. A soaker! I expect you heard from that."

"I did."

"Did they yelp?"

"They did."

"Threaten?"

"What could they threaten?"

"That's true; what could they?" repeated the other thoughtfully. "They wouldn't know where to have you. You're an undetermined quantity to them. And as such they don't know your price. Have they tried to find it out?"

"Not openly enough to be caught at it."

"They've been trying to get at mine ever since I came to the Legislature as a grass-green young kid of an Assemblyman. I guess they'll find out yours about the time they find out mine. And, for a further guess, the two prices will be about the same. Eh?"

"That also is possible," conceded the editor demurely.

"The Record didn't spoil you. I was afraid it might. They're so slick and respectable over there! But as soon as you began to get your muscle into The Guardian's editorials, I saw which side you were on. And the tax attack settled it in my mind that you're for the public and against the corporation grafters."

"I'm against the corporations when they don't play fair."

"That's good enough for me! They never do play fair. Not in politics."

"I don't go that far," said Jeremy.

"You will," smiled the other. "Give you time. You'll come to it. You're with us and you're going to be with us stronger and stronger."

"It depends on who 'us' is, and what policies are involved," replied the editor, not wholly pleased at being thus confidently catalogued.

"The radicals. The clean, common voters who believe that the people should run their own government for themselves."

"So far, all right. I'm for that."

"I knew you were. And here I am." The smile now fairly surcharged the little office.

"And here you are. What can I do for you, Senator?"

"Wrong, my boy! Wrong for once. It's the other way around."

"What can you do for me, then?"

The smile was replaced by a look of candor and earnestness. "Mr. Robson, you've got to increase the sale of this paper, haven't you?"

"Yes."

"I can boost the circulation of The Guardian a thousand copies. Perhaps fifteen hundred."

"Will you take the job of circulation manager?" asked Jeremy, smiling.

"That's another point. I'll come to that later. Now, there's no bluff about this, Robson. I'm in dead earnest."

"If you can tell me how to put on circulation without its costing all I've got—"

"It'll cost you nothing. Absolutely nothing."

"Then it will be different from any circulation scheme I've heard of yet."

"Listen. Up in the Northern Tier I'm strong. They know me. They believe in me. If I pass the word that The Guardian is my organ—"

"The Guardian is nobody's organ."

"I understand. The mouthpiece of our policies, I should have said. The policies and principles you and I stand for, reform and anti-dollar-domination. If I pass that word about The Guardian they'll take it like the Bible."

"There might be something in that," conceded the editor, who knew the almost idolatrous quality of Embree's following in his own district.

"Make no mistake about it. It'll mean four or five hundred copies in my own town, and it ought to run to a thousand more in the county outside."

"That won't help much in getting local advertising, here in Fenchester."

"No. But it will help out your foreign advertising."

"How do you know so much about the newspaper game?" asked the editor, struck by the other's use of the technical term. "Ever been in it?"

"I study everything that has a bearing on politics in this State. I could pretty nearly tell you how much The Guardian stands to lose this year."

"Don't!" said Jeremy, with a wry face.

"Unless you can raise your rates. And I'm showing you the way. Right here in Fenchester, as soon as the common people are satisfied that you really represent their interests, subscriptions will flood you."

Suspicion of the phrase beset Jeremy. "I'm not going in for any demagogue, yellow journal stuff."

"Nobody wants you to. Just a decent, clean, fair-minded, progressive radicalism. If I can stand up in my next campaign and say honestly that there is a newspaper at the State capital, in the stronghold of old-line politics and graft, that represents what I stand for, that newspaper is going to boom. And I'm ready to do it."

"On what terms?"

"None."

"Just out of regard for my fascinating personality?"

Martin Embree's smile appeared again, conciliatory, persuasive, earnest. "Let's understand each other, Robson. I'm convinced that you're on the level. That's the first point. I'm convinced that you're honestly a radical, even if you're a mild one. That's the second. Barring differences on minor policies which are bound to arise between independent-minded men, you and I stand for the same principles. You know my motivating ambition?"

"The governorship," replied Jeremy innocently.

A furrow of annoyance appeared between the lofty brows of the Senator. "The ambition of my life," he said emphatically, "is to serve the people of this State by delivering our government out of the clutches of the corporations. To that end I will accept any office, high or low, within the gift of the voters."

Oratorical as was the delivery, there was a certain ring of enthusiasm which went far to convince the editor. In the years to come, of constant alliance with Martin Embree, Robson satisfied himself of the man's essential devotion to the cause which he had made his own, a devotion second only to the monstrous egotism which subordinated all causes and all principles to his own rodent ambition, or, rather, merged and absorbed them in that ambition.

"Of course; of course," apologized the editor. "But you *do* want to be Governor, don't you?"

"I'm going to be Governor," was the positive response. "Not all their money can stop me. This campaign of mine for reelection to the Senate is really a preliminary skirmish for the bigger thing. I could be reelected without lifting a finger, so far as that goes. But I want to hammer home the State issues. And if you and I hammer at the same time, it isn't going to do either of us a bit of harm! By the way, you ought to have agents on the ground to boost your circulation in the places where I campaign. Who's your circulation manager?"

"A routine scrub. No good. I'm shipping him. Do you happen to know of anyone?"

"Yes. I've got the very man for you, if he'll come. Max Verrall, a live wire on The Forreston Tribune. He's a youngster, but a hustler. I think I can get him for you."

"I'll take him on your say-so."

"Now, let me give you a pointer or two on getting hold of the country districts.[1] We're streaky on nationalities out through this State. There's a point to play for. Get after their feelings for the home country with a tactful editorial or a bit of translated matter now and then if you can lay your hands on it. Tickle their little vanities. That's what I do on my speaking tours. If it's a Swedish community, I tell 'em the Scandahoovians are the backbone of the Middle West. In a German district—and the State is thick with 'em—I boost German efficiency, the system to which the rest of the world goes to school."

"Speaking of Germans *and* schools," remarked Robson; "I'm told that they don't even teach in English in some of the country districts. I've been thinking of starting a campaign on that, one of these days. Americanization[2]—that ought to be a good slogan."

"Off it, my boy!" said the Senator emphatically. "Hara-kiri is cheaper. Nobody is so touchy as your German-American on the subject of language and race. Don't butt into a stone wall."

"Wymett had a pet theory that Germany is getting ready for a world-war and the German-Americans are already at their propaganda to influence this country."

"Bosh! I never could quite make out whether Wymett was more crazy than crooked, or *vice versa.*"

"Just the same, I've noticed that quite a little reprint stuff boosting Germany drifts into this office. Anecdotes about the Kaiser and that sort of thing."

"Print 'em! Print 'em all. It'll make the paper solid just where you most need support."

"So I do, some of 'em, on their merits. It's good stuff when fillers are needed. Only, when the propaganda side is too plain, I can it."

"Get your mind off this propaganda notion," pleaded his adviser. "The Germans are the best element of our citizenship today, and any man or institution that goes up against them is *through*. Some lunatics are trying to make a political issue of it. Magnus Laurens is. And they're talking of running him for Governor next time, because they think they'll need a respectable figurehead rather than one of the old, discredited gang to beat me with. Lord! I'd ask nothing better than to have Laurens against me, with his crank Know-Nothing conservatism that he calls Americanism."

"I liked Mr. Laurens," said Jeremy.

"You won't when you've fought him as long as I have. Speaking of Germans, do you know Emil Bausch?"

"Only by sight."

"He's president of the Fenchester Deutscher Club and a mighty good friend of mine. He wants to get in touch with you."

"He called once, but I was out."

"Bausch is a little ponderous at first, but he's all right when you get used to his ways. And he's a power among the Germans. Don't forget that."

"Between you and Wymett and Eli Wade I'm not likely to forget the Germans," laughed Jeremy.

"Wade? Poor chap. That was an unfortunate thing, that row of his. Well, he's good on the feet, but weak in the head. Do you know Milliken, his crony?"

"Yes. He hasn't much use for you."

"So he tells me every time he sees me. He considers me a slinker because he says I'm a Socialist at heart, but my heart is weak. Socialism is all right in its way. It's a good vaccination, but a bad disease. Milliken's working in your shop now, isn't he?"

"Is he? I didn't know it."

"Stick to me and you'll learn a lot of things," smiled the politician. "Yes; he's assistant to Big Girdner in the press-room. There's another German for you, Girdner, and a good one. Well, I'll tell Emil Bausch to come in again to see you." At the door he paused. "By the way, are you likely to be interested personally in politics?"

"Office for myself? No. I've got my hands full now."

"Later, perhaps. Well, if you should want anything for any of your friends, let me know. Perhaps I could manage it."

"Could you? Locally?"

"I have a little influence locally, as a member of the Cities Improvement Committee."

"We were speaking of Eli Wade a moment ago," said Jeremy. "Something I wrote in The Record helped to get him out of a job he was very proud of."

"The Public Schools Board? Yes: I know."

"It was tough on the old boy. I'd like to make that up to him. Do you think you could get him put back?"

"Hardly that. You see, he got the Germans stirred up. He was out of place on the Board, anyway. Education is the special political bent of the German-Americans, you know. No; I'm afraid he's finished there. But I might look around and see if there isn't something else that would be just as good for him. It's just the little honor of having an office that flatters his type of mind."

"I'd be mightily obliged if you could," said Jeremy.

Martin Embree lost no time on the Bausch matter. On the morrow of his interview with Jeremy, there stalked into the editorial den of The Guardian, a tall, plethoric form buttoned within the frock coat and wearing the silk hat of high ceremony. The form introduced itself with a pronounced guttural accent as President Bausch, of the Deutscher Club, removed the hat, unbuttoned the coat, took from the breast-pocket thereof a document formidable with seals and tape, dandled the precious thing reverently in its hands, and addressed the editor with solemnity.

"I have here somedthing of grade importance for your paper."

"Take a seat," offered the editor.

The document-bearer complied. "Id is a ledder from Prindz Henry to the Cherman Singing Societies of America."

"The original?" asked Jeremy, regarding the waxed and tapered curio with interest.

"Certainly not! The orichinal is mounted and framed in New York. This is the official copy."

"It certainly looks official."

"Id iss to be printed on Ventzday."

"You mean that it is released for Wednesday."

"Id iss to be printed on Ventzday," reiterated the solemn emissary. "It should appear on your frondt page."

Had Mr. Bausch but known it, this landed him full upon the editor's pet toe: a toe, moreover, by this time angrily sore from over-frequent treadings. It was no time to be telling the new proprietor and editor of that free and untrammeled organ, The Guardian, what to and what not to print, or where to locate it.

"It will if it's worth it," stated that gentleman briefly.

"Wordth? Id iss *most* important," his visitor assured him. "I have also here the material from which could be derifed a valuable editorial—"

"I can't really see that such a letter, even though it be news, is a subject for editorial comment in The Guardian," said Jeremy impatiently.

"Do you understand *whoo* this ledder iss from?" cried the other. "Prindz Henry! Our Kaiser's brother. And you tell me—"

"Whose Kaiser's brother? Not mine."

An incredulous and pious shock passed over the face of Mr. Emil Bausch. "Not yours! What matters you? The Kaiser of all goodt Chermans." He contemplated the young man with gloomy severity. "If id was the Prindz of Vales I will bet you prindt it."

Unversed in the carefully inbred German hatred and jealousy of all things British, Jeremy was mildly puzzled.

"Why so?" he asked.

"I bet you are a Inklish-lover. I bet you are a Cherman-hater. You would prindt the Prindz of Vales ledder. Hein?"

"Just as much or as little as I shall print of this."

"As liddle? You will edit *this*; Prindz Henry's own words?"

"If there's too much of it."

Dumbfounded at the proposed sacrilege, Mr. Bausch retrieved the precious roll and held it ready to thrust back into the pocket of the frock coat. "All or nothing," he said.

"Nothing, then."

"I will rebort this at the next meeting of the Deutscher Club," growled the departing Teuton.

"Send us a copy of the minutes," retorted the exasperated Jem. "Perhaps we'll give you an editorial on those."

He finished his writing and leaned back to meditate upon the possible results of this encounter when a well-remembered voice in the hall spoke his name, in a tone of business-like inquiry, to the youth on duty there.

"Come right in, Buddy," called Jeremy.

Buddy Higman entered. He was dressed with extreme correctness, even to the extent of a whole and intact pair of suspenders, and his Sunday coat which he carried genteelly over his arm. Jeremy pointed an accusing finger at him.

"I know what you've come here for."

"Gee!" murmured Buddy, impressed.

"You've come to tell me how to run my paper."

"Me?" said Buddy.

"Or to order something put in."

"What—"

"Or kept out."

"No, sir," said the astounded Buddy.

"What!! Don't you know how to run my paper better than I do?"

"N-n-no, sir."

"Then you're unique in this town. Come to my arms. I mean, sit down. What's that you're trying to get out of your pocket?"

"A—a—a letter, sir."

"Hah! I knew it. From the Kaiser!"

"No, sir. I don't know him," said Buddy nervously.

"What are you calling me 'sir' for?" demanded Jeremy, suspicious at this unaccustomed courtesy.

"I want a job."

"Oh, you want a job! Here?"

"Yes, sir."

"What are you good for in a newspaper office?"

"Nothin'."

"That's a fine recommendation. Do you expect to get the job on the strength of it?"

"Yes, sir. No, sir. On this."

After much painful struggling the urchin succeeded in extracting from his pocket a note which he placed in Jeremy's hands. At sight of it, all residue of raillery died out of the editor's face. Though he had but once seen Marcia's writing, he knew, at the first glance, the bold, frank, delicate, upright characters for hers. The note was undated. He read, with a feeling that the world had changed and sweetened about him, her words.

*Dear Jem:*

If you ever can, give Buddy a chance; some work that will not interfere with his schooling. I wish you two to look after each other.

And, oh, my dear, do please not quite altogether forget

Marcia

Jeremy sat in a long silence. The boy did not disturb it. Finally the young man looked up.

"When did she give you this, Buddy?"

"Before she went away."

"All right. You get the job."

"Thanks. I knew I would," said the urchin confidently. "I c'n start in tomorrow." He watched, sympathetically, the other fold the note and bestow it in his pocket.

"Mr. Robson," he said. "She said a queer thing when she gimme the letter."

"What was that?"

"She said—you know how her eyes get solemn and big and—and kinda light up, deep inside, when she means a thing *hard*—she said, 'Buddy, I shall like to think that you and he are looking after each other.' What did she mean by that?"

"I don't know. I'll have to think it over."

"Well, I been thinkin' it over an' I don't get it." He paused. Then with the self-centered simplicity of boyhood, "Mr. Robson, I miss her somethin' fierce. You don't know how I miss her."

"Don't I!" retorted Jeremy involuntarily, with a stab of pain.

"Nobody could," stated the other with conviction.

So Jeremy and Buddy Higman became fellow-workers. Buddy's job was decidedly indeterminate. It didn't matter. In taking him on Jeremy was performing his first definite service to Marcia.

A week later his second was completed. Eli Wade was appointed a member of the Library Board. The Guardian chronicled the appointment more conspicuously than its unimportance as news warranted. Jeremy hoped that in some manner Marcia would see or hear of it.

## 15

MARTIN EMBREE MORE THAN fulfilled his word. As if a royal patent had been issued in favor of The Guardian, the Senator's zealous partisans of the Northern Tier bestowed upon it their patronage. Max Verrall, who revealed himself as a brisk and unfettered spirit with political ambitions and a slavish fervency for Embree, did the actual work of establishing the circulation in the district, and did it so well that Jeremy Robson had no misgivings in turning over to him the circulation managership of the paper.

In Fenchester the paper held about even for a time. The new features which Galpin had put on gained readers, though not as fast as he had hoped. To offset this, there had been some loss among the more rabid element of the Deutscher Club, Bausch having spread the report that the new ownership was anti-German. On his next visit to Fenchester, to deliver the formal address at a school dedication, Senator Embree reproached Jeremy for his tactlessness in handling the Prince Henry message.

"Don't stick your fighting-jaw out at me, young Robson," he added cheerily. "Keep that for your enemies. Now you put in a nice, good-tempered philosophic little editorial paragraph on the 'entente cordiale' line."

Jeremy began. "I'm da——"

"No, you're not," broke in the other. "Listen. Here's the idea." And he outlined an editorial so tactful, so deft, so diplomatic whilst still independently American in tone, that for sheer pleasure in good workmanship the editor agreed to adopt it.

"And I'll square it with Bausch," said Embree. His smile expanded and enfolded the other. "Better come hear me speak tonight. I'll have something to say about The Guardian. Watch the effect of the spread of the gospel for the next few days."

The one brief reference to the paper in Senator Embree's address said little but implied much. Jeremy was inclined to be disappointed. He looked for no results. But the following day brought in thirty-seven new subscriptions, with others trailing in their wake at the rate of a dozen per day. Furthermore, a batch of letters to the editor urged upon him a more definite political stand, or invited (in one instance challenged) him to state his attitude regarding Embree and the new policies frankly. Since his taking over the paper, politics had been at slack tide in the State. Jeremy had wisely refrained from committing himself definitely. All his instinct was for independence of thought and speech. When the issues were cast, The Guardian would take its stand. But he had reckoned without that pervasive and acute political self-consciousness of the Middle West which expects every citizen to be definitely one thing or the other, and be it promptly! His tax editorials, he found, had already committed him in the general mind to the radical side. Whoever attacked the railroads was a Friend of the People. To be sure, Jeremy's attack had been addressed to a few specific and flagrant instances; but the public does not discriminate finely. And Senator Embree's word-of-mouth "gospel" had already premised for The Guardian a course which would considerably have surprised its proprietor.

That keen-scented legal prowler, Judge Selden Dana, became uneasy. Young Robson, he feared, was getting deep into "Smiling Mart's" toils.

"It's time we took a hand," he warned Montrose Clark. "Don't you think I'd better see Robson and have a talk with him?"

"I will do it myself," said the public utilitarian. "I have had more experience than you in handling newspaper men."

"All right. But—easy does it. Remember, this is no A. M. Wymett."

"If it were, I should leave it entirely in your hands," retorted the magnate.

Judge Dana left, reflecting pungently upon his employer's capacity for unnecessarily disagreeable speeches.

"If he tries that on Robson he'll get bumped, or I miss my guess," he surmised, and found some satisfaction in the thought.

Nothing, however, could have been farther from the mind of President Clark. He purposed treating the young newspaper man kindly.

Firmly, but kindly. Even benevolently. Point out to him the error he was committing: show him that he was unwittingly an enemy to civic interests and progress which could best be left to those equipped by experience and under Providence, for handling large affairs: indicate to him, delicately, wherein his own interests and those of his newspaper were consonant with the interests of such public benefactors as Montrose Clark and the P.-U. That was the way to handle a presumably reasonable young fellow with a property to consider! In his satisfied mind, the public utilitarian outlined the course of the conversation, with himself (naturally) as converser and his visitor contributing the antiphony of grateful assent. Summoning the hand-perfected private secretary, Mr. Clark entrusted to his reverent care a summons for Mr. Jeremy Robson.

The message was duly transferred to the 'phone. It found the editor imparting some instructions to his new office boy and loyal personal heeler, Burton Higman. At the call which informed him that the Fenchester P.-U. Corporation office was on the 'phone, Jeremy's mind reverted to the interview of some months before when Mr. Montrose Clark had issued his god-like directions to the fuming but helpless "rippawtah" from The Record, and an unholy light shone in his eye.

"What is it?" he asked.

"This is Mr. Garson, Mr. Montrose Clark's private secretary."

"Go ahead."

"Mr. Clark wishes to see you."

"What about?"

"Is that necessary?" queried the voice, in a tone of startled rebuke.

"It's usual."

"He will doubtless explain, himself," said the voice, after a pause.

"All right," said Jeremy.

"Three o'clock this afternoon," specified the great man's mouthpiece, and shut off.

Such was the Montrose Clark method with inferiors. Time and the wish were stated. The place was assumed. A newspaper man was a natural inferior according to the Montrose Clark measure. The weak point of the theory, in this instance, was that the other party to the transaction had not subscribed to it. He returned to his writing. At three-ten the hand-perfected private secretary was on the 'phone again.

"Mr. Garson speaking. Mr. Clark is waiting."

"So am I."

"I don't understand." The tone was incredulous.

"Put Mr. Clark on the 'phone," suggested the editor. "He may be quicker of comprehension."

The suggestion was not adopted. But in fifteen minutes the secretary, one button of his black cutaway flagrantly unbuttoned, was being admitted to the den by Buddy Higman.

"This is most extraordinary, Mr. Robson," he protested.

"What's extraordinary in it? Mr. Clark wants to see me on business, I assume?"

"He does."

"This is my place of business."

"This is—you—you are going out of your way to be offensive," accused the scandalized visitor.

"Not going out of my way at all. I'm sitting tight. You might have noticed that yourself."

"Mr. Clark—that is to say, the Public Utilities Corporation has been a good friend to The Guardian."

"It's been reciprocated in the past," returned Jeremy dryly.

"In the past? Am I to understand that the attitude of The Guardian toward the Corporation has changed?"

"If Mr. Wymett was accustomed to run around whenever Mr. Clark chose to push a button, it has. Them good old days," said Jeremy enjoyably, "is gone forever."

"Mr. Wymett returned courtesy for courtesies."

"So shall I. When I receive the courtesies."

"The advertising patronage—"

"Don't talk to me about advertising," broke in the editor. "The few dollars that your concern pays into our cash drawer don't entitle Mr. Clark to regard this paper as his errand boy."

Mr. Garson's sensitive ear fixed upon the word "few." "We aren't doing much advertising anywhere just now," he explained with a conciliating purr. "There will be more soon. Quite soon, in fact. But there were other ways, you understand, in which Mr. Clark's friendship was useful to The Guardian—to Mr. Wymett."

"For example?"

"News items. Inside information. Advance information, I may say, on the stock market, for instance, amounting to really advantageous opportunities."

"I see!"

"Such information is still—er—available."

"I see, again. Would Mr. Clark confirm the proposition, do you think?"

The hand-perfected private secretary beamed. His mission, self-inspired, was prospering famously. "Undoubtedly," he averred.

"In writing?"

"Mr. Clark's word is—"

"As good as his bond. Naturally. I was merely thinking of such a letter not necessarily as a guarantee of good faith, but for publication."

A thin, gray veil appeared to draw itself across Mr. Garson's countenance, out of which his eyes stared with an aspect of surprise and fright. This animal had claws!

"For publication?" he gasped.

"That's it. You don't think he'd do it? Well, he's wise—to that extent, anyway. Now, you go back and tell Clark that when we open up for bribes we'll take cash—and publish the news in the paper."

"What did you do to little Eddie Garson?" asked Andrew Galpin, coming in a moment later. "I just met him in the hall."

Jeremy explained.

"You're a rude thing!" grinned the general manager. "What's your idea in going up against the P.-U.?"

"Partly personal," confessed Jeremy. "That puffy Clark thing rasps my nerves. Anyway, I don't like the P.-U. methods, public or private, and I'm not going to stand any bulldozing."

"Going to fight?"

"If it comes to that."

"Know what it'll cost us?"

"No."

"More than a thousand a year if they pull out all their regular advertising."

"It's tough, Andy. But I don't know any other way to run a paper."

"Oh, I'm not kickin'! It ain't my money. I enjoy it. Maybe he won't pull out, unless we go after him first."

"I'm going after him, though, the next raw deal the P.-U. tries to put through."

"Let's pray they'll be good, then," said Galpin.

Upon receipt of the hand-perfected private secretary's report, though it was carefully edited to avoid too unbearable offense, Mr. Clark waxed exceedingly wroth. His first intent was to order all future advertising in The Guardian stopped. Passion always had the first word with Montrose Clark, but shrewdness had the last. Shrewdness said, "Wait." Montrose Clark could be a good waiter. He waited.

Jeremy Robson didn't. He published on the following day an editorial, "Public Utilities and Public Rights," stating unequivocally The Guardian's attitude, which gave deep scandal to President Clark and inspired the darkest misgivings in the mind of the diplomatic Judge Dana. The lawyer hurried around to see his principal.

"What did you do or say to young Robson?" he demanded.

Outraged innocence sat blackly on the presidential brow. "Nothing," he declared. "He—he sent me an insulting message. He refused to come and see me. I'll smash him."

"Very likely. Meantime he's smashed our transfer scheme. Or he will smash it when the time comes."

"I shall go ahead with it just the same."

"You'll be swamped. He's dug up some tax assessment material on us that wouldn't look pretty in print if he sprung it now. We'll have to go slow."

The President of the P.-U. swallowed his desire for immediate reprisals. He felt that his prey was sure in the long run. No newspaper could offend consistently the important people and interests of a community as The Guardian was doing, and continue to make a living. That way bankruptcy lay!

Personally, Montrose Clark declared against this young upstart a war of extermination. He would eliminate the noxious creature. He would make the town too hot for him.

Vast would have been his rage could he have known that, at the same time, the editor was meditating much the same design concerning himself. War to the finish, on both sides. And all, in the first instance, because of a minor affectation expressed in the pronunciation of the hybrid word "rippawtah." Of such petty stuff are human complications constructed, and thereby the plans of the mighty brought to dust!

POLITICS AS SUCH HAD never greatly interested Jeremy Robson. The trivial and blatant insincerities of party platforms offended a mind naturally direct and sincere. As he saw the game played at the Capitol, it seemed to consist mainly in clumsy finesse directed to unprofitable ends, on the part of the lawmakers, back of whom sat the little tin gods of finance and commerce, as players sit back of the pieces on a chessboard. Only, it dawned upon Jeremy, in this game it was the public that paid the stakes; the public which Jeremy intended that The Guardian should represent. His platform was "Fair play all around and a chance for all."

Being of such mind, he was naturally sympathetic to the fervent and altruistic radicalism of Senator Embree. Almost before he knew it, he was committed to the broad, general policies of a new faction whose immediate object was to capture the party machinery and elect Embree Governor. Farmers, the more thoughtful class of labor in the industrial centers, and that floating vote which is always restless of party control, made up the bulk of "Smiling Mart's" support. His newspaper backing was scanty. In Bellair, the chief city of Centralia, The Journal lent its valuable support to most of his measures and to his general policies. A score of country journals were thick-and-thin adherents. The Guardian soon began to be classed with these for loyalty and with the Bellair Journal for weightiness, in support of the new movement.

Jeremy Robson's spirited editorial attacks upon the controlled State administration were now establishing his paper as a gospel to the fermenting political elements and had earned the indignant distrust of those interests which base loud claims to impregnable respectability upon the ground of returning reliable dividends to their stockholders. To these he was anathema; a "dangerous radical," a "half-Socialist," an "enemy of the American institutions," a "confessed demagogue," and the like impressive and silly characterizations. The Guardian was quoted, confuted, and abused over the State. It had become a power.

While Jeremy and Andrew Galpin and their lesser aids were struggling with various immediate and insistent problems of a newspaper's existence and sustenance, and establishing their organ before the public as genuinely independent in thought and unhampered in the expression of it, political prestige, which is not acquired in a day by a newspaper any more than by an individual, steadily accrued to it. Jeremy Robson had owned The Guardian for a year before he fully realized his political responsibilities in that what was said editorially in his paper greatly mattered to some thousands of earnest and groping minds. Not only this. He himself mattered, individually, as controlling The Guardian. His visiting list became inconveniently large. People took to dropping in at the office to discuss, advise, approve, or object, particularly visitors from outlying districts who deemed it an all-sufficient introduction to state that they were "friends of Mart Embree." Whether through the direct procurement of that energetic campaigner or otherwise, Jeremy found that The Guardian was considered to be not only the representative but the proprietary organ of the new movement. Financially this was an important asset. Nevertheless, the editor disrelished it. Remembering A. M. Wymett's disquisition, he heartily resented his newspaper's being regarded as the horn to anyone's phonograph! Moreover, all these calls ate up time. But that paid for itself in widened acquaintance and a more sympathetic understanding of the people who, after all, made up the Commonwealth of Centralia. He made friends readily with them. They liked him as soon as they adjusted themselves to the shock of his apparel which they deemed dudish.

The World-War was still more than a year distant, still but the dream of such pessimistic and flighty minds as A. M. Wymett's, when politics began to boil again in Centralia, and in that steaming stew of policies, principles, pretenses, ambitions, and chicaneries there simmered, all unseen, one of the minor but far-spread schemes of the Teutonic war-lord's propaganda[1]. It came to Jeremy's ears through a call from

Magnus Laurens, already the subject of frank rather than well-judged comment, in the pages of The Guardian, as representing franchise-holding control of government. The water-power magnate looked squarer, ruggeder, more determined and formidable even than on the occasion when Jeremy had first seen him grimly facing the ridicule of the German societies. He was nearer sixty than fifty and walked like a football captain, and the blue eyes under the severe brows, as they met Jeremy's, were alert and hard. The editor rose to greet him, holding out his hand.

"I didn't come here to shake your hand," said Laurens quietly. "I came to tell you something."

Jeremy sat down. "Tell ahead," said he.

"You've been using my name too freely in your paper."

"You're a public character."

"My name is my own. I'm particular about it. I keep it clean. Your paper has coupled it up with names that aren't clean."

"Did I choose your political associates, Mr. Laurens?" said Jeremy keenly.

"Political criticism is one thing. Innuendoes of crookedness and graft are another."

"We'll reach no common ground as regards your water-power operations. I'm against you there. You're selling to the people, at a profit, power that should belong to them."

"That's theory. With that I've no quarrel. But when your paper moralizes about franchise-grafting, and hints at bribery, leave me out of it."

The editor reflected. On Martin Embree's representations, he had assumed Lauren's operations to be founded in corruption. But what proof had he, after all?

"The Dollard's Falls Charter—" he began and was cut short.

"The records are open to you. The books of the company are open to you. I'll even go that far, if it's facts you're after. Or is it hush-money?"

"Which do you think?"

The hard, blue eyes looked at him with a more interested scrutiny. Magnus Laurens grunted. "Bird of a different feather from Wymett," he surmised doubtfully.

"A little."

"Well, I'm different from Sellers and Corey and Bellows and that lot. Bear that in mind. If you couple me up with them again, I'll be back here for *real* trouble."

"Coming back to lick the editor?" asked Jeremy, contemplating the muscle-packed figure of the other with a smile. "If so, I'll lay in a length of lead pipe."

"Lay in for a lawyer and a good one," advised the visitor grimly. "For I'll be after you for criminal libel. No fiddling little damage suits for me. That's what I came here to tell you."

"All right. I've got it. Anything else?"

"No."

"Then it's my turn. You control the Oak Lodge Pulp Company."

"I have an interest in it."

"The Guardian buys its print paper from you."

"Yes."

"When you came here did you have in mind any—well, exchange of courtesies, editorial for business consideration, in respect to future deals?"

"I did not. I don't do business that way," retorted Magnus Laurens with emphasis.

"Did you think that perhaps I was aiming in that direction, with my comments on you?"

The magnate changed color a little. "I might have suspected something of the sort."

"You were wrong."

"Very well. I was wrong. Anything else?"

"Yes. If I'll undertake that The Guardian shall say nothing more along the line which you find objectionable without specific and definite charges taken from the records, will you acquit me—that is, will you consider that you've scared me sufficiently?"

Magnus Laurens blinked. "I'm not a fool," he said presently. "Scared you? You're no more afraid of me than I am of you."

"Then you've done better than scare me. You've convinced me that you mean what you say. You and I can fight fair."

"I'll shake hands now," said Laurens, and did. "You're all wrong. You've been misled by that quack, Embree. But I suppose a man can be wrong and still be straight."

"Exactly what I'm supposing about you," retorted Jeremy. "Now, sit down, Mr. Laurens, and tell me some real political news."

Laurens drew a chair up opposite the editor. "Do you think you'd print it?"

"News is The Guardian's stock in trade."

"Here's some, then. A bill is going to be introduced this fall to Germanize our public schools farther."

"What's the substance of it?"

"Making German practically compulsory in the grade schools."

"They'll never pass it."

"Watch them! What leader is going to oppose it? In a governorship election year?"

"Who will introduce it?"

"Some nonentity. It will have the most powerful radical support. You can guess from whom."

"I don't guess, professionally."

"Then I'll tell you. Martin Embree."

"I don't believe it."

"Ask him. My sources of information are reliable."

"Can I get a copy of the bill?"

"Here's a rough outline of it. It isn't fully decided on yet, as to details."

"Who drew it up?"

"The Reverend Theo Gunst, Henry Dolge, and Professor Brender, of the German Department at Old Central, on the basis of a plan which Herr Professor Koerner left when he was here. It's one of the moves in the development of 'Deutschtum.' Have you ever seen the Germanizing scheme for Centralia gotten up in the eighties?"

"No. I've heard there was such a thing."

"Colonization up to a certain point. Then the establishment of a Little Germany through making German the official language of the schools, the courts, and the Legislature. Peaceful conquest idea."

"And this bill is a revival of that plan, you think?"

"It has that appearance. Will The Guardian support it?"

"No."

"Will it oppose it?"

"Who's doing this interviewing, you or me, Mr. Laurens?" smiled Jeremy.

"Call it an exchange."

"All right. Yes: we'll oppose it. What about you?"

"It's well enough known where I stand."

"As a private citizen, yes. But as a candidate for Governor?"

"I am not a candidate for Governor."

"Not formally. But you're going to be. What about this German school bill then? Will you oppose it?"

"I certainly won't dodge it. Are you going to pass on this conversation to 'Smiling Mart' Embree?"

"Not if it's confidential."

"Then I think this latter part is, for the present. To be quite frank, I don't want to meet that issue till I have to."

"You're right. It'll probably beat you."

"Possibly. But if the issue is once raised, it won't die out of people's minds readily. That's something." He paused, then added casually. "By the way, our first meeting was in a pretty German atmosphere. Do you recall the meeting where little Miss Ames stood up for the flag? That took character."

Jeremy's face became wistful. "Do you ever hear from her—Miss Ames?"

"Eh? My daughter does. Did you—Why, you were the one that put her on the golf team, weren't you! I'd forgotten. You must be a good teacher."

"She was a good pupil. Never knew when she was beaten."

"It didn't happen often enough for her to know, I guess," laughed the magnate. "She came out to visit Elizabeth and made a fool of me on my own course. I owe you a grudge for that, young man! Will you take me out and show me some of the tricks some time when I'm down here? We'll talk politics while we go around, so you can soothe your conscience for taking the time off."

"Glad to. Miss Ames and I used to lay in the early morning, but I guess I can take an afternoon off when you come down. By the way, where is she?"

"In Hamburg, I believe. There was some hint of an engagement—a relative of her stepfather's, I believe. Very advantageous match."

Jeremy heard the reply "Is that so?" in a tone of flat and polite simulation of interest, issue upon the air. It was obviously the result of a mechanical ventriloquism of his own, for he was quite sure that his lips had been for the moment incapable of speech. Of course he had always known that it must come. Inevitable with a girl like Marcia. But hope, though it withers, clings hardily to the last pulsing of secret life in the young. Even in the heart-emptiness of a long year of silence—except for the one note delivered by Buddy Higman—Jeremy had cherished a delusion dear as on the day when her first met her. . . . He became aware that Laurens was saying something to him. Politics—that was it. He had to fix his mind on politics, and though life had abruptly become sterile of hope and dreams, nevertheless there was a job to do. For the next twenty minutes, Jeremy passed through an ordeal which entitled him to a hero's medal. He forced his aching mind to take in what Laurens was telling him, and afterward he fashioned it a skilled and dispassionate interview.

After Lauren's departure the editor opened the drawer in his desk which was always kept locked. Therein were a dozen golf scores—he was still very young, and his stock of souvenirs had been pathetically scant—her note and the little photograph. He understood, now, why she had written him no letter. When she gave him up, she had mapped out her course for herself. If she were not formally betrothed then, she had determined upon the step. And having determined, she ended it all, then and there. It was the honorable way. It was the direct, definite, frank way. It was the right way. It was Marcia's way.

He looked yearningly at the photograph. Wonderful how that tiny oblong of paper, touched with a few flat tints, could evoke the very essence and fragrance and challenging sweetness of her! She looked out at him, all soft radiance in the hard radiance of the sunlight which flooded her, and his fingers, bidden to tear the likeness to fragments and scatter it—not in resentment but as a sacrificial formality—trembled and slackened. What harm, after all, in keeping the picture? It meant nothing—and therein Jeremy Robson lied to his own soul. It meant that he still clung to his vision, which nothing had blurred. For no other woman had so much impinged upon the outskirts of his imagination. There was neither time nor space for women other than Marcia. He restored the picture, the note, the prim numerals of the golf scores— how vividly he could see the full, lithe swing of the young body vivid with untainted health and vitality as her brassie flicked the ball cleanly from its turfy lie!—and locked the drawer again. There lay hopes dead and ideals still unconquerably alive.

Reading the Laurens interview, conspicuously played up, on its merits as news, Martin Embree felt rise within him dark misgivings as to his supporter. He was of that type which, in its self-centered mind, forbodes disloyalty and suspects betrayal in any divergence of opinion or policy from its own standards. But his smile was as brilliant as usually, perhaps even more so, when he sat next to Jeremy.

"Pretty handsome send-off you gave Laurens."

"Yes. I like him. He's straight."

"So's a snake—when it's dead. I told you to look out for him."

"I did," said the editor good-humoredly. "I don't think he fooled me any. Or even tried to."

"He's likely to be the man we've got to fight for the governorship."

"We'll fight him, when the time comes."

"And meantime you boost him."

"You'll never understand the newspaper game, Martin. That was news; therefore worth printing."

"I understand this, my boy; that you can't afford to mix up with Laurens and his gang."

"Oh, cheer up, Martin! I don't intend to. But I can't take your point of view in everything, much as I appreciate what you've done for the paper."

Indeed, Jeremy had always given ungrudging acknowledgement of Embree's services to The Guardian. That first boost in circulation through Embree's efforts in the Northern Tier had been invaluable. And now, through his strength in local labor circles, Embree was being of assistance to Jeremy, in preventing strikes, and allaying trouble in the press-room. The center of disturbance there was the most white-haired, sharp-tongued Socialist, Nick Milliken. Most correct in his attitude toward his employer in work hours, Milliken asserted his independence outside the "shop" by invariably addressing him as "young feller" and usually reproaching him for "hanging onto a half-mile-post, like Mart Embree," instead of coming out fair and square for Socialism and the millennium. As against him Embree played the big, stolid German-American foreman Girdner, who had influence among the men, and who was a political adherent of the Northern Tier Senator's. On the whole the internal affairs of the office were satisfactory. Another connection between Embree and The Guardian office was maintained through Max Verrall, the Senator's protégé, who, having made good as circulation manager, was now handling the paper's advertising, as sub-head of that department under the general supervision of Andrew Galpin.

For all favors The Guardian repaid Martin Embree by its loyal and effectual political support. If the Senator's friends were not always acceptable to Jeremy's somewhat squeamish political standards, at least his enemies were The Guardian's enemies. No "conspiracy of silence" on the part of the press opposed him now. The Guardian paid so much heed to his utterances that The Record was forced to take them up as a matter of news. Without this aid, Embree could not have been certain of the nomination for Governor at that time. Now it was practically assured to him. The account between him and Jeremy Robson stood fairly balanced to date.

Jeremy wondered how hard he would take the projected editorial campaign against the Germanizing of the public schools.

THAT PHENOMENON OF FINANCE which has relegated many a business man to a pained and bewildered retirement, increase of receipts attended with a parallel deficit, had marked The Guardian's first year under the new control. No question but that The Guardian was a much livelier, newsier, more influential, and better paper. No question but that the public appreciated this. The increased and steadily increasing circulation bore proof. With reluctance the local advertisers also accepted the fact. Rates had been raised, to the accompaniment of loud protests, which were largely formal, for the merchants paid the higher charge, and, in many cases, increased their advertising appropriation. The Guardian was recognized as a necessary medium. When a newspaper reaches that point, its fortune is made.

But a newspaper is like an automobile or a loaf of bread in this fundamental respect, that it costs more to make a good than a bad one. All the special features which Andrew Galpin had put on, mounted up into money. The staff was more expensive. The telegraphic service cost more. At no time had swelling revenues quite overtaken rising expenditures. Galpin, however, who had originally suggested to the new boss A Short Life and a Merry One as The Guardian's appropriate motto, was now optimistic. He confidently believed the paper to be within measurable distance of assured success.

"But we're pretty near at the end of our rope—my rope," Jeremy pointed out.

"Ay-ah. There's other ropes dangling around loose. Why not hitch to one?"

"Borrow?"

"I've heard of its being done in business," replied the general manager quizzically. "Somebody's got to help the banks make a living."

"How much do you think we need?"

Galpin juggled with a pencil and a sheet of paper. "Let's get enough while we're at it. Twenty thousand ought to be the last cent we'll ever have to ask for."

"Can we get that much?" asked the other doubtfully.

"On the security of the plant? Easy."

Jeremy's money was in the Fenchester Trust Company, of which Robert Wanser was president. No difficulty whatsoever was made by him when Jeremy called. Wanser was an anomaly in national sentiment. The grandson of a leader of the Young German movement who had found refuge in this country from the rigorous repression of Germany in '48,[1] the son of a major who fought with distinction for the Union through the Civil War, he remained impregnably Teutonic in thought, sentiment, and prejudice. He was a large, softish man who suggested in his appearance a sleek and benignant walrus. He sat back in his chair and listened and puffed and nodded, and when the applicant was through, made a notation on a bit of paper. The rest was merely a matter of "Jeremy Robson" at the bottom of a dated form, and "Do you wish to draw it now or leave it on deposit, Mr. Robson?" To the borrower it seemed like the nearest thing to magic since his great-aunt's bequest.

"And how is the paper getting on, Mr. Robson?" asked Wanser benevolently.

"First-rate. We can feel it taking hold harder and harder every day."

"Ah!" Robert Wanser's "Ah" had just the faintest touch of a medial "c" in it; just a hint of the guttural, the only relic left in his speech of a Teutonicism which three generations have failed to Americanize. "That must be a great satisfaction."

"It is."

"And a great responsibility. What a power for good a newspaper may be, even in a small community such as this! Or for evil. Or for evil," he repeated sorrowfully.

Jeremy waited.

"It can radiate enlightenment. Or it can scatter poison. The poison of class hatred, of political unrest, of radical dissension." He sighed.

Always for the direct method Jeremy asked, "You think The Guardian is too radical?"

"A(c)h!" said Robert Wanser. "I have not assumed to criticize."

"I'm asking for information. That's the only way I can make the paper better. By finding out what people think of it."

"A(c)h, yes! There is much to commend in your paper. Much! But it is not always quite kindly, is it? Not quite kindly."

"Probably not. What have you got in mind?"

"Nothing in particular," disclaimed the banker. "I feel that in our complicated system there is room for all classes of thought, and that all of us who are, in a sense, leaders should set the example of a broad tolerance. The imputation of unworthy motives, for example, can do nothing but harm. A community such as this should be a brotherhood, all working for the common good of the town. Don't you agree with me, Mr. Robson?"

To agree with so pious a banality would have been easy; was, in fact, almost a requirement of politeness. But Jeremy was wondering what lay behind all these words. "I don't know," he said. "It sounds all right. But I don't get your real meaning."

Mr. Wanser hastily disclaimed any real meaning, and the interview proceeded in a mist of steamy generalities contributed by the banker, of which one alone impressed the editor as embodying a kernel of a thought.

"You may gain temporary circulation by making enemies, but you lose support."

"But a newspaper has got to take sides on public questions," protested Jeremy.

"Why so? Why should it not be a lens, to collect and focus facts for the public's attention?"

"It should, in the news columns. But editorially?"

"Comment," said Wanser blandly. "Simple, explanatory, enlightening comment."

"It won't do the business. Take this tax matter—"

"A(c)h! Very unfortunate! Very unfortunate!" murmured the banker.

"Of course it's unfortunate," returned Jeremy warmly. "It's unfortunate that those best able to pay taxes should get off light at the expense of those less able to pay."

"That is not what I meant. These attacks upon property—"

"They're not attacks on property, when property plays fair. Would a simple comment have brought old Madam Taylor to time?"

"Perhaps. Why not?"

Jeremy rubbed his nose thoughtfully. "Perhaps it would. The facts were enough just as they stood."

Madam Taylor, the daughter of the dead statesman who had founded The Guardian, was not only the richest woman in Fenchester, but was also a highly respected and considerably feared local institution. Because of that her taxes had not been raised in thirty years, though her property had quadrupled in value, until The Guardian shocked the community by running afoul of her.

"You might have so enraged her that she would have left Fenchester forever," accused Wanser.

"Small loss, then," returned Jeremy heatedly, he having been the victim of the old lady's spiciest line of commentary, after publication of the article.

"A(c)h! It would be a misfortune to the town," said the banker, thinking, on his part, of the heavy balance in the name of Taylor at his bank.

"Anyway, Mr. Wanser," said Jeremy, rising to go, "I'm not neutral. I'm for or against. And, in reason, The Guardian will be the same. Maybe I'm wrong. But it's the only way I know. If it makes enemies, I'm sorry."

Indeed it had seemed to the young editor that circulation for The Guardian and enmities for its owner were inevitable concomitants in the making. Every local question upon which he took sides landed him upon somebody's tender toes. Much of the news that he printed—such as had not been printed for fear of hurting some more or less influential person's feelings, before The Guardian espoused the policy that news is a commodity to which the public is entitled by virtue of its purchase of the paper—exasperated and even alienated the sympathies of the formerly favored elements. But it didn't cause them to stop buying the paper, because they shrewdly hoped to find equally interesting and annoying items, later, about their friends. Then there was the matter of special consideration to the advertising patrons; a principle by which the mercantile crowd resolutely held, despite Jeremy's pronunciamento at the luncheon. At least three fourths of the advertisers in town, Jeremy estimated, were fitfully concerned either in getting into The Guardian matters which didn't belong there, or in keeping out matters which did; or, if not they, themselves, then their wives, children, or intimate associates. With respect to all these requests, he cultivated a determined and expensive habit of saying "No." Thereby, if the paper became newsier and scored more than occasional "beat" on its rival, The Record, it also became a heavier burden to carry, as the wrath of the afflicted gathered stormily about its head.

Through local advertisers resented the policy of the paper, they appreciated its value. That is all that kept them in. Verrall, in his activities as advertising manager, was constantly reporting evidences of a hostile spirit. Half of the big stores in town, he said, would knife The Guardian in a minute if they dared. He resented himself as being obliged to spend more time in diplomatic soothings than he could well spare from the routine of his work, and while advocating the utmost freedom of criticism in public matters, as befitted a follower of Embree, was mildly deprecatory of what he termed "Mr. Robson's hedgehoggishness toward advertisers." Malicious tongues, moreover, had been at work among the Germans, who formed an important part of the local mercantile world, spreading the report that The Guardian was secretly anti-German. If Mr. Robson could see his way clear to giving the German-Americans an editorial pat on the back occasionally, it would aid Verrall considerably in building up his space. Mr. Robson replied that, as it was, he was publishing a fair amount of German press-stuff, and he saw no reason to do any editorial soft-sawdering for Mr. Bausch and his faction.

Foreign advertising, such as the nationally exploited automobiles, soaps, razors, breakfast foods, and the like was now coming in in good volume, a most encouraging development, for these big advertisers exercise a keen discrimination in the matter of newspaper space, and their general support not only makes a paper "look good" to the technical eye, but also gives it a certain cachet among lesser concerns. To the high-grade national businesses The Guardian had made special appeal by expelling from its columns[2] the fake financial, oil, gold, rubber, and real-estate dollar-traps, and the quack cure-alls, whose neighborhood in print the reputable concerns resent.

To offset this, the paper had lost in volume of local advertising. Several of the large stores had cut down their space, in token of resentment over the raise in rates, and had restored it only gradually and not to the full. Barclay & Bull had stayed out for more than six months. But this helped more than it hurt The Guardian, for their business showed a marked falling-off and their being obliged to come back in, rather shamefully, was testimony to the paper's value. Turnbull Brothers, of The Emporium, the largest of the department stores, had, however, cut off The Guardian wholly, in consequence of reporting a fire in the local freight yard, with the detail that a large consignment to The Emporium of the bankrupt stock of Putz & Lewin, of Chicago, was included in the losses. As the arrival of this consignment was coincident with the announcement of The Emporium's annual "Grand Clearance Sale," the effect was, as their advertising manager passionately stated to Jeremy, "derogatory as hell." He demanded a retraction. The editor politely regretted that facts were both untractable and unretractable matter to deal with. The Turnbulls threatened libel. Jeremy told them to go ahead and promised to print daily accounts of the proceedings. The Turnbulls resorted to violent names and called off their contract for advertising. Jeremy dismissed them with his blessing, and told them not to come back until they had learned the distinction between advertising and news. Thereupon Verrall bewailed the sad fate of the advertising manager of a paper whose chief was an irreconcilable stiff-neck, and appealed to Andrew Galpin, but got nothing by that step other than unsympathetic advice to confine his troubles to his own department lest a worse thing befall him.

There was the case of Aaron Levy, of The Fashion, who, starting on the proverbial shoestring, was building up a wide low-class trade, and spreading his gospel through the columns of The Guardian, to the extent of occasionally one-eighth pages. One phase of the Levy trade was a legal but unsavory installment business, the details of which were frequently threshed out in petty civil court actions. One of these, with a "human interest" end, was reported in The Guardian. Mr. Levy promptly called on Jeremy.

"What do you want to do? Ruin my business?" he demanded.

"Is that account true?" asked Jeremy.

"Neffer mind if it's true. It didn't have to get printed."

"Your business ought to be ruined, from what the court thinks of it."

"You take my money for advertising it all right," the protestant pointed out with justice.

"So we do. We won't anymore. The Guardian won't carry your installment business, Mr. Levy."

"Maybe you're too good to have my ads in your paper at all!"

"Oh, no. We'll be glad to have everything but that one line."

"You can't run my business for me, don't you think it!" adjured Mr. Levy in one emphatic breath, and departed with a righteous conviction of unmerited injury.

The Fashion's one-eighth pages no longer graced The Guardian. Too shrewdly devoted to his trade to stay out entirely, Mr. Levy confided himself to terse announcements in the briefest and cheapest possible space. He also helped spread the evil rumor that young Robson was "sore on the business men of Fenchester." Business men there were, however, shrewd, fair-minded, and far-seeing enough to appreciate The Guardian's one-standard policy, even while they deprecated what they regarded as its abuse of independence. These formed a strong minority of defenders and supporters. Andrew Galpin's optimism, and the debt which represented it, seemed fairly justified as the election of the fall of 1913 drew near.

Already The Guardian had far outstripped The Record in circulation and in advertising revenue. The rival paper was being hard pressed to make a respectable showing, and had adopted a decidedly acidulous tone toward Jeremy and his publication, letting no opportunity pass to impugn its motives and jeer at its principles. Ever ready for a fight, Jeremy was for joining issue on the editorial page, but Galpin's wiser counsel withheld him.

"Nobody cares for newspaper squabbles but newspaper men," said that sage. "We're not making a newspaper for newspaper men. We're making a newspaper for Bill Smith and Jim Jones and their missises. And we're getting 'em!"

But Jeremy Robson was making a newspaper to meet another, more demanding, more changeful standard which was yet in a great measure the same. He was making a newspaper for Jeremy Robson; for Jeremy Robson, who, with a surprised and humble and hungry mind, was being educated by that very newspaper which he himself was making. More and more Jeremy Robson, editor of The Guardian, was identifying himself in mind and spirit with Bill Smith and Jim Jones and their missises, readers and followers of The Guardian. Because of that fellowship, because of the implied link of faith and trust that had grown up, impalpable, between them, evidenced in hundreds of letters to and scores of calls upon "the editor," there had been established standards to which The Guardian was inviolably if tacitly committed. There were things which The Guardian might not do. There were things which, when the time came, it might not refrain from doing. An implicit faith was pledged. So and not otherwise does a newspaper become an institution.

Yet The Guardian was Jeremy's very own. He felt for it the proprietary pride and interest of a man with a growing business and a growing influence to wield, and, added to that the affection of a child for a toy machine—which actually goes! He coddled his paper and petted it, and treated it, when he could, to new and better equipment, and awoke one day to the unpleasant realization that the editorials which he so enjoyed writing, and the growing, widening response to which constituted his most satisfactory reward, were physically a blotch and a blur and an affront to the staggering and baffled eye. The Guardian needed a new dress and needed it badly!

Now the garmenture of a newspaper is of a costliness to make Paquin, Caillot, and their Parisian congeners of the golden needle appear like unto ragpickers when the bills come in. Jeremy bought The Guardian a new dress of type. It made a hideous hole, a chasm, an abyss in the loan negotiated from the Trust Company. But the paper became a festival to the proud eye of its owner. Galpin helped salve his chief's conscience by agreeing that they would have had to do it sooner or later anyway.

Well advised of the loan, the status of the paper's finances, and the new plunge, Montrose Clark and his legal satellite, Judge Dana, held consultation. Now, they decided, was the providentially appointed time for trying out the transfer ordinance in the City Council. The Guardian, whose opposition they had feared, had put itself in a position where it must "be good."

"That young cub," said Montrose Clark confidently, "will have to come into line."

"With management. With careful management," amended Judge Dana.

"Anyway!" returned the public utilitarian. "He'll need every cent he can get and when he sees five or six hundred dollars as his share of our advertising campaign of education, with more to follow, he'll take his orders like the others. I'll send for him in a day or two."

"What, again?" said Judge Dana.

The puffy jowl of Montrose Clark deepened in color. "I shall not tolerate any more of his impudence," he declared. "He will come when sent for or—"

"Now, Mr. Clark, this is a case for diplomacy."

"For you, you mean, Dana."

"What do you employ me for?" soothed the lawyer. "Just you have a copy of the ordinance drawn up. Tell Garson to get up the advertising figures and give them to me. I'll talk to young Mr. Robson."

The magnate assented, though with an ill grace. "Will you take up the matter of your candidacy with him at the same time?"

Matters were so shaping themselves in politics, that with the figure of Martin Embree looming and the probability of a strong radical vote in the Legislature, the P.-U. and its allied traction interests in the State deemed it advisable to place a safe representative on the Court of Appeals bench, where much may be done by "interpretation" to offset destructive legislation. Dana had been selected as the man. In his early days the Judge had weathered, with difficulty and not without damage to his reputation, two or three legal tempests, one of which had all but caused his disbarment. Had not Montrose Clark, already finding him valuable as a clever quasher of damage suits in their early stages, employed his influence, the Judge would have ceased to ornament the legal profession. He had since gone far to rehabilitate himself in the eyes of the public, by sticking close to the high-class, quiet (not to say secret) corporation work. But the better men of his own profession, while recognizing his abilities, were still suspicious of him, though not to the point where any protest was likely to be made in the face of such powerful interests as were backing him.

Judge Dana pondered his patron's question. "That depends on how he takes the transfer plan," he replied.

"You gave me advice about him," said Montrose Clark rather maliciously; "to handle him with gloves. You see how it came out. Now I'll give you some in return. Put the screws on the young fool!"

"Not my way. And not his description. He's got a lot to learn. I'm going there as his teacher. I wouldn't be, if he was a fool."

Channels of communication bring information (and even more misinformation) from many sources into an editor's office. Through one of these Jeremy had learned of the projected transfer plan's recrudescence. Therefore he was prepared when Judge Dana, having called by appointment, stated the case flatly.

"We want your support," he said.

"This is a pretty raw deal, Judge Dana," remarked Jeremy.

The lawyer's thin and solemn face did not alter its expression of bland disinterestedness. "Not if looked at in the right light."

"What is the right light?"

"The P.-U. needs the new arrangement in order to perfect its service to the public. The greatest good to the greatest number."

"Number One," suggested Jeremy. "Mr. Montrose Clark."

"Setting aside any personal prejudice in the matter, what have you got against the Public Utilities Corporation?"

"It doesn't play fair. It is always begging for special privileges and then establishing them as rights after it has got them."

The lawyer reflected that this theory, presented and amplified editorially in The Guardian, would be unpleasantly difficult to refute.

"After all, it performs a public service," he pointed out, a bit lamely.

"The public could do it for itself better and cheaper."

"That's Embreeism. It's Socialism."

"Call it what you like. It's common sense."

"Let me advise you, in the friendliest spirit, not to take up any such scatter-brained theories in your paper. They'd wreck it."

"That may come later. I'll tell you this now, Judge. We won't support the transfer plan."

"I never thought you would," said the lawyer calmly.

"What's the idea of this call, then?"

"To suggest that you keep your hands off and let us fight it out in the Council."

Jeremy laughed outright. "You don't ask me to hold the easy mark while you go through his pockets. Only to stand by and not interfere."

Judge Dana grinned. "I don't care much for the style of your metaphor," he confessed.

"Judge, I'm afraid it's no go. You can easily bulldoze or bribe the Council, if we keep our hands off."

"Fair words, my boy! Fair words! Hasn't The Guardian ever done any bulldozing?"

"I expect it has—in a good cause."

"This is a good cause. It's going to be good for you as well as us—and the public."

"How so?" queried Jeremy.

"Our plan is to present the new system to the public through a series of advertisements. Education, you understand. The modern way: through the press. Would you like to see the outline?"

"Come to the point. What's the amount?"

Where the hand-perfected Garson would have seen hope in the question, the warier lawyer scented danger to his plans. Nevertheless he went ahead. "Five hundred, minimum. Perhaps as high as a thousand, if the public is slow to learn. Our total advertising appropriation this year," stated Judge Dana with great deliberation, "will run to five thousand dollars. There is no reason why The Guardian should not get a half of it. At least a half."

"Did Mr. Clark ever get the message that I sent him by Garson, as to bribes?"

"Bribes?" The lawyer looked properly startled. "I don't know. I doubt it."

"I sent word to Clark that when I got ready to take bribes, I'd take them direct, in the form of cash."

"But I'm not offering to bribe you or The Guardian," protested the other. "It's a matter of simple business. We institute an advertising campaign in a newspaper. We don't ask it to advocate our measures; to a finicking mind that might seem to be a form of bribery. No; we only ask that, having published our advertising and accepted us as customers, the paper refrain from rendering the service we've paid for useless or less than useless, by attacking our arguments editorially. Isn't that fair and reasonable?" pleaded the lawyer, with a plausible gesture of laying the matter out for equitable judgement.

Jeremy passed the argument. "Do you think Garson ever delivered my message?"

"I should think it unlikely," returned the other, taken slightly aback.

"Afraid?"

"Politic."

"The same thing, usually. Are you afraid of Montrose Clark?"

The lawyer reddened. "I came here as one gentleman to another—"

"With an offer of hush-money," broke in the editor. "Come, Judge; you and I are down to hard-pan. We can dispense with bluff. However, if you don't like the word 'afraid'—I don't like it much, myself, but that's because there's so many things that I'm trying not to be afraid of—I'll take it back. Now; will you take my message to Clark, as Garson wouldn't?"

"No; I will not."

"Then I'll have to write it to him. Or, I might print it in The Guardian, in the form of an open letter following this interview."

"This is a confidential visit," cried the lawyer, shocked clean out of his professional calm.

"You've got me there," admitted the other. "I've got to play square if I put up the bluff, haven't I, Judge? Even with you."

"I'm damned if I understand you, young man."

"Cheer up. We've got many long years to learn all about each other in."

"You think The Guardian will last?" Dana could not resist the temptation to impart the dig.

"It'll be remembered, if it doesn't," promised its editor. "Won't you reconsider the matter of that message, Judge? You can tone it down, you know, and temper it to the dignity of the great little man, whereas if I write to him—"

"I'll do it," declared Dana suddenly. "And I won't tone it down."

"And you'll enjoy it," added Jeremy with a grin, which met an unexpected response. The two men understood each other. In a certain complimentary sense they were even sympathetic to each other.

Devastating was the wrath of Montrose Clark upon receipt of Judge Dana's report, wholly unexpurgated. He fumed, first redly, then purply, as if some strange chemical reaction were taking place inside him; and from the exhalations of that turmoil, there crystallized a most unwise decision. Montrose Clark decided upon reprisals with his enemy's own weapon. He had Garson write several personal attacks upon Jeremy Robson, and intimidated Farley into publishing them in The Record, at special advertising rates, a procedure decidedly painful to Farley's views of professional ethics and journalistic fellowship. Jeremy retorted with a series of hasty but rather brilliant imaginary interviews with one "President Puff," which all but drove the subject of them into an apoplexy, and were a source of joy to the ungodly, albeit discreetly subdued as to expression, for the P.-U. head was a man of power in many directions. At this point the Church rushed into the breach in the person of the Reverend Mr. Merserole, Montrose Clark's rector, and the beneficiary of a five thousand dollar gift to the fund of the Nicklin Avenue Church only a week previous. Both the high-minded Mr. Clark and the high-church rector would have been profoundly and quite honestly shocked at the suggestion that there was the faintest element of financial influence (in impious circles called "graft") in what followed. But the reverend gentlemen preached an able and severe sermon upon the topic "Poisoned Pens," in which a certain type of reckless, demagogic, passion-inciting, self-seeking, conscienceless journalism was lifted up to public reprobation in a pillar of fiery invective. The Guardian violated all precedent by publishing the livelier portions of the sermon under the caption, "Whom can the Reverend Gentleman Mean?" and followed this up with a report on the Clark contribution, paralleled with further excerpts from the more spiritual and lofty portions of the sermon, headed with the text "Where your treasure is, there will your heart be also." The reverend Mr. Merserole was pained and annoyed for the remainder of the week by a steady influx of marked copies of The Guardian. He was stimulated to a holy but helpless wrath by the subsequent discovery that he, the impeccable pastor of the fashionable Nicklin Avenue Church, had been impiously dubbed "the Nickle-in-the-Slot rector." This ribaldry he ascribed to Jeremy Robson's unprofessional wit, wherein he was wrong. As a matter of fact, it was a flash from the quaint mind of Eli Wade, the Boot & Shoe Surgeon. But Jeremy had earned another implacable enemy.

The Guardian did not get its share of the $500-or-more educational advertising from the P.-U. Indeed, there was no educational advertising. The transfer issue was passed, for the time, rather than venture into the open where, as Judge Dana observed, "The Guardian was waiting for it with a fish-horn and a brick"; and the P.-U.'s legal lights set about drafting a blanket franchise for the consideration of some future legislature, which should enable the corporation to do about what it pleased without reference to dubious councils or pestilent journalistic demagogues.

CRYSTALLIZING POLICIES LEFT BUT two figures in the field for the campaign of 1913. That Martin Embree would carry the radical banner was a foregone conclusion. Magnus Laurens was logically the man to oppose him. To the Clark-Wanser-Dana wing of the party, who owned the then Governor, a weak-kneed, feeble-spirited, oratorical creature, Laurens was distasteful. He was far more prone to give orders than to take them. But on fundamental issues he was "right"; a sound conservative, reliably hostile to all the quasi-socialistic theories threatening the control of the State. Moreover his personal and political rectitude was beyond suspicion. Like or dislike him, he was the only man in sight with a chance of beating Embree.

Meantime "Deutschtum," that world-wide, subterranean propaganda of German influence, German culture, German hopes and ambitions and future dominations which had for a quarter of a century established itself reproductively as the ichneumon parasite affixes its eggs to the body of the helpless host which, later, their brood will prey upon and destroy—Deutschtum was scheming out the peaceable and subtle conquest of Centralia through capture of the minds of the coming generations of citizens. The Cultural Language Bill was quite harmless in appearance, so astutely had it been drawn. Under pretense of giving parents of public school pupils the right to secure for their children, by petition, instruction in foreign languages, it actually established German as a "preferred study" with the heaviest ratio of credits, and, in the advanced schools, as practically a compulsory subject. This meant the addition of some four to five hundred teachers of German throughout the State, every one of whom would be a propagandist of Deutschtum. As a side issue, the determination of the textbooks on European history was left to the German staff. The school boards of the State being already pretty well Teutonized, it was evident that, should the bill pass, history as taught in the Centralia school system would be censored agreeably to the purposes of His Imperial Majesty Wilhelm of Germany.

Originally it was intended to present the measure, backed by a formidable list of names from the academic world, with a sprinkling of "prominent citizens," and push it quietly through as a purely educational and technical matter into which, the professionals and professors having said their say in advocacy, the public need not trouble itself to examine. Leave these esoteric matters to the specialists! The list of endorsers was prepared. It was comprehensive, as regards the colleges and schools, the pedagogic element being influenced by the natural academic sympathy for the German educational system which honors scholarship so highly. Prominent citizens lent their names as prominent citizens always will when a petition not affecting their own pockets (though it may affect the national integrity of their own country) is presented. A committee, graced by the presence of Emil Bausch, Professor Brender, head of the German Department of the local university, Professor Rappelje, of the Economics Department, Judge Dana, the Reverend Mr. Merserole, Farley of The Record, and others, with Robert Wanser as chairman, made a formal appearance as sponsors. It was a solemn, dull, and impressive occasion, and The Guardian representative sent to report it almost yawned his head off. He sadly envied his boss whom he had met coming out of the office juggling two white and gleaming golf-balls. He wished he owned a paper and could devote a morning to pure sport whenever so minded!

The golf-balls did not indicate unmingled recreation for the boss of The Guardian. He was responding to a telephone challenge for a match with Magnus Laurens. Since the agreement in the editor's den, the water-power magnate had made rather a habit of dropping in upon Jeremy when he came to Fenchester. He would stretch his powerful figure in Jeremy's easy-chair, open the friendly hostilities by proposing to him that, since he believed in other people's property being taken over for the public good, he should deliver The Guardian to Nick Milliken and real Socialists; shrewdly discuss politics and the practitioners thereof; and invariably wind up on the main interest which the two men held in common, the Americanization of their hybrid State.

Even at its best, Lauren's golf-game was not redoubtable to a player of Jeremy's caliber. On this particular morning it was far from its best. Turning to his opponent after a flagrant flub on the ninth green, the older man said:

"My mind isn't on the game today. Let's get an early lunch, and talk." As soon as they were seated at the table, he opened up the subject.

"You're against me, of course, in the campaign."

"Certainly. We're for Embree."

"That's all right. What I'm going to say doesn't contemplate any possibility of your changing. Have you read the Cultural Language Bill?"

"No. I've sent a man up to cover the hearing."

"Why didn't you read it?"

"I understood it wasn't of any special importance."

"From whom? Embree? Never mind," added Laurens, smiling. "You needn't answer. Remember our conversation about Deutschtum in the schools?"

"Yes."

"This is it."

"As this bill was explained to me, it isn't at all the measure you described in outline."

"Not on the surface. They've changed it. But it's even worse in intent."

"You made a study of it?"

"They asked me to sign it. I refused."

"Who asked you?"

"In confidence, Robert Wanser."

"Why, he was one of the leaders in the movement for your nomination."

"As he took pains to remind me."

"Is this likely to be made a political issue?"

"I don't think so. Not in the party sense. The German crowd want to push the bill through as quietly as possible."

"That's natural. Once they get their system fastened on the schools—"

"It's there to stay."

"I guess I'll get back to the office, Mr. Laurens. I want to get in touch with our reporter at the hearing."

Olin, the reporter in question, abruptly ceased yawning his head off upon receipt of instructions to follow closely the representations made for the bill. His story, edited by Jeremy himself with illuminating side touches, turned that innocent-seeming measure inside out and revealed some interesting phenomena on the inner side. One remark of Magnus Laurens—"I got my first schooling in the Corner School-House and I want to see it stay as American as it was in my day"— stuck in Jeremy's mind. Out of it he constructed an editorial on the Corner School-House as the keystone of Americanism, never for an instant foreboding that the phrase would become the catchword of a bitter campaign. The first effect of the editorial was to bring Embree around to the Club at dinnertime to find Jeremy.

"What on earth did you make that break for?" cried the harassed statesman.

"Break? It wasn't a break. That bill means more than you think."

"It means nothing serious. Or it wouldn't have, if you hadn't made an issue of it. Now, the Lord knows what we're in for!"

"An open discussion is my guess. That was the object of the editorial."

"Oh, you'll get that! If that were all—or half!"

"We haven't killed the bill, have we?" asked the editor hopefully.

"No. But it will have to be cut and pruned a good deal, to meet arguments."

"Will that hurt your feelings?"

"I care nothing about the bill. It's only a sop to the harmless vanity of the Germans. But you've got them down on you again. And they blame me for it."

"*Do* they! Why?"

The Senator laughed in a half-embarrassed way. "Well, you know, Jem, I'm credited with having some influence with The Guardian. I wish I had half I'm credited with."

"You mean you're supposed to control the paper's policies."

"Don't get disturbed over it. I can't help it."

"Nor can I, apparently," returned the editor, frowning. "People absolutely refuse to believe that a man is responsible for his own paper—except when there's something to kick on."

"What are you going to do now about the bill?"

"Let it simmer. Take another shot at it when it comes up again."

"Do you want me to lose the election?"

"Come out on the other side if you want to, Martin."

"I am for the bill."

"Make a speech and say so, then. We'll report you in full, and give you a leading editorial courteously regretting that so brilliant and far-seeing and sturdily American a statesman should be in error on this one point."

An answering smile game into Martin Embree's expressive face. "Go a little light on the sturdy American feature."

"But you are that, aren't you?"

"Of course I am. Just on this bill, though, I don't care to ram it down the Germans' throats."

"You'll never teach me politics, Mart," sighed the other. "I'm too single-barreled and one-ideaed."

"One-eyed, my boy, one-eyed. Try to see the thing from another fellow's point of view."

"Your point of view at present is that I've gone astray from your good influence. Is that it?"

"There are other influences, Jem." The Senator's smile was broad and golden as a bar of sunlight. "I hear you were out at the swell Country Club this morning with Magnus Laurens."

"Your information is O.K."

"Did he talk to you about this bill?"

"He did."

"Is he against it?"

"He is. Refused to sign the memorial."

Embree's face grew heavy and thoughtful. "Did he so! I wonder if we could get him on record?"

"Magnus Laurens isn't likely to dodge an issue."

"He's a queer associate for the editor of The Guardian."

"I pick my own associates," retorted Jeremy shortly.

"Or let them pick you. Until they get ready to drop you again. That's the way with those fellows that have too much money."

"He isn't likely to buy me away, Martin," replied Jeremy, recovering his temper.

"I'm not worrying." The Embree smile was on duty again. "What bothers me is what the Germans will do to you for today's paper."

What the Germans did to Jeremy Robson was, in the terse slang of the day, a plenty. The German press[1], religious and lay, attacked The Guardian as an exponent of narrow and blighting Know-Nothingism. One or two small German organizations passed high-sounding resolutions of reprehension. There was a flood of letter and enough "stop-the-paper" orders to afflict the soul of the much-tried Verrall. The most definite response came from Bernard Stockmuller, the jeweler, a generous advertising patron of The Guardian. On the morning following the hearing on the bill he met Jeremy on the street and stopped him.

"Vot you got against the Chermans, Mr. Robson?" he demanded truculently.

"Not a thing in the world."

"Emil Bausch told alretty how you turned down Prinds Henry's ledder."

"I did not."

"He says you are a Cherman-hater. If you are a Cherman-hater," continued the irate jeweler, overriding the other's protest, "I guess a Cherman's money ain't good enough for you. My advertising you don'd get any more."

"I don't need it on those terms," replied the owner of The Guardian. "And you may tell Mr. Bausch from me that he lies."

No other advertiser actually deserted the paper, though Verrall reported much ill-feeling among the German mercantile element. The sturdy jeweler alone was enough a man of principle to make his nationalism superior to his business.

"Is it worthwhile?" was the argument posed by Embree, a fortnight later when the bill, in re-amended form, was coming up again, and Jeremy was whetting his pen for another tilt at it. "You've done the job. Can't you drop it now?"

"Have we done the job, though?"

"Surely. Look at the bill now. Practically everything you objected to is out. I'll guarantee it harmless, myself."

What he said was in a sense true. Practically every point made in The Guardian had been speciously met in the new draft of the bill. But, in essence, it remained the same, an instrument of Deutschtum. Jeremy did not look at the amended measure more than give it a hasty glance. He accepted it on the Honorable Martin Embree's word; and as he did so was conscious deep within himself that he was dodging responsibility; that he really did not want to know too much about the new form. The Stockmuller incident had disturbed him, for he liked the little, impetuous jeweler. Then, too, the accusation that he could endure with the least equanimity was that of narrow-mindedness. Men whose sound Americanism was as trustworthy as their technical judgement had endorsed the measure. The Guardian went off guard. The bill became a law.

Unforeseen concomitants marked its political course. Embree, playing expert politics, so arranged matters that Magnus Laurens was challenged repeatedly on the "Corner School-House" issue. It did not lie within Lauren's vigorous and frank nature to refrain from declaring any principle which he held. He replied in speeches which, slightly and cleverly distorted by the trained German-language press, gave profound and bitter offense to the German-Americans, even the best of them. Taking up the controversy at the politically effective moment, Embree pushed it, making the most of his adversary's alleged prejudice and narrowness, particularly in the foreign-born districts. Long before the election it was evident that the school-house slogan alone would beat Laurens. He was heavily defeated. That morning's golf with Jeremy did it.

In honor, The Guardian had refrained from making use of the "Corner School-House" issue against Laurens. Jeremy at least would not play the turncoat. He persuaded himself that, in resisting Embree's arguments for a strategic change of base, he was doing all that could be required of him. Nevertheless, it was with an inner qualm that he met Magnus Laurens, a week after the election, their first interview since the golf-game.

"Well, Mr. Laurens," he said, "you made a good fight. We can't all win."

"But some of us can stand by our colors even if we lose," said the downright Laurens, and passed on.

"Can't stand defeat," said Jeremy to himself.

But the explanation did not satisfy his inner self. Deep down he was conscious of his first surrender.

## 19

Six weeks after Martin Embree's triumphant election to the governorship, the owner of The Guardian visited the Fenchester Trust Company for the formality of renewing his note. He was referred to President Robert Wanser. More walrus-like than ever, the president of the institution looked this morning as if he might have eaten a fish that didn't quite agree with him. Jeremy stated his errand. Mr. Wanser ruminated.

"Difficulties have arisen," he presently announced.

"What difficulties?" asked Jeremy, startled.

"The Trust Company does not see its way to renewing your note at this time, Mr. Robson."

"What's wrong?"

"I have not said that anything is wrong. It is merely a matter of business policy. The loan is a heavy one."

"It is well secured."

"I do not question that."

"The paper has turned the corner. We are making money today."

"Today—you are."

"And we shall make more from now on."

"A(c)h!" observed the banker with his buried guttural. "That is prophecy."

"Based on facts and figures. I can show them to you."

"No need."

Jeremy reflected, with an unpleasant sensation of being spied upon, that probably the local banks knew as much of the financial side of his business as he himself did; perhaps more.

"Do you consider The Guardian weaker security than it was?" he inquired.

"I have not said so," replied the impassive walrus.

"You haven't said anything. Do you intend to, or am I wasting my time?"

Jeremy arose, looking at the financier with a lively eye. This was not at all what Wanser desired. He intended to read this young sprig of journalism an impressive and costly lesson, after first reducing him to a condition of affliction suitable for the punitive exercise. It annoyed him to find that Jeremy did not reduce; on the contrary, that he was likely to escape uninstructed in that discipline to which he, Wanser, was leading by gradual stages. Forced to a shorter cut he said oracularly:

"A newspaper's best assets is its friends."

The editor's regard continued intent.

"Its heaviest liability is enemies."

Still no response from the beneficiary of these pearls of wisdom.

"A newspaper is on the down-grade when it makes unfair and prejudiced attacks upon—upon any class of people."

"Talk plain, Mr. Wanser. You mean the Germans."

The walrus, startled by this abruptness, began to bark. "That's what I mean. That's exactly what I mean. You've got a grudge against the Germans."

"Not I."

"You have. It proves itself. The Germans are the best citizens in the State."

Jeremy laughed not quite pleasantly. "I was betting myself you'd say that next."

"Say what? I don't understand you."

"Every German-American I've ever talked with tells me sooner or later that the German-Americans are the solidest or the best or the most representative citizens in the country. If not the most modest," added he maliciously.

Like most retorts inspired by annoyance it was a tactless speech. The walrus bristled. "You see!" he growled. "There's your prejudice."

"No prejudice at all. The Germans considered as people are all very well. I like them and respect them. But there are other people in America, you know—Americans, for instance."

"We all know how you feel. We all know why you fought our school bill."

"I didn't fight it. I let up on it."

"You let up on it when you were afraid to go on," taunted the other.

Jeremy's face flamed. "You're a—" he began, and stopped short, swallowing hard. "You're right," he said with quiet bitterness. "I was a quitter. It serves me right that you should be the second man to tell me so."

"You quit too late." The walrus was enjoying himself now.

"Evidently. All right, Mr. Wanser. The note will be paid when due. At least I'm glad we understand each other."

The walrus, briefly meditant upon this, didn't like it. "Don't be so sure you understand it all," was his parting word, by which he really meant that he failed to understand Jeremy. There was a large leaven of timidity in his imposing bulk.

To Andrew Galpin the interview as detailed by his boss proved no great surprise. "Dutch Bob"—thus he irreverently dubbed Fenchester's leading banker—"is sore on two counts. You mussed up his bill. That's the first and worst. The other is our support of Mart Embree."

"But Embree and Wanser worked for the bill together."

"Ay-ah. That's all right. Wanser is all for Embree when he's a German booster. He's all against him when he's a radical. It's one of the twists of politics."

"Why are they so hot about this school business anyway? It almost makes me believe that Wymett and Laurens are right in their Deutschtum theory."

"Don't you go seeing ghosts, Boss," advised the general manager, good-humoredly.

"Then don't put any stock in the notion."

"About the Germans? Oh, I don't know. Let 'em play with their little Dutch toys. I guess we're a big enough country to absorb all the sauerkraut and wienerwursts they can put into our system. What's the use of being cranky about it? It only gets the paper in wrong."

"We're certainly in the wrong with Wanser. And now we're out. Got twenty thousand dollars up your sleeve, Andy?"

"No. I've spent my week's salary," answered the other with a grin. "The Drovers' Bank would be my best guess."

To the Drover's Bank went the owner of the Fenchester Guardian, a daily with a rapidly rising circulation of eleven thousand, an increasing advertising patronage, and a fair plant. He was courteously received by the president of the institution, an old, glossy, and important looking nonentity named Warrington. Mr. Warrington listened with close attention, made some thoughtful figures on a blotter, and requested Mr. Robson to return that afternoon when a positive answer would be given. But Mr. Warrington thought—he was quite of the opinion—he confidently believed—that there would be no difficulty.

"There's one thing that worries me, Boss," commented Andrew Galpin as the pair sat absorbing coffee and pie into their systems at a five-cent, time-saving lunch-counter near the office.

"Pass me the sugar—and the worry," requested Jeremy.

"Why should Wanser close down just at this time?"

"Why not?"

"Well, safely secured loans of twenty thousand dollars aren't the kind of business a bank chucks to another bank."

"Didn't I indicate to you that his loyal German heart was sore?"

"Why wasn't it sore last summer, when the bill was up?"

"Do you think somebody's been stirring him up to go after us?"

"More likely he's got some reason to think we're up against it."

"Hoots! We were never in such good shape."

"That's our view. I'm wondering if, maybe, Bausch and his lot are putting up some kind of a game."

"What kind of a game can they be putting up?"

"I'd have to understand German to read their minds. Maybe they'll stir up advertisers against us. Like Stockmuller."

"Any local advertiser that thinks he can do business without The Guardian," stated the owner arrogantly, "is suffering from an aggravated form of fool-in-the-head."

"That's good doctrine. If only you can make 'em believe it."

"They believe it all right."

"Say, Boss. Why not get Mart Embree's view on it?"

"Good idea."

Jeremy went to the Governor-elect. "What did you expect?" asked that acute commentator on men and events. "Can't you understand that you insulted every good German-American by attacking them on the point where their pride is most involved, the superiority of their educational system?"

"Allowing that, is this just a belated revenge on Wanser's part?"

"No. It's business."

"To drop $1400 a year interest on a good note?"

"It would have cost the Trust Company more than that to carry you."

"I don't get the point, Martin."

"Deutscher Club account. Emil Bausch's account. Henry Vogt. Arndt & Niebuhr. Stockmuller—have I said enough?"

"They would have withdrawn? Are they as sore as that?"

"One of these days you'll realize the truth of what I told you about committing hara-kiri, Jem. There's only one safe way with the Germans. Let them alone and they'll let you alone."

"Oh! Will they! That shows how one-sidedly you look at it. They've begun flooding the office already with their press-work for the winter Singing Society festival."

"Perfectly harmless. You certainly can't see anything objectionable in that."

"No; I can't," admitted Jeremy.

"Run a lot of it, then. It costs nothing, and it will help square you for the school bill break."

Which Jeremy found good advice and resolved to follow. He said as much and was approved as one coming to his senses after regrettable errancy.

"How much pull do you think the Deutscher Club crowd have with the Drovers' Bank?" asked Jeremy.

"Not so much. If you do have difficulty there, let me know. I could probably fix you up in some of the out-of-town banks."

The Drovers' Bank made no difficulty. Mr. Warrington was most amendable when Jeremy returned. This helped to reassure the borrower that no financial plot threatened his newspaper. He would have felt less happy had he known that the interval between his visits had been utilized by Mr. Warrington to pay a call of consultation upon a certain florid and self-important gentleman, no lover of The Guardian or its editor since he had suffered indignities of print as "President Puff" from Jeremy's satiric and not always well-advised pen.

"Let him have it," directed the public utilitarian. "Three months' note."

Montrose Clark smiled puffily upon Judge Selden Dana later at the club.

"I thought he would come around to us," he stated.

"What will you do now?" asked the lawyer.

"Wait," replied the magnate.

Which might have been regarded as either a direction, threat, or declaration of intent, and partook of the nature of all three.

## 20

BUDDY HIGMAN, PROSPEROUS IN a new blue-and-yellow mackinaw (Christmas), a pair of fur mittens (New Year's), and high snow-boots (accumulated savings), entered the Fenchester Post-Office with the mien of one having important business with the Government. Four dollars a week was now Buddy's princely stipend from The Guardian, for working before and after school hours at a special job of clipping and sorting advertisements from the press of the State, for purposes of comparison.

Occasionally Buddy brought in an item of news, with all the pride of a puppy bringing in a mouse, and beat it out with two fingers on a borrowed typewriter. Such of these contributions as got into print were paid for extra. Thereby Buddy was laboriously building up a bank account. It was young Mr. Higman's intention to be, one day, Governor of the State. But in his wilder and more untrammeled flights, he hoped to be an editor like Mr. Robson. Buddy was an enthusiastic, even a hierophantic worker at his job. He was worth all that The Guardian paid him. Even had he not been, the Boss would have kept him on. For he was, all unknowing, a link; decidedly a tenuous link, but the only permanent and reliable one, between Jeremy and a foregone past.

At the stamp window Mr. Burton Higman, dealing with the United States Government, produced a silver dollar and gave his order in a firm and manly voice.

"Hullo, Buddy," greeted the clerk. "Still got that girl in Yurrup, I see."

A fire sprang and spread in Mr. Higman's face. "And the rest in postal-cards," he directed with dignity.

"You're our best little customer," continued the flippant clerk. (The little customer murderously contemplated arranging with The Guardian, later, to write an editorial about him and get him fired!) "Write to her every day, don't che?"

"Shuttup, y' ole fool!" retorted the infuriate youth, stepping aside to reckon up his purchase, lest it might be short.

"Yessir," continued the blatant gossip, to the next comer. "He sure is the ready letter-writer, only *an'* original. Don't see how he has time to help you edit your paper, Mr. Robson."

Mr. Robson! The shock diverted Buddy at the twenty-eighth count. He looked up into the friendly face of the Boss.

He hastened to defend himself.

"I yain't, either, Mr. Robson. 'T ain't letters at all. They're fer noospapers."

"Are they?" said his chief, walking out into the wintry air with him. "I didn't know we had so much foreign circulation, Buddy."

"No, sir; we ain't. Say, Boss," he added after a pause, "we gained five new ads on The Record this week, an' they only got one that we didn't."

"Good business, Buddy."

"An' I had two sticks in the paper yesterday. Dje see it? Story of the kid that fell through the ice."

"You'll be a reporter one of these days, son."

"Oh, gee!" said Buddy ecstatically. Then, with resentment, "What's the good of school, anyway?"

"If you're going to be a real newspaper man you'll need all the education you can get."

"Yes, sir." The aspiring neophyte sighed. "That's what She says."

There was but one "She" in the vocabulary of the exclusive and worshiping Buddy. Her name was never pronounced in the conversations on the subject between himself and his Boss. There was no need of being more specific, for either of them.

"It's good advice."

Buddy marched along beside his employer, obviously wriggling upon the hook of some pointed thought. Presently further reticence became impossible.

"Mr. Robson!"

"Well?"

"Them stamps—"

"What would the blue pencil do to a sentence beginning that way, Buddy?"

"*Those* stamps—it's like I told the fresh guy at the window."

"They're for the circulation department?"

"No, sir. But they're for circulation all right. I been sendin' the paper every day to Hamburg."

Jeremy's pulses quickened. "Your own idea, Buddy?"

"Nope. I'm sendin' it to Her. It's Her idear. She reads it reg'lar. She's deeply int'rusted in my cay-reer."

"Where did you get that? It doesn't sound like Her."

"It ain't. Got it out of a book," confessed the boy. "I write to Her, too," he added happily. "She ast me to."

"What does she think of your work?" inquired the Boss gravely.

"I ain't heard from Her since I began gettin' my stuff in the paper. But I guess She likes the paper all right. She tells me in most every letter what a big thing it is to help make a noospaper."

"Does She? What else does She say?"

"I dunno." The boy lost himself in thought. "It's just a little here an' a little there. She never says much; not any one time. But you can see She thinks a lot of the Business."

"Now, you wouldn't suppose that, would you?" said the artful Jeremy, feeding his hunger for the mere, dear memory of her brought back and made real by speech. "It must be because you told her you were going to be a newspaper man."

"That's it. She thinks it's like being a preacher, only more so. She says you mustn't ever be mean or give away a friend or take advantage of having a noospaper to write for. An' She says you got to always write what you honest-to-God think, because it's yella to do the other thing. I guess She wouldn't stand for a fake, not for a second! I bet She'd take the hid off'n some o' them—o' those Record guys. An' She says the hardest thing'll be some time when there's somethin' a fella oughta write an' that'll get him in the wrong if he does write it, for him not to lay down an' quit on it. An' She says never, never to be afraid o' your job, because that makes the job your boss an' not you the job's boss.

An' She says unless a guy can't trust himself nobuddy can trust him an' be safe, no matter how much they want to. I guess that's about all right! Ain't it, Boss?"

"It's about all right, Buddy," said Jeremy with an effort. That final bit of philosophy had stabbed.

After the presses had stopped and the offices had emptied, that evening, the editor of The Guardian sat at his desk with the little photograph of Marcia Ames before him. He looked into the frank and radiant face; into the eyes that met the world and its perplexities so steadily, with so pure and single-minded a challenge.

"You didn't ask much, did you, my dear!" he said softly to the picture. "You only asked that I should be straight and honest; not a shifter and a coward. Well, it was too much. Buddy may do better. I'll help him as far as I can. That's a promise, my dear."

He heard the departing Buddy whistling outside. His footsteps approached the door. Jeremy slipped a hand over the picture.

"Anythin' more you want me for, Boss?" asked the boy, appearing in the doorway.

"No, Buddy. Good-night."

"'Night." He paused. "I dunno's She would have wanted me to tell you about the paper," he said. "She never told me not to, though. I kinda thought you'd wanta know. I guess we got a man-size job makin' a paper good enough for Her to read, ain't we, Boss!"

"I guess we have," said Jeremy steadily.

The door shut and he returned to his contemplation of the picture. "You read me, my dear," he said. "You were reading me all the time. You read me in the Eli Wade story. And in the golf story. And perhaps in others I didn't realize. You knew I'd come eventually to do such a wretched crawl as I did on the German school bill. You knew that you never could trust yourself to me. You'd seen me go back on myself. You knew that a man who would go back on himself would go back on you when the test came." He mused bitterly. "As I would have done," said Jeremy Robson.

No man ever pronounced upon himself a harsher judgement.

"Boss," said Andrew Galpin.

He had come in and perched himself upon a corner of Jeremy's desk, swinging his long legs. A folded copy of that day's Guardian served him for a fan, which he plied languidly, for it was the early hot spell of June, 1914. The regard with which he favored his chief was both affectionate and quizzical.

"Well?" queried Jeremy.

"D' you know we're pretty near two years old?"

"That's right, Andy. We are."

"D' you feel it?"

"Yes, and a couple of hundred years on top of it."

"So bad as that! We're some old for our age, I'll admit. But I don't see any signs of senile decay, yet."

"Oh, we can still stir our bones enough to get off the press on time."

"What do you think of this feller's paper, anyway, Boss?"

"What do *you*?"

"Pretty well satisfied, thank you. We've got fourteen thousand circulation that you couldn't pry loose with a crow-bar."

"Couldn't we? I'm not going to try."

"Not going to? You *have* tried. You've stepped on every cussed one of their cussed toes, one time or another. Dam' fi don't think you've got 'em so they *like* it."

"Queer way they've got of showing it, then. Do you ever read the editorial correspondence?"

"Oh, that's all right!" The general manager waved such matters loftily away. "They quit the paper, sore. Then they get over it and come back. If they don't, there's plenty of others to take their places. Even the Dutchers"—this being, at the time, Mr. Galpin's term indicative of that powerful and flourishing organization, the Deutscher club—"have come around."

"Not all of them. Stockmuller is out still."

"He's a stiff-neck. He's the only one."

"Not the only advertiser. The Laundry Association have never got over Wong Kee, the yellow peril. The Emporium takes as little space as possible. And I don't notice the P.-U. crowding any contracts on us, Andy."

"Verall tells me they're coming back. At least, they're showing flirtatious signs."

"No! I wonder what kind of bargain they'll offer now."

"You ought to curb that mean, suspicious nature of yours, Boss," reproved Galpin solemnly. "Now, *I* set it down to force of habit on the P.-U.'s part. Something's in the air. Therefore they begin to advertise. It's the cuttle-fish principle. Only they use printer's ink."

"What's their little game?"

"Self-defense, I guess. The Governor is sharpening up his Corporation Control Bill."

"We'll be for it. The P.-U. advertising won't make any difference. Montrose Clark ought to know that by this time. If he knows anything," qualified Jeremy.

"Don't worry about President Puff. He knows a lot of things he didn't know before The Guardian tackled the job of his education. One of 'em is that the P.-U. is going to need just as much friendship and just as little enmity as it can get when this bill comes up."

"And Clark is going to smooth us down with his advertising, eh?" Andy lifted up his voice in pertinent song:

"There was a young man who said, 'Why
Can't I look in my Ear with my Eye?
   If I set my mind to it
   I'm sure I can do it.
You can never tell till you try.'

There's the P.-U. motto," he added; "and a noble one it is. 'You never can tell till you try.'"

"Let 'em try somewhere else than in The Guardian."

"Not so, Boss," argued Galpin. "This bill is rough stuff. It'll pretty near wipe out the P.-U. They're entitled to a yell, at least. Even Verrall admits that. And what Verrall won't swallow whole, when it comes from Mart Embree, must be tough swallowing."

"Verrall wants to make his advertising total as big as possible."

"Being human—although an advertising manager—he does. Well, he's got no kick coming. Look at the clippings of your young friend and disciple, Mr. Buddy Higman. The Record is nowhere. Respected Sir and Editor, as your correspondents from the cheese district write; we are making money this year. Real, guaranteed money."

"Enough to take up our note?"

"Why worry? The bank doesn't. Old Warrington purrs like a cat every time he meets me. You can read in any witch-book that a banker purring like a cat is a sure sign of prosperity."

"What's it in your scheme-hatching mind to do with all this prosperity, Andy?"

"New press," returned the general manager, who had been leading up to this point.

Pro and con they argued it, the owner finally agreeing.

"We really owe it to the advertisers as well as the readers" had been Andy's best argument. "Look how they've stuck."

"They've had to," returned Jeremy grimly. "Half of 'em would have got out at every bump if they hadn't been afraid."

"Well, we're solid with 'em now. Look what we did to 'em in April. Hiked the rates a clean ten per cent all around. And did they peep?"

"They did not. They howled."

"Force of habit again. They all came through, didn't they? We're making it pay 'em."

"We're giving them all the return they're entitled to," agreed the editor. "I wish I were as sure that we're giving the reading public as good."

"Don't hear many kicks, do you?"

"Lots. If I didn't I'd *know* we were rotten."

"Ay-ah. That was a fool question of mine. But I mean, you feel the paper taking hold all the time, can't you? We're certainly putting it over. We've made a Governor already. What do you expect? Want to elect a President and Congress?"

"The Governor is one of my troubles, Andy."

"Butting in?"

"You can't call it that."

"What can you call it?" demanded the downright Galpin.

"Well, boosting. Without him we wouldn't be where we are."

"Nor anywhere else," added the other with emphasis.

"Probably not. I appreciate that. I'd *give* him the paper, if he needed it, as far as that goes. But as long as my name is on it, I want it to be my paper."

"Well, 'Smiling Mart' isn't trying to pry it away from you, is he?"

"Of course not. It's hard to put into words. But I feel as if I—we— The Guardian were being surrounded by a sort of political web."

"The Governor being the spider?"

"No. It's his web, in a way; but he isn't spinning it. It's being spun for him and for us. All our readers identify us completely with his policies. If I say anything editorially, it commits the Governor. People take it for granted that we're his mouthpiece. It's isn't fair to him or to us."

"Does he take advantage of it?"

"We—ell; I don't know. He doesn't mean to. Every now and then, though, something will come up where he wants us to do this or not to do that—always some unimportant thing—because of its influence on more important things that we're both interested in."

"As for instance?"

"Take all this boosting, press-agent stuff that comes along and that Embree wants in," replied Jeremy. "Sometimes it's political. Sometimes it's personal. Sometimes it's the German stuff that Wymett used to talk about. I've got to admit that Embree's view is always for the practical good of the paper. By following his advice, we've held sulky advertisers more than once. But I know this, I'm doing for him—and for the politics of it—and for the paper itself, in a way, I guess—what I wouldn't do for any advertiser. And sometimes it's been a matter of principles. Not very important, maybe, but principles just the same. Compromise, Andy."

"Life's mostly compromise, I guess. There's a little more of it in the newspaper game than in other lines because the newspaper touches life at more points than any other business."

"I've always thought," pursued Jeremy, "that when I came to own a newspaper it would be independent if it wasn't anything else. Well, look at The Guardian!"

"Ay-ah. I'm looking at it. What's wrong with it?"

"It's ducking a little here, and dodging a little there, and trying to be cautious about this issue and polite about that man, and so on. That isn't my notion of being independent."

"What is? I guess we're as cocky as any paper in the country. You can't tell all the people to go to hell all the time," pointed out the general manager, reasonably.

"I don't want to. But I want to be able to if I do want to. Am I talking like a fool, Andy?"

"I don't know," answered the other, troubled.

A silence fell between them. Galpin whittled a pencil to so careful and delicate a point that it immediately broke. He repeated the experiment with like result before he spoke.

"Say, Jem."

The other looked up, attentive. Seldom, since their new relationship had the older man employed any formula of address other than the half-jocular, half-official, "Boss."

"Say it, Andy."

"Who are you making this paper for?"

Across the editor's face passed a swift shock, as of thought surprised and betrayed.

"Making it for?" he said slowly.

"Ay-ah. For yourself, I guess. Huh?"

"Yes."

"And it don't suit?"

"Not altogether."

"Not good enough?"

"No."

"Ay-ah. I see." One of those extraordinary flashes of intuitive insight which sometimes pass electrically between surcharged and kindred minds, culminated in the general manager's next question. "What does she think of it?"

"Who?" The startled counter-question represented less than Jeremy's normal frankness.

Andy rose and stood above the other. "How should I know who? If I did I'd know more about the paper."

"You're right." For the moment Jeremy was as intuitive as his friend. "You think it would have been more honest of me, as I'm making a paper for someone else, to let you in on it."

"What does she think of The Guardian?" persisted Andy.

Jeremy stared out into the gray and bleak spaces. "God knows," he said. "I've no way of finding out."

Andy turned and went to the door. "Forget it," he said. The tone was his sufficient apology.

That night of June, 1914,[1] two years after Marcia Ames's lips had pressed themselves to his cheek, and he had felt her sobbing breath on his face, Jeremy went again to the bridge where they had stood. A barge filled with young people passed the turn of the lake. A canoe bearing a boy and a girl—how young they seemed to lonely Jeremy, and how enviable!—floated beneath him, and their speech came up to him, dim, tender, and murmurous. Then, sped by a poignant magic, the blended voices of Marcia's song were wafted to him across the waters.

> "Who wins his love shall lose her,
> Who loses her shall gain,
> For still the spirit wooes her,
> A soul without a stain,
> And memory still pursues her
> With longings not in vain!"

He could hear in the distance the faint plash of the oars that drove the boat of song. The fairy voices, fainter, sang:

"He loses her who gains her,
Who watches, day by day,
The dust of time . . ."

The words were blurred as the unseen boat passed behind some unseen cape; then the music died on the breeze. Jeremy bent over the railing, where Marcia's hand had rested.

Half a world away an obscured fanatic, unknown to the world and today almost forgotten by it, was gloomily, lonelily, dreamily blending those common, inexpensive, terrific chemicals whereby he was to plunge civilization in carnage. The happy boats passed on. The happy voices blended again and were silenced. The busy presses chronicled the events of unsuspecting nations to little folk of souls yet untouched who, sleeping, "rose up to buy and sell again." Then the bomb of the dreamy fanatic was flung, and in the force of that explosion, the wave of war, which had hung crested and suspended, broke and whelmed the world in such flood that the quicksands upon its edges spread even to far-away Fenchester.

# PART III

STRICKEN, AT FIRST, BY the unimaginable vastness of the tragedy which had befallen Europe, the State of Centralia quickly recovered, and lifted up a thousand voices of acclaim. Germany was being splendidly victorious.[1] Nothing could stop the Kaiser's perfected war machine; nothing could stand against the valor and discipline of the field-gray legions. Triumph was a matter of only a few months; perhaps only a few weeks. France would be crushed; Russia humbled; England, the faithless and foolhardy, penned in her island and slowly starved to submission. Deutschland, Deutschland über Alles! The loyalest Imperial colony could hardly have rejoiced more openly or fervently than did Centralia, a sovereign State of the United States of America. Slow, still, systematic, scientific propagation of Deutschtum throughout the years now reaped its due reward.

Those there were in the State, and many, who revolted from the brutality of Germany's war-making. But what voice they could find in Centralia, where politicians and press and pulpit were dominated either by the influence or the fear of organized German sentiment? Let a man but speak a word against Germany's cause, and the anathema of Deutschtum descended upon him. A highly practical anathema, too; directed to his business affairs and even his social relations. The accusation of prejudice, of Wall Street influence, of British sympathies lay against any who dared question or criticize the "necessary rigor" of German methods. The rape of Belgium[2] was hardly more triumphant than the seduction of Centralia.

Most conspicuous of the few who braved the local power of Deutschtum was Magnus Laurens. Less than a month after the declaration of war he spoke at a Manufacturers' Association convention dinner in Bellair, the metropolis of the State. "America and the Future" was his topic. It should have been a safe topic; safe and sane, and in the hands of a less obstinately courageous partisan would have been. Indeed, for twenty minutes, it was. Then the speaker, setting back his massive shoulders, and with a significant deepening of his voice, challenged the sense of justice of the gathering, in these words:

"What future can America hope for if the policies of nations are to be dominated by the nation to whom the sacredest pledge is but a scrap of paper when it conflicts with her blood-stained ambitions?"

Gordon Fliess, the head of the great Fliess Breweries, was on his feet instantly. "Order!" he shouted. "The speaker is out of order, Mr. Chairman."

Echoes came from all parts of the banqueting hall, mingled with cries of dissent. Laurens raised his great voice, and dominated the tumult. It was a reckless speech; it was violent; it was, in parts, unfair. But it raised a voice in Centralia that arraigned the State before a court of honor for self-judgement; a voice too powerful to be silenced, too clear to be ignored.

Yet, instantly, the silencers were at work. Their first attempt was through the toastmaster who laid an arresting hand upon the speaker's arm, only to be shaken off with a violence which sufficiently warned him. Shouts, hoots, hisses, and cat-calls failed to make any impression on Laurens. Galvanized into action the reporters were taking down every word. But there descended upon them an emergency committee hastily constituted by Fliess, Mark Henkel, of the Henkel Casket Company, and other reliable Germans who not only warned them against publishing the proceedings, but also manned the telephones and issued their directions through owners, advertising managers, and editors regarding the event. Out of six dailies published in Bellair, only The Journal, already under suspicion because of its independence, reported the one sensational and interesting speech of the occasion. That single publication, however, gave the matter currency. The German dailies took it up virulently. The Journal was all but swamped with protests.

Political matters had, on the day when the Laurens speech was published, brought Cassius Kimball, the managing editor and dominant spirit of The Journal, to Fenchester to see Governor Embree, whose fortunes the paper had early backed. After his call, the Governor sent for Robson. They had not seen each other since the war began. Martin Embree's smile was that of a boy.

"Well, Jem," was his greeting. "We've got him this time."

"Who?"

"Magnus Laurens. Didn't you see this morning's Bellair Journal?"

"I've just been reading it."

"That kills Laurens."

"For what?"

"For everything and anything in the State. Governor—Legislature—dogcatcher; he couldn't get elected to anything, if this is handled properly."

"I'm giving his speech in full, in tonight's paper."

"That's it! And a slashing editorial to follow tomorrow. Eh?"

"Slashing which way?"

"Why, into Laurens."

"Not me," declared Jeremy with more emphasis than grammar.

"You wouldn't back him up!" cried Embree.

"Not in everything. There's a good deal in that speech, though, that needed to be said; that was *right*."

"Jem, are you off your head?"

"Never felt saner in my life."

"They always say that just before they begin to bite the paper off the walls," smiled the other. "Come, Jem! Here's our chance to put Laurens out of the game once and for all. Give me a column and I'll do it myself."

"The chance'll have to wait."

"Until when?"

"Until he isn't as near right as he is on this."

"Jem," said the Governor suddenly growing grave, "why is it you're always pussy-footing when Laurens is in question?"

"I don't like that word, Martin."

"Word the question to suit yourself, then."

"And I don't like the question. It reminds me that the last time I pussy-footed was on an issue that Laurens met fair and square."

"And it licked him."

"There are worse things than being licked."

"That's cant," retorted Embree promptly. "When you're licked politically, you're through. You can't get anything done. Oh, I don't mean that I'm afraid to fight a losing fight when a big principle is involved. My record shows that, plain enough. But this war isn't our fight."

"What's your view on the war, Mart?"

"It came in the nick of time."

"For what?"

"For us. For our programme. We can put through pretty much anything we want in the line of reform legislation. As long as the war continues, the German vote will stand by us almost solidly, if only we play fair with them. Even men like Wanser and Fliess and the big business crowd that have always fought us are ready to swing into line, if we don't rush things too hard. Why, Jem,"—the keen, fine face lighted up with enthusiasm,—"we can make Centralia the banner State of the country in social reform and popular rule."

"As to rushing things, isn't this Corporation Control Bill a little rough?"

"It's meant to be. It'll be toned down in conference. We made it pretty stiff to throw a scare into the P.-U. crowd. There won't be anything we can't do to those fellows, if the war keeps on long enough."

"What do you really think about the invasion of Belgium, Martin?" asked Jeremy abruptly.

"I don't like it."

"I hate the whole business."

"But I don't like war, anyway. And this is part of war. I'm going to keep my hands off. Neutrality is our watchword,[3] Jem. The President has given it to us, and I guess in international affairs we can afford to follow the President. Let Magnus Laurens and his gang do the fireworks. They'll only burn their fingers."

"Belgium was neutral," said Jeremy gloomily.

"Let Belgium alone and 'tend to Laurens."

But this the editor of The Guardian would not do. He ignored the Manufacturers' Association banquet incident editorially. Publication of the mere report of the Laurens speech, however, stirred up a volume of local displeasure chiefly on the part of the Deutscher Club element, and The Guardian received some pointed letters on the subject of neutrality.

"Neutrality," commented Andrew Galpin thoughtfully to his chief. "That's good business for Mart Embree. He can preach neutrality and tickle the Germans at the same time, for our kind of neutrality in Centralia is sure hall-marked 'Made-in-Germany.' But how neutral are *we* going to be?"

"There's no such thing as 'how neutral.'"

"Oh, isn't there! Look here, Boss; what's practically every paper in this State, on this war, except The Bellair Journal?"

"German. They're not afraid to be."

"Suppose a paper is really neutral; gives both sides an equal show. What'll it look like where all the rest are pro-German? What'd it look like in Germany?"

"I get your point, Andy. It will seem to lean to the Allies by contrast."

"There you are! Well, what are we going to do?"

"Play fair."

"Sure. But we can be cagey about it, can't we?"

"To what extent?"

"Enough to live. I don't want to see The Guardian mess up in a fight that's none of our fight and get done up so bad we can't help win the fight that is our fight. Let England lick Germany. Our business is to play the game here and lick the corporation crowd for legislative control of the State. Don't you think it's going to be a cinch, either, just because we've elected Mart Embree Governor!"

"Expediency is a queer text for you, Andy."

"I'm all for expediency as against idiocy."

"What about butting into the Wade riot?"

"That was for a friend. War, right there under my nose. The other thing is four thousand miles away. And I hope it stays there!"

"Andy," propounded his chief, "what do you really think of the Governor?"

"'Smiling Mart'?"

"Is that an answer?"

"Ay-ah. I always wonder about one thing. If you brushed that smile off quick, what'd be under it?"

"He asked me to sit in his box at the convention meeting of the Federated German Societies."

"Oh, you got an invitation from the Societies, did you?"

"Yes. Issued by Bausch as secretary."

"I bet he spit in the ink before he signed it. Going?"

"What do you think?"

"Sure."

"Expediency again, eh?"

"Ay-ah. There's no principle in turning down an invitation, even if it *will* do us some good!"

"All right, Andy. I'll go," laughed the editor.

He sat in the Governor's box at the meeting. There was the same pan-Germanic atmosphere that there had been two years before, but magnified. The Imperial banners were more flamboyant, more triumphant. The verve and swing of "Deutschland, Deutschland über Alles," was more martial; it defied the world. The speeches were more fiery, more challenging, more instinct with the fierce pride of a dominant nationalism; and again Jeremy felt resentfully, in the references to the adoptive republic, that tone of bland and intolerable condescension to a lesser people.

The Governor's box was that which Mangus Laurens had occupied in 1912. Sitting well back in it, Jeremy faced the high balcony. In the far corner a fat, steamy German in a fancy waistcoat roared out "Hochs!" of assent and applause to the speakers. But before Jeremy's wistful vision he dissolved, giving place to another figure; a figure slender, gallant, boyish, erect. Martin Embree's touch on his knee recalled Jeremy to realities.

"Wake up, Jem! What ghosts are you seeing?"

"None. Nothing," muttered Jeremy, and stood while the fervid gathering sang thunderously "Die Wacht am Rhein."

STEP BY STEP THE Guardian followed the war through its pregnant early days. In presentation of the news, both Jeremy and Galpin strove to be conscientiously neutral. For Galpin, this was simple enough. It accorded with his creed, that the news should stand of itself and for itself and let the people judge. Jeremy took it harder. There were times when, in the security of his den, he fingered his pencil with a fierce and mounting resentment which cried for expression toward Germany's savagery and terrorism. On the other hand, he knew that to incite prejudices, wrath, and hatred within America, and particularly within so divided a State as his own, was to thrust the other nation nearer to that hell's caldron wherein Europe agonized. The President had prescribed neutrality. That, Jeremy recognized, was part of the statesmanship. He appeased his own soul with the argument that it was equally the part of honorable journalism.

If he had thought by editorial silence to satisfy or even conciliate the propagandists of Deutschtum in the State, he was soon undeceived. The process of the absorption of Centralia by the German-Americans was swiftly progressing, and as a newspaper of influence, The Guardian came within the purview of their programme. Daily the mail deposited on his desk a swelling flood of proselytizing literature; pamphlets, reprints, letters to the editor from writers whom he had never heard of (and who in many cases had no existence) as well as from his own clientèle, excerpts from the German press, editorials from that great and malign force in American journalism[1] who, already secretly plotting with Germany, was playing the game of Teutonic diplomacy by inciting fear and distrust of Japan and shouting for war upon and annexation of Mexico. He could not have published one twentieth of them. He did not publish one one-hundredth of them. Hardly a day passed without his being stopped on the street by some sorrowful or accusing or indignant subscriber who wished to know why The Guardian had not reproduced Pastor Klink's powerful editorial on "The Crusader Spirit of Germany," or how it happened that The Record printed Mr. Woeker's letter on Belgian provocations while The Guardian hadn't a word of it. Suspicion established itself in the editor's mind that some person or persons were making daily and scientific analysis of his newspaper for the purpose of forcing propaganda upon it by the power of protest. He suspected, and with reason, the Deutscher Club.

The matter of news soon became an irritant to the apostles of Deutschtum. To the layman, news is simple fact, the product of the world's activities, finished and ready for the press. To the expert journalist news is a theme and the printed page is an instrument whereon he may render that theme by an infinite variety of inflections and with infinitely varying effect upon his public. Headlines and sub-heads alone may vitally alter the whole purport of an article not otherwise garbled. So long as Germany's record was one of consistent victories, the course of Centralia newspapers was clearly marked. They had but to print the cables with captions appropriate to the facts, in order to appease their self-appointed masters, the German-American public. But Russia now made her sensational advance. Victory in the West was threatened by disaster in the East. Much ingenious and painful juggling of cable news was imposed upon the harassed journalistic fraternity of Centralia by this unfortunate development. Relegating the Russia campaign to nooks and corners of the inner pages and qualifying it by indeterminate or sometimes satiric headlines, was the most generally approved method. The Guardian, however, printed the news. It printed it straight, for what it was worth, and under appropriate captions. Somewhat to Jeremy's surprise and more to his relief, the Governor had no criticism to make of this course.

"So long as you stick to facts, we've got a good defense," was his view. "They'll kick. Of course they'll kick. Let 'em. In time they'll come to see that they're really just kicking against the facts, not against The Guardian. Just now our German friends are pretty excited and touchy and nervous. If you could give 'em a little more show on the editorial page, while this Russian business is on, it'd help."

Kick the German-Americans it certainly did, by pen and voice. No less a person than Robert Wanser, who had maintained a mere bowing acquaintance with Jeremy since the Cultural Language Bill episode, took it upon himself to voice a protest to General Manager Galpin.

"Why print this Russian claptrap at all?" he asked.

"All the papers are carrying it," answered Galpin.

"Not so much of it, and not so prominently as The Guardian."

"We're giving it what it's worth as news, just as we give the German advances in the West."

"Everybody knows that it isn't news. It is British fabrications, put on the tables to fool—er—influenceable newspapers."

"Influencable, eh?" said Galpin, annoyed. "Everybody knows, do they? You prove it to us, and we'll print it, all right."

"You are making a mistake," pronounced the banker severely. "For a newspaper to take up the British side is very suspicious."

"Bunk! The Guardian's been square, and you know it. But we're not going to stand for being censored by a lot of organized letter-writers."

"A(c)h, censored!" The banker's guttural almost emerged upon the troubled surface of speech. "The censoring is inside your editorial office, if anywhere. You refuse to publish our letters—"

"'Our'? Have you been writing letters?"

"I have sent you letters." Mr. Wanser's face became red.

"Funny! I don't recall any. Sign 'em?"

"They were signed," returned the other, with an effort at loftiness.

"With what name?" demanded Galpin bluntly.

"I am not here to be cross-examined by you."

"You started this. And now you want to duck it. Nothing doing! You let out what we've suspected; that a lot of those letters are machine-made, and sent in signed with fake names or with real names stuck on as a blind for some committee. That don't go, in The Guardian. We've had too much stuff put over on us."

The banker's dignity dissolved in wrath. "Don't you get fresh with me, young man. I guess you and your boss, too, are going to learn something one of these days! Going out of your way to insult the best citizens in the State every time your dirty, pro-English paper—"

"Oh, you make me sick!" said Galpin, and marched away, leaving Wanser brandishing a denunciatory fist at nothing.

The split between the Germans and The Guardian imperceptibly widened, as time went on, through minor incidents, arguments, and abortive attempts at influence. Seizing upon its opportunity, The Record accepted the whole programme of local German censorship, published nothing that could possibly offend, trimmed its news to the prejudices of the dominant element, and by these methods cut in upon its rival's local circulation. Verrall, however, reported that as yet there was nothing to worry about, while at the same time earnestly advocating an inoffensive foreign news policy for The Guardian. So 1914 passed into 1915, and the paper held its own.

On a mid-April day of 1915 there appeared upon an inner page of The Guardian, an item of such overwhelming importance, that when the editor and owner read it, all other news of the day receded and blurred into a dull, colorless mist of insignificance. The article stated briefly that Miss Marcia Ames, cousin of Miss Letitia Pritchard, of 11 Montgomery Street, who was well known to Fenchester society, not only for her charm and beauty, but also as being the only lady intercollegiate golf-player in the country, had left Berne, whither she had gone after the breaking-out of the war, and was visiting friends in Copenhagen. Her many and admiring friends would be glad to learn, etc., etc., in the best society-reportorial formula. After thoroughly absorbing that paragraph into his inmost being, Jeremy sent for Buddy Higman, who had now taken on the additional duty of marking each day's paper, from the assignment book, article by article, with the name of the writer of each.

"Buddy," said the editor, "whose is the Ames story?"

This being an official query, Buddy made pretense of consulting his marked file. "Higman, sir."

"Oh! You wrote it! Did you have a letter?"

"Yes, sir. But I didn't write it from that. I wouldn't make a story out of a letter from Her. That's personal," said Buddy, proud in his rigid sense of ethics.

"Then where did you get it?"

"I figured that like as not Miss Pritchard would get one by the same mail. So I went an' ast her."

"And she had?"

"Yes, sir. I told her I was there for The Guardian an' was there anything she could give out. An' she gimme the story."

"Buddy, if you don't look out you're going to be a real newspaper man one of these days!"

"I wisht I was one now," returned the boy wistfully.

"Do you? What would you do?"

"I dunno, exactly. Somethin'."

"You'd need a more definite policy than that, son, if you were in the bad fix of owning a newspaper."

"I'd do somethin'," persisted the boy. "I'd soak the Germans. Say, Boss, how old do you have to be to get into the National Guard?"

"A good deal older than you are. Why all this martial ardor, Buddy?"

"That's what She'd do, if She was a man."

"Did the letter say so?"

"Yes. Can a feller—is it ever all right for a feller to show a lady's letter?"

Wondering again as he had wondered before whence this freckled scrub of a boy had derived his instincts of the gentleman born and bred, Jeremy answered gravely: "It might be. That's for you to decide, Buddy."

"I kinda guess She'd like for you to see this." He dug out of his pocket a crumpled sheet, covered with the strong, straight, beautiful script of Marcia. "Read there, Boss." He indicated an inner page.

". . . or later it must come," the letter ran. "As soon as you are old enough you must learn to be a soldier. Everyone in the world who can, must learn to be a soldier. I cannot tell you, Buddy, of the terrible thing that German national ambition is; how it reaches out into every nation to make that nation its tool; how it aims to overrun the world and make it one vast Germany. You will be old enough to see what it is doing in your own little city, so far away. Perhaps you do not comprehend. Perhaps you will not understand even what I am writing; but you may find someone on your paper who will know and will explain."

"I think, perhaps, I was meant to see this, Buddy," interjected Jeremy.

"But I guess I know what She was drivin' at all right," replied the boy.

"How can America be so blind!" Jeremy read on. "How can its newspapers be so blind! The last numbers of The Guardian I saw, no word of arousing the people to a sense of what all this means. Oh, Buddy, Buddy! If you were only a man and had a newspaper of your own! I have written your aunt about the books and . . ."

The bottom of the page terminated the reading. Jeremy, with his lips set straight and hard, handed back the sheet. The boy faced him with a candid eye.

"Boss, you're a man," he said.

"Am I?" said Jeremy, more to himself than in reply.

"And you got a noospaper of your own."

"Not of my own, wholly."

"Ain't it?" cried Buddy, amazed. "Who's in on it?"

"The people who read it, and believe in it. It's partly theirs. The men I work with to help keep politics straight and fair. I have to think of them."

Buddy sighed. "It ain't as big a cinch as it looks, ownin' a paper, it is!"

"Not these days, son."

"Anyway, I guess She knows," asseverated the stout little loyalist. "She's lived there an' she oughta know. What She says goes, with me."

The clear single-mindedness of a boy! How the editor of The Guardian, feeling a thousand years old, envied the lowliest assistant! How the unstilled ache for Marcia woke and throbbed again at her words! She had begged him not wholly to forget her. Had it been a spell laid upon him it could have been no more compelling. He wondered whether, twenty years hence, her influence would have become less vital, less intimate upon him, and, wondering, knew that it would not.

He went home deviously by way of Montgomery Street.

The early shoots had lanced their way into the sunshine of the Pritchard garden, and Miss Letitia was making her rounds, inspecting for the winter-killed amongst the tenderer of her shrubbery. Jeremy leaned upon the fence saying nothing. There were reasons why he felt hesitant about approaching Miss Pritchard. In his campaign against the tax-dodgers he had fallen foul of old Madam Taylor, one of her particular friends.

Shortly after the publication, Miss Pritchard, meeting Jeremy at her own front gate as he was about to enter, had presented the danger signal of two high-colored spots upon the cheek-curves, and a pair of specially bright eyes; also the theorem, for his acceptance, that a newspaper ought to be in better business than attacking and abusing lone defenseless women. Declining to accept this theorem without debate, Jeremy was informed that Miss Pritchard would disdain henceforth to harbor The Guardian upon her premises. Interpreting this to mean that the editor of that fallen sheet would be equally unwelcome, the caller had departed, divided between wrath and melancholy. Up to that time the Pritchard house had been one of the few ports of call in his busy but rather lonely life. Now, another of those gossamer links with Marcia Ames was severed. Miss Pritchard soon came to regret her severity, too; for the steadfast, unspoken, hopeless devotion of the boy—he was still only that to her—to the memory of her golden girl, had bloomed for her like one of the flowers in her old maid's garden.

Now, seeing the lover, forlorn and mute, outside what was once his paradise, she gave way to compunction. But not wholly. There was a sting in her first words.

"Are you reckoning up taxes on my place, Mr. Jeremy?"

"That's been done long ago," he said uncompromisingly.

"When are you going to print it?"

"As soon as you try to dodge 'em."

He looked very tired, and his voice had lost something of the buoyant quality of youth which she had always associated with him. A different note crept into her own voice when she spoke again.

"I had a long letter from Marcia today."

"Is she well?" The tone was politely formal, but she saw the color rise in his face and marked the pathetic eagerness in his eyes.

"She's the same Marcia Ames. Even to the name."

He caught at the opportunity. "She's not married yet?"

"No. Her fiancé is fighting. Somewhere in the remote colonies, I believe."

"Fiancé?"

"Surely you knew that she was engaged; a young cousin of her step-father's. It was an affair of years."

"Not when she was here," Jeremy blurted.

Her surprised regard challenged him. "You seem very certain," she observed.

Jeremy recovered himself. "I had heard rumors, but nothing formal," he said. "I thought perhaps you would have told me when it was announced."

"I assumed that you knew."

What Miss Pritchard meant was, "I assumed that she would have told you." She perceived that there were depths in this affair of which she knew little or nothing.

"German betrothals are curious and formal things in her class," continued the old maid. "When she came here to 'see America first,' I believe it was understood that nothing was to be settled until her return. She went back, and the formalities were arranged. At the outbreak of war her fiancé was somewhere in Africa and, I believe, is still there."

"I see," said Jeremy dully.

"Marcia still sees The Guardian." The spirit of romance in the spinster heart *would* force the words.

"I know. And that helps. Good-bye and thank you."

"Come to see me and let's be friends again," said the warm-hearted lady.

Most of that night Jeremy spent on the tramp, thinking of The Guardian in terms of Marcia's letter; haggardly struggling to harmonize cross-interests, cross-purposes, cross-loyalties. Out of the struggle emerged one clear resolve. What next the progress of the war should produce that intimately touched his conscience, should be the signal, the release. Upon that The Guardian should speak its owner's mind though damnation follow.

Three weeks later the Lusitania[2] was sunk.

LIKE A PORTENT OF stern events to come, The Guardian's Lusitania editorial laid hold on the collective mind of Fenchester. It was a hand set against every man's breast, bidding him to stop as he went about his occupations, and summon his own soul to ponder what a German war might mean. "The Black Flag," Jeremy had captioned it. Simple and grim words were its medium, and the burden of its charge was plain murder.

The first effect was that of any profound and pervasive shock; the community lay quiet, collecting and rallying its forces. Until now, no newspaper in the State of Centralia had dared lift voice against the cumulative outrages of the conquerors, fearful as all were of the coördinated forces of German sentiment, ready and under arms for the call. To what the initial outbreak might spread, no man could foretell. It was not so much a high explosive as a fire-bomb that The Guardian had cast.

The German press ravened. The dailies howled for the blood of the dastardly and treacherous Robson. They called upon the authorities to suppress The Guardian, without troubling to specify upon what ground. They summoned the Governor to cut loose from a supporter so violent, so vicious, so filled with the spirit of hatred and contention. The German religious press backed up the attack, and even improved upon it. It declared The Guardian and its owner enemies to an all-wise, all-beneficent, and all-German Gott, and shrieked inquisitorially for a holy ban upon it. All of which, combined, failed to keep Jeremy awake o' nights. Indeed, it had quite the reverse effect. For the first time in months he fell asleep at peace with his own soul, and awoke with untainted, new-found courage to face whatever the day might bring.

One day brought Cassius Kimball, of The Bellair Journal. He was a slow, cautious, weary, high-minded, and plucky man of forty-five who looked sixty behind his lines and his glasses, and he eyed Jeremy, his devoted admirer, with a benign but puzzled expression as he sat in the office spare chair.

"I wish I'd said it first," was his opening remark.

"I wish you had," returned Jeremy, quite honestly.

"I never say anything first. That's why I'm really not much good."

Jeremy laughed. From the most independent and battle-scarred veteran of Middle Western journalism, this was funny.

"It's a fact, though," continued the tired voice. "I always think too slow. What are you going to do next?"

"Next?"

"About the Lusitania issue. You've started it in Centralia. Nothing can put out that fire. It may die down and only smolder. But the embers will be there. And nobody can tell when they'll reach a powder magazine. Have you seen the recent Eastern papers?"

"Some of them."

"A lot of them are yelling for war. It's going to be put up to the President pretty stiff. What are you going to do about that?"

The gravity of the tone, almost amounting to deference, made Jeremy tingle. Here was the greatest journalistic power in Centralia, a man whose clarity and courage of spirit had won for him an almost hierarchic ascendency in his profession, ascribing such importance to the course of The Guardian that he had taken the four-hour journey from Bellair to consult its owner. To do Jeremy justice, his pride was for the paper, semi-impersonal, rather than for himself. To the question he had no ready answer.

"I hadn't thought it out yet. What's your idea?"

Kimball took off his glasses and wiped them carefully. His eyes, without them, seemed squinted and anxious. He drummed on the desk a moment before replying.

"There's a man down in Washington," he said in his gentle, reasonable voice, "with a hard job on his hands. He has a lot of decisions to make every day. We newspaper men have the same kind of decisions, but where ours affect a few thousands, his affect a hundred millions.

From now on he's going to have bigger decisions put up to him. He can lift his hand and there'll be war tomorrow, and six months from tomorrow there'll be thousands of us back home here in mourning. It's a hard decision, Mr. Robson. You and I did our best to beat the President for election.[1] We've differed from him in many things. But this isn't politics. It's something else now. And, knowing what he's got to face, I don't feel exactly like yelling in the President's ears." He resumed his glasses. "Seen the Governor since your editorial?"

"No. He's up at his home in Spencerville."

"It's going to be put up to him pretty hard, too. Your outbreak is responsible."

"How?"

"The German legislative outfit in Bellair," said Kimball, who had an uncanny knack of knowing things before they were ready to be known, "is cooking up a bill to offset your editorial. They intend to put the State on record. The bill will call on the President and Congress to declare that any American sailing on a ship of a belligerent nation forfeits all right to the protection[2] of his own country."

"What will The Journal do about that?"

"Fight it."

"Can we beat it?"

"No. But the Governor can."

"Will he?"

"Ah! What do you think? You're closer to him than anyone else."

Jeremy shook his head. "Not on the war. I don't even know what he's thinking, most of the time. Your paper has more influence with him than The Guardian. If I could think of Martin Embree as being afraid of anybody, I'd say he was a little afraid of The Journal."

"Of course, he doesn't want to lose us," answered Kimball reflectively. "He can't afford to lose us. But there isn't much danger of that." He rose. "I'll send you a word before the bill is ready. They intend to spring it suddenly."

Jeremy thanked him, and after he had left, sat down to think out the Governor's situation. He could appreciate its perplexities. He could foresee that Embree would blame him for stirring up dissension unnecessarily, when he might have held his peace. Therefore he was prepared for a difficult interview when, on the Governor's return, he was invited to lunch with him. But "Smiling Mart's" smile was as open and friendly as ever.

"You dipped your pen in earthquake and eclipse that time, my boy," he observed.

"I had to speak out or blow up, Martin."

"Therefore you did both. Up in the Northern Tier you're not precisely popular."

"No. The circulation reports show that. We're getting two or three dozen stop-the-paper orders from there per day."

"I've done my best for you, there. But I can't hold the more rabid elements. There's one saving grace, though."

"That's—?"

"You've gone no further than criticism. You didn't even hint at war."

"And I'm not going to. Not on this issue."

Martin Embree drew a long, slow, luxurious breath. "Thank God for that! At least they can't identify us with the war-howlers in the East."

Jeremy passed the "us." "What's your view of the Lusitania sinking, Martin?"

"It's damnable. But it's war."

"German war. They're holding jollifications over it here. There's to be one tonight at the Deutscher Club."

"Not a formal thing?" cried the Governor.

"Bausch and Henry Vogt, the florist, are engineering it, I understand. It isn't exactly a club affair."

"Ah! That's not so bad. You're not going to print anything about it?"

"I'd print their remarks about The Guardian if I could get 'em," grinned Jeremy. "They'd be spicy. But of course they won't admit reporters."

"What goes on at a private dinner is nobody's business," said the relieved official. "So you don't need to stir up any more trouble for yourself on that score. Some of the smaller German organizations have been passing resolutions about The Guardian. That will cut into your circulation, won't it?"

"To some extent. But we're holding up."

"Just keep your head, Jem, and we'll be all right," advised the Governor anxiously. "Don't forget we've got measures to put through here at home more important than a war four thousand miles away. Harvey Rappelje, of the Economics Department of the University, is working on the Corporation Control Bill now. I'm going to have him talk it over with you when it's ready."

"Glad to see him. Speaking of bills, Martin, what do you know of a bill drawn by a bunch of Bellair Germans, to keep Americans off British passenger ships?"

"Nothing. And I don't want to until I have to."

"That'll be soon," prophesied Jeremy. "I'm going to fight that."

"I don't know about that," doubted the other. "There are two sides to all these questions, remember."

"There are two sides to the war. Admitted. But there's only one side to Americanism. And this is a question of American rights."

"But is it quite fair to our Cause, to endanger it now for an issue that you aren't called upon to report?"

"If our cause isn't American, then The Guardian is going to quit it," retorted Jeremy heatedly. "What's more, Martin, if I ever had to suspect that when the issue comes you wouldn't be for America against—"

"Stop right there!" the other adjured him, laughing. "When you hear me speak an un-American word or see me do an un-American act, it will be time enough to worry. But in the business now on hand we need those German votes, and I'll do just as much to hold them as you can do to drive them away."

On his return trip to the office, Jeremy encountered Eli Wade, the Boot & Shoe Surgeon, and Nick Milliken. Wade shook hands with him, and looked at his feet.

"You're standing solid now, Mr. Robson," he said. "I went on my knees and thanked God when I read your editorial."

"Not me," put in Milliken. "That ain't my God. I don't worship Mars."

"Don't heed him, Mr. Robson. He'll fight, too, when the time comes."

"In a capitalistic war? Do I look as soft a mark as that!" retorted the socialist disdainfully.

"It's an American war," said Eli Wade.

"Don't you think it! Nine tenths of the people are dead against the war. There's a bill coming up this session that'll tell the war-birds where they get off."

"Where did you learn about it?" asked Jeremy.

"The Party is going to back it. It'll carry without any trouble. The yellow-bellies won't dare kick for fear of the German vote."

"Then they might as well raise the German flag over the Capitol," declared the Boot & Shoe Surgeon fiercely.

"German nothing! We'll have the red flag of brotherhood here yet, Eli."

Considerations of the policy delayed the presentation of the bill. When it was offered, Jeremy put it on record all over the State, in an editorial of protest, dubbing it the "Surrender Bill." But no leader could be found in the Legislature who dared back this bold course. German intimidation had done its work well. The most that the opponents of the bill ventured was to obstruct its passage by parliamentary obstacles. Even that much brought down upon the offender the threats of an organized Deutschtum. But the matter bumped and dawdled along the legislative road all that spring and summer before the bill passed to a final reading. Jeremy published his last editorial on the subject, "Hands Off the President," solemnly warning the Legislature against interfering in international matters of which they could know little or nothing. The Record replied with a scathing "leader" denouncing The Guardian, under the caption "An Insult to Our State," the purport of which was that Centralia possessed the patriotism, statesmanship, and wisdom embodied in its Legislature to lay out the course for the ship of state through the most perilous waters. It was the kind of claptrap which rallies pseudo-patriotism and emboldens vacillating politicians.

The bill passed in the fall by a ratio of two to one. Deutschtum rejoiced exuberantly.

Jeremy hurried to the Executive Mansion. "Governor, are you going to veto that bill?"

"Is this for publication, Mr. Editor?" smiled the Governor.

"Yes."

"Then I will say that the matter is still under advisement."

"It's a rank surrender, Martin."

"It's a silly bill, Jem. But where's the harm? Let 'em blow off steam."

"Then you won't veto it?"

"I certainly shall not. Does The Guardian propose to scarify me?"

"My Lord, Martin! A matter as serious as this—I don't see how you can take it so lightly."

"Philosophy, my boy. With our Corporation Bill coming on soon I'm certainly not going to compromise its chances by flying in the face of the whole German-American vote."

"But on a question of natural honor—"

"National flapdoodle! Our national honor is safe enough as long as we keep our heads. Will you see Rappelje tomorrow about the Corporation Control Bill?"

"Yes. Tomorrow afternoon."

The lean and dry authority on economics, an ardent apostle of Embree's policies and his chief adviser on all corporation matters, spent an hour in the editorial den of The Guardian. All points of the bill were carefully discussed. Jeremy committed his unqualified editorial support to it.

"Will you forward it to Mr. Kimball, of The Bellair Journal?" asked the professor.

"Yes, if you wish."

"We can be sure of his aid?"

"Probably. Though he will be very sore on Governor Embree if the 'Surrender Bill' is signed."

"That has no bearing whatsoever upon this measure."

"Only as a matter of political barter and trade. What do you think of the 'Surrender Bill' yourself, Professor Rappelje?"

"I was requested to come here to discuss the Corporation Control Act," returned the economist austerely.

"Another dodger!" thought Jem disgustedly, as he bade his visitor a somewhat curt good-day.

Such advisement as Governor Embree bestowed upon the "Surrender Bill" was brief. Two days after its passing he signed it without comment. Jeremy's editorial on the final step in the enactment was dignified and regretful, but carefully guarded against offense. It indicated plainly that there would be no split between The Guardian and the Governor.

On the morning following the signature, as Jeremy was at his desk, Andrew Galpin burst in upon him, his face vivid with emotions in which unholy glee, such as might be evoked by some Satanic jest, seemed to predominate.

"Come out here!" he gasped.

"What's the matter?" demanded his Boss, struggling against a powerful grip.

"Come out. I can't tell it. You've got to see it."

Galpin hurried him downstairs and out upon the sidewalk. The street was full of people with faces turned upward and to the northeast where Capitol Hill reared its height. The typical characteristic of the faces was a staring incredulous eye and a fallen jaw. Jeremy followed the line of vision to the dome wherefrom projected the State's official flagstaff.

In the place of the Stars and Stripes there blew, stiff in the brisk wind, the banner of Imperial Germany.

## 25

PHENOMENA DO NOT OCCUR upon legislative flagstaffs without due process. The astonishing manifestation of sardonic intent above the unconscious lawmakers of Centralia was not the fruit of magic, black or white, but of a simple and easy substitution. The legitimate ornament of the staff was lowered each evening into a box, where it lay, still attached to its halyards, and was raised therefrom in the morning by an assistant janitor who, operating the rope from within the dome, never saw the flag as it mounted to its peak. What more easy, since the dome was always open and unguarded, than for some demoniac-souled satirist to ascend to the repository and substitute an alien banner, always supposing him able to lay possessive hands upon such a thing? Since the Lusitania rejoicings, German flags had blossomed broadcast in the streets of Fenchester, and each new submarine success had brought them forth afresh. As a matter of fact, the satirical substituter had borrowed the Deutscher Club's proud insignium.

How would the German-Americans take it? That was the first question in the minds of Jeremy Robson and Andrew Galpin alike. When the first shock of amazement wore off, it began to appear they were taking it with a certain gusto. A joke? Oh, certainly! But a joke with a deserved sting in it for the "Know-Nothings," the jingo-patriots who could admit to no other nationality than their own to any rightful say in American affairs. Privately they were much inclined to chuckle. The forehanded among them hastened forth with cameras to perpetuate the spicy relish of their flag exalted in the high place of the State. While the click of shutters was at its height, the flag came down. Somebody in the Main Square shouted "Hoch der Kaiser!" and there was a burst of laughter and applause.

But for that, casual and insignificant as it was, Jeremy Robson might have treated the matter tactfully, or jocularly, as did The Record. But that heavy, Teutonic mirth roused a dogged wrath within him. What he composed for a "box" on that evening's editorial page was unpleasant writing and extremely unpleasant reading. There were but few sentences, but they stung. And that which rankled was the suggestion that the insult to the State and the Nation was fittingly typified in the flag from that organization which had jubilated in wine and song over the murder of American women and children aboard the Lusitania.

Before the editorial had been out two hours there were rumors of a mob that was to be raised against The Guardian. Jeremy returned to the office. So did Galpin; also Verrall, white with consternation and chagrin over the reckless challenge of the editorial which could not fail to prejudice the circulation and advertising of the paper; and a dozen other of the staff. At eight o'clock the rhythm of marching feet sounded, and the tumult of voices. Five hundred undergraduates from Old Central massed in the street before the office and gave the University's three times three for The Guardian and its owner. The rumor had come to them. They were there to tackle any mob that arrived seeking trouble. None materialized. The students stayed and sang and cheered until midnight, and then dispersed. More than the protection offered, to those of The Guardian, was the proof that Young America at least was still American to the core, without taint of doubt or hyphen!

The mob-rumor had been a canard. Organizations such as the Deutscher Club do not raise mobs. They sit in solemn conclave, when action is called for, and appoint proper committees. Insult gross and profound having been offered Fenchester's leading social organization, its president summoned the Board of Governors, which in turn appointed a Special Committee with instructions. The first act of the committee was to advertise a liberal reward for the "apprehension of the criminal miscreant"—to such heights of expressiveness did righteous indignation run—who had filched the club's flag. The second was to send a sub-committee to call upon Mr. Jeremy Robson, owner and responsible editor of that libertine sheet, The Guardian. Chance may or may not have dictated that two of the committee, Arnold Bla-

sius, the hatter, and Nicholas Engel, the local grocer, should be important local advertisers. The chairman was Emil Bausch.

Forewarned of their coming, Jeremy had Andrew Galpin on hand.
The two young makers of The Guardian, shirt-sleeved and alert, received
the black-coated delegation of clubmen, formal and accusing, into the
inner den.

"We have come to demand a full retragtion," Emil Bausch opened
the ball.

Unhappily, since his first interview with that dignitary, Jeremy had
been invariably afflicted with mingled exasperation and amusement
at Bausch's every action. The apostle of Deutschtum roused within
Jeremy an impulse of perversity which flatly refused to take the heavy
German seriously.

"All right. Go ahead and do it."

"Do what?" Bausch's eyes goggled at the editor suspiciously.

"Do what you came to do. Make your demand."

"I do do it."

"You make a formal demand on behalf of the Deutscher club for a
retraction of my editorial?"

"We do."

"Declined, with the editor's thanks."

Mr. Bausch's neck showed signs of swelling beyond the confines of
his collar. "You refuse to accebd the rebresentations of this commid-
dee?" he inquired, with a thickening accent.

"Don't know. Let's hear 'em."

The chairman produced from the official pocket a document which
he proceeded to render vocally. It was quite grave and awful in ver-
biage, and there was a great deal of it, rising through a spiral of where-
as-es to a climax of denunciation. At the conclusion the editor held
out his hand.

"If you please."

"You want this?" queried Mr. Bausch doubtfully. "What for?"

"For tomorrow's paper."

"You wish to publish it? Why?"

A glint appeared in Jeremy's eye. "It's so prettily worded," he explained with sweet simplicity.

Bausch turned the characterization over in his heavy mind. "Pretty," he said. "*Pretty?* I do not think—"

"He's making a fool of you, Mr. Chairman," broke in Engel, a little neat, nervous man. He turned on Jeremy. "You insult our club and now you insult us."

"Apropos of insults," retorted Jeremy: "what about this document that Mr. Bausch has just read so expressively? Murder seems to be about the only thing that isn't charged in it. Would you call that a testimonial of regard?"

"Consider the provocation," said Blasius. "Be square about this thing, Mr. Robson."

"Give me a chance," returned the editor promptly. "Don't begin by holding a gun to my head."

"The case is blain," stated Bausch in his heavy accents. "You cannot deny the editorial charching that we made a festivity over the Lusitania."

"Evidently not."

"We demand a retragtion of that."

"On what ground?"

"Because it was an outrache on a high-toned, representative organization, a private—"

"Wasn't it true?" Andrew Galpin's sharp-edged voice injected a new and brisker element.

"Huh?" The interrogation seemed to have been jolted out of Chairman Bausch's volume from somewhere below the Adam's apple.

"Wasn't it true that there was a dinner at the club to celebrate the Lusitania?"

"That is not the question."

"It's my question."

"It's the only question," put in Jeremy.

"You refuse to apologize—"

"For commenting on fact? Certainly."

"While we're on the subject," pursued Galpin, "isn't it true that

Professor Brender, of Old Central, came in when the dinner was half over, and gave you all hell for pulling such a rotten stunt?"

"Gott im Himmel!" muttered Blasius. He turned to Bausch. "Is that true?"

"That he said his heart was all for Germany, and that if submarine warfare was necessary to her success it must go on; but that the man who rejoiced over its necessary tragedies was a reckless fool who put every decent German-American in a false light? Isn't that true?" continued the restless voice of Galpin.

"Are you going to prind that?" muttered Bausch.

"The newspaper doesn't print everything it hears. If we could have verified it, we would have printed it, at the time."

"We shall come back to the point," said the chairman, recovering himself. "The Guardian editorial is an affront to a respected and valuable element of the community."

"We don't respect child-and-women murderers," flashed Jeremy, "nor those who honor them."

"It all comes to this, Mr. Robson." This was Blasius. "Is your paper for or against Germany in this war?"

"The Guardian is neutral."

"Neutral!" snorted Bausch. "A straddler."

"Is that editorial neutral?" demanded Engel.

"Not neutral as regards piracy," answered its writer steadily. "Neutral as regards legitimate warfare."

"Of which you are the jutch," sneered Bausch.

"So far as my paper is concerned."

Bausch returned doggedly to the charge. "The Deutscher Club is a private organization of gentlemen. For what goes on within its doors we are not resbonsible to any outsider. The Guardian has traduced and defamed us—"

"Sounds like an action for libel," interpolated Galpin. "Who drew that up: Judge Dana?"

Again the chairman gulped in unpleasant surprise. But he recovered and continued: "—and in the name of the club we demand a full and fitting apology—"

"Hold on!" cried Jeremy. "It was a retraction just now."

"Retragtion or apology," amended the baited chairman. "It is all the same."

"Quite different. A retraction admits an untruth. An apology merely says we're sorry."

"I guess either will do," muttered Engel uncertainly, perceiving that matters were not improving by discussion. "We'll leave it to you which."

Jeremy stood up significantly. "Neither," said he.

The other two committeemen led out their chairman whose Adam's apple, though pumping furiously, was missing fire so far as vocal result was concerned. Their excited interchange of views died away in the hall.

"I guess we've invited Old Miss Trouble in to tea this time, sure," observed Galpin.

"You didn't tell me about the Brender outbreak, Andy."

"You were away at the time and had enough troubles, anyway. We couldn't get it in any such shape that I dared print it."

"Wouldn't Brender talk?"

"Tried him. Tight like a clam. Murray, who was assigned to tackle him, said he looked like a man who had lost something."

"His country, maybe," surmised Jeremy.

"Ay-ah. I wouldn't wonder. I tell you, Boss, there's a type of German-American that is going through hell and out the other end before this thing is over. Me, I'm glad I'm not one!"

"I'd rather be that kind than belong to the Bausch species, though. Let's start a Back-to-Germany movement in The Guardian, Andy, and nominate Bausch for the first departure. Wouldn't that nominate us for the Suicide Club!"

"Don't trouble yourself, Boss. The Dutchers will save us the trouble of suicide, if they can."

And on the following day, he bore the news of the first attack to his chief.

"Boss, prepare! The blow has fell!" he proclaimed tragically.

"Who's been denouncing us now?"

"Worse. We're excommunicated. The Deutscher Club has expelled the paper from its sacred precincts. Out we go, lock, stock, and barrel: bell, book, and candle. Two whole copies lost to circulation at one swoop."

"Mild, Andy, mild! Verrall's got a list of thirty-seven quits by this morning's mail. He'll die of heart-failure superinduced by bad circulation if you and I don't stop running this paper into the ground."

"Verrall's an earnest soul," observed the general manager, "but he's always on the borderland of hysteria, and if an advertiser looks cross at him, over he flops."

"Yes. He had an attack this morning. Blasius is out."

"Entirely?"

"Five inches double; three times a week. Gone glimmering into the jaws of Hun ruthlessness."

"Anyone else?"

"Threats of reduced space. If only they dared, Andy, what wouldn't they do to us! But they need us in their business."

Confirmation in part of Verrall's dismal forebodings came from Arthur Betts, of Kelter & Betts, who dropped in to see Jeremy. Since the first struggle with the Retailers' Association, Betts had proved himself a "good sport," as he would have wished to have put it, in admitting The Guardian's right to editorial independence, which did not in any measure inhibit him from trying to "put one over" on the paper whenever he thought that he saw a chance. That was part of the game. Though usually worsted, he sometimes succeeded in landing a bit of free advertising. But, like a sound opponent, he had become a strong partisan of Jeremy as against the field.

"You sure put it to the German lot in that editorial," he observed with a shining eye.

"They had it coming to them," returned Jeremy.

"Right! But they're sore clean though. Any cancellations?"

"Blasius."

"Yep. He's a dachshund all right. Do you know what they're stirring up in the Retailers' Association?"

"No."

"This is rank treason and betrayal of secrets and so on; but they're talking down your circulation. Are you losing much?"

"Some."

"Enough for 'em to demand a lower rate?"

"They can demand. They won't get it. We've got a comfortable margin left."

"Well, of course I'm for it, officially. Here's another point. Some of our customers are beginning to talk to the salespeople and department heads about The Guardian. 'Do you advertise in that paper? What do you do that for? It's no good. Waste of money. I wouldn't believe a thing I read in it, not even an ad.' You know the line of stuff."

Jeremy did know it and knew how dangerous it was. "Who are they?" he asked.

"Hans, Fritz, and Wilhelm," grinned the other. "They aren't scaring us. But you may get a kick-back from some of the other stores that are timider than we are."

"I'll keep an eye out, Betts," said the editor.

Thus the anti-Guardian campaign simmered, bearing testimony to a steady fire and a slow boiling beneath the surface. Said Judge Selden Dana to Montrose Clark:

"Our young cub of The Guardian is getting in wronger every day. I think a polite call is about due."

## 26

DEUTSCHTUM MOVES SLOWLY, BECAUSE it moves methodically. No general and open manifestation against The Guardian had followed the Lusitania editorial. None retaliated for the attack on the "Surrender Bill." But, little by little, there became apparent a guerilla warfare upon the paper. Manufacturers of certain products widely circulated in the State, particularly beers and soft drinks, began to withdraw or decrease their advertising. In every instance it was noteworthy that these concerns bore German names. Furthermore, small and casual advertisers of Teutonic cast of name and mind—For Sale, Want Ads, and the general line of "classified"—switched from The Guardian to the more amendable Record.

Despite all this The Guardian made a clear and pretty profit in the busy year of 1915. Ups and downs marked the course of its circulation, but the general tendency was upward. The Retailers' Association had given over any hopes of a successful drive against its advertising rates. Indeed, the best they could look for was that there would not be another increase. Success, however, had entailed special expenses. A new press had been installed. The working force was increased. An active and discontented element in the press-room, led by Milliken, had compelled an expensive readjustment of the wage scale, and the combative Socialist was already lining up his men for another raid. Thus Jeremy had found it expedient to renew from time to time the twenty-thousand-dollar note at the Drovers' Bank. No difficulties had been made over the renewals. Nor was the owner of the paper much concerned with the matter. From the time that his property had turned Prosperity Corner into Easy Street, to adopt Andrew Galpin's term, Jeremy had been content to leave the business and financial details to the general manager and Verrall, reserving himself for editorial problems. Even Verrall, of the twittering nervous system, was now ready to admit that the paper was winning and would soon be an established property, if Jeremy would tactfully refrain from further and gratuitous depredations against Teutonic sensibilities. Verrall did not appreciate, to the full, the unforgiving tenacity of Deutschtum.

Fortunately for Jeremy Robson, the campaign for the State offices of Centralia, in the fall of 1915, took precedence over everything else in the public mind. The reelection of Governor Embree on the anti-corporation issue was all but conceded. But it was not the issue that insured him victory. The solid German vote did that. Orders had gone forth to the German-language press that Governor Embree, even where special conditions made it impracticable to support him, must be recognized as an authority on international complications and a statesman of national caliber. For Embree's reelection meant that he would be next in line for the Senate vacancy, three years hence, and Deutschtum needed sympathetic souls, such as it deemed Martin Embree to be, in the high places of government. The real fight of the old-line crowd was for control of the State Legislature. For this they were quite ready to sacrifice their gubernatorial candidate, one Tellersen, a stock war-horse of the political stables. A safe representation in either legislative house would mean that Embree's pet corporation measure, aimed specially at the P.-U. and its branches, but affecting all railroads in the State, was scotched. It might even mean that the Blanket Franchise Bill could be put through. As a further safeguard to corporate interests, the P.-U. intended to put forward, later, its own legal adviser for a place on the Court of Appeals bench.

The campaign drew the Governor and Jeremy Robson closer together than they had been since the Lusitania editorial. Where no vital matter of principle was involved, The Guardian was quite willing to keep off German toes. On his side, the campaigning Governor consented to emphasize Americanism while still maintaining his attitude of sympathy for the sentiments of the German-Americans. Embree won by a large majority, the German districts giving him a preponderance of votes which gravely troubled Jeremy when the figures were analyzed. But on the legislative side it was conceded that only the brilliant campaign of The Guardian in Fenchester and The Journal in Bellair had averted a signal defeat. Widespread "trading" of the German-American vote had favored the P.-U. plans. So close was the result that, when the figures were all in, no man could say which side had won. Taking both houses together there were at least ten indeterminate votes. Plainly the battle for control of the State would be fought out in the spring session between the corporation interests, locally represented by Montrose Clark and Judge Selden Dana, and the radicals led by Governor Embree. Through that winter Jeremy, scenting the lesser battle from afar, cried "Ha-ha!" editorially with frequency and fervor, relegating the greater cause to the background for the time. Herein he was honest enough, as well as politic. He believed that the action and course of the United States was in abeyance until the people should have opportunity of making themselves heard in the presidential decision of the upcoming year. Hence he was content to wait, always providing that no major issue imperatively called for an expression of policy. For a time, too, Germany seemed more inclined to respect the dictates of humanity[1]. Locally, Jeremy found the atmosphere clearing. The Governor's triumphant reelection had pleased and appeased the Germans, and they were inclined to accord a certain measure of credit to The Guardian. Jeremy was sensible of an improved temper in many members of the Deutscher Club as he met them casually. But Blasius was still out of the paper; Stockmuller as well. And Emil Bausch, when he encountered Jeremy on the street, became absorbed in the contemplation of the Beautiful as exemplified in cloud-shapes.

Virtuously unconscious of any backsliding or suspicion thereof, Jeremy was surprised at being made the target of a direct attack by Miss Letitia Pritchard, whom he was passing with a bow on Bank Street one March day of 1916, when she held him up with a lowered umbrella.

"Mr. Robson, have you gone over?" she inquired, her eyes snapping fire into the query.

Naturally, Jeremy asked what she meant.

"I've been taking The Guardian again ever since the Lusitania editorial, because I just had to have an American newspaper in the house. Are you still that?"

"Do you doubt it?"

"Could anybody help but doubt it!" challenged the vigorous lady. "Politics, politics, politics! Nothing but stupid politics! Don't you know that the greatest war in history is coming closer to use every day?"

"I hope not closer to us."

"A fool's hope! Do you know your Bible, Mr. Robson?"

"Not as well as I ought."

"Better read it more. Those writers weren't afraid to speak their minds in a good cause."

At the ugly adjective Jeremy flushed.

"But that's beside the matter," she pursued, twinkling at him suddenly. "I came across a quotation that the Deutscher Club ought to send you, suitably illuminated. Isaiah, 14, 8; the last sentence. Look it up."

"I will," promised the editor.

"And you can come and tell me how well it fits," she threw back at him over her departing shoulder.

Important telegrams claimed Jeremy's attention on his return. Having disposed of them, his mind reverted to Miss Pritchard's suggestion for a Deutscher Club quotation for him.

"Buddy," he said to the industrious Mr. Higman, "look up the fourteenth chapter of Isaiah, copy the last sentence of the eighth verse and bring it to me."

Protesting under his breath that this was no time for Sunday-School exercises, Buddy interrupted the composition of a Social Jotting, and set about the errand. When he returned there was a pleased expression upon his face. He presented his chief with a slip of paper thus inscribed:

"Since thou art laid down, no feller is come up against us."

"What's this, Buddy?" demanded the chief sternly. "I said the Bible."

"That's where I got it," returned the appreciative Buddy. "Some of those old guys could sure sling the up-to-date stuff."

"Bring me the Old Testament." Jeremy looked up the text and, to his surprise, verified the exact words. But when he saw the context he laughed. And that evening he made one of his rare calls.

"Isiah is no prophet so far as The Guardian is concerned," he declared to Miss Pritchard. "And the style of that sting rings familiar. Where did you get it?"

"It was written on the margin of an old Guardian."

Jeremy raised questioning eyes to her face. Miss Pritchard nodded.

"Yes," she said. "She was back in Berne when that was sent."

"All right?" Jeremy was conscious that his voice was less *insouciant* than he could have wished.

"Quite. She will go back to Germany after the war, I suppose."

"Will you give her a message for me?"

"If you wish."

The dry, slightly hesitant tone meant, "If you *will* be so foolish."

"Tell her for The Guardian," said Jem, "that this feller hasn't laid down. Tell her that he won't lay down"—he paused, and then completed the paraphrase—"though Hell from beneath is moved for him to meet him at his coming."

"Put that on your editorial page," said Miss Pritchard, with a thrill in her voice. "I'd like Marcia to see it there."

"Perhaps I will when the day comes," he answered and took his leave.

It was the first message that he had sent to Marcia Ames since they had parted at the door of the Pritchard mansion nearly four years before. Every sense of her, every thought of her, was as vivid, unblurred, untainted by time as if she had gone from him yesterday: "the loveliness that wanes not, the Love that ne'er can wane." Now, even by so tenuous a thread as his impersonal message for The Guardian, he held to her again. And in his heart sang something lesser but sweeter than hope.

## 27

WORDS OCCASIONALLY TAKE EPIDEMIC FORM. Such was the course
of the word "hyphen" through the United States in the year 1916, with
its alternate phases, "hyphenate" and "hyphenated." Centralia, however, established a quarantine against the terms. They were checked
at the borders of the State. Where they did creep in and break out into
print, it was but a sporadic appearance, the references being both cautious and resentful that such a characterization should be allowed to
the license of an unbridled Eastern press. None was willing to admit
that the hyphen could be an issue in the future.

It fell to The Guardian to make the first use of "hyphenate" as a term
carrying a suggestion of reproach. Quite casually, indeed carelessly, it
was written in a sentence of no special import in one of Jeremy's editorials. Where bolder and more direct offense might have passed with
no more than the usual retaliation, this by-word was seized upon by the
enemy. It came in the more pat in that, since Jeremy's talk with Miss
Pritchard, The Guardian had assumed a more positive tone upon war
issues. Now the hyphenated press again fell upon him tooth and nail.
The Marlittstown Herold und Zeitung sounded the keynote in declaring that The Guardian, not content with playing England's game and
misrepresenting Germany's part in the war, had now descended to calling the loyal German-Americans foul names. "Hyphenate" didn't seem
to Jeremy a very villainously foul name. He was much inclined to dismiss the whole thing from mind as a petty excuse for renewed hostilities, had not the flood of letters in his mail apprised him that the chance
word had been salt upon the raw surfaces of the Teutonic skin. Select-
ing a typical letter, he replied to it in a moderate and good-tempered
editorial, pointing out that in the hyphen[1] itself was no harm; but that
essentially the Nation had a right to expect every German-American,

Irish-American, Swedish-American, or other adoptive citizen, to consider the interests of this country as paramount in any crisis. Far from soothing the exacerbated press, this seemed rather to inflame them. Their principles were not clear (other than that they were not to be "dictated to" by Jeremy or anyone else), but their temper was. That one misstep had landed The Guardian in a hornet's nest.

Just about the time when the buzzing and whirring were the loudest, Judge Selden Dana called to see Jeremy, and requested the favor of half an hour's uninterrupted conference upon a subject of importance. When the long-jawed, sleepy-eyed, crafty-spoken lawyer settled down to his topic, it manifested itself as the imminent fight in the Legislature over the public utilities bills. On behalf of certain clients, Judge Dana would be pleased to know what attitude The Guardian might be expected to assume.

"Don't you read The Guardian, Judge?" inquired its editor.

"Always. I may add, carefully."

"Then do you have to ask where we stand?"

"Circumstances change, Mr. Robson. Conditions also. Sometimes opinions."

"Changed circumstances or conditions might alter The Guardian's opinions. Is that the idea?"

"I suppose that The Guardian's circumstances are changed," murmured the lawyer.

Jeremy's easy smile vanished. "The Guardian is able to take care of itself."

"Up to a point. That I will concede. But, all things considered, would not the paper do well to make some friends now, instead of enemies?"

"That depends on the price to be paid."

"Small. Ridiculously small." Judge Dana spread out a pair of candid hands. "Mr. Robson, I'm not going to ask that The Guardian oppose the Corporation Control Bill when it comes up."

"Indeed!"

"Nor that you'll support the Blanket Franchise Bill."

"I appreciate your forbearance."

"But The Guardian has professed a profound regard for neutrality."

"As to the war only."

"Neutrality," repeated the lawyer, "as to the war. Whether you have practiced what you preach is another matter. Some of our most influential citizens and business men—*and* business men—appear to think not. I don't know," he continued with intent, "whether The Guardian's note for a considerable amount—say, well, twenty thousand dollars—would be considered safe today by the best of our local banks. I say, I don't know."

"There's very little you don't know, isn't there, Judge?" retorted the editor evenly.

"I try to keep informed; I try to keep informed." The long jaw relaxed a trifle. "Now, Mr. Robson, a reasonable neutrality as to these pending measures would be greatly appreciated by us."

"Appreciation is a vague sort of thing."

"Don't think you're going to trap me, young man," warned the visitor keenly. "I'm not here to make offers. Every man may have his price, but I don't happen to be fool enough to think that I know yours or could pay it if I did. I want to appeal to your sense of fairness."

Jeremy laughed, not unpleasantly. "Don't scare me, Judge."

"No. This is plain talk. The P.-U. intends to open up soon its extensive educational campaign of advertising, to instruct the public on these new issues."

"Through the newspapers?"

"Through the newspapers. Would The Guardian refuse that advertising?"

"I don't see any reason why it should."

"Very good. Would it accept the advertising and take our money in payment for value received, and then turn about and destroy all the value to us by attacking our arguments editorially?"

"Very ingenious," smiled Jeremy. "But we've been over that before, haven't we?"

"Not ingenious. Simple fairness. Isn't it?"

"Maybe it is."

"Then—"

"Then it's quite plain that we can't take your aids. In other words, Judge Dana, you can't buy our editorial opinions."

"See, now, how you divert my meaning," reproached the lawyer. "I've distinctly said that all we expected in The Guardian is neutrality."

"You can't buy our silence, either."

"What'll you take for The Guardian?" asked the lawyer abruptly.

"The Guardian's not for sale."

"It will be before the year's end."

"As a prophet you don't qualify, Judge."

"As a man who knows what is going on, I do. Figure out what the loss of the P.-U. advertising will cost you; the present advertising and the coming campaign. Figure on top of that the other railroad advertising affected by this strike bill of Embree's. Add what you're losing every day by your war-policy. Then figure out where you're going to get your next loan. After that, come and see me. Delighted to have you call at any time. Good-bye."

"Now, I wonder how much of that is bluff," Jeremy communed with himself, after his caller had left.

He had not long to wonder. The P.-U. contract was cancelled on the following day: a sure sixteen hundred dollars and a potential twenty-five hundred dollars a year. On top of that every railroad company advertising in The Guardian gave notice of withdrawal.

At least four thousand dollars more, gone. True, Jeremy might have brought suit, but the contracts were so loosely drawn that the issue would have been doubtful. As if by a preconcerted signal, various concerns in Bellair and the other large cities, which had been consistent patrons of The Guardian for years, dropped out. One chum manufacturing company was quite frank as to the reason. So much criticism had poured in from the German farmers, against The Guardian and anyone supporting it, that the concern deemed it wise to remove the cause of offense. Jeremy pondered upon the probability that the P.-U., represented for political reasons in the Deutscher Club by Judge Dana, was working with the hyphenate element to down the paper. He foresaw that he would need all his resources, editorial and financial, to weather the storm. No hope, for the present, of paying off that twenty-thousand-dollar note at the Drovers' Bank. Upon the heels of the thought, he recalled Dana's innuendo.

He went at once to the bank and asked for the president, Mr. Warrington. Mr. Warrington was gently regretful, but could not see his way to renew the note. No, not even for half the amount. Money was in great demand. Newspaper security was proverbially unstable. Finally: "One of our directors who is in a position to be informed strongly advises against continuing the loan." Knowing beforehand what name he should find, Jeremy looked up a list of the directors. There it was, "Montrose Clark, President Fenchester Public Utilities Corporation."

Pride, an excellent quality in an editor, is no asset to a borrower. Swallowing his, Jeremy made a pilgrimage of mortification to the offices of the P.-U. Corporation, where he presented to Garson, the hand-perfected secretary, his application to see Mr. Montrose Clark. Garson, discreetly and condescendingly smiling from above the carnation in his curvy black coat, said that he would see if it could be arranged. Thereafter Jeremy had leisure to do more swallowing, for he was kept waiting a humiliating and purposeful hour. Admitted, at length, to the presence, he went at once to the point.

"Mr. Clark, it is going to be very inconvenient not to have The Guardian note renewed."

The president of the P.-U. was no foe to time-saving directness. "It would be very inconvenient for us to have The Guardian misrepresenting the new franchise plan."

"That's not a franchise. It's a Hudson's Bay Company charter. It would give you the right to do anything from conducting a revival to raising beans on the right of way. It isn't even constitutional."

"Lesser legal authorities than yourself venture to dissent," returned the other, sardonically. "Such as Judge Dana."

"He's paid to."

"As you are paid for your partisanship, in circulation among sensation-seekers, and in the favors of that blatherskite, Embree."

"The Guardian stands by the Governor in this fight."

"Go to him for your loan, then."

"Am I to understand that unless I play the corporation game here, the banks are closed to me?"

"Not from anything I have said."

"*Said*: no. It's pretty plain what you mean. Well, the plant is good security. I can get money from the Chicago banks."

"Probably not," was the quiet retort.

It fell upon Jeremy's consciousness, with chill foreboding, that this might be true. Little though he knew of banking, he guessed that any large, out-of-town banks would take counsel of the local institutions before making a loan. What information would thus be elicited would hardly be favorable. He rose.

"All right, Mr. Clark. If you're going to fight that way, it can't be helped. The Guardian isn't going to back down. We'll fight you on your own terms, to a finish." The red face of the local great man grew redder. "With this difference, that we'll fight fair." The face turned purple. "I bid you good-day, sir."

"What do you mean by talking to me about fairness?" burst out the other. "You don't know what fairness is."

"Call it patriotism, then. If I were in your position, Mr. Clark, I don't think I'd care to make a deal with the Deutscher Club committee, to try and ruin a newspaper for daring to be American and not hyphen-American."

Montrose Clark bolted up out of his chair. "It's a lie," he roared.

"It's the truth. Ask Judge Dana. You're going to put him up for the Court of Appeals, I hear. Let me suggest that you read his record first. Or, you can read it later in The Guardian."

"Don't you threaten your betters, sir." Jeremy laughed. "Let me tell you before you go," pursued the exacerbated banker, "that I haven't forgotten your impertinence in pretending to expect me to trot around to your wretched little newspaper office."

Instead of annoying, this final flash of pettiness rather cheered Jeremy. After all, he reflected, on his way back, a man so small-souled could not be a very formidable opponent. Montrose Clark, he surmised, was powerful chiefly because nobody had ever boldly challenged his power. Nevertheless, Jeremy did not under-reckon the seriousness of his situation. Money the paper must have, and at once. By gutting his reserve and selling some high-grade stocks in an unfavorable market, he could pay off the note. But, in that case, The Guardian would have to continue on a shoe-string, and with obvious troubles looming ahead. He laid the problem in conference before Andrew Galpin and Max Verrall. Verrall, who for weeks had been prowling about the office with his pale and bony fingers plunged in his brickish hair, ready at any moment, one might infer, to pluck out some desperate handfuls, promptly made the same suggestion that Montrose Clark had proffered, though in a different tone.

"Go to the Governor."

"How would he have any spare money?" demanded Galpin.

"He can get it easy enough. His name on a note would go with any bank in the Northern Tier."

"No. That won't do," objected Jeremy. "We're too close politically. That would compromise The Guardian if it were ever known."

"Let him fix it up for you, then, without his endorsement," insisted the other. "I'll go up and see him now."

Arrangements were quickly completed. Nothing easier, the Governor had said, smiling. He had sent Verrall up to Spencerville with letters. All was concluded that evening. The Spencerville Agricultural Savings Bank would be glad to loan to Mr. Robson, on the security of The Guardian plant, any sum up to twenty-five thousand dollars. Verrall brought back the glad news in the morning.

"Too easy," grumbled Galpin. "Don't close yet," he advised his chief privately. "I'm taking a day off."

The general manager made a flying trip to Spencerville. On his return, he held a long conference with Jeremy, the upshot of which was that the Governor was warmly thanked for his kind offices, but informed that the loan would not be needed as another arrangement had been made. The other arrangement was a second-mortgage loan on the building for fifteen thousand dollars. This, they hoped, would pull them through.

Andrew Galpin had won his point by a silent exhibit of a snap-shot taken in Spencerville. It showed the obliging bank, with its front window bearing this inscription:

"Landwirtschaftliche Spar-Bank."

The lettering was German text.

Mighty was the clash of political lances, that spring of 1916, in Fenchester. Senate and Assembly alike rang with noble phrases and high sentiments. The mortal agony of a world across the seas, locked in a conflict which should determine the future of civilization, became a quite unimportant matter to those embattled souls on the hill. Let outer and lesser history take its course; it was theirs to decide whether the State of Centralia should or should not thenceforth emancipate itself from the rule of its former and uncrowned dictators. From the front pages of the local press, a committee vote was likely to evict an Italian battle, or an interview with Montrose Clark or Governor Embree take precedence over a peace-hint from Baron Burian. All of which meant, if you read The Record, that the radical and socialistic element were undertaking to slay the fairy-babe, Blanket Franchise,[1] and substitute the horrid changeling, Corporation Control; whereas, if you pinned your faith to The Guardian, it indicated the final struggle of an oppressed people to writhe out from beneath the heel of a conscienceless, tyranny of dollars. Amidst all this sound and fury Judge Selden Dana's candidacy, signifying much but saying little, was pressed. Only one reference had the Judge made to Jeremy's warning about his past record.

"Remember that libel is criminal as well as civil, my young friend."

To which Jeremy replied cheerfully: "Let us know when your formal announcement is made, Judge. We'll give you a good show."

"Agreed," said the lawyer. "And I'll give you some advertising, too. I've got to convert some of your deluded followers."

Already the advertising campaign of the P.-U. was in full swing. Part of it had been offered to The Guardian, in spite of Judge Dana's earlier threat. That had been partly bluff. The astute politician knew that an element, not otherwise attainable, could be reached with argument through the radical paper. Only with great difficulty had he persuaded Montrose Clark to this view. Said the public utilitarian, reluctantly according his assent:

"I haven't forgotten that that cub accused us of playing the Germans against his paper. I gave him the lie."

Judge Dana, who knew far more about the Deutscher Club's internal operations than he cared to have his principal realize, passed this observation with a non-committal smile.

"I'm going to advertise my own candidacy there," he pursued. "To get converts you've got to go after the other side."

After having prevailed upon the public utilitarian to adopt his view, Judge Dana was chagrined at having the proffered advertisements rejected by the owner of The Guardian.

"But why?" he demanded, his sleepy eyes lifted to Jeremy's with a candid and injured expression.

"You want too much. I remember your learned and able argument as to editorial forbearance toward advertisers, Brother Dana."

The lawyer shifted his ground. "Is it fair to deny the other side a hearing?"

"That's where you've got me," admitted Jeremy. "It isn't. But if I take your ads and then go after you editorially, you'll claim that we are double-crossing you."

In fact this is precisely what the ingenious Dana had purposed doing, through the lips of his campaign speakers. But he came back promptly with "The ads are offered without stipulations."

Jeremy considered. Setting aside the money consideration, the mere appearance of the P.-U. advertising in The Guardian would notably add to the paper's prestige, as an admission that its advertising pull was essential even to a hostile campaign. He very much wanted that advertising. Picking up a pencil he scribbled a sentence, conned it, amended, elided, copied it fair and full and handed it across to the other.

"Provided that every ad carries this footnote," he said.

Judge Dana read. "You young hellion!" he murmured, and grinned aslant and ruefully. He repeated the words on the paper. "This paid advertising is submitted and accepted without reference to what may appear upon the subject in the news or advertising columns of The Guardian."

"All right, isn't it?" asked Jeremy, in the tone of innocence.

"You young hellion!" said the Judge again, almost affectionately, this time. His double-cross accusation was gone glimmering. "I'll go you, anyway," he decided. "Do you want the same footnote on my campaign stuff?"

"No. That'll speak for itself."

"Let it speak fair. That's all I ask. And see here, young man. Twenty years ago isn't a fair basis to judge a man on."

"It is, if the man hasn't changed," Jeremy shot back.

At what was judged to be the psychological moment, the news was permitted to seep into the papers of the State that the eminent jurist Judge Selden Dana was being urged to become a candidate for the vacancy on the Court of Appeals bench. The method was sedate almost to demureness. Immediately there blossomed forth fragrant and colorful editorials, from all corners of the State to form a wreath for the blushing and débutante candidacy. These constituted an enthusiastic and determined public demand. Judge Dana urbanely announced that he would accede to it. The Guardian carried the announcement as news, giving it due prominence. Thereafter, for several days, Judge Dana, Montrose Clark, and a number of other important and interested persons, secured early editions of The Guardian each day with more interest than they would have cared to admit. When the attack did come, it was in such peculiar and indeterminate form that there was a general sigh of relief over a venture foredoomed to fall flat.

On his editorial page, Jeremy had "boxed" a double-column at the top, with what was obviously the outline of a half-tone photographic rectangle. But the interior was a blank. Below it ran the legend:

A CANDIDATE

(Fill in the Picture to Suit Yourself)

This was followed by one of the most biting poems from the grimmest volume of modern American literature, with the attributive line:

*From Edgar Lee Masters'[2] 'Spoon River Anthology.'*

I was attorney for the Q.
And the Indemnity Company which insured
The owners of the mine.
I pulled the wires with judge and jury
And the upper courts, to beat the claims
Of the crippled, the widow and orphan,
And made a fortune thereat.
The bar association sang my praises
In a high-flown resolution
And the floral tributes were many—
But the rats devoured my heart
And a snake made a nest in my skull!

Deeming this a flash-in-the-pan, the Dana partisans reckoned with-out the terrible power of allusiveness. Ugly memories rose to meet, iden-tify, and confirm the portrait. Day after day, Jeremy reprinted it, without comment. The press in other places took it up, and in an unbelievably brief time it had spread throughout the State, a strangleweed upon the growth of the candidate's tender young chances. Conferences were hastily called. Ways and means of curbing The Guardian's destruc-tive activities were projected, canvassed, and dismissed. Apparently there was no way either of "handling" Jeremy Robson, or of uproot-ing a poem once planted and spreading in the public consciousness. The candidate himself, depressed but philosophical, pointed the way out. A substitute, stodgy but honorable, was found, and the regretta-ble but timely return of an ancient liver trouble compelled Judge Dana to withdraw from the exigent demands of a political campaign to the seclusion of certain reconstructive hot springs.

What effect this might have upon the legislative fight, no man could foretell. Many thought that the Judge's candidacy had, in itself, impugned the P.-U. before the public. Certainly the leaders of the Blan-ket Franchise movement missed his shrewd judgment, for he would never have let them make the first move in a losing fight. In his absence Montrose Clark forced the issue. Embree's forces lined up against him, and beat the Franchise Bill in the Assembly by a round dozen of votes. Encouraged by this, the other side thrust forward Governor Embree's Corporation Control Bill as revised by Professor Rappelje. Now it was time for the public utilities of the State to rally to the last man, for this was a battle to the death. The Guardian did yeoman work in this as in the first action; but the weight of resources was on the other side. On the final vote the public utility interests won by a scant but triumphant margin of three. Thus the whole campaign had resulted in a draw. If Centralia had, on the one hand, repudiated corporation control, on the other it had balked at the radical measure put forth by the Governor. All that ground must be fought over again. The one clear triumph had fallen to The Guardian, in the ousting of Judge Dana.

How the Judge would take his enforced temporary exile was a speculation which sprang into Jeremy Robson's mind when, the smoke of the corporation battle having cleared away, he met the shrewd jurist, brown, hearty, and with no slightest liverish symptom, in the hotel restaurant. Would he ignore Jeremy's existence? The younger man gave him credit for being too sound a sport for that. But he rather expected to be held at a distance. Not at all. Dana came up and shook hands.

"Glad to see you looking so well, Judge," said Jeremy, and meant it.

"Liver isn't much if you take it in time," returned the other gravely. Then, "You still wield quite a lively pen, my young friend."

"As a weapon of defense, it's useful."

"Look out that the point doesn't turn in on you."

"Warning or threat, Judge?"

"Professional advice. Something I seldom give gratis."

"I'll bear it in mind. No ill-will, Judge?"

"Oh, I can take as well as give," answered Dana, who prided himself on never admitting and never forgetting an injury. "This is no kid-glove game. But I wouldn't have thought poetry had such a punch in politics. I'll have to look into that line a little closer."

As an example of what the Judge could give in return for what he took, there presently descended upon The Guardian a small but lively swarm of libel suits. All were traceable, directly or inferentially, to the office of Dana & Dana, a firm which did not ordinarily cater to this class of business. Four were wholly without merit; two were of the kind that can always be settled for a hundred dollars and counsel fees, and the remaining one hinged upon an unfortunate and ambiguous sentence in the tax-dodging charge against that aged but vigorous lady, Madam Taylor.

"Hold-ups, pure and simple," said Andrew Galpin indignantly. "Dana has drummed them up."

"Can you trace them to him? Safely enough so that we can print it?" asked his chief.

"Print a libel suit against ourselves!" said the general manager, scandalized at this threat against one of the most rock-ribbed principles of a tradition-choked calling.

"All seven of 'em. Tying each one up to Dana. No comment. The public will supply that for themselves."

The result more than justified the experiment. Dana & Dana, who had not considered the possibility of this simple *riposte*, hastily withdrew the four weakest suits, amidst no little public amusement. The other three, however, were pressed, causing a continual wear-and-tear of worry and expense, which was their object. Every charge against The Guardian's exchequer now meant less fighting power later when the test should come.

Politics succeeded politics in Centralia, meantime. Hardly was the legislative campaign over when the presidential election began to loom. Herein Jeremy found fresh source of difficulty and indecision. By training and natural affiliation he was opposed to the party of the President. In so far as The Guardian was committed at all, it was Republican in national politics, and more Republican than anything else in State. Undoubtedly the popular thing to do would be to enter upon a virulent attack against all the presidential policies. Embree urged this. It would go far to reconstitute the paper with the German-Americans who had already instituted the nation-wide campaign of the hyphen in favor of the President's opponent, taken by them on trust, as nothing was known of him in a world-political sense other than that he was a sturdy and fearless type of American. Possibly it was the very vehemence of the hyphenates that impelled Jeremy to a cool-headed course. Virulent he could not be; there was no venom in him. His first formal pronouncement upon the campaign was to the effect that the United States had never before had a choice between two alternative candidates of such high character and attainment; and this he heartily believed. The Guardian would support Hughes.[3] But it served notice on all and sundry that it would be no party to rancorous, unjust, and un-American attacks upon a President whose path had been more beset with difficulties and perils than any leader's since the day of Lincoln. In a State so violently preoccupied with political prejudices as Centralia, this course was regarded as weak. It lost support to The Guardian.

Throughout the ensuing campaign, Jeremy never seemed able to get his hands free from politics sufficiently to take up and develop a distinct attitude toward the deepening, threatening problems of the war. Embree deemed this fortunate. So did Galpin, upon whom the financial weight of the burden of conduct was heavily pressing. The fewer superfluous enmities The Guardian now stirred up, the better, to his way of thinking. Verrall was all for peace at any political price. But though the World-War was relegated to a place of secondary importance, in the main, it was not consciously neglected or belittled. Slowly there had grown up in The Guardian's environment the feeling that, after all, here was the one paper which was honestly undertaking to present the news as it developed. This helped to hold its circulation, even among those who bitterly resented its editorial attitude on the submarine, the bombing of defenseless cities, and similar war enterprises. So the paper won through the summer and fall of 1916, losing but little under the secret unremitting pressure of Deutschtum. When the President was reelected, Jeremy Robson spoke out frankly and clearly the mind that was in him, calling for a united nation to be ready for what events might come upon it.

Back at the base of Jeremy's hard-thinking brain there lay a lurking self-accusation. Had he not used the political stress as a convenient alibi? Had The Guardian truly stood on guard against the subtle and powerful inner war being waged across the hyphen? What of the promise, deadly serious despite its quaint Isaian twist, given to Marcia Ames? He sensed the looming conflict. He shrank from the terms of fulfillment to be exacted from him. But take up his pledge he must, when the hour came, though Hell from beneath were moved for him to meet him at his coming.

DUMBA[1] HAD GONE. VON BERNSTORFF was preparing for departure. The atmosphere which they had created under the cloak of diplomatic privilege was malodorous with the taint of plottings, corruption, and chicanery. Grain elevators were developing extraordinary tendencies toward spontaneous combustion. Munitions plants were dissolving into fiery fragments, in numbers beyond the reckoning of insurance-risk experts. Strikes were materializing in the most unexpected places and for the most unexplained reasons. An informal morning call upon a peaceful and businessless "advertising agency"[2] office in lower New York had laid bare to the heads of Government the extent of Germany's official treachery, and inklings of it were beginning to leak out to the public. Strident politicians were filling the atmosphere with irresponsible clamor. The American representatives of Deutschtum were frantically explaining, denying, palliating, sulking, or plotting. No corner of the horizon but bristled with imminent lightnings. The earth underfoot trembled with the rumble of coming events. So the old year of 1916 which saw civilization fighting with its back to the wall, the great bubble of Russian might and Russian nationalism already dissipating, France staggering though still resolute, England facing terror and herself the more terrible in that grim confrontation, the lesser nations opponent to Germany crushed to a mere welter of blood, the Hun savagely certain of his triumph, and on this side of the ocean, the United States being slowly, steadily, unwittingly, powerfully drawn and bound by the gossamer threads of a nation's psychology to the great purposes before it—so 1916 passed into 1917.

With it passed United States Senator Eugene Harter, of the State of Centralia. Time was when Senator Harter had been a useful figure in the Senate, rather by the possession of a vote than for any other and more forceful reason. But even his vote had been lost of late, for the exigencies of war-complications had terrified him and a nervous and overfed stomach had opportunely collapsed. The Senator fled to the tropics for surcease from troublous national questions and in search of health, and there encountered a mosquito in search of dinner. The mosquito being infected with one of the regional fevers, his victim passed, six weeks later, to that country where politics have been unknown since Lucifer's insurgents met their historical downfall. Thus was left as heritage to the Senator's already sufficiently bemuddled State a legacy of further complications, in that his successor must be elected in the early fall. Here was benign Fate moving to meet the welcoming smile of Martin Embree, well ahead of schedule. As soon as official decency permitted, he announced his candidacy for the senatorship. With his German following nothing, he believed, could defeat him. The path of glory extended, broad and unobstructed, before his eager feet to the Capitol at Washington; and thence—who could tell? His campaign prospered from the first.

Imagination could picture nothing less like a lion in Martin Embree's path of progress than the old man who, on a harsh March night of 1917, sat in a scholar's book-lined study, painfully writing. A bust of Goethe looked benignly down upon him. There were pictures on the walls of Schiller, of Lessing, of Beethoven, of Wagner, and the table was strewn with German publications. By every bond of the old man's lonely life, he should have been at the Deutscher Club, for good news of the great war had come through private channels, and the *brüdern* were meeting that evening to celebrate, in good German drink, and hearty German song, and sturdy German sentiment, the promised triumph. Though an American since early boyhood, Professor George Brender had grown old in these associations. He was a lover of sound Rhenish wine and of the noble literature of the mighty German poets, and of that tenderest and loveliest and simplest of all music, the *Lieder* of the Fatherland, and above all, of the close comradeship of the German-American clan. Tonight he was giving them all up. He had been forced to the sternest decision of his life. Quite simply he wished that he might have died before his seventieth year had set a sword in his hand wherewith he must now sever himself from past loyalties and fellowships. It amounted to that. For, torn to small fragments in his waste-basket, was a letter upon which he had pondered for a week; a letter from another German-American, a man wise and informed and clear of vision and of spirit, and that letter summoned him, in the name of a lifelong friendship, now to declare himself. From the first reading, he had known how the decision must fall. The Germany of world-domination, of the "will to victory," of the torn and dishonored "scrap of paper," of terrorism and the slaughter of the helpless, and violation of humanity's laws—that was not his Germany. To it he owed no real allegiance. As between it and his adoptive country he could no longer hesitate. He was an American. And as the first step toward justifying himself to his own soul, George Brender, Doctor of many degrees from Universities German and American, head of the German Department of Old Central, feared of its undergraduates for his caustic tongue, loved of its graduates for his leal and generous heart, had resigned from the Deutscher Club of Fenchester, with all that the action implies.

The gravest events of the cumulative international crisis did not more deeply stir Fenchester than the resignation of Professor Brender. Of such import to us human toads are the giant ripples upon the tiny puddles wherein we mightily splash! Rumors of the most violent and inspiring nature were passing from mouth to mouth before his letter was formally announced but verification of his intent had been wanting. Neither local paper had touched it, therefore. So the story grew and took on strange embellishments. Professor Brender had torn down the German flag from over the Deutscher Club door and resigned rather than be expelled. Professor Brender had called upon the Deutscher Club to rise and sing the "Star-Spangled Banner," and had resigned in fury when they refused. Professor Brender had denounced the Club as traitors and been thrown out bodily by President Bausch. Professor Brender was going to sue the Deutscher Club. The Deutscher Club was going to sue Professor Brender. Gossip, untrammeled by the responsible restraints of print, was having a gala day over the affair. Yet all that the old German scholar had done was to resign, on the ground that his sympathies must henceforth be American and not German.

Now he sat in his study, sorrowful and lonely, seeking to stem the tide of rumor by a plain statement to the press. He wrote in German, for thus his deeper feelings best expressed themselves, then translated into simple and gracious English. This is the letter of Professor George Brender, as offered to and refused (for reasons of policy) by The Record, but published conspicuously by The Guardian:

> I have grown old and gray in the service of the German tongue and German letters in America. One of the most vivid recollections of my childhood is the positive declaration of the German elders that I was not a German but an *Amerikaner*. On the other hand, the Americans were just as emphatic in their declaration that I was a German. Then the "hyphen" came to the rescue and I blossomed out into a German-American with a *dicken Bindestrich* (thick hyphen). Later I heard that the Kaiser had given it as his opinion that there were only Germans and Americans. The true Americans of my own country endorsed this point of view. So I concluded that I would have to make a place in the sun for myself.
>
> And now, with the snow gathering on my hair, I am an American only: nothing more (if there be such) and surely nothing less.
>
> In my American heart there is and always will be a shrine dedicated to that which came into my life from the soul of my father and mother. But they have long ago gone into the land from which no traveler returns and they have left a son who can love but one flag, although he has often nailed the Star-Spangled Banner to a staff of good solid German oak.
>
> I am now an old man, whose work is almost done. I cherish but one more great hope—that on the stars and stripes of my country's flag there shall ultimately be written the gospel which will redeem the world— the fatherhood of God and the brotherhood of man.

When he had finished reading that letter, Jeremy Robson dropped his head between his doubled fists and lost himself in thought. It was not pleasant thought. Self-reproach was a burning element in it. Here was a man German-born, German-bred, German by every tie of life except the profounder bonds of conscience and patriotism, saying to the German-Americans of Centralia, in no uncertain tones, that which he, the editor of The Guardian, had had in mind to say—when the time should come. And, behold, the time had come! Any hour in which a man great of soul and clear of vision to meet the issue would speak out, was the appointed hour. He, Jeremy Robson, despite all his good intentions and brave promises, had procrastinated and paltered and dallied, while another, with far more to lose, had lifted the banner and set it up for a challenge to the disloyal, the unloyal, and the half-loyal. A sorry enough champion Jeremy Robson seemed in his own eyes! Doubt of his own courage, smothered under the pressing emergencies of the past few months, lifted up a strident and whimpering voice. And that was a doubt with which young Mr. Robson could not live on any terms.

When the threat of war had loomed, with the dismissal of the German Ambassador, The Guardian had broached the project of a State Council of Defense in a plainspoken but moderate editorial. Further, it had urged it upon the Governor who, with unaccustomed vacillation, had evaded and procrastinated, arguing that the time was not yet ripe, and that the plan would needlessly complicate matters. Naturally the more rabid German press fell foul of it with their accustomed shrillness. Rather than embarrass Embree at the time, Jeremy had refrained from following up his first editorial, but had pressed the scheme upon the Governor by private persuasions. Now, in the stir caused by Dr. Brender's call to the flag, he would bring it out again. If necessary he would force it upon Embree, who could not well withstand a direct challenge to his patriotism. He sketched out three leaders on the topic; then put them aside and wrote the opening sentence of that editorial which was to declare unequivocally the status of The Guardian. Thus to declare was to declare war.

"The hyphen has two ends but no middle."

Mild to the verge of banality, in wording. Yet the writer well appreciated the high-explosive potency of that aphorism. Even without what followed, it would be taken up as a defiance, the first open defiance since Magnus Laurens's speech, to the German-Americans of the State. It would be the first step toward putting them on record. No one knew better than the owner of The Guardian that upon the editor who should first demand of the Centralia hyphenates that they declare themselves as for or against the United States, who should assume the initial responsibility for making the polyglot Commonwealth a house divided against itself in treacherous and deadly enmities, the united and deliberate vengeance of Deutschtum would fall in every practicable form of reprisal. Sharp as was the offense he had heretofore given, it was upon issues of minor import as compared to this. This was final.

When the emotions are deeply engaged, a practiced pen follows the thought of the writer almost without interruption. At the conclusion of his work, Jeremy read it over, altered a word or two, not in the way of modification as is the tendency of re-casting, but from weaker to stronger; then, after a moment's thought, resumed his pencil and with extreme care and neatness—as a young officer going into desperate action might meticulously brush and set his uniform—inscribed the caption, "Under Which Flag?"

He then did an unaccustomed thing. He made a complete tour of The Guardian plant. Why, he could not have said, at the time. Afterward he realized. It was the pride and satisfaction of proprietorship feeding itself. Beneath it lay the unvoiced monition, warning him that it might not be for long. Nevertheless, Jeremy was happy. He had been in a defensive fight for a weary length of time. Now, at last, he had hit out from the shoulder.

Transferred into typewriting at the hands (two-fingered at the exercise) of Mr. Burton Higman, the editorial had gone upstairs. It returned, galley-proof, in the hands of Nicholas Milliken.

"This yours?" he asked of the editor.

"Yes. Why?"

"Didn't carry any O.K. For today?"

"Yes."

Milliken lingered.

"Well?" said Jeremy sharply.

"Pretty hot stuff," observed the Socialist. "It'll start something."

"It probably will."

"Somebody pulled a couple of extra proofs on me."

"Somebody? Who?"

"Dunno. Only I don't want to be held responsible if they get out of the office in advance."

The proofs were already out of the office and on their way to the Deutscher Club, a fact concerning which Mr. Milliken probably had his shrewd suspicions, had he cared to voice them. But the hyphen editorial was not destined to burst upon the German-American world of Fenchester that day. For, at noon, Max Verrall entered the editor's den, his brisk eyes alight.

"Did the Governor get you?" he asked.

"No. What's up?"

"State Council of Defense.[3] He's going to put it through. I've just seen him."

"Good business!"

"Better call him up. He'll tell you more."

Jeremy did not get the Governor, but his private secretary verified Verrall's report. "Yes. I've been trying to get you. The preliminary conference is set for tomorrow at ten."

"Short notice," said Jeremy, surprised.

"Call's gone out over the wires. Will you come to the Capitol this evening to talk it over with the Governor?"

Jeremy assented. He imparted the good news to Andrew Galpin, whom he had sent for to run over the hyphen editorial. "The State Council of Defense is going through, Andy."

"'Smiling Mart' has climbed off the fence, has he? Or did we push him off?"

Jeremy frowned. "Nobody pushes Martin Embree."

"All right, Boss," conceded the other good-humoredly. "He can certainly push himself ably when the occasion arises. I reckon this is part of his push for the senatorship."

"Anyway, Andy, you'll admit that this State Council move proves where he stands on Americanism."

"I'll admit that," said the cautious Galpin, "when I see it—in The Guardian."

"He'll be all right," said his supporter with conviction, "now that the issue is getting clear."

"What about your editorial, now?"

"Well, what about it?"

"Hadn't that better wait a day or two? You don't want to muddy up the water unnecessarily. If the State Council move is on the level, your hyphen stuff will only make hard sledding for Embree."

"That's right, too. I'll put it on the hold-over hook."

Arriving at the Executive Office at seven-thirty, Jeremy was conscious of effort in the Embreean smile, conscientiously directed upon him. That fine wave of the gubernatorial hair, too, so suggestive of uplift in its stressful rise from the broad, even forehead, seemed to droop a bit. Smiling Mart Embree looked like a man who has passed the night in a sleepless torment of the mind.

"Any late news on the wires?" he asked anxiously.

"A little. All of one kind."

"Pointing toward war?"

"War," said the editor gravely.

"There must be some way out!" The Governor lost himself in a maze of thought. "This is a terrible thing!" he muttered bitterly.

"It was bound to come."

"A terrible thing," repeated Embree, "for me."

"For you?" Jem stared, startled at the out-cropping of egotism.

"For all of us," hastily amended the other. "For the Nation."

"I'm not so sure. It may be that we needed it, to save us from ourselves."

"What is one to do? How is a man to tell what course he can safely take?" said the Governor, pursuing his own line of thought.

"It isn't exactly a time for Safety First, is it? There's only one course for a decent American."

"That's so like you," fretted the other. "You see your own side and nothing else."

"What else do you see?"

"I see this great State of Centralia which has chosen me for its chief official," retorted Embree with a touch of that exaltation which, his enemies sneered, invariably crept into his speech when it dealt with his political self. "I see it torn and racked from end to end, and aflame with hatreds, dissension, and distrust. I see all the long fight that I've made—that we have made—against corporation control of the State gone for nothing in the new political issues. Have you thought of that?"

"Yes."

"Well?"

"It doesn't matter."

"Not matter!"

"Not if we go to war. Nothing else matters then but ourselves and Germany. We've got to think of the country as a whole and of ourselves just as a part of it."

"Oh, I'm for the country!" proclaimed Embree. "Of course! But I'm not for this war if it can be avoided."

"It can't be."

"Not by any such hot-headed, reckless course as The Guardian is laying. You're doing everything but yell for war and the blood of your own neighbors."

Jeremy's lip protruded obstinately. "Is that the view you take of it? We'll do more tomorrow."

"For God's sake, Jem! What has got into you? How can you commit yourself to such a policy of savagery?"

"This isn't going to be a polite war, Martin. But if I'm a savage, at least I'll be an American savage; not a German savage. That's all we're committed to in The Guardian."

"That's too much. It isn't the time for it."

"Not when every national right has been violated?"

"Forget your newspaper rhetoric and listen to common sense. Jem, will you be discreet for once in your editorial life?"

"I doubt it."

"This is deadly serious. Listen: Congress is going to hear from the country. Appeals are going to be made—"

"Which country?" asked Jeremy with intent.

"Try to be reasonable about this," pleaded his friend. "These appeals are going to pour in on Washington, to stop while there's time."

"More German propaganda. You've answered my question."

"The demand of a peaceable people for peace," controverted the

Governor heatedly. "At the same time the newspapers all over the country will be urged to use their influence toward keeping us out of a war that can mean nothing but injury to their business. We'll show that blundering fool in Washington—"

His visitor stiffened perceptibly in the chair. "Are you speaking of the President of the United States?" he demanded.

"Oh, between four walls," Embree deprecated. "Since when did you swing around to the Schoolmaster?"

"Since he gave the word to close ranks."

"He's never given it. His whole attitude is a big bluff. The only danger is that the hot-heads will make capital of it. He doesn't intend to go through with it."

"You're wrong there."

"If he does, he can't do it. Congress has the final word. And Congress is responsive to the newspapers. Now, Jem, when the arguments from the other side come to The Guardian—"

"We're being swamped with 'em already; machine-made letters to the editor, fresh every hour from the Deutschtum factory."

"Give them a fair show. Publish them."

"I'll see them damned first!"

"Neutrality!" commented the Governor acidly.

"War!" retorted the owner of The Guardian.

With an obvious effort "Smiling Mart" summoned his beam from out the gloom and set it on guard again.

"When it comes to the pinch you'll find me as ready to fight as anybody," he asserted. "The only difference between your position and mine is that I want to be perfectly sure it's right and inevitable."

"The State Council of Defense is a long step in the right direction."

"It mustn't be too long a step, though," the Governor pointed out. "It's defense, not offense, that's our purpose. By the way, do you know that there is an old act of the Legislature empowering the Governor to appoint such a body?"

"Fine!" said Jeremy heartily. "Then you can do the whole business at tomorrow's meeting."

"Yes; but I thought it advisable to have the formal approval of a

State-wide representative body, such as I've called together, for the moral effect—and the political," he added.

"You've made it non-partisan?" asked Jeremy.

"Yes, yes! Of course! And representative; representative of all classes. To make it so I've been obliged to include some of the German element."

"Certainly. That's all right, as long as they aren't the 'Deutschland über Alles' lot."

"Some of them, I'm afraid, don't like you much; or you them. Now, Jem, don't go off at half-cock," he added persuasively as the other looked up at him with a gleam of discomposure. "I can't ignore my best political friends and supporters, can I? And you know we have no solider, more influential citizens than our Germans."

"But what about their loyalty?"

"Don't expect too much of them right now. They'll be all right when the test comes."

The editor thought it over.

"Yes; I get your point. If you go back on 'em now they'll slaughter you for the senatorship." In spite of himself, "Smiling Mart" Embree winced. "Well, a few of 'em in the conference, or even on the council, can't do any harm; in fact, it may serve to bring 'em around, unless they're too far gone. A lot depends on whom you appoint chairman."

"What's your idea on that?"

"Magnus Laurens."

"Why a corporation grafter?" challenged the other, eyeing him narrowly; "and one that's always fought us and may fight us again for the senatorship?"

"He isn't a grafter."

"He's an associate of grafters."

"And if he has fought us, he's fought fair. Also, he's one hundred percent American. That's the big consideration in this matter. But if you won't stand for him, how about Corliess, of the Lake Belt Line. Cassius Kimball vouches for him."

Governor Embree stared. "First a water-power baron and then a public-utilities manipulator," he commented. "You're chumming up with some queer friends, for a radical, Jem."

"They're no friends of mine," retorted the editor. "You know that. But they're men we can trust to be right on this war question. However, anyone will do, provided he's big enough, loyal to the bone, and representative."

"Leave it to me, Jem," said the Governor with his warmest smile.

Returning to his den for the purpose of preparing an editorial boosting the new project as an accomplished fact, Jeremy saw a light in the business office. Amid ledgers and files of The Guardian sat Andy Galpin, figuring profusely upon sheets of paper.

"Hello, Boss!" was his greeting. "I'm trying to find out where we stand now."

"What do you make of it?"

"Hard sledding; but we'll pull through. Always supposing that the dam' Botches"—thus, now, did the general manager at once anathematize and Americanize that element whose solidity and good citizenship all political parties so warmly and officially endorsed—"don't lift too much of our advertising, in return for your few well-chosen remarks upon the hyphen. They'll be after us hot-foot, sure." After a pause he added: "They've been working on 'Smiling Mart.'"

"It hasn't done them much good so far."

"On Verrall, too. He's so far up in the air that his nose is turning blue. And something's up in the press-room. I think it's that big gorilla, Girdner. He's a Botch; belongs to their club. Milliken; he's another trouble-hunter. The Socialist. Wish I could pin something on him and fire him. Well, you've got troubles enough without that. Sorry I spoke. . . . Have a pleasant evening with the Governor?"

"Pleasant enough."

"Hope the morning will be as good," retorted Galpin, and hunched himself back into his calculations.

THE HYPHEN EDITORIAL SPENT the following morning on the hook. Its author gave it an affectionate and yearning glance as he passed early to his desk to touch up his substitute leader on the State Council of Defense. Once fully determined upon the casting of his verbal bomb, he was eager for the explosion and the resultant battle which should end the armed truce. But, as Andrew Galpin had said, fair play demanded that he hold off now, lest he hamper the development of the Governor's new plan. Any time was suitable for his challenge. Meanwhile copies of it from the stolen galleys had been circulated among the elect of Deutschtum, and a synopsis taken to Governor Embree. He had bidden his informants not to worry. There would be no occasion for the publication of that screed. A plan was already completed which would take care of Mr. Robson. It was observed that the Governor looked weary but optimistic.

Short though the notice had been, the invited conferees responded to the official call for a meeting upon the State Council of Defense plan, almost unanimously. It was a curiously assorted gathering that surrounded the long table in the council room, when Jeremy Robson arrived, a trifle late from his work of re-casting the day's page. That it was broadly representative was beyond denial. Yet as the newcomer reckoned it up, he felt a more than vague uneasiness.

Appropriating the nearest vacant chair he found himself between a down-state lawyer and politician named Lerch on one side, and Cassius Kimball, of The Bellair Journal, on the other. Next to Kimball sat State Senator Bredle from Embree's county, beyond him a lake-district dairyman of indeterminate political sympathies, and then Gordon Fliess, of the Fliess Brewing Company, the Lieutenant-Governor, an imposing and obsequious puppet of the Governor's, and Ernst Bauer

of the Marlittstown Herold und Zeitung. Bunched at the upper end
of the table were an ill-assorted trio of The Guardian's enemies, Montrose Clark, Judge Dana, and that anomaly of Teutonic type-reversion,
Robert Wanser, grandson of the Young Germany of '48.

In the other direction, the prospect was no less puzzling nor more
reassuring. Half a dozen men from the Southern Tier, a section unfa-
miliar to Jeremy, suggested a predominance of the Swedish type, which,
in Centralia, meant anti-war sentiment. Concerning the next figure,
tall, plethoric, ceremonially garbed, there was at least no uncertainty.
Emil Bausch's local letter-writing bureau of German propaganda[1] was
at that moment represented in The Guardian's waste-basket by half
a dozen grossly pro-German and subtly anti-American communications to the editor. Bausch had for neighbor that fire-eating Seminar-
ian, the Reverend Theo Gunst, next to whom, in turn, sat Arthur Betts,
of Kelter & Betts, looking uncomfortable but flattered. Milliken, pre-
sumptively representing the Socialist element, flanked him on the far
side with Girdner, appearing for Labor, on his left.

But when Jeremy's anxious glance finally reached the Governor's
high chair he breathed a temporary sigh of relief. In the place of honor,
on the right of the gubernatorial smile, sat Magnus Laurens. Surely
that indicated an acceptance by Embree of Jeremy's argument; Laurens was to be appointed chairman of the council, after all. The Governor's left was occupied by Ensign, the millionaire absentee owner
of The Record. In a less crowded moment Jeremy would have given
some thought to this curious preferment. Directly across the table
from the central group there protruded loftily from between a pursy
judge and a northwestern corn-raiser, a figure tall, stiff, and meager, a
lean, hard-wood lath of a man lost in the dim, untroubled contemplation of an awful example of political portraiture on the far wall. Why
Professor Rappelje should have been included, Jeremy could not surmise, unless it was that Governor Embree could count upon him as an
unquestioning follower through thick and thin. In fact the whole composition of the meeting suggested that the summons had been apportioned with a view to safe control by the Governor.

To the watchful Jeremy it seemed that Governor Embree was nervous. The smile at the comers of the conciliatory lips was disturbed by a restless twitching. After an anxiously calculating glance over the assemblage he began to read from a typed sheet a preamble, concluding: "Therefore, I present for the consideration of this honorable body the following names to constitute the Centralia State Council of Defense."

The first nomination fell upon Jeremy's ears like a burst of thunder. It was that of Emil Bausch, chairman.

The second nomination fell upon his brain like a bludgeon. It was that of Jeremy Robson, vice-chairman.

From down the table he caught the confirmatory sneer of Montrose Clark. His eyes darted to Magnus Laurens, squarest and most honorable of enemies, and met in his face a wrathful contempt. Cassius Kimball leaned to him and whispered:

"First you knew of it?"

"Yes."

"He's put it over on you."

Jeremy sat in a daze. His mind was confused by the suddenness of the thrust; his will was blurred. Instinctively he felt that he must do something. But what? Protest? Decline to serve? Announce his attitude? And already his time was past! The monotonous, fateful reading had gone beyond him.

Wanser and Fliess, Kimball, Laurens, ex-Governor Scudder, Montrose Clark, the Reverend Theo Gunst, Lieutenant-Governor Maxwell, Ensign, Bredle, Girdner, Ivanson, the Swede, and so on with the German and pacifist element always slightly but safely in the majority. Not a word was spoken, except once when in a brief breathing-pause someone shot out, like an arrow through the tense quiet, the contemptuous monosyllable:

"Packed!"

Jeremy thought that he identified the voice as that of Judge Selden Dana. Then the reader pronounced the name of Professor Harvey Rappelje.

"Wait!" said that gentleman.

"Order! Order!" protested Wanser and Bausch with suspicious readiness.

"I am in order," retorted the economist, rising in his place to confront the Governor opposite.

The Governor smiled, but thrust out a nervous tongue and licked the corners of the smile. The professor's face was as set and still as a frozen river, and much the same color. Embree, motioning with a placating hand for silence, resumed: "The Honorable Carter N. Rock—"

"Wait!" The scholar's keener voice cut off the reading. "I rise to a point of order, sir."

"State the point."

"Governor Embree, is that your honest conception of a council to fight this war?"

"Out of order!" cried Bausch again, and was reinforced by Girdner, Fliess, and others. "Who said fight?" "We are not making war." "Keep to the point." "Discussion is not in order." "Sit down."

But the hard challenge of the professor's glare compelled the Governor. "It is my carefully considered selection," said he with a suggestion of sulkiness.

There leapt from Rappelje's lips a blasting oath. From any mouth in that environment it would have been startling. From the lean dry, silent, repressed scholar it had something of the shock of nature's forces in outbreak. Not less appalling was the single word to follow:

"Treason!"

Embree's smile did not fade; but it shriveled into a masklike grimace, the rictus of a child before the convulsion racks it.

"You—you will retract—" he began chokingly.

Two astounding tears welled from the scholar's pale eyes, tears of a still man's uttermost fury.

"I will demonstrate to you," said he precisely, "what it is to fight."

He launched himself across the table at the Governor's throat.

The steel-framed Laurens seized and forced him back; but not before Embree had collapsed into his chair. From his place, up the table, the Lieutenant-Governor, quite beside himself, squealed for a totally imaginary sergeant-at-arms. The corn-belt farmer, in thunderous tones with a wailing inflection besought any and all not to forget that they were gentlemen. Girdner, huge and formidable, had jumped to his feet. The white-haired, alert Milliken caught up a heavy paper-weight. Bausch was solemnly, almost sacrificially taking off his coat. A medley of voices demanded "Order!" "Throw him out!" "Arrest him!" There were all the elements of a lively and scandalous mêlée, waiting only the fusing act.

Laurens checked it with one sufficient threat. Brandishing the weighty official gavel of lignum vitæ, he stood, a modern Thor, in the unconscious pose and with the menace of the Berseker, and, in a full-throated bellow proclaimed:

"I'll brain the first man that strikes a blow."

Before that intimidation they dropped into their chairs. There was a ripple of the shamed and foolish laughter of self-realization as the strain eased. The warrior-scholar's neighbors, who had been holding him in his chair, felt his limbs relax, and mistakenly thinking his effort spent, released him. Instantly he rose.

"I apologize to this honorable body," he said with quiet courtesy, "and to the State of Centralia as represented by its chief executive. And, as a question of privilege preliminary to my resignation, I ask whether the list as read is to stand."

"I will not submit to be bulldozed or intimidated," declared the Governor huskily.

"The list stands?" persisted the other.

"It stands, subject to the approval of this body."

"Doubtless you can carry it," conceded the objector, ranging the assemblage with his clear and contemptuous glance.

"Vote," piped up an uncertain and tentative voice.

"But you would be well advised not to make the attempt."

Martin Embree conceived that the proper course now was to ignore this unforeseen assailant of his plan. "I will proceed with the reading," he announced.

"I beg your pardon," said the relentless and polite voice. "One moment. You will have until this evening to withdraw your list."

"And vot then? Vot then?" broke in Emil Bausch, thrusting upward a truculent face.

"Do you want civil war in this State?" challenged Fliess.

"If necessary," retorted Rappelje, and stared him down with a steady and intolerable eye. He turned again to the Governor. "Unless that list is withdrawn before night, Martin Embree," said he solemnly, "so help me the God of my country, I will raise the University and hang you to the highest tree on the campus."

He made a stiff, formal, absurd little jerk of a bow and marched from the room.

"By gosh! He's the boy could do it," confirmed Milliken in an unexpectedly cheerful chirp.

"Finish the reading," said somebody weakly.

"Vote! Vote!" came a mutter of several voices.

No vote was taken. Under the corroding acid of the professor's passion the fabric of that meeting's purpose dissolved. The session did not adjourn. It disintegrated. Jeremy Robson stood irresolute as the groups edged past him.

"Congratulations, Mr. Vice-Chairman," purred Montrose Clark. It was the first time since the interview about the note that he had conceded the fact of the editor's existence.

"Bad politics, my boy! Bad politics!" said Judge Dana, his head wagging with reprehension, but a malicious twinkle in his somnolent eyes.

Cassius Kimball set a friendly hand on Jeremy's shoulder. "Pretty shrewd of old Martin, eh?" he observed. "But we can square that, among us. Let me know what you want The Journal to do."

Jeremy nodded his gratitude, but did not move. Laurens was the man he wanted to see, to set himself right before. Moreover, with him as leader a counter-stroke could be planned to bring Embree to his senses. The viking form strode toward him.

"Mr. Laurens," began Jeremy, "I want—"

"Stand out of my way!" warned the magnate, and swerving not an inch from his stride, he jostled the other aside. But for Kimball's quick interposition Jeremy's fury would have launched him upon the insulter.

"Steady!" soothed that experienced diplomat. "You come outside with me, and cool off."

"No," said Jeremy, mastering himself. "I've got to wait. I've got to see the Governor."

"But has he got to see you?" inquired the other suggestively.

"He has," said Jeremy with grim positiveness.

Governor Embree had closeted himself with Wanser, Bausch, and Fliess. He sent out word that he would see Mr. Robson in half an hour.

Jeremy telephoned to Andrew Galpin to hold the editorial page make-up open. He strolled to the window and got an unpleasant shock. Montrose Clark, Judge Dana, and Nicholas Milliken were standing in earnest conference, near one of the park benches. The Socialist, the public utilitarian grafter, and the legal manipulator! It came back to Jeremy's mind that, according to Galpin, there was a leak of information from The Guardian office to the Fenchester Public Utilities Corporation. Milliken was perhaps the go-between, unlikely though such an association might seem, at first thought. He would speak to Galpin about it. Meantime he had another editorial to outline, and set about it, seated at the table across which the first real action of the war in Centralia had just been fought to an indeterminate result.

A buzz of guttural voices inside the door interrupted him. Glancing at the clock he was astonished to see that it marked twenty minutes of one. The half-hour had grown into more than an hour. An inner door opened and the waiting man heard Smiling Mart Embree's weary but clear-toned "That can wait, gentlemen." The Germans passed Jeremy, Wanser giving him a civil word and Bausch nodding sardonically, as one might to a none-too-welcome accomplice by compulsion.

"Come in, Jem," summoned the Governor, and the editor of The Guardian advanced to confront his longtime friend, aide, and ally.

ADMIRATION WAS JEREMY'S FIRST impulse as he faced Martin Embree. The man had so quickly and surely recovered his poise. Serenity was in his tired smile, and the assurance that from Jeremy he would have understanding and sympathy. To destroy that childlike and beaming confidence was a thing smacking of brutality. Jeremy fought off a temptation to temporize and went to the point at once.

"Why did you appoint me vice-chairman without consulting me in advance?"

The Governor's smile became both confident and confiding. "Because you're the man for the place. We need you there."

"Or because you thought it would tie my hands."

"Tie your hands?"

"Keep The Guardian quiet."

"The Guardian has to keep quiet, anyway. It's the only course open to it."

"Is it?" said Jeremy significantly.

"Isn't it? Reason it out for yourself. Either we're going to get into this war or we're going to keep out of it."

"We're going to get into it."

"I don't believe it. But admit that we are. Until we're in it, it's our business, those of us who have influence, to use it in keeping peace at home."

"While the Germans at home work out Germany's plans."

"Bosh! Germany's real plans are to keep this nation at peace. She doesn't want us in the war. And we certainly don't want to get in."

"No. We don't want to. But we're being forced to."

"Wait until the real underlying public sentiment asserts itself."

"It's asserting itself now."

"No, no, Jem. Jingoism always makes the loud noise. But jingoism isn't Americanism. The one thing America won't do is to go into a losing war."

"We can make it a winning war."

"If it were truly our war, we could. But the people aren't for it. They never will be for it. Now look at the situation in this State, in the light of what is coming in Europe. Germany is sure to win. This State splits about even now between German sympathizers and the others represented by the pro-British and those who don't really know where they do stand. Only, the Germans have got the solidarity and the others are divided."

"You're right in that, anyway."

"Very well. After Germany has won, it'll be all pro-German here. That's our American way of it. We're all for success. Then where will a newspaper be that has taken the losing side?"

"Can't you see, Martin, that we're practically in the war now?"

"Jingo talk! If the capitalist crowd could drive us into it we'd be in now. It's the duty of good Americans, and particularly of every American newspaper, to stand solid against it."

"Is that the principle on which you appointed your State Council of Defense?"

"Of course it is! I've drafted a body of men who can be trusted not to rush us madly into this damnable mess. That's our real, our best possible defense—to keep at peace."

"Very pretty sophistry! How far do you think it would go with a real American? Harvey Rappelje, for instance?"

The Governor's eager face darkened. "That crazy fool!" he blurted out. "Who could have foreseen that he'd break over!"

"He did what each of us ought to have done in his turn."

"Don't say that, Jem!" implored the other. "I'm about beside myself over this Rappelje business now."

"Afraid?" Jeremy looked at him curiously.

"Of his mad-dog threat? No."

"Yet the boys at Old Central would follow him in anything. Curious that such a type should take hold on the youngsters' imagination, isn't it? It's the fire at the heart of him, I suppose."

"The maggot in his brain!" returned the other fiercely. "He's crazy enough to try his mob scheme."

"If he tries, he'll carry it through."

"Against a company of the National Guard?" said the official contemptuously. "I could have them here in ten minutes."

"That would mean bloodshed."

"It's what I dread. Some of those young idiots might be killed."

"And their ghosts rise up between you and the senatorship," pointed out Jeremy. "If the charge of official murder were raised against you, it would kill your chances. Rappelje may have figured that out, though I wouldn't suppose he'd be so keen in politics."

Black shadows of brooding settled upon Embree's handsome face.

"I'll arrest that frantic fool of a professor," he muttered. "I'll arrest him now. Nobody can call me a traitor!"

Jeremy made up his mind, and struck:

"Can't they? Read tonight's Guardian."

"T-t-tonight's—Wh-wh-what!" stuttered Embree. "Jem! You're not going back on me?"

"Going back on you! Haven't you gone back on me? Haven't you gone back on the State? On the country? Didn't you pledge yourself to appoint a representative American Council of Defense? Where did you get your list? By cable from Berlin?"

"What are you trying to do? Provoke a fight?" retorted the other fiercely.

"Make you wipe out that council of Germans."

"I won't be bulldozed and blackmailed!" shouted Embree in the loud wrath of a weak man cornered.

"Then it's the lynching party and the end of you politically. We'll have an interview with Rappelje in this evening's paper. He'll talk. That silent kind always do, once they break over."

The Governor collapsed.

"Wait!" he pleaded. "Give me time to think."

He walked to the window and stared out toward the east—his Mecca—Washington. When he turned, his face was so haggard that Jeremy felt a stab of remorse; but Embree contrived to summon the fleeting wraith of that once bounteous smile.

"You've got me," he admitted. "I'll make another list. Wait while I outline it."

"No. I've got to go to the office."

"Come back here in an hour, then. I'll have it ready."

The hour Jeremy put in in outlining to Galpin and Verrall the probable new course of the paper. Galpin was grimly pleased.

"I knew we'd have to quit him."

"It's the end of the paper," prophesied Verrall, pale and shaken.

Governor Embree was almost his normal self with almost his normal smile, when Jeremy returned to the Capitol. His revised list was one which needed no defense. It was preponderantly American, though with many of the prominent German names left, it is true, and the addition of Professor Brender and another loyal German-American. Magnus Laurens had been substituted for Bausch as chairman. Jeremy's name remained as vice-chairman.

"Is that good enough?" asked the Governor.

"Yes. That's a real Council of Defense."

"Then The Guardian will stand for it?"

"To the finish."

Smiling Mart Embree swallowed hard and beamed anxiously upon the other.

"What about me?"

"No." The negative was bluntly final.

"My God, Jem! What more could you ask?"

"A leader who can be trusted to be American."

"This is the parting of the ways, then?"

"The finish." Something in Jeremy's throat was hurting him so that he could hardly speak. And he could not, for anything, look at Martin Embree. Then Embree made it easier for him.

"And after all the years I've stood by you!" he cried angrily. "You turncoat! You don't know what loyalty is!"

"I've got pretty definite notions as to disloyalty."

Embree seized a pen and crossed Jeremy's name off the revised list, with a pen that ripped through the paper.

"All right," said the victim evenly. "Who goes in as vice-chairman?"

"That's for me to say."

"You're still expecting The Guardian to support the council?"

Embree's throat contracted with impotent fury. "I'll put in Clarence Ensign."

An impulse of pity rose within the other. "You can't do anything with The Record crowd, Martin," he said. "How can they play your game? I don't suppose you're going back on your corporation policies."

"No, I'm not. But you—"

"Not a bit of it. We'll be with you on that."

"With me, after you've stuck a knife in me!" The conviction of having suffered unmerited wrong, ever at call in an egoist's soul, surged to Embree's pale lips. "You've sold out to the corporation gang. That's what you've done," he accused. "You've sold me out."

The bitter and withered face of the man who had been his friend oppressed Jeremy with a sense of tragedy.

"Good-bye, Mart," he said. "I'm sorry it—it had to be this way."

"You have cause. You'll be sorrier." The smile was a little crooked now, with a hint of fangs at the corner. "I'm a poor forgetter, Robson. Particularly when it's my friends who betray me," he added, calling out the last words after the departing visitor.

So there was no interview with Professor Rappelje in that evening's paper. Nor did any account of the vivacious proceedings of the conference appear. These the editor of The Guardian deemed to be confidential. Nevertheless, there was no dearth of interesting matter in that issue. The announcement of the State Council of Defense personnel stirred up hearty approval among a large element and grievous surprise and wrath in other quarters. Further to enrage the aggrieved Germans, The Guardian's clear challenge, "Under Which Flag?" retrieved at the last moment from the hook and double-leaded for emphasis, set the two ends of the hyphen to bristling mutually, and surcharged the air with more electricity than it could comfortably contain.

In its next issue, The Guardian sprang another sensation by formally forswearing its support of Governor Embree. Its leader for the day, under the heading "He Who is Not For Us is Against Us," established a local and definitive test of Americanism, and declared all other questions and issues subordinate to the critical interests of the Nation as a whole. The Guardian would remain steadfast to the internal policies and reforms which Governor Embree had instituted. It could not and would not support him for the United States Senate, believing, as it must, that to elect him would be to place a putative enemy agent in that body.

Martin Embree answered through the columns of The Record. The slanderous assertions of The Guardian, he stated, would later be cited for proof before the courts. The Record gave him two mildly supporting editorials, but did nothing to indicate an alliance. Thus Embree was forced to enter the crucial campaign of his political career without local editorial support. At the same time The Bellair Journal quit him.

The greater necessity was that he should keep himself before the public in the news. His projected libel suit against The Guardian would be one method. After considerable delay the suit was filed.

But here again the unlucky politician missed fire. Nobody paid much heed to his libel action. For, on the day when it was instituted, the patience of a long-enduring President and people broke and the Government of the United States of America bared the sword[1] between the flag and its insulters overseas.

## 32

How essential a prop Martin Embree's influence had been to the threatened fortunes of The Guardian, its editor was now to learn. Where, hitherto, the paper had offended, "Smiling Mart" had palliated, explained, excused, defended, spreading the soothing oil of his diplomacy with expert healing. Now the bland oil was supplanted by salt to rub into the wounds. At this, too, the Governor plied a master hand. The "firebrand" interview, given to the papers of the State, in which he solemnly and all but officially anathematized The Guardian as an incendiary and anarchical agency, rallied the forces of peace-at-any-price and helped to organize them for the ruin of The Guardian. This was in the interval between the establishment of the State Council of Defense and the declaration of war, a period when Centralia still blundered about in a fog of delusion, blindly discrediting the inevitable.

Vainly a few dailies strove to force the truth upon them; The Bellair Journal, The Guardian, a handful of lesser papers. It was to be read between the lines of the German-language press, exhorting their people to be firm of spirit and stand together whatever might betide, warning them that British agencies were in control of the Administration, openly flouting and vilifying the Government of the Nation at a time when politicians of all parties but the Kaiser's had forgotten every consideration but loyalty, extolling and exalting Germany, snarling at the military "pretensions" of the United States, appealing to racial divisions in a last-hour attempt to devitalize the war-spirit. But the Centralians, breathing the murky air of their pacifists' paradise, were in no mood to read between the lines. For them the assurances of the great bulk of their newspapers sufficed. These, either themselves deceived, or fearful of reprisals, or simply accepting that old-time tenet of the pander "Give the public what it wants," would not admit the possibility of this Nation's being drawn into the struggle. War? Those who prophesied it were fools playing with fire. They were in Wall Street's pay. They were traitors to a peace-loving people. And Centralia, for the most part, read and believed.

All that man could do to foster this creed, Martin Embree did. To do him justice, he did not admit to himself the imminence of the conflict. His was the type of mind, characteristic of the self-centered, which translates hopes into expectations and expectations into belief. On the whole he thought the time and opportunity favorable for a brief, preparatory campaign for the senatorship. On anti-war, pro-German sentiment combined, he felt sure that he could ride to victory, when the time came, atop the crest of an irresistible wave. He made a short speaking tour in the Northern Tier, where The Guardian as his representative organ had so prospered. Wherever he now appeared, The Guardian's circulation withered. He had but to quote from the "Under Which Flag?" editorial, with such intonations as he well knew how to impart, and the Teutonic fury of his audiences did the rest.

At home in Fenchester the paper showed a slight but steady loss of circulation. Verrall went about the office looking, as Andrew Galpin indignantly observed, "like a sob-sister on reduced salary." The circulation and advertising manager was frankly of opinion that The Guardian was done for. If the hyphen outbreak were not, in itself, enough, the split with Governor Embree was the final madness. Personally he maintained unbroken relations with the Governor. He did not despair, he told Galpin, of bringing about a practicable adjustment if not an actual reconciliation between The Guardian and Embree. How was the Governor to mature his senatorial plans without at least one important newspaper through which to express himself? he argued. The Bellair Journal, never reliably loyal, was now violently opposing him. The Record was out of the question on the political side. He needed The Guardian and The Guardian needed him. The thing ought to be fixed up—he put it squarely to Galpin. Couldn't it be fixed up?

Galpin, regarding him with a sinister eye, opined that it might, what time fried snowballs were a popular breakfast food in Sheol.

Since the publication of the fateful editorial the Deutscher Club had been, officially, mute. Even though, in a later effort from Editor Robson's pen, it had been invited to gladden the eyes of Fenchester by displaying the Stars and Stripes above its building, it made no retort. Neither did it display the Stars and Stripes. It was quietly busy with other considerations.

"The Botches are at it," announced Galpin one morning.

"What's their line of action?"

"Boycott. The Deutscher Club is running it."

"Old stuff, Andy."

"Not this. They've got a committee and an organized campaign."

"Print their names," suggested the editor with a cheery but baleful smile.

"In a minute if I could get 'em! They aren't so brash as all that. It's all very pussy-footed. Nothing to put your hands on legally."

"How are they working it?"

"House-to-house canvass, I'm told. That would fit in with our circulation returns. We're shy about eight hundred right here in town, Boss. They're claiming fifteen hundred."

"Claims won't hurt us."

"Don't you believe they won't! They're going to our advertisers. The Record is in on it."

"Naturally. They could use some added advertising space if they could get it away from us."

"They're getting it; a little. They'll get more if we hold up to our present rates. The Retailers' Association had that up in meeting again, and we'll probably hear one of their mild suggestions about a reduction soon."

"They don't get it!" said Jeremy angrily.

"No. If we let down now, we'll be on the slide. Besides, we sure need the money. Those libel suits of Dana & Dana are going to cost something. They're juggling 'em that way."

"Any other cheer-up news today, Andy?"

"No-o. Nothing special. We're up against a new paper contract. Verrall's looking after that. Something's going on under the surface in the press-room. Maybe the Deutscher Club has a committee at work there, too. I'd like to catch 'em at it—with a press-hammer handy," he concluded, licking his lips. "It wouldn't hurt my feelings at all to have to slaughter a few Botches."

"Well, you may get your chance. Andy, what would you do if war were declared?"

"Who? Me? Get out a special, with the American flag all over it, if it was at 3 A.M."

"That isn't what I mean. What would you do personally?"

The general manager's face fell. "Nothing. I couldn't. No good." He stretched his long and powerful arms and gazed at them sorrowfully. "Old lumber, Boss. They wouldn't take me." He touched his injured eye.

"No!" exclaimed Jeremy. "That's tough. Are you sure?"

"Tried it. No go."

"Tried it?" returned Jeremy, surprised. "How? When?"

"Went to Doc Summerfield. He's been down on the border. Knows the game. He said no go right away. Not a chance."

"So you did that," mused Jeremy with growing wonder. "You never peeped to me about it."

"Didn't want to bother you."

"I'm mighty sorry for you, Andy," said his chief. "But I'm mighty glad for The Guardian. We need you here. And we're going to need you worse."

"How's that?" The other looked up with swift suspicion.

"Andy, you could take hold and run The Guardian if—"

"Not by a dam' sight!" shouted Andrew Galpin. "*You* can't quit. Not now."

"But if it comes to war—"

"*This* is your war. You've got your fighting cut out for you right here. It's a dandy scrap if there ever was one."

"It isn't the same."

"Ay-ah! Sure it isn't. Hasn't got the headline stuff in it. 'Gallant Young Editor Goes to War.' Hey? Is that what you're after?"

Jeremy sat silent, disconcerted by the bitterness and anger in his associate's voice.

"You were going, if you could."

Again Andy winced. "That's different. You could run the paper without me—"

"Not for a week!"

"You're saying that to make me feel better about it. Jem, you *can't* quit. This is your job."

"Until a bigger one turns up."

"There isn't any bigger one," retorted his general manager with profound conviction.

In the ensuing days it seemed to the owner of The Guardian that there could be no more racking one. For, step by step, as war drew nearer, the revenues of The Guardian declined. The secret committee work of the Deutscher Club was as effective as it was quiet. Uncertainty in business conditions was producing a logical letup in advertising, and the boycott was borrowing impetus from this tendency. A committee from the Retailers' Association had approached Jeremy on the subject of a reduction of rates. He had retorted hotly upon them that they were making themselves the agents of an attack upon The Guardian because of its Americanism. Matthew Ellison had attempted to smooth matters over with a "business is business" plea; but Ahrens, of the Northwestern Stores, had sneered at The Guardian for making capital out of cheap jingoism, and the session had ended in taunts and recriminations. Its echo had followed in the loss of some minor advertisements. The department stores, however, could not yet bring themselves to abjure so valuable a medium, no matter how defiant its attitude. Business *was* business to that extent.

Meantime Jeremy, amidst all his worries and troubles, was conscious of a great and unwonted inner peace. He was doing his job as it came to him to be done. The present was engrossed in the fight, growing sterner and more demanding day by day. His future was clear before him. He knew what course he must steer. If The Guardian were driven upon the rocks, or rather if the submarines got her (he grinned with cheerful determination over this preferred metaphor), at least she would go down fighting, and the flag that she had flown would be caught up from the flood and carried on. Wavering and uncertain notes from that quaint herald-figure, heading its pages, were a thing of the past. At last it had "sounded forth the trumpet that shall never call retreat." And, when the crash came, he, Jeremy, could find refuge in his country's armed service. That was an unfailing comfort.

More potently sustaining, even, than this was the thought that the dear and distant and unforgotten reader of The Guardian overseas must, now and to the end, believe in it.

## 33

UNDER THE FAR SHOCK of declared war, the sovereign State of Centralia, unready and unrealizing, was rent and seamed from border to border with seismic chasms across which brother bandied threats with brother, and lifelong friends clamored for each other's blood. Politicians and newspapers, who live chiefly (and uneasily) by grace of public favor, stepped warily among racial pitfalls set with envenomed stakes. Having so befooled the public, and in thus doing lulled themselves to a false security, they were now in a parlous state, not daring to affront a nation in arms, fearful of the unmeasured power of their alien supporters, afraid alike of truth, falsehood, and silence.

But it was the dear-bought privilege and luxury of The Guardian in these great days to speak that which was in its owner's soul. Straight and clear it spoke, while for the first fortnight after the declaration the editor hurried about the State organizing the trustworthy newspapers into a compact league of patriotism, meantime living, sleeping, and writing on trains, in automobiles, in country hotels, those editorial battlecries that variously rasped, enthused, infuriated, or inspired, but always stirred and roused, the divided and doubting people of Centralia.

After the first stunned inaction and uncertainty of surprise, there crept through the German communities of the United States a waif word of strange import.

"Deutschtum is bent, but not broken."

From mouth to mouth it passed. It was spoken in German clubs and societies. It was proclaimed in lodge-rooms. Presently it appeared in print. Bauer's alien-hearted Herold und Zeitung published it once and again; first, cautiously, tentatively; the second time, building upon its own impunity, and the incredible tolerance of the stupid Yankees, repeating it as the text of an editorial word of good cheer for struggling

Germany—with whom the United States was at war! The Reverend Theo Gunst's religious weekly spread the rallying cry; and fervent theologians preached it in its own tongue from their pulpits. Soon it had permeated the whole German fabric of Centralia, with its message of aid and comfort to the enemy: "Deutschtum is bent, but not broken!"

And the Deutschtum of Centralia, unbroken and scarcely bent, set about fulfilling its vengeance upon The Guardian and Jeremy Robson.

The first attack was a blast of letters, signed and anonymous. Correspondence enough was daily piled upon the editorial desk of The Guardian to have occupied all of Jeremy's time had he undertaken to answer it. Most of it was denunciation, protest, warning, threat. Several weak-kneed politicians, followers of "Smiling Mart" Embree's political fortunes, had written pressingly for appointments, evincing in every line their perturbation lest The Guardian's course might compromise them in one way or another. One correspondent had contented himself with a spirited but unsigned free-hand drawing of a noose overhanging a skull and crossbones.

In the middle of the heap was a brief and simple note of commendation for The Guardian's course, from the hardest-worked, most sorely pressed and anxious man in America. It was headed: "The White House." All but this Jeremy shoveled into the waste-basket; then plunged into his work with renewed spirit. The anonymous threats had cheered him only less than the President's word. They showed that his work was striking home.

Uncertainty was what Jeremy found hardest to endure in those days. And the local advertising situation seemed to be about fifty-one per cent uncertainty, and the other forty-nine probable loss. Contracts both yearly and half-yearly were renewable on May 1st. There appeared to be an almost universal indisposition on the part of the local stores to commit themselves to any definite figures or estimates in advance. In the case of the German advertisers, or of the few which still maintained rancor against The Guardian because of its independence in business matters, this was quite explicable. But no such reasons applied in the case of the large majority which were holding off. Nothing in the way of enlightenment could be elicited from Verrall. He "didn't understand it at all." He'd "done his best." Business was "very uncertain." Probably that was it. They were waiting to see the effect of the war. If anyone should be in a position to make a guess, Verrall was the man; for he was spending enough of his time among the stores. At least he was certainly not spending it at his desk.

Extra work was thus thrown upon the overworked Galpin. No dependence could be placed upon Jeremy from day to day now. At any hour, the demands of State-wide newspaper organization were likely to call him away from town, and relegate to Galpin all of his duties other than the actual writing of editorials. There were mornings when the general manager would arrive at the office before eight o'clock to find three hours' work by his chief already completed and on his desk with a note: "Meetings at Fairborn and Rocola today and tomorrow. Back Thursday." To be obliged to handle part of Verrall's desk job also, in these circumstances, struck the patient and dogged Galpin as excessive. Besides, there were matters in Verrall's department which puzzled his tired mind.

After one of Jeremy's flying trips into the country, he returned to find Andrew sitting at Max Verrall's desk. Instead of responding to his employer's greeting, the general manager asked abruptly:

"Verrall was a sort of political pet of 'Smiling Mart's' when we got him, wasn't he?"

"Yes. Embree recommended him to me."

"He's quit."

"No great loss; he's been laying down on his job lately."

"He's been doing worse than that. He's been tying us up in a double bowknot. Boss, did he have authority to make print-paper contracts?"

"Yes; all supplies."

"Then God help The Guardian!"

"What's wrong?"

"He's contracted for our next year's paper at four cents and a quarter."

"Four and a quarter! That's half a cent above the market, isn't it?"

"All of that."

"What concern did he buy of?"

"Oak Lodge Pulp Company."

"Magnus Laurens's outfit! They never tried anything of the kind on us before. It looks queer, doesn't it!"

"Worse than that."

"But, see here, Andy. They can't make that stick. Half a cent above market for that grade of paper—"

"Which grade? There's the kink. Verrall's tied us up on a special quality."

"Good God!" said Jeremy.

He sat down heavily. A clean blotter on the desk offered him a field for calculations. For a few moments he busied himself with a pencil. When he looked up, his face was queer and drawn. Andrew Galpin waited.

"It'll be a pull, Andy," said Jeremy. "It'll be a hell of a pull! It'll suck the yolk right out of my surplus. But we can pull through yet if—"

"If what?" demanded the general manager, for his chief had stopped.

"If we can hold the big local advertisers."

Galpin looked down on his employer with sorrowful eyes. He cleared his throat, scratched his head, spat upon the floor, and was apologetic about it; hummed, hawed, and glowered. Jeremy regarded these maneuvers with surprise.

"Baby got a pin stickin' into ums?" he inquired solicitously.

"Oh, hell, Boss!" broke out the other. "I hate to tell you. They're on our trail now. The Botches' game is working. Ellison, of Ellison Brothers, is in your office waiting to see you."

Jeremy left for his own den and the interview.

Visibly ill at ease, the head of Fenchester's oldest department store rose to greet Jeremy, resumed his seat and proceeded volubly to say a great deal of nothing in particular, about the uncertainty of the business outlook and the necessity, apparent to every thoughtful merchant, of retrenchment. Adjured to get down to details, he painfully brought himself to the point of announcing that Ellison Brothers felt it best to drop out of The Guardian's columns.

"Just temporary, Mr. Robson, you understand," he said in a tone which assured his auditor that it was nothing of the sort. "We hope to resume soon."

"But, Mr. Ellison," said Jeremy in dismay, "there must be some reason for this. Is it our editorial course that you object to?"

The visitor began to babble unhappily.

"No, no, Mr. Robson! You mustn't think that. I—I quite approve of your editorial course. Quite! Personally, I mean to say . . . As a merchant—Well, of course, you have been a little hard on our German fellow-citizens. Haven't you, now? You must admit that, yourself . . . Oh, it's all right, of course! Very praiseworthy, and all that. Loyalty; yes, indeed; loyalty above everything . . . But for a business man—We can't afford—"

"Wait a minute, Mr. Ellison. How many of your German customers have given notice to quit you unless you quit The Guardian?"

"Oh, none, Mr. Robson," disclaimed the tremulous Ellison. "None—not in those terms."

"I understand, Mr. Ellison. And I'm rather sorry for you. Who are the boycotters?"

"Oh, really, Mr. Robson, I couldn't—"

"No. Of course, you couldn't. By the way, you're an American, are you, Mr. Ellison?"

The merchant drew himself up. "My folks have been in this country for seven generations. Why do you ask?"

"Just to be disagreeable," replied the other softly, and left Ellison to make what he could out of it.

Bad though this was, the owner of The Guardian comforted himself with one assurance. No store in Fenchester could do business by advertising in The Record alone, against other stores which advertised in both papers. Therefore, Ellison Brothers would soon discover, in the harsh light of decreasing trade, that they could not afford to ignore The Guardian. Unless, indeed, the other stores also—Before the thought was fairly concluded, Jeremy had seized his hat and set out to obtain instant confirmation or refutation of his fears. His natural source of enlightenment was the loyal Betts, of Kelter & Betts, but Betts was out of town. The next store was The Great Northwestern. There could hardly have been a worse choice from one point of view, for the Ahrenses had from the first resented The Guardian's independence, and, moreover, were members of the Deutscher Club in good and regular standing. But Jeremy was in a hurry. Friend or enemy, it made no great difference, if he could arrive at the facts. In the seclusion of his inner office, Adolph Ahrens bade his visitor sit down, with an anticipative smile.

"I ain't seen you," he said slowly, "since that elegant hyphen editorial, to congrach'late you on it."

This was Refined Sarcasm, according to the Ahrensian standard.

"The events since have backed it up," said Jeremy shortly.

"Must be great," surmised the other, "to be a big enough Smart-Allick to rough up decent folks' feelings whenever you want to."

"There was nothing in what I wrote to offend any good American."

"I guess you ain't the only good American in Fenchester! I guess I'm as good an American as you are, if I have got a German name. You ain't an American! You're a England-lover and a German-hater."

"Perhaps you haven't heard that we are at war with Germany, Mr. Ahrens," said Jeremy with rising color. "We've been at war for three weeks."

"Never mind your funny jokes with me! I know about the war. Does that make you right to insult every German—German-American, I mean? You think you got us merchants where you want us with your verfluchter— your be-dammt paper. Well, you ain't! Not anymore. I got somethin' to tell you about next year's contract."

"Tell it."

"I'll tell it, all right," jeered the other. "I'll tell you where you get off. Half of last year's contract. Not a line more."

"That's less than The Guardian's fair share."

"Surprisin', ain't it?" snarled the other.

"Yes, it is. Unless on the theory that you expect a decrease in your trade." Ahrens flushed.

"Not in our trade," he asserted; "in yours. The Guardian's a losing proposition."

"You know why it's losing—temporarily," replied its owner, keeping his temper.

"It's losing because it steps on too many folks' toes. From now on we don't need but half as much Guardian in our business. That's all."

"I see. This is our punishment, this half-space allowance."

"You can call it that if you like."

"Then, just to make it even, I'll throw out the other half."

"Wha-at?" gasped the thunderstruck merchant.

"You understand me, Ahrens. You're out—every line of you."

Ahrens became suddenly timorous. "Wh-wh-why?" he stammered.

"Because I don't take punishment lying down. Not from you, Ahrens. You're going to find out whether you can do business without The Guardian, losing proposition or not!"

He left the worried store-keeper and continued his rounds. Nearly everywhere he found the same prospect; appropriations cut from a third to a half, but mostly a third. Something definite was back of it. Of that he felt sure. But what it was he could not discover.

Enlightenment was waiting for him at his office, through the medium of Galpin. That usually self-contained person looked haggard. "Verrall has been here since you left, Boss."

"What did he want? His job back?"

"No. He's got another."

"Good riddance. What is it?"

"Boss, the cat's out of the bag. I don't know how they ever kept her in so long. Her name is The Fair Dealer; morning paper with Amalgamated Wire Franchise; scheduled to start next month. And she ain't a cat. She's a skunk."

"Who's back of it?"

"Can't you tell from the sniveling, canting, hypocritical name? 'Smiling Mart' Embree—damn his soul."

"So that's it," said Jeremy slowly. "That explains Ahrens's attitude. Of course they can get along with less space. And Ellison's. Wants to try out the new, and save money on the old. We might have known! Embree has to have a paper here for his senatorial campaign. If he gets us, on the side, so much the better."

"But does he get us?"

"It doesn't look pretty, Andy. I can't pretend I like the scenery. There isn't room for three papers in Fenchester. Somebody's going to get bumped."

"Maybe it'll be The Fair Dealer."

"All the Germans and the anti-war crowd will get in back of it. I shouldn't be surprised if Montrose Clark and his gang were financing it—to kill us off. If we can pull through this next year—But there's that print-paper contract pinching us. Any details about the new paper?"

"Verrall claims it'll start with twenty-five thousand circulation all over the State. He was in here this morning to see me about—well, about something else; and to give us the news of the new paper. I told him we'd print it when released; wouldn't give him the satisfaction of thinking we were afraid to."

"Right! If we've got to die we'll die game."

"It makes me sick!" growled Galpin. "Oh, I ain't kicking, Boss! Only it'll be a tough game if, after all our scrapping, right and wrong—and we haven't always been a hundred per cent right, you know—we get ours from a bunch of half-breeds and double-facers, like the Governor and his crowd, because we wouldn't straddle a hyphen."

There followed a thoughtful silence between the two. Then the owner spoke:

"Did Verrall make you an offer, Andy?"

"Kind of hinted round."

"How much did he hint? In dollars?"

"Oh, a little raise. Nothing much."

"I can't honestly say"—Jeremy spoke with an effort—"but what the new paper's a better prospect than this, as things stand. I think you ought to consider it carefully."

"That's your best advice, is it?"

"I guess it is, Andy."

Galpin wandered about the room, arriving by a devious and irresolute route at the door. He opened it, shut it, opened it again, stood swinging it with a smudged hand. "Boss," he said insinuatingly.

"Well?"

"Speaking as man to man, and not as employee to employer—"

"Don't bleat like a goat, Andy."

"—you can take your advice and go to hell with it. I stick!"

## 34

ANNOUNCEMENT OF THE NEW paper was not to be formally made as yet. Its projectors had other possible plans in mind. Already, however, its competition bade fair to be fatal to The Guardian. Simple mathematics proved to the complete dissatisfaction of Jeremy and Andrew Galpin that a store's advertising appropriation of twelve hundred dollars yearly, say, divided between two papers would give to each six hundred dollars revenue; whereas divided among three papers it would afford only four hundred dollars apiece. Therefore, quite apart from German boycott, The Guardian might expect a loss of thirty-three and a third per cent of the income from such advertisers as the department stores, which would naturally use all local mediums.

But in this case, the purity of mathematics was corrupted by complicating human elements not all of them adverse. Reports of the Ahrens interview had drifted through the mercantile world. It became known, too, that Ellison Brothers had dropped out of The Guardian; been "bluffed" out, rumor said, by pressure of Deutscher Club threats. The Germans, so the word passed, were now openly out to "get" The Guardian. As a gleam in the gloom Galpin was able to report one morning a cheering sign:

"We're beginning to get a little reaction from the Botches' attack. Remember the Laundry Association who lifted their contracts in a bunch early in the game?"

"Because we took Wong Kee's ad? I remember."

"They're back with the American flag over their copy. Lamp this, Boss."

The note he tendered was written in the most approved style of business-college condensation, and read as follows:

*To the Pub'r of the Guardian. D'r Sir*: A Chink may not be White but he is a Long Sight better American than any Kaiser-hound. Inclosed please find contract renewals.

Resp'y, for the Com'tee,
The Spotless Laundry.

J. Corby, *Prop'r.*

"At least we're making a few friends," Jeremy commented.

"The trouble is, they're not organized. Our enemies are. It's organization that counts."

Friends counted, too, however, in practical as well as in moral support, and they materialized in the least expected quarters. The Emporium, which since the early quarrel had withheld all but occasional special-sale advertising, now came in with a full contract. "And I take off my hat to The Guardian," said the obstinate and combative Peter Turnbull. "I've learned to do that when I see the flag passing by, no matter who carries it!"

Barclay & Bull restored their full original space and added to it. No comment accompanied the order. But Galpin went around to the store to explain that The Guardian understood and appreciated. Then there was Aaron Levy, of The Fashion, who had never forgiven The Guardian's attitude toward his installment trade. The dogged, hard-bitted, driving Jew came to The Guardian office and was received by Andrew Galpin.

"Mr. Galpin, I hear Ellison Brothers is out."

"Ay-ah. They are."

"What for?"

"Didn't you hear that, too?"

"I heard something."

"What you heard is right."

"Mr. Galpin," said Levy slowly. "I been running a two-inch three-time card in The Guardian."

"Yep."

"It ain't that I want to; but it brings trade. It's small; but it'd have been smaller if I could afford to make it. You know why."

"Sure."

"Now I hear there's a new paper coming in. I gotta go into that. That's business."

"Ay-ah."

"But I'm going to stay with you. That's business too. And I'm going to double my space and go in daily. That ain't business; but—but you know why?"

"I do not."

"Mr. Galpin, I'm a Jew. I was raised on kicks and crusts in Mitteldorf. I came here a boy and got a living chance. I'm worth fifty thousand dollars today. I can't fight, myself; but I'll help any man who fights the Germans, at home or over there. You have, maybe, all the fight you can handle, and more. Yes? Well, that's my help. No; you don't have to thank me. It ain't for that. I don't like you or your paper any more after the war is over."

He stumped out, leaving in The Guardian office a vivid contrast in practical patriotism between an Ellison seven generations in the United States, and a Levy, German-born and American-hearted.

Even among the Germans of a certain type the strange reactions of the war dissolved old enmities. Coming out of the Post Office one evening, Jeremy found himself approaching Blasius, the little German-born hatter, who had withdrawn his thrice-a-week announcement from The Guardian, after the Lusitania editorial. Upon sighting the editor, Blasius squared his shoulders to a Prussian stiffness, set his lips, and all but goose-stepped up to the other.

"I wish to say a word to you," he announced precisely.

"Say it."

"Those Deutscher Clubbers; they are after you—not?"

"They are. Are you?"

"Mr. Robson," said the hatter gravely, "while we are at peace I think of my good people in Germany and I hope we remain at peace. When we are at war once, I think of myself, a citizen of this United States; and I am at war too. As you are," he added. "And I want my advertisement back in your paper, double space."

"I'll be mighty glad to have it there, Mr. Blasius," answered Jeremy heartily.

"I thank you. This that I have told you I say to the Deutscher Club at their meeting. And what do they do? They fire me out! That is, I think, strainch," reflected the sturdy little hatter.

To Jeremy it did not seem "strainch." Men like Professor Brender and Blasius would find no fellowship in the Deutscher Club now. He knew too much, however, of the retentive power of Deutschtum to believe that the schism in the club would be important.

But for every patriot who came to the aid of the sorely beset Guardian with financial support there were ten who were swayed adversely by resentment or fear. Meantime expenses went merrily on, increasing as they went. The Guardian's surplus was already enlisted in the fight. Jeremy's small reserve was compromised. Even Andrew Galpin, against his chief's protest, had scraped up two thousand dollars which he insisted on putting in, as he blithely observed, "just for the hell of it." That, Jeremy prophesied discouragingly, was about all that he might expect to get out of it!

With true Teutonic effrontery, the propagandists of Deutschtum continued their attempts to use the paper whose ruin they were encompassing, until the inutility of this procedure was at length borne in upon them by the adverse experience of Henry Vogt, florist and heavy advertiser, who personally approached Jeremy with a long and thoughtful screed in the best Teutonic-pacifist style of reasoning. This, Mr. Vogt argued, with the assurance of an old-time patron, would well beseem the editorial columns of The Guardian. The editor thought otherwise. As a result of that difference of opinion the remnants of the Vogt advertising disappeared from The Guardian's pages just one degree less promptly than Mr. Vogt himself disappeared from its precincts. In a rather testily conceived editorial entitled "Local Dummkopfheit" Jeremy set forth the principles of his paper regarding propaganda. In response to this he received three threats of extinction, eleven of ruin, and two of unprintable language, which served to restore the level of his overtried temper.

While he was perusing this mail, his general manager came rambling in, with a queer light in his eye.

"Want to sell, Boss?"

"Sell what?"

"Sell out. Sell the paper."

"Tell me the rest of the joke, Andy, and get out. I'm busy."

"Joke nothing! We got a buyer. He's in my office."

"Is he violent?"

"Boss, it's A. M. Wymett."

Jeremy straightened in his chair. "Wymett! What's he doing here?"

"Wearing lovely clothes and looking prosperous. He *is* crazy, Boss. He wants to get back into the game." Two minutes later, the ex-proprietor of The Guardian was confirming this latter statement.

"Yes," he said. "The crave is in my blood. It's worse than drink. I've quit drink. But not the other."

"You've been back in it?"

"Mining journal in California. I made a little money at it. But there's no life in that. You're in a back-water. I want to get into the main current again."

"What made you suppose The Guardian was for sale?"

Wymett lifted the heavy brows above his weary, cynical eyes, as if with an effort. "Aren't you going into the service?"

"I may," said Jeremy shortly.

"Oh! I beg your pardon. I thought you were under thirty." The tone was courteous but indifferent. It stung.

"I'm over. A little."

"In that case you're not *obliged* to go, of course. Then you won't consider an offer for The Guardian?"

"I didn't say that." Jeremy's mind revolved many things swiftly. The Guardian's days were probably numbered anyway. If he could sell at a decent price now, he could retrieve part of his own fortunes and make a fresh start after the war. Besides, there was Andy and his hard-scraped two thousand dollars. No one could criticize him for selling out with a view to making the larger sacrifice and going into the army. But in his heart he knew it was the lesser sacrifice. He knew it would be a surrender, with a salve to his conscience; knew it and would not confess the knowledge to himself.

"Ah, well!" said Wymett's even, tired voice. "I wish I were young enough to get in."

Jeremy's head lifted. "When do you want an answer?"

"You gave me one hour," Wymett reminded him.

"So I did." Jeremy smiled. "Times have changed since then. Or you wouldn't be back in Fenchester," he added rather brutally.

"Tactful of you to remind me," returned the other, unperturbed. "People's memories are charitable—and short. Suppose we say tomorrow?"

"Three days," amended Jeremy. "That will be Monday. By the way, whom do you represent?"

"Myself."

"Of course. But who's behind you?"

"Ah! Is that wise?" drawled the other. "In the interests of your own unprejudiced decision?"

It was on Jeremy's lips to return a definite refusal then and there. But, after all, what harm in considering?

"The money will be forthcoming," Wymett assured him. "Shall we discuss terms?"

"Let that wait."

The other assented, and took his leave. By a roundabout course he made his way to The Record office, and there consulted Farley. The result of the conference was that A. M. Wymett contributed a trenchant and bitingly worded editorial to that evening's issue of The Record entitled "Lip and Pen Patriotism." It was conceived in the old and waning style of personal and allusive journalism, and contained pointed references to young men of means and sound physique who preferred staying at home and preaching the patriotic duty of others, to shouldering a gun and doing their own part. The shrewd, tired eyes had seen Jeremy wince under the sting of the war-query. Their owner judged that a little impetus might decide the matter. And Farley, for reasons of his own and The Record's, was only too glad to lend a hand toward getting Jeremy out of the way. He knew, what Jeremy only suspected, that Wymett in nominal control of The Guardian meant Embree in actual control, and hence two papers instead of three in Fenchester, as The Fair Dealer would then be dropped.

Had the writer of the editorial been present to mark the effect upon its unnamed subject, he would have been gratified. Jeremy cursed fervently. He then summoned Andrew Galpin.

"Andy, I'm going into the army."

"Ay-ah?"

"What do you think?"

"Going to sell the paper?"

"Might as well sell it as wreck it."

"Ay-ah?"

"For God's sake, Andy," broke out his chief; "can't you say anything but 'Ay-ah'?"

"I've said my say once."

"That was before we were surely down and out."

"I haven't changed my mind."

"I'm sick of a losing fight."

"Good thing there's folks in the world that aren't. The French, for instance."

Jeremy cursed again, wildly and extravagantly. "You're trying to make me out yellow!"

"Boss, your nerves aren't all they ought to be. Why don't you drop in on your doc?"

"I'm going right from here to Doc Summerfield's."

"Ay-ah? You *are* feeling shaky, eh?"

"No. I'm not. But I want to be sure that I'll get through all right on the physical examination."

"Ay-ah. I guess you'll do—physically." Andrew Galpin turned and left. His head was hanging. He looked like a man ashamed. Jeremy knew for whom he was ashamed. Again he cursed, and this time, himself. All the catchwords in the vocabulary of patriotism could not now exorcise that inner feeling of surrender, of desertion.

A figure emerged from a forgotten corner. It was Buddy Higman.

"I heard you," said the boy in a lifeless voice. "Are you goin' to quit?"

The final word flicked Jeremy on the raw. "I'm going to fight."

"What's goin' to become of us?" said Buddy simply. Jeremy stared at him without consciously seeing the open, freckled face of the boy.

What he saw was the letter of Marcia Ames in which she had committed Buddy to his care.

"Become of you, Buddy?" he said.

"Of us. The paper. It won't be us anymore with you out of it."

"No. It won't be," sighed Jeremy. "But I'll arrange to have you kept on."

The boy shook his head. "Nothin' doin'. She wanted me to have a job with you." Suddenly he brightened up. "Boss, could I have a half-day off tomorrow?"

"Take it all if you like. Looking for another place?"

The boy thanked him without replying. Jeremy went to Dr. Summerfield's office where he was duly stripped, prodded, poked, flexed, and stethoscoped by that slim, dry, brief-spoken physician. When it was over the doctor leaned back in his chair and contemplated his caller. "Want to get into the army, eh?"

"Yes."

"What for?"

"To fight, of course."

"Isn't there enough fight right here?"

"It isn't the same."

"Certainly it isn't. No flags. No ta-rum-ta-ra. No khaki, brave soldier-boy, hero-stuff. Eh?"

"I notice you went, fast enough. And you're going again, aren't you?"

"Different matter. I don't own a trouble-making newspaper. What are you going to do with it?"

"The Guardian? Sell it."

"To whom?"

"A. M. Wymett."

"He's a figurehead. What's behind him?"

"I don't know."

"Nor want to, I guess."

"I don't care."

"'I don't care,'" mimicked the physician. "You talk like a spoiled kid. Are you going to act like one?"

"I want to get in it! I want to get in it!" cried Jeremy.

"Or out of it? Which?"

"Doc, if you weren't an old friend—"

"You'd punch my nose. I know. You'll do 'most anything to prove to yourself that you'll fight 'most anything. Except the enemy that most needs your kind of fighting."

"I've been doing nothing but fight," said Jeremy wearily.

"And now you want to quit."

"I've had about enough of that word, quit."

"Somebody else been using it to you? Ugly little whippet of a word, ain't it! Well, you're not going to profit by it, at least not with any nice, little, heroic, ready-made excuse to comfort yourself with. That much I've just heard over the telephone."

"Telephone?"

"This one." He tapped his stethoscope. "Straight from Central. Were you in athletics in college?"

"Yes. Golf. Some football. Cross-country run."

"That's it; the distance run. Been under some nervous strain, lately, too?"

"Try to run The Guardian for a month and see!"

"Well, the college athletics began it, and overwork and worry have brought it out. Those endurance tests will get a boy's heart—"

"Heart! Have I got heart-disease? What kind?"

"Never mind the big names. Nothing to worry over. You'll live a hundred years for all of it. But it's there all right."

"I don't believe it."

"Try another physician, then, my spoiled child."

"I beg your pardon, doc. Of course, I know it's right if you say so. But it—it's—"

"Rather a soaker, eh? Don't let it worry you. You're sound enough to go ahead and raise any amount of Hades here, so far as your heart goes. I won't say so much for your nerves."

"It isn't that."

"No. I know. It's the being counted out." He wrote a prescription, looked up from it to study the silent and downcast patient, then tore it up and flung the pieces in the air. "I'm not going to coddle you with minor dopes," he declared vigorously. "Jem, I read The Record editorial this evening. How much did that have to do with your warlike ambitions?"

"It hurt," confessed Jeremy.

"It was meant to. Know who wrote it?"

"Farley, I suppose."

"And you call yourself a newspaperman! Farley's got the malice, but not the sting."

"Who did, then?"

"Wymett."

"Wymett?"

"I'd spot his style across the continent even if I didn't know he was here. Don't you see the game?"

"No."

"Wymett has come on at Embree's call. Embree is behind his bid for The Guardian. He'd rather buy The Guardian than start his new paper. Quicker and cheaper. Farley'd rather have him buy The Guardian than start the new paper; only one competitor in the field instead of two. Wymett sees he has you going; but he isn't certain. He borrows The Record's columns to force your hand. And you want to run away and play soldier!"

"I've got to! I've got to!" cried Jeremy, beating the arms of his chair with violent hands. "And now you tell me I can't."

"Steady! I never said you couldn't play soldier."

"My heart—"

"You're a border-land case."

Jeremy's face lighted with hope.

"You can get in all right. I've passed cases like yours. But let me tell you what it means. It means that you'll never see active service. It means they'll make use of your brains somewhere, in a perfectly honorable, perfectly safe office job where the only gunpowder you can ever smell is by getting to leeward of the sunset gun. Mind you; you'll get all the credit. You'll go marching away in uniform with Committees handing out flowers and tears and embossed resolutions, and everybody will regard you as a hero, except perhaps me—and yourself. You've got to reckon it out with yourself whether you'll put on uniform and shirk or stay home and fight."

Strangely enough, at this bald summons there stood forth in Jeremy's working mind two incongruous figures, each summoning him to judgment; Marcia of the clear, instinctive courage, and Andrew Galpin. Were they ranged in opposition to each other? Or were they not, rather, united in impelling him to the simple and difficult course? More strangely still, it was the thought of Andrew Galpin which predominated at the last; Galpin who, facing disaster and the ruin of his dearest projects with an alternative clear and easy and not dishonorable, had made his choice of the hard path and the forlorn hope, without so much as a quiver of indecision.

"I stick" he had said.

Jeremy lifted his head. He rose and held out a hand as steady as a rock in farewell, to Dr. Summerfield who bestowed a passing and self-gratulatory thought upon the stimulant effect of psychologic suggestion properly administered. The physician took the hand.

"Well," he said. "Which?"

"I stick," plagiarized Jeremy.

Andrew Galpin's relief when the decision was reported to him was almost pathetic. "Boss, if you'd laid down on this I was about through with human nature," was his comment. "And now, what's to come?"

Jeremy's lined face puckered into a cherubic smile. "The last trench, and a damned good fight in it," he said softly.

## 35

MR. BURTON HIGMAN MOUNTED the stairs of The Guardian office, dressed in his best suit of clothes. A powerfully inferential mind might have derived from his proud and important bearing that he had matters of moment on his mind; might further have deduced that he had been on a railway journey, from the presence of a cinder in his ear. He wore the air and expression, sanctified, as it were, all but martyr-like, as of one who, if he had not already died for his country, was at least prepared to. For young Mr. Higman had been performing that miracle, forever dear to dreaming boyhood; he had been saving the world. Such, at all events, was his own glorious interpretation of his enterprise.

The clock, pointing an accusing digit at V, was the only sign of life in the inner den. Buddy went to Mr. Galpin's office. Empty also. So there was none to apprise him of the Boss's final determination. A group of printers, scrubbed and clean, clumped down the stairs, still discussing the exciting rumor that somebody had bought out Robson; for every press-room is a clearing-house of gossip, technical and other.

"Hey, Buddy," one of them hailed. "Got a new job yet?"

"Good-bye the easy snap," added another. "The old Guardian's sold again."

"Much you know about it," retorted Buddy, stoutly and scornfully. But the statement struck a chill to his ardent soul. Could it be that he was too late? Surely the deal couldn't have been fixed up overnight!

On Mr. Higman's official desk was a heap of mail which, in size, would have done credit to a correspondence school. It was Mr. Higman's present professional duty, interrupted by his brief leave of absence, to sift out the anonymous communications, with special reference to those of a spicy and murderous character, and deliver them to his chief. To Jeremy's journalistic instinct, it had occurred as a sprightly idea to make up a special page for publication of these epistolary efforts. It would be interesting to his readers, and would serve further to enlighten them as to the extent and virulence of local German sentiment. Perhaps, too, it would check the flood. So Mr. Higman sorted and divided and contributed marginal marks, and finally delivered a large packet upon the editorial desk for the Boss's professional consideration, when he should return that evening, which, his young aide felt sure he would do, even though it was Saturday. Few, indeed, were the evenings that did not see a light in the den, close up to midnight.

Doctors' protests to the contrary, notwithstanding, Jeremy came back to the office that evening, after a hasty dinner. Overwork might be bad for that second-rate and shop-worn heart of his. Loafing on the job would be a thousand times worse. That was one thing which his temper positively refused to endure. As he ran through the pile of letters, terminating in such suggestive and enticing signatures as "Vengeance," "Outraged justice," "Member of the Firing Squad," "Old Scores," or (with appropriate and blood-curdling commitments) those old familiars, "X," "Y," and "Z," he realized that the threats were getting on his nerves. He was becoming bored, with an unendurable, deadly boredom, at their repetition. Nor could he deny to himself that they were affecting his actions, though in minor respects. For a week he had gone a block out of his way at night, not to avoid but to pass a certain unlighted alley-mouth wherein, so "Well-Wisher" and "Warned-in-Time," two (or perhaps one) depressing correspondents had informed him, in feminine handwriting, lurked his intended murderers. Silly though it was to pay any heed, he had to do it. He had to prove to himself the futility of any such intimidation. In vain had Andrew Galpin tried to prevail upon him to carry a revolver. It was the common-sense, reasonable, unromantic thing to do. Jeremy wouldn't do it. He wouldn't even have one in his desk. But there were times in the long solitary evenings at the office when the unexplained creaking of floor-boards, or that elfin gunnery carried on by invisible sharpshooters in the woodwork of old buildings during nights of changing temperatures, produced sudden effects upon his handwriting which the two-fingered typist, Mr. Burton Higman, subsequently found disconcerting.

On this Saturday evening, he had set aside nearly enough episto-lary blood-curdlers for his make-up, and was deleting certain anatom-ical references unsuited to fireside consumption from a rather illiterate but highly expressive letter, when he became aware that a draft from below was driving some papers along the hallway outside. A high wind off the lakes was making clamor through the street, but it had no busi-ness inside The Guardian building, and couldn't have got there unless someone had opened the front door. He listened for footsteps on the stairs. Nothing. He returned to his editing.

"Getting your throte cut some dark nigt is too Good for you," his correspondent had written, and suggested, in unpolished terms, dis-agreeable and lethal substitutes of almost surgical technicality.

Jeremy was Bowdlerizing these, when he stopped and put down his pen. The floor-boards in the hallway were creaking intermittently but progressively. Through the noise of the wind he thought that he could catch fragments of a whispered colloquy. Then, quite plainly, there was a retreating tread, which, however, left something. What? An infernal machine? Infernal machines do not linger, striving and forc-ing themselves to the determining action; theirs is a simple and direct method. And Jeremy could feel, through the noisy darkness, the strug-gle of a will, agonizingly fighting for expression, through dread. Him-self, he was not conscious of fear. But every nerve was tense. He sat looking at the door.

For what seemed an interminable time nothing happened. But the Something outside drew slowly, painfully nearer. The knob of his door moved, a thing suddenly inspired to life. Jeremy gathered himself. It turned. The door was drawn open swiftly. A blur came upon Jeremy's vision. His heart bumped once in a thick, dull way, then swelled intol-erably. He half rose, sat down again heavily. His eyes cleared and the clogged blood in his temples flowed again.

She stood framed against the stirring, whispering darkness beyond. Her breath came quick and light. She was white to the lips, and more lovely even than the dreams of her, cherished through all those ach-ing years.

"Jem," she said.

"Marcia!"

She made one eager step forward. A vagrant gust, ranging the darkness, caught the door and drove it savagely to, behind her. She threw a startled glance back. It was as if the impalpable fates had cut off the last chance of withdrawal.

"I have come back to you." The sweet precision of her speech was the unforgotten same, blessedly unchanged in any intonation. But wonder held Jeremy speechless. He stood, his hands knuckling the desk, and devoured her with his eyes.

"Will you not speak to me?" she said, with a quick sorrowful little intake of the breath. "You frighten me. You look so strange. Have you been ill?"

At that he came forward and took her hand, and drew out a chair for her. "Not ill," he heard himself say in a surprisingly commonplace voice. "Sit down."

She shook her head gently. "I can look at you better, standing."

Her candid eyes swept over him. She saw a face thinner and more drawn than she had remembered it; bitten into by stern lines about the mouth; the eyes tired but more thoughtful, and just over the temple nearest her a fleck of gray in the dark sweep of his hair. Involuntarily she put forth a swift hand and touched it.

"Oh, Jem!" she whispered with quivering lips.

He seemed to brace himself against her light touch. "That?" he said. "Oh, that isn't anything."

"How came it there?"

"Honest toil, I hope," he returned cheerfully.

Her inventory was completed with a smile. "You are quite as carefully turned out as ever," she commented.

"Habit."

"Oh, no! Not habit alone. Character. And you stand as straight and square as you used."

A curious expression came into the weary eyes. "Straighter," he said. "That's your doing, Marcia."

"How mine?"

"It's rather complicated and long. I don't know that you'd understand."

"Make me understand."

"Give me time. This has been—well, startling. I think I'm a little dazzled and—and dizzy."

And, indeed, Marcia Ames, as she stood there beneath the hard, revealing light of the overhead arc, was a vision to dazzle any man, and, taken on an empty heart, to make him dizzy. The years had fulfilled her; had added splendor to her compelling beauty without withdrawing that almost fantastically delicate and elusive challenge of youth. She seated herself, and Jem took his accustomed position behind the editorial table.

"That is well," she said lightly. "Is that how you receive callers on business?"

"Yes."

"Very well. I have come on business."

"Where did you come from? I can't quite believe it's really you—here!"

"From Chicago. Buddy brought me."

"Buddy Higman?"

"He came after me. He told me that you were in great trouble."

"He told you that I was going to desert the ship."

"Oh, no! Buddy is your loyal subject. The Boss can do no wrong."

"The Boss has reached the point where he isn't sure what's wrong and what's right."

"I am not afraid of that." There was an implication of pride and of proprietorship in the words which shook Jem's hard hold upon himself.

"Were you coming here, anyway?"

"Later."

"Then I should have seen you." He seemed to be puzzling out some inner problem.

"I had thought you would have been in the army."

"So I should, if I hadn't been told that I'm a useless bit of wreckage."

"Please! I know all about it. I have seen Mr. Galpin. Your war is here. If you had decided otherwise than you did I should—I should—"

"You're trying to make it easy for me," he accused.

"I should have come back to find another Jem from the one I have learned to believe in."

"To believe in, Marcia? How's that?"

"'Seein' 's believin','" she laughed. "I once heard Buddy's aunt give out that word of wisdom. I have been seeing The Guardian and reading it, and reading you in it, ever since the war."

"More than me. Galpin and Cassius Kimball; yes, and old Eli Wade, and others that have helped keep me straight. We haven't always gone straight, Marcia. There have been issues of The Guardian that I'd hate to have you see."

"But I have seen them. All."

"And you didn't lose faith?"

"I never lost hope that—that you would be what I wanted you to be. Jem, Mr. Galpin says that the paper is losing."

"It is."

"Can you go on?"

"For a while?"

"Could you go on if you had more money?"

"For a while longer. There'd be a chance of our pulling through. But only a chance."

"Will you take mine?"

"Great God! *No!*"

"Why not?"

"I tell you, it's almost sure loss. There's a new paper coming into the field—"

"You said just now that it was my doing that you—you stood straighter than you used. Did you mean The Guardian?"

"The Guardian. Myself. It's the same thing."

"Then does not that give me a right in the paper? A moral right?" she argued with bewitching earnestness.

"Granted. Put in anything you like but your money."

"Jem! Please!" she pleaded. "Will you not take it if—"

"Not with any if."

She rose and came to him around the corner of the table, and set her hand on his shoulder. Her eyes were steady, clear, courageous upon his, but her whole face flushed into a glorious shame and her voice shook and fluttered as she spoke again. "Not if—not even if—I go with it?"

"No," said Jem. But his face was like that of one in a mortal struggle.

For a moment there was a flash of fear in her regard. "Jem! There is not—someone else?"

"How could there be?" he said simply.

"How could there be!" she repeated with a caressing contentment. "I knew there could not be."

"There never could. How did you know?"

She stepped back from him. "By what I felt, myself." She laughed a little tremulously. "I should have read it in The Guardian. Between the lines."

"But—" he began. "There was—Miss Pritchard told me—"

"Yes," she assented gravely. "There was. It was a formal betrothal. But when I saw him again I knew that I could not. It was no fault of his—nor mine. I remembered," she said very low, "that night. That last night. On the bridge. Four years ago. My dear! *Was* it four years ago?"

Her eyes, her voice yearned to him, wooed him. Jem's knuckles were white with the force of the grip wherewith he held to the table.

"Marcia!" he began.

"It made no difference," she went on dreamily, "whether I was ever to see you again or not. I did not believe then that I ever should. But whether or not, there could be no one else. Some women are like that, Jem. 'Once is forever, and once alone!' I think a woman wrote that . . . And you have not even said I was welcome."

"I daren't!" he burst out. "I daren't tell you what I feel—what I'm struggling against. Marcia, I'm down and out."

"Does that matter?" she broke in proudly.

"It matters everything. I can't take your money. I can't ask you to marry me. There's nothing ahead of me."

"Mr. Galpin says that The Guardian is the one big, fighting energy—"

"Andy Galpin is a loyal fool. He's the best and finest and stanchest friend ever a blunderer like me had. Poor devil! He's put every cent he's got into the fight—"

"And you will not let me put in my share?"

"Share? Don't talk nonsense, Marcia. No."

"Not even a little part?"

"Not a cent!"

"And you will not even marry me?"

"No," groaned the sorely beset Jem.

"Very well. I think it very hard." There was a palpable, even an exaggerated, droop to the tender and mobile lips; but in the depths of Marcia's eyes twin devils of defiance and determination danced. "Good-night, Jem. No! You shall *not* take me downstairs."

In the motor outside the scandalized Miss Letitia Pritchard, after a wait of an hour and five minutes, commented significantly and with a down-thrust inflection: "Well!"

"Well, Cousin Letty," said Marcia demurely.

"Are you going to marry that young man, Marcia?"

"How can I? He has refused me."

"Refused you!" gasped Miss Pritchard.

"Precisely. I am a blighted maiden."

"Snumph!" sniffed Miss Pritchard. "Don't you tell me!"

"Must you hear it from him to believe it?"

"Marcia Ames! I've watched that boy since you set your seal on him four years ago. I've seen him grow into a man, and fight his way wrong and right, and take his loss of you like a man and make a religion of it, and run his life by it, and if ever a chit of a girl ought to be proud of something too big and too good for her that she's thrown away—Don't you tell me, Marcia Ames! I—I don't positively know what to say of such doings."

The little electric, equally scandalized, suddenly lost its head, rushed upon an unoffending hydrant, sheered off, made as if to climb the front steps of the bank, performed an impossible curve, chased two horrified and incredulous citizens (who had never seen Miss Pritchard under the influence of liquor before, and so reported to their wives when they got home) up against a railing, and finally resumed the road with a sickening lurch, all of which may have been due to the fact that the usually self-contained Miss Marcia Ames had abruptly buried her face in Miss Pritchard's shoulder, and clutched at her blindly.

"Say it again," quavered Miss Ames, when the errant electric had squared away for home. "Say it again, Cousin Letty! I could not make him say it. And oh! how hard I tried."

"Land sakes! Then you are going to marry him!" exclaimed Miss Pritchard.

"But he does not know it," replied Marcia, suddenly demure.

## 36

Had anyone informed Governor Martin Embree that Miss Marcia Ames was again embellishing Fenchester society, he would have dismissed the matter as of no political moment. That is to say, of no importance whatsoever. Politics was now the exclusive and feverish preoccupation of "Smiling Mart" Embree's days and nights, "Aut Senatus aut nullus" the motive guiding his every action. Miss Ames was not even a voter, having no residence in the State. Yet, by those devious ways in which women work and quite as unknown to herself as to Martin Embree, she was preparing a pitfall for the aspiring feet of Centralia's most bounteous smiler.

Strange organizations were now coming to birth in every part of the State visited by "Smiling Mart." They were self-assumed to be exuberantly patriotic and violently American, and their slogans were, "American Blood for American Soil," "Our Army for Home Defense," "America for America," "One Soldier Here Worth a Hundred in Europe," and the plausible like, the underlying purpose being to keep the American forces at home and thus out of the war until the Kaiser could successfully finish his job in Europe. Considering the super-quality of Americanism in the claims, the proportion of Teutonic names among the membership was striking. Open pacifists, covert pro-Germans, and political straddlers made up the strength of these bodies, while in the background warily lurked Martin Embree, moulding their activities to his own purposes of advancement. Deutschtum, bent but not broken, was become his chief political asset.

Presently these bodies merged into a State-wide and single entity, the Defenders of Our Land—"Our Land" ostensibly meaning the United States, though another interpretation might have been present in the minds of some of the participants. All was going prosperously with the enterprise; new members were flocking to its banner; the weak-minded and short-sighted were responding to its proselytizing methods, when, one day, the Fenchester Guardian, with that unparalleled and foul-minded brutality to be expected from a bloodthirsty jingo like young Robson (to paraphrase the impromptu but impassioned German of President Emil Bausch at the Deutscher Club), set the German flag above the platform of the organization, and below it the conjoined portraits of Governor Embree and Kaiser Wilhelm wreathed in the olive. Thereafter recruiting lessened.

Never before had Governor Embree so felt the need of reliable newspaper backing. Upon the rejection of his offer for The Guardian, A. M. Wymett had thrown all his energy into organizing the new paper for his backer, the Governor, and the sub-backers, Bausch, Wanser, Fliess, the Deutscher Club, and the German Societies of Centralia. Ostensibly it was to be loyal, as the Defenders of Our Land were loyal. "An American Newspaper for Americans" was to be its catch-line, and its main editorial precepts were to be the already somewhat blown-upon "Keep the Boys at Home" slogan, and "A Rich Man's War." Other than propaganda, its chief purpose, of course, was the election of Governor Embree to the vacancy in the Senate. As the Governor, perforce, was drawn by his all-excluding ambitions deeper and deeper into the pro-German campaign, newspaper upon newspaper had fallen away from him, some, like The Bellair Journal, from principle, others from fear of committing themselves too far. A powerful daily with a State-wide circulation was now absolutely essential to the success of his candidacy. The Fair Dealer was to supply the want.

As to circulation, that was arranged in advance. Max Verrall's boast of twenty-five thousand, assured from the start, was no great exaggeration. Embree's political agents had worked hard and well. Throughout the State the pro-Germans and pacifists were prepared to accept The Fair Dealer as their political mouthpiece from the day of its appearance. The difficulty, which now grilled the souls of Embree and Wymett, was the delay inevitable and unforeseeable attending the institution of a newspaper plant. Meantime The Guardian's editorial page had become at once a beacon-fire for the patriotic elements and a searching, searing flame for the pan-Germanic scheme of which Embree was the local figurehead.

At length the path of the new daily seemed to be clear of reckonable difficulties. Wymett decided that it was safe to go ahead. Spacious announcements flared forth on the city's hoardings, confirming what rumor had more accurately than usual presaged of The Fair Dealer's principles and purposes, and setting July 5th as the date of publication. Thereupon, as at a signal, part of the remaining bottom proceeded to fall out of The Guardian's advertising. Not only did the local situation develop a more disastrous decrease than had been looked for, but some two thousand dollars' worth of products, manufactured in other parts of the State by German or pacifist concerns, decided that a morning paper was better suited to their needs than an evening.

With his final determination not to sell, Jeremy had shifted upon Andrew Galpin the entire financial responsibility for and conduct of the paper.

"Here's the extent of my pile," he had said, turning over a statement to his coadjutor. "You know where the paper stands and what it owes better than I do. Take charge. There's a worry I make you a present of. I'm out of it. I prefer the editorial kind of nerve-strain, anyway. If you come to me with any unnecessary information, Andy, I'll have Buddy fire you out."

"Don't you want to know *anything* about it?"

"You might tell me, from time to time, how long the patient has to live. But not too often, Andy. I don't want to be distracted by—er—irrelevant details."

So, on the day of The Fair Dealer's announcement, Galpin approached his chief.

"We've slipped a couple of extra steps down the slide, Boss."

"Is that all?"

"Ay-ah. But we aren't so blame' far from the bottom, you know."

"Give us five more months, and we may get Mart Embree's hide to cover our lamented remains with."

"Five months! Not on the cards, Boss. Call it three."

Jeremy sighed. "Don't bother me with it now," he said testily. "I'm busy. Didn't I specially make you a present of that worry?"

Diplomacy was not Andrew Galpin's strong point. Most injudiciously he conceived that now was the time to advance a project which he had held in reserve, awaiting such an opening.

"Boss," he said, "there's another buyer in the field for the paper."

"Who's the crook?"

"It isn't a crook."

"Who's the fool, then?"

"I am."

With a deliberation and accuracy worthy of a better action, the owner of The Guardian thrust his editorial pen in the glue-pot.

"Oh, *you* are, are you? And how much do you propose to pay for this valuable property?"

"Well—er—say fifty thousand. And assume the mortgage."

"Fine! You've got the fifty thousand ready, I suppose? In your little leathern wallet?"

"It's real money," retorted the other, with a touch of resentment.

"Real, of course. But whose?"

"I'm not instructed to state."

"Are you instructed to take me for a boob? Do you observe a blithe and vernal touch of green in my eye, Andy? When did Miss Ames put you up to this?"

"Well, it's good money, ain't it?" blurted the discomfited general manager.

"Too good. You ought to be ashamed of yourself."

"D' you think I *wanted* to do it!" retorted his aide in outraged tones. "She made me. Did you ever try not to do something that little lady wanted you to do? It can't be done," asserted Mr. Andrew Galpin positively.

"Andy, as a self-excuser you're—"

"Ay-ah! I know. But you've been running this paper like you thought she wanted it run over four years' time and three thousand miles of ocean," accused the other with unexpected vigor. "Have you or haven't you?"

It was now the editor-in-chief's turn to be disconcerted. "I'm busy," he said. He reached for the implement of his trade. "Who the hell put that pen in that glue-pot!" he vociferated. Then, relieved by his little outburst, he added, "Tell her we're not for sale"; and, after Galpin's retreating back, he fired, "And tell her that as a secret negotiator you're about as subtle as a street-piano."

Rejection of her bid did not appear to surprise Miss Ames. Coming upon the proprietor of The Guardian on the street, some days later, by chance (or did she, as Miss Pritchard accused, cunningly plan the encounter?) she inquired if the price were not high enough.

"It's no use, Marcia," said Jem. "You can't get in. I'm not going to let you commit financial suicide."

Marcia was in teasing mood that day. "I should be hardened to disappointments and withered hopes, I suppose," she sighed mockingly. "Jem?"

"Yes?"

"Will you walk along with me? Or do you think it compromising to be seen on the streets with the girl you have rejected?"

"Marcia," groaned the tormented lover. "If you don't stop that I'll— I'll grab you up right here and carry you off."

"That would commit you fatally," she reminded him. "By the way, are you never coming to see me again?"

"I'm all tied up with evening work, now."

"Of course," she assented with a gravity which, however, roused his suspicions. "Are you going to Madam Taylor's tea?"

"I'm not on Madam Taylor's list, since I called her a tax-dodger."

"I cannot imagine her dodging anything; not even a taxi, let alone a tax. She is so dignified and positive and 'sot.' Will you come if I get you an invitation?"

"What for?"

Marcia's delicate mouth drooped exaggeratedly. "If I must be a sister to you," she murmured, "that is surely no reason why we should not meet occasionally."

"Oh, I'll come!" said Jem wildly. "I'd walk from here to New York just to see you in the street, and you know it."

"Jem!" she said with a change of tone. Her fingers just touched his hand lightly. "It is a shame to tease you. But your Spartan rôle is such a temptation!"

Madam Taylor, though she adored Marcia, flatly declined to invite the editor of The Guardian. "That young mud-wasp" she termed him, and advised the girl to beware of his specious claims to fairness and rectitude. There would be plenty of other young men, far better worth meeting, at her tea than young Robson. It was not any other young man, however, whom the lovely Miss Ames selected for her special attention at the tea, but, vastly to his surprise and not a little to his gratification, Mr. Montrose Clark. There was nothing of the gallant about the public utilitarian; he was the highly correct head of a devoted family. But even in such, the aesthetic sense remains, and Mr. Clark was conscious of a distinct interest arising from his being selected for the special ministrations of the most attractive young woman in Fenchester. When she had duly hemmed him into the corner of an arbor with an impregnable fortification of Dresden and selected viands, he made the start himself.

"I surrender," he announced with ponderous playfulness. "What do you want of me?"

"How unkind of you, Mr. Clark! I was about to try my craftiest wiles upon you," returned Miss Ames regretfully.

"Then it's a subscription. I withdraw the white flag. I'll fight."

"Please! That is exactly what I do not wish you to do. I wish you to make peace."

"Have I a quarrel with you?"

"Not yet. With some friends of mine. With The Guardian."

The public utilitarian's expression changed; became more impersonal and observant. "Young Robson," he remarked. "He's been talking to you."

"No. It was Mr. Galpin that told me about it."

"You're his emissary?"

"Oh, no! You must not suppose that. I come to you quite of my own accord."

"Why this extreme interest in The Guardian, Miss Ames?"

"Because I—There is a reason for—Circumstances—"

"Over which you have no control," suggested her vis-à-vis.

"Over which I have no control," she accepted, and her hand went to her throat—(Mr. Montrose Clark, seeing the swift color pulse into her face, discarded Andrew Galpin from consideration and came back to Jeremy Robson and wondered whether that pernicious journalist knew how lucky he was), "have given me a—an interest, a responsibility—" Marcia Ames was experiencing unwonted difficulties in explaining what was perhaps not fundamentally clear to herself.

"I see," answered the magnate mendaciously.

"If you saw as I see," she retorted earnestly, "you would not be opposing and trying to ruin The Guardian."

"But bless my soul, my dear young lady! That is precisely what The Guardian has been doing to me. You haven't been reading it these few years past."

"Oh, yes. Every day. I do not pretend to understand that part of it. But I do know this; that Mr. Rob—that The Guardian is making a fight single-handed for the Nation and the war, and is being beaten because those who should stand by it are not patriotic enough to forget old scores. Have you stopped to think of that, Mr. Clark?"

The magnate shifted uncomfortably in his seat. To say that he had stopped to think of this would be untrue. Rather, the thought had essayed to stop him and force itself on his consideration with increasing pertinacity of late, and he had barely contrived to dodge it and go on about his lawful occasions. Now it challenged him in the clear regard of a very beautiful and very determined young woman.

"No. Yes," said Montrose Clark, and left that for her to take her pick of. "One wouldn't think you the kind to take such an interest in politics."

"Is this politics—exactly?" she asked quietly.

Upon Montrose Clark's chubby facial contours appeared a heightened color. "No; by thunder! It isn't. Will you sit here, young lady, and keep out of sight of pursuers until I can catch and fetch Selden Dana?"

Marcia had not long to wait. The Judge was retrieved from a circle of the elderly, harmless, but influential, with whom he had been discussing cures. The two men sat and drank more tea than was good for them, while Marcia made her argument and plea. Then said Selden Dana to Montrose Clark, smiling: "Let's buy out The Guardian and turn it over to her to run."

"We might do worse," conceded the magnate.

"It is not to be bought," said Marcia.

"Have *you* tried?" the lawyer flashed at her. "You have," he answered himself, marking the response in her face. "Well, I *am* dashed!" He and Montrose Clark exchanged glances. "Business is business," observed the lawyer with apparent irrelevance, but in the tone of one who strives to recall a wandering purpose.

"Quite so!" murmured Montrose Clark. "Quite so!" But there was a lack of conviction in his voice.

"Miss Ames," said Dana, "I pride myself on being a judge of character. Sometimes I meet a problem that puzzles me. Why hasn't Jem Robson gone into uniform?"

"Do you think Mr. Robson is a slacker?" she shot back at him.

"Not if I read him right. That's what puzzles me about his staying behind."

"Did it not occur to you that he has a more important fight here than there?"

"It might occur to me," admitted the lawyer. "But I don't know that I'd care to have it occur to a son of mine."

She gave him her flashing smile. "That is clever of you," she said. "I like that! And now I will violate a confidence, but it must go no farther. The doctor would not pass Mr. Robson for active service. Mr. Galpin told me."

"I never take an afternoon off," sighed the lawyer, "but some obtrusive business crops up and ruins the day's sport. Let's go down to the office, Mr. Clark, and talk this over."

One more bit of meddling with the irresponsible fates which rule men and newspapers was committed by Miss Ames that afternoon. Magnus Laurens, just off a train, came in late to the tea, and was straightway seized upon.

"Uncle Magnus! Where have you been, all these weeks and months?"

"Well, Marcia!" He took both her hands and looked down into her face. "What a sight you are! If you're ever allowed to get away from America again, I'll lose all faith in our young manhood . . . Where have I been? Here and there and everywhere. Organizing the State Council of Defense. Raising money. Trips to Washington. Letting family and business go to the bow-wows."

"Are you in touch with Fenchester matters?"

"Hello! What's this? You're talking like a politician. After my vote?"

"Do you know that The Guardian has been making the fight almost alone here against the anti-war crowd?"

Magnus Laurens rubbed his big, gray head perplexedly. "I've got to look into that situation. When Jeremy Robson went back on us—"

"Jeremy Robson never went back on you! At least, not since war was probable. And—and your company is choking The Guardian to death with a contract dishonestly made by Senator Embree's man, Verrall."

"The devil! I beg your pardon, Marcia. Where did you learn these interesting facts—if they are facts?"

"From Mr. Galpin."

"Oh! Hardly a disinterested witness."

"Uncle Magnus, I wish you to promise me just one thing."

"Not so foolish! What is it?"

"I wish you to go to the Library this evening—no matter how busy you are—and go over the files of The Guardian since last March."

"I'll do that much," he agreed.

"Then you will do more," said Marcia contentedly. That first day's confabulation between Marcia and Galpin, the scope of which its object, Jeremy Robson, little suspected, was bearing fruit.

LONG YEARS UNHEARD YET unforgotten, the voice of Edwin Garson, President Montrose Clark's hand-perfected private secretary, warbled with a mellifluous intonation over the telephone wire into the surprised ear of The Guardian's editor and owner.

"Hello! Hello? *Hel*-lo . . . This Mr. Robson? . . . Office of the Fenchester Public Utilities. Mr. Montrose Clark wishes to see you."

An unfortunate formula. It recalled the vivid past. One sweetly solemn thought in Jeremy's mind was forthwith transmuted into one briefly pregnant speech which shocked the private secretary clean off the wire. Jeremy resumed his editorializing. His next interruption, to his incredulous astonishment, took the important form and presence of Mr. Montrose Clark himself. Mahomet had come to the mountain.

At Jeremy's invitation Mr. Clark disposed his neat and pursy form upon the far edge of a chair impressively, yet with obvious reservations, as one disdaining to concede anything to comfort. Embarrassment might have been conjectured in one less august. His voice was as stiff as his posture as he began:

"I had my secretary telephone you, Mr. Robson."

"I got your message."

"And I your reply, which, as transmitted to me, was that I might go to the devil!"

"I think I mentioned the place, not the proprietor."

"It does not signify. I am here"—there was no glimmer of light on the round red countenance to suggest an ulterior meaning—"I am here on a matter of business, in my capacity as acting president of the Drovers' Bank in Mr. Warrington's absence. As such, I have to inform you that we stand ready to make you a loan on favorable terms upon the security of The Guardian."

"Wh-wh-why?" stammered Jeremy, taken wholly aback. "Do you consider the paper a sound risk now?"

"Sufficiently sound."

"Up to what amount?"

"Any amount you need."

Jeremy stared at him, unbelieving.

"No security I can furnish now is as good as that which you rejected before."

"That may very well be true."

"Yet your offer is still open?"

"It is."

"Ah, yes!" said Jeremy, thinking slowly and carefully. "You're assuming that, with the change in the local political situation, The Guardian is going to shift its principles. Well, Mr. Clark, if you expect that we're going back one inch from the stand we've taken on public utilities, and the P.-U. Corporation in particular, you're badly fooled. We're just as much against you as if we were still for Governor Embree. I thought I had made that clear to Judge Dana."

"I have proposed no bargain," stated the magnate aridly. "I make an offer. No conditions are attached."

"Then I've got to tell you frankly that we're not doing very well."

"So I am informed. What appears to be the trouble? Will the new paper cut into your circulation to an extent—"

"Newspapers do not live by circulation alone, Mr. Clark, but chiefly by advertising."

"Certainly; certainly. Local merchants appear to be pretty well represented in your pages."

"At reduced space—or worse. Take the case of Vogt, the florist, who has always been good for a hundred dollars a month with us. Perhaps you can point out Mr. Vogt's present space in The Guardian."

The visitor ran through the paper handed to him.

"I fail to find Mr. Vogt's advertisement."

"He's out."

"Why?"

"Because The Guardian has been 'corrupted by British gold.'"

"Indeed! Did he express that theory to you personally?"

"He did. He also instructed me as to running my paper, and gave me the outlines of an editorial demanding that none of our soldiers be sent abroad to help in the war. When I said that I wasn't interested in pro-German strategy he said something else, in German, which unfortunately I understand a little; and then 'Police!'"

"Police?" repeated Mr. Clark, with hopeful interest. "Why did he say that?"

"I suppose he thought I was going to throw him downstairs. I wasn't. I left him carefully on the top step."

Signs of perturbation appeared upon the visage of the little magnate. He rose. His projective eyes appeared no longer to feel at home in his face. They roved afar.

"Police!" he murmured, and added "Ah!" in a curious, relishing tone. Suddenly he thrust out a pudgy hand, clawed at Jeremy's unready fingers, murmured "Count on us, Mr. Robson, for anything we can do!"—and stalked out.

"Now, how do you account for him?" inquired Jeremy, referring the matter to Galpin, who had come in to announce another withdrawal.

"Oh, him!" Galpin turned the public utilitarian over in his mind, considering him on all sides. "Wants to use us to club the Governor, I reckon. Now that we've quit 'Smiling Mart,' plenty of our old enemies will be willing to play with us on the theory that there'll be a change in policy."

"They'll have to make a better guess than that."

"I guess you're right, Boss," sighed the other. "Even if we did borrow, it'd only be postponing the finish. Things won't get any better for us while the war is on. And when the showdown comes where would The Guardian be if we were in for twenty thousand more?"

"In the hands of the Drovers' Bank."

"There or thereabouts. Well, I can't just see us being editorial copyboys for President Puff. Can you?"

"Not exactly! Yet, you know, Andy, he gave me almost the impression of being really for us."

"Well, it's possible, Boss; it's just possible"—the other's shrewd face was puckered in conjecture—"that he might consider this war thing more important than his own little interests. A man who thinks different from us on every other blooming subject under the sun might be every bit as real an American when it comes to the pinch. Ever think of that, Boss?"

"Not just that way."

"Time enough to find out. Where the lion jumps, the jackal follows. See if Old Slippery Dana doesn't come round in the next few days."

Come round Judge Dana did. That candid honesty of expression and demeanor which had aided him in pulling off some of his most dubious tricks was never more markedly in evidence than when he shook hands with Jeremy.

"Ever give any thought to the libel suits against you in the office of Dana & Dana?" he began.

"Some."

"Bother you any?"

"I'm not losing sleep over them."

"Now, I'll admit candidly," said the lawyer, "that a couple of 'em are no good. They're dead. But there's merit in Madam Taylor's case. You went too far there. Your own lawyers will tell you that."

"They have," said Jeremy incautiously, and bit his lip.

"Well, in spite of that, I've come to tell you that we've advised our client to withdraw the action."

"Have you?" said the editor warily. "Why?"

"Call it friendship."

"On your part? For The Guardian?"

"We-ell; say it's because I foresee that the paper is going to have plenty of troubles of its own without our adding to them."

"You haven't always been so solicitous as to The Guardian's welfare."

"Meaning that you would like to understand the reason for my present solicitude?"

"*Timeo Danaos*,"[1] quoted Jem. "I fear the Danas bearing gifts."

The lawyer smiled his appreciation.

"I've given you the best reason I know."

"Did Montrose Clark send you here?"

"You don't like Mr. Clark much, do you?"

"Not particularly."

"Nor me, either, perhaps?"

"I blush to say that I rather do."

"But you don't trust me."

"Oh, come, Dana! What would you expect!"

"Just for relaxation of the mind, my young friend, what do you think of me?"

"Straight?"

"Straight."

"I think you're a slippery old legal crook," returned Jeremy without hesitation.

"And I think you're a flitter-witted young fool—ninety-nine times out of a hundred!"

"And the hundredth?"

"That's what I'm looking at now. By God, you're an American, anyway! Here, Jem," he leaned across the table, extending a bony and argumentative forefinger; "if you and I were in the trenches, fighting shoulder to shoulder, it wouldn't make a pickle's worth of difference whether you were a sapheaded loon or not, or whether I was a crook or a thief or a murderer, or not. All we'd have to ask of each other would be that we were fighting in the same cause, and with the last drop of our blood, and to the finish! Am I right?"

"I guess you're right."

"Well, then! What's this we're up against right here in Fenchester? Are we fighting? Or playing tiddledywinks?"

"There's very little tiddledywinks in it, so far as The Guardian is concerned," confessed Jeremy with a wry face.

"So far as any of us are concerned. It's coming to the place where it's a case of get together and stick together for us Americans. Seen Magnus Laurens since the Governor's little soirée?"

"No," answered Jem, flushing.

"Laurens thought you were in on Embree's deal. Why don't you put him right?"

"He can put himself right," returned the editor shortly.

"Hardly that; but he can be put right. There are a lot of things that ought to be put right for you, my boy. Things that have been wrong for a long time."

He leaned to Jeremy again, his long face alight with an eager and innocent candor.

"Jem, there's no use fighting your friends. The people that can help you, the people that are the real Americans of your kind, you've always opposed. Come in with us now. There's nothing that won't be done for you and The Guardian. I'm going to talk plain talk. Isn't it about time you made up your mind to be good?"

"How be good? What's on the carpet now?"

"Why, this fight against the pacifists and pro-Germans."

"You don't have to tell me to be good for that. Something else is up." He eyed the lawyer with a bitter grin. "I might have known you had something up your sleeve. What is it, the Blanket Franchise Bill again?"

"That's a perfectly fair bill," defended the visitor. "But for The Guardian, it would have gone through before. Now—"

"Now we'll kill it again if it shows its crooked head. Tell Montrose Clark that from me. And tell him that I won't need any loan from the Drovers' Bank to do it."

"Very well," sighed the lawyer. "No hard feelings, my boy. Business is business."

Reporting to his chief, Dana stated:

"He won't dicker."

"As I told you," replied Montrose Clark in pompous self-appreciation of his own prophecy.

"Well, no harm in trying . . . We can pass the Blanket Franchise Bill after The Guardian is dead."

"How long can it last?"

"Not three months, according to what I can gather."

The president of the Fenchester Public Utilities Corporation began to puff up and grow red in the face and squirm in his seat. Finally it came out explosively:

"Dana, I don't want to pass the damned bill—at that price."

"Neither do I."

"You know, I—I almost like that young fool."

"So do I."

"Well, what are we going to do?"

"Pull him through whether he wants our help or not. We can fight him for the Franchise Bill after the war."

"Go to it!" returned the president of the Fenchester Public Utilities Company with unwonted energy and slang.

As the first fruits of that confabulation between two of Jeremy Robson's oldest enemies The Guardian received on the following day a contract from the P.-U. for advertising space amounting to sixteen hundred dollars a year. Jeremy reckoned that with grim satisfaction, as giving the paper a few days more of life. On the following morning there came a far more important help in the form of a brief and characteristic note from Magnus Laurens, the pith of which was in these sentences:

> I hope you will accept my sincere apologies. Enclosed find contract with the Oak Lodge Pulp Company, which, I have reason to believe, was made under a misapprehension as to quality of paper. Kindly make out new contract at three cents and three quarters if acceptable.

Andy Galpin's philosophical estimate—"Every bit as real an American, when it comes to the pinch"—reverted to Jeremy's mind. A sudden humility tempered his spirit. He felt that The Guardian was a pretty big thing and he a pretty small one. Well, in what time remained he would fight with a new vigor and for a broader ideal. It would not be long. Magnus Laurens's generosity meant only a respite; perhaps two or three months extra of fighting the good fight. In the owner's heart was no self-deception as to the inevitable outcome. Meantime the paper might yet beat Martin Embree and save Centralia from the disgrace of sending the chosen prophet of Deutschtum to the United States Senate.

And just for itself, how well worth fighting for and with to the finish was the battered, gallant old Guardian! Jeremy thought of his paper as a Captain might think of his ship staggering, unconquered but hopeless, through her last storm to her last port; thought of her with that sort of devotion, of passion. And the precious freight of hope and faith and belief that she carried, the loyal confidence of the simple, clean, honest people for whom he had made the paper!

Strange and unexpected accessions had come to that number; none stronger than the stubborn and violent jeweler, Bernard Stockmuller, who had abused Jeremy on the street after the first trouble with the Deutscher Club.

On the morning after the Constantia was sunk, with the first American naval victims, an event upon which Jeremy had poured out the hot fervency of his patriotism, his door was thrust open and the powerful form of the German burst in. His face was a dull, deep red. His eyes protruded. He was gasping.

Believing that he had to do with a man crazed by fury, Jeremy jumped to his feet and set himself. The expected rush followed, but ended in a stagger, a gulp, and a burst of unashamed tears.

"Dot bee-ewtiful tribude!" sobbed the emotional German. "Dot bee-ewtiful tribude dot you haf printed in your paper to our boys. To my boy!"

"Your boy? Why, Stockmuller, I didn't know—"

"All the boy I got. My nephew, Henry. Him I brought up and put through the Ooniversity. He iss dead. He hass gone down in the Constantia. I am glad he iss dead so splendid! I am proud when I read what you have written. Und—und, Mr. Robson, I wand you should—I wand you should—"

"Go on, Stockmuller," said Jeremy gently, as the other stopped with a pleading look. "Of course I'll do it—whatever it is you want."

"I wand you should take my ad back," said Stockmuller as simply as a child.

"You bet I'll take it back!"

"Mind! I dink you wass wrong, first off," said the honest and obstinate German. "I dink Inkland made dis war. But my Henry, all the boy I got, if he iss only a nephew, iss dead for dis country. And now dis iss my country and my war!"

"All right, Stockmuller. Glad to have you with us," was all that Jeremy, pretty well shaken by the other's emotion, found to say. The visitor produced a large and ornate handkerchief, wherewith he openly wiped his swollen eyes.

"Also, dere is someding else," he stated, lowering his voice. The editor looked his inquiry. "Monkey business with your printer-men."

"Yes; I know something about that."

"Do you know when they strike?"

"No. When?"

"The day before the new paper comes out."

Jeremy whistled softly.

"Of course! That's when they would, assuming that it's a put-up job from outside. Where do you get your information?—if it's a fair question."

Stockmuller turned a painful red.

"I was on der Deutscher Club committee," he said. "The segret committee. No more!"

"Who are the men in our press-room they're working through?"

The visitor shook his head. "'Weiss nicht," he murmured.

"Never mind; I know! I'll start something for 'em before they're ready."

Jem had now definitely fixed upon Nick Milliken, the white-haired, vehement Socialist, as the chief instigator of trouble upstairs. He no longer suspected Milliken of being in the underground employ of Montrose Clark and Dana. He believed him to be the agent of Bausch and the Deutscher Club committee. He sent for the man and discharged him. Milliken took his discharge, at first, in a spirit of incredulity.

"Me?" he said. "What have you got it in for me for?"

"You're a trouble-maker. That's enough."

"Because I'm a Socialist? Look-a-here, Mr. Robson—"

"There's no use in arguing, Milliken. I won't have you around."

"Give me a week," said the other. "I can tell you some—"

"Not a day! Get your pay this noon."

The man hesitated; then with a sardonic, but not particularly hostile grin he bade his employer good-day.

"Now for the strike!" said Jeremy to Andy Galpin.

But the strike did not come. Evidently the manipulators in the background would bide their own time.

## 38

B<small>EHOLD</small>, <small>NOW</small>, M<small>ISS</small> M<small>ARCIA</small> A<small>MES</small>, conspiratress, seated in the depths of the Boot & Shoe Infirmary, deep in converse with Dr. Eli Wade, Surgeon of Soles and Healer of Leather. Opinion was always to be had at the Sign of the Big Shoe; often information; sometimes wisdom. Miss Ames was seeking light upon her problem wherever she might find it. Her scheme for Magnus Laurens had been successful; that in which Montrose Clark was to have played the Beneficent Influence, had prospered in part; yet The Guardian's downhill pace had been only mitigated, not checked. Methods more radical must be found. Eli Wade proved at least a friendly, if not a broad-visioned consultant.

"A fighter, thet young man is," said Eli Wade. "He don't go stumblin', anymore. Straight, he goes. And if he falls at the end, it'll be in the best fight any man ever made in this town against a gang of snakes and traitors."

"But he must not fall, Eli!" cried the girl. "We must not let him fall."

"Ah! Thet's the talk! If them as had oughta stood by him had done so, he'd be all right today."

"Who? Why have they failed him? Is it that they do not understand?"

"Blind," said Eli Wade. "They don't see. They're millin' round wherever the Germans and the slick politicians drive 'em. If ever I was fooled in a pair o' shoes it was them Number Eights of 'Smilin' Mart' Embree's."

"But your kind of people, Eli! Simple, straight, honest people. Why would they not stand by The Guardian?"

"Bless your soul! They do. They're solid. It's the advertisers thet are trippin' up his feet."

"So Mr. Galpin says. The stores."

"Yes. The stores support the newspapers with their advertising, an' so they rule or ruin 'em."

"When have they ruled The Guardian?"

"Never. Nick Milliken says thet's what's wrong. Thet's why they're against it. He says if you could get at what supports the stores an' work on thet, The Guardian might be pulled out yet. I got my own notions about thet."

"About what supports the stores? The public, does it not?"

"Part of the public."

"What part?"

"Women-folks," said the Boot & Shoe Surgeon tersely.

Upon that pronouncement Marcia Ames pondered. There seemed to be a gleam in it. The more she thought, the more the gleam expanded. It became a ray of light.

"The women!" she said. "Of course they do. Who ever saw a man in a department store?"

"Well, I wouldn't go thet far," returned the Surgeon. "I reckon they's a few. But they don't wear out much sole leather there. And if anyone was to say to The Big Shop or The Northwestern, or Ellison Brothers or any of them big advertisers, 'We'll take the women-folks away, but you can keep the men,' thet store would about close its doors next week."

Marcia Ames rose out of her deep chair. There was a glow on her face. "Eli Wade," she said, "you are a great man!"

"No, *ma'am*," disclaimed the other. "Jest a handy man with leather."

"Well, you are a dear! And that is better. I believe—I do believe—you have shown the way. If only there is time! I am going to take your big idea to high legal talent for consultation."

"Hain't had any big idea sence"—his old, keen eyes twinkled—"sence the State Capitol flew the German flag in honor of the Surrender Bill. But who's your legal talent?"

"Judge Selden Dana."

"You're the wonder, Miss Marcia. How'd you know you could trust him? He ain't always been reckoned trustable."

"No? But in a matter like this—I am sure."

"Kee-rect! You got him. He's marchin'."

"Marching?"

"To the music of war. He's quit slinkin'. Left—right, left—right! True to the drum. Watch his feet."

"Good-bye, Eli Wade," said Marcia. "If your big idea works out—I shall love you forever."

To Judge Selden Dana, when she unfolded it, it seemed more like her own idea. Unquestionably, however, it was a promising one. If there were only time! If the scheme could be set afoot before The Fair Dealer was in the field; if some way could be found to delay the publication—at which point Judge Dana fell to thinking powerfully. All the pleasant candor went out of his face, as he pondered, and it became subtle and secret and dark. Yet the girl, watching, liked it and trusted it none the less in this manifestation. She knew that the mind within was working to good ends. At length he spoke.

"I've got a plan for The Fair Dealer. No; never mind what it is. Forget that we even spoke of it."

"It is forgotten."

"Go ahead with the women. Mr. Clark and I will help where we can. You can organize the University girls?"

"Yes."

"Good! One more thing. Not a whisper of this to Jem Robson."

"Mr. Robson knows nothing of it. What I have learned has been from Mr. Galpin."

"Nor to Galpin, either. Or anyone else at The Guardian."

"Have you a fancy to play at mysteries and secrets, Judge Dana?" teased the girl.

"Mysteries? Secrets? Great Scott, young woman! Collusions and conspiracies! Trust an old fox of the law. If it should come to an issue and it could be shown that The Guardian people had knowledge of your precious little plot—well, I shouldn't care to have the case to defend. So, work as quietly as you can. I think a hundred women—if they're representative, mind you,—will about do the business."

He contemplated her, with a gentle light in his pinched, wrinkled, shrewd old eyes. "My dear," he said, "I remember four years ago, at the Federated German Societies, how you stood up, straight and brave, before all of them."

"Do you?" said Marcia, answering his smile.

"You're still doing it. Still standing up as you did then. I'd do a good deal for you, if it were only in memory of that."

"Thank you, Judge Dana," she said simply.

"And I'd do a good deal for that young hot-head, Jem Robson. About anything I could do, I guess."

"Thank you," said the girl again, but there was a thrill in her voice this time.

Into the devious ways of the legal profession and of railroad operation when they run parallel it is not meet for the layman to inquire too closely. Suffice it to say here that Judge Selden Dana took a brief trip to the office of a certain railway system, and thence followed up a certain consignment of freight which subsequently became the innocent victim of cross-orders to the extent of getting itself mysteriously and obscurely side-tracked while certain interests in Fenchester afflicted the heavens above, the earth beneath, the Postal Telegraph, the Western Union, and all the long-distance wires with frantic inquiries. Further it may be stated that this sort of law-and-railroad practice is such as would have been severely condemned by Mr. Jeremy Robson, editor of The Guardian, had he known of it. He knew nothing. There were many and important matters happening at this time whereof he knew nothing.

This matter having been arranged, Judge Dana made an appointment by telephone, and called to see Jeremy.

"Got another dicker to suggest, Judge?" the editor greeted him, with indulgent raillery.

"No," returned the caller slowly; "no dicker. This is serious business, young man. How long are you going to be able to hold out?"

"Don't you worry about us," said Jeremy, who hadn't the smallest intention of betraying the paper's status to the wily lawyer. "There's a lot of fight left in the old hulk yet."

"What about this strike?"

"So you've heard about that?"

"I've seen Milliken."

"Milliken is fired."

"So he told me."

"How came you to be on such close terms with a rank Socialist?" taunted the editor.

"I'll be on terms with a rattlesnake if he'll play my game," replied the lawyer with one of those bursts of frankness wherewith he occasionally favored Jeremy. "Never mind Milliken now. Can you beat out this strike if it comes?"

Suddenly Jeremy looked tired and old.

"I don't know," he said lifelessly.

"Is there any danger of The Guardian having to give up in the next month?"

"It's getting harder sledding all the time," confessed Jeremy. "The strike might finish us, at that."

"Publication date of The Fair Dealer is postponed two weeks," observed the lawyer.

"No! What's caused that?"

"How should I know? They say part of the machinery has been lost in transit. It was shipped via the Lake Belt Line, for which I happen to be counsel. But I can't imagine"—he paused, and Jeremy saw a distinct, enlightening flicker of his left eyelid—"I can *not* imagine what has caused the unfortunate delay! I should think there might be danger of their losing some of their promised advertising!"

"Oh, their contracts are all made. Trust Verrall for that."

"Doubtless. But will they hold? I understand they specified an issue of July 5th."

"What of it?" said Jeremy wearily. "The advertisers will make new contracts. You couldn't pry 'em away from that twenty-five thousand circulation at the low rate given."

"Who knows what the morrow may bring forth?" said the lawyer oracularly. "'I could a tale unfold'—" He stopped, with a large gesture.

"There's always a cloven hoof that goes with your kind of tail," retorted Jeremy. "But if you've really got anything cheery up your sleeve, spring it. I could do with a little cheering-up right now. That postponement of publication is a good start. What's next?"

"My son, the less you know just now, the better. But I'll tell you this: Some of us who are—well—interested in The Guardian, for reasons of our own, are skating on the thin edge of conspiracy, treason, stratagem, and crime, as it is. Do you want in? You do not want in! You stay out and keep a stiff upper lip. Can't use any of our spare cash? No! Well, if your neck was a little stiffer it'd break! Good-bye, and hang on!'"

All of which Jeremy promptly retailed to the faithful Galpin with the comment:

"Something's certainly up, but how much is for us, and how much for Clark, Dana & Company, I don't know."

"You got a mean, suspicious sort of mind, Boss," grinned the general manager. "But I admit I don't get that bunch yet."

"Nor I. But I'm watching."

"Somebody's pushing on the reins upstairs again. If the strike don't bust this week, I'm a goat! I caught Milliken hanging round yesterday and chased him out. Gave him the police talk."

"Dana knew all about Milliken and the strike. Had it from Milliken himself."

"Wheels and wheels and wheels!" commented Andy, making expansive and elegantly rounded gestures. "Wheels within wheels; wheels without wheels; wheels going in opposite directions and at different speeds. They make me dizzy!"

They made Jeremy dizzy, too. At least, something made him dizzy. He was dizzy a good deal of the time, and tired. Very tired. He thought that some vague and hopeful day he'd take a week off. When things quieted down. When Andy's anathematized "Botches" let up on the paper. When advertisers ceased to trouble. When the whole show was over and the final issue of The Guardian had closed with its final challenge to the forces of Deutschtum. When his heart stopped crying out for Marcia.

Meantime he wearily wished he could get a night's sleep.

## 39

S<small>UCH</small> <small>ADVANTAGE</small> <small>AS</small> <small>THE</small> bee may boast over the butterfly is pro-verbially supposed to inhere in its industrious habits. But Miss Mar-cia Ames, now adopting the schedule of the bee at its busiest, found her earlier butterfly proclivities of advantage in that they had put her in touch with certain flowers of Fenchester's social world with which the harder-worked honey-collector might not have been so familiar. Visiting these upon her proselytizing errand, this enterprising flitter, still trailing clouds of glory from her butterflyhood, left behind her the fructifying pollen of the Great Idea. In one respect—to carry the ento-mological metaphor a step farther—she was like a moth rather than either the butterfly or the bee, since her good works, to be effective, must needs be carried on in the dusk of a semi-secrecy.

Behold our bee, now, hovering about the garden of that ancient but still lively wasp, Madam Dorothea Taylor, until bidden to alight and state her errand, whereof the venerable one, having already received some hint from her friend, Letitia Pritchard, is alertly suspicious. Accept-ing the invitation, the visiting bee leads up diplomatically to the first point of risk, the name of Jeremy Robson.

"A slanderer!" rasps the wasp. "A character-robber. A rag-tag and bob-tail cheap-and-nasty politician!"

The bee goes on with her musical, conciliatory, and soothing song, and presently mentions The Guardian.

"Don't name the rag to me!" blares the enraged wasp. "A filthy sheet! The poison of asps! A mud-slinger! A tool of that torch-and-scaffold, anarchistic harlequin, Martin Embree."

"Have you read it lately?" queries the bee.

"God forbid! I wouldn't endure a copy in the house."

"How fortunate," hums the bee sweetly, "that I brought only small portions of one or two copies."

Cleverly stimulating the other's curiosity, our cunning bee succeeds in persuading her to look at the clipping wherein Martin Embree, Emil Bausch, and the Kaiser stand forth wreathed in the olive of a mock-pacifism. Now is the wasp's angry voice hushed, as she peruses this and follows it with the now famous "hyphen" editorial, and the political quittance of Martin Embree.

"He appears to have lost none of his venom," observes the reader, "though he is now turning it against his own kind."

"They are not his own kind!" The bee for the moment forgets that she is committed to the soft footing of diplomacy. "I will not hear it said that they are his own kind! We are his own kind: we Americans!"

"Hoity-toity and here's a to-do!" cries the aged wasp. "Are we, indeed? Not I, you minx! That gullible old fool, Selden Dana, has been preaching from the same text. He wheedled me into withdrawing my libel suit against the young backbiter. Why I was silly enough to do so, *I* don't know. Now, what are you asking me to do?"

"Help," answers the visiting bee, and sets forth a general outline of her plan.

"Boycott," observes the shrewd old wasp, after turning it over in her mind.

"Oh, not in the least!" disclaims the bee. "That would be illegal."

"Pooh! Who cares for laws! Boycott it is, against any merchant who won't support The Guardian. Isn't it?"

"It might appear—"

"Appear! Don't hem-and-haw with me, Miss Pert. I can hire Dana to do that. You're asking the women of this city to boycott the stores that boycott The Guardian."

"Dear me, no!" returns the bee demurely. "We are only suggesting a practical method of showing appreciation of Mr. Rob—of The Guardian's patriotic course. And if you will join our little association and bring your Red Cross work down with you for a few minutes each morning, that is all we ask of you."

"Of me! There's the point. *Me!* I've been libeled and slandered and traduced and held up to public scorn," sizzles the wasp (who had, since the withdrawal of the suit, enjoyed one last reading of Judge Dana's comprehensive complaint with stimulating influence upon her style), "and now you have the assurance to ask me to rush to the aid of this reckless young muck-raker. It's absurd! It's outrageous! It's an impudence! It's an imposition! It's—it's—I'll do it."

"I knew you would," softly says the bee (who hadn't known anything of the sort, and has, indeed, dreaded this visit above all others). "I do not think you will ever be sorry."

"I hope *you* won't," retorts the wasp vigorously and significantly. "That's a dangerous character, that young Robson. Have a care of him!"

Having made captive her most difficult subject, the missionary bee now descends upon one hardly less difficult, Mrs. Vernam Merserole, wife (and, if rumor be correct, head of the house) of the "nickel-in-the-slot" rector. Mrs. Merserole, looking meek, according to her practice, but stubborn, according to her character, harks back to past injuries, and talks darkly of defamers of character as one might say "persecutors of the saints."

"That was before we were at war, Mrs. Merserole," her caller reminds her.

Mrs. Merserole looks up quickly from her clasped hands. "You think that today Mr. Robson would not make an unprincipled attack upon—upon a clergyman who did nothing more than his duty?"

Diplomatic though her errand be, Marcia will not pass this challenge to her truthfulness. "I do not say that. Nor do I admit that what he wrote was unprincipled. He wrote what he believed. He would do that again tomorrow. But I do know that he is a broader and more charitable man than he was then."

"War does not change men's characters, Miss Ames," says the rector's wife austerely.

"Then God help the men!" bursts out Marcia. "And God help the country!"

"Why, my dear!" says the older woman, shaken by the girl's vehemence. "You think it does? Perhaps you're right. Yes; I think you're right. But Mr. Robson—"

"Mrs. Merserole," breaks in Marcia with apparent irrelevance, "I have heard that your boy picked out the aviation service because it is the most dangerous, and that you told him that he had done what you would choose him to do."

The other does not reply. But her lips quiver, and her tightly clasped fingers press in on each other. Marcia lays her warm, strong little hand over them.

"You have done a great thing like that. And now I ask you to do a little thing. To forget an old injury."

"But Mr. Merserole—he feels toward The Guardian—I cannot express it to you," falters the other.

"The Guardian is a forlorn hope," returns Marcia. "Mr. Robson is sacrificing it and with it all his ambitions and his future for the sake of a principle. That is his part in the war; the only part he can play."

"Is it? I had heard otherwise."

"What have you heard?"

"That he persuaded a doctor to declare him unfit."

"That is a lie," declares Marcia calmly, and gives the facts. "Who told you the lie?" she asks, at the close of the recital.

The other hesitates. "Mrs. Robert Wanser," she says, at length. "I will speak to the rector about your plan," she adds, and, by her tone, Marcia knows that she has won another recruit.

So from house to house flits the busy bee, arguing here, pleading there, feeling her way cautiously in doubtful places and always imposing secrecy until the organization shall be completed; enlisting trustworthy lieutenants,—Miss Pritchard; little Anne Serviss, vice-president of the senior class at Old Central; Magnus Laurens's daughter, who comes down from the country to hot and dusty Fenchester to help; Miss Abbie Rappelje, sister of the Professor of Economics; Mrs. Montrose Clark; and, chiefest of all, the wary and wily Judge Selden Dana, . . . who, by the way, is working out a little scheme of his own all the time, in which Marcia is no more than a pawn, and without saying a word to her about it. Trust Dana for that!

While these processes were moving more or less bumpily on their appointed course outside The Guardian office, those wheels within wheels, upon which Andrew Galpin had philosophically animadverted, were whirling at an accelerated pace inside. The postponement of The Fair Dealer's publication day had been a blow to certain developing plans in The Guardian's press-room. When a labor leader has sedulously fomented ill-feeling, worked it almost to the point of explosion, promised the malcontents another job at increased pay if they strike to order on a certain date, and then had that date unavoidably postponed, his position becomes difficult and his next step doubtful. Such was the situation in the press-room of The Guardian. It was accentuated by the fact that The Guardian's editor had taken to editorializing quite frankly upon certain developments in the labor world outside, thereby furnishing extra incentive to the waiting strikers, for, radical though he was, Jeremy held himself as free to criticize labor as capital when he deemed it in the wrong. In fact he was in the midst of a mid-afternoon editorial for the morrow on "Labor and the War," when he came out of the fog of mental toil into a sensation of something wrong, something lacking. The presses had stopped. Surely it wasn't time for the run to be over! No; his watch marked four-ten.

From above sounded the scuffling of feet; a door opened and a furious, hard-breathing voice shouted an oath. Now there was a hubbub of voices, dull in the distance, and the floor shook lightly under some impact. Jeremy got to his feet, shaking and sweating. To such a condition of nerves had the overwork and overstrain of the last few weeks reduced him. He forced himself toward the door—when, with a roar and a clack, the presses took up their rhythm again, making sweet music for the relief of his beleaguered mind.

He returned to his editorial. But the savor of the work had gone. He was too deeply preoccupied with what had happened upstairs. That was Galpin's department; he made it a practice not to interfere. Yet, until the last run was off the presses and the machinery was silenced, he sat, intent and speculating.

The clang of a gong sounded outside. From his window he caught a glimpse of a departing ambulance. Was there some connection between that and the turmoil above? The men had not come down, though it was past time. He decided to go to the press-room and investigate.

On the top step he stopped short. Somebody was making a speech. Surely that was Nick Milliken's voice—Milliken, who had been threatened with arrest if he returned! Milliken's voice and Milliken's propaganda, for he was saying:

"Someday we'll own this stick-in-the-mud old plant, all of us together. We'll own it and run it for the common good and the common profit. Someday we'll own all production, and run it for the common good and the common profit! That'll come. But that ain't our job now, comrades. We've got something else on hand, first."

The editor and owner of the plant, thus cavalierly committed to common control, laid his hand on the knob of the door, but paused to hear the speaker's next words:

"Now about this strike: I'm for the strike. I'm for any strike—at the right time. But this ain't the time. Lemme give you a little parable, comrades."

Jeremy sat upon the top step and listened to the parable of Milliken, the Socialist. When it was over he tiptoed quietly down the stairs and into his own office. There he lay in wait until he heard the meeting break up and the tramp of descending feet. Standing sentry, he intercepted the speaker and called him into the sanctum.

"Will you come back to the job?" said Jeremy.

"Sure!" returned the other. He was spent and haggard, but his eyes were alight with triumph. "I was never off it."

"I heard your speech—part of it—enough so I knew I had you wrong."

"It did the business. The strike's spoiled."

"Off?"

"Might as well be. There'll be six or seven Germans quit. But they can't do much without Girdner. He's the one that's been playing merry hell with the whole show."

"Where's Girdner?"

"Hospital."

"What happened to him?"

"He fell downstairs," said Milliken casually but happily.

"Oh! Unassisted?"

"He threw me out of the meeting. Easy picking for him. You'd be surprised to see how quick he hustled me through the door," said the other regretfully. "He might have hurt me bad; I wouldn't be surprised. He was real rough with me. Then, just as we got to the top of the stairs, one of my arms took to flopping round kind of general, and he got hit on the jaw. Queer how things come back to you!" observed the white-haired Socialist, with surpassing innocence. "It never came into my mind till then that I once spent two years in a fighters' stable."

"I see," said. Jeremy thoughtfully. "No—I don't know. I thought you Socialists—"

"I thought you capitalists—" interrupted the other with instant retort. Jeremy laughed.

"I guess you were an American before you were a Socialist."

"When I can't be both I'll quit being either," answered the other fiercely.

"I do see!" said the other. "You're in that same trench with Judge Dana, where it makes no difference who or what a man is so long as he fights on the level and to a finish."

"I guess I am—comrade!" said Milliken, the Socialist.

## 40

SOMETHING QUEER HAPPENED TO young Mr. Jeremy Robson on the night of July 10th. Despite a lumpy sensation in the back of his neck and his habitual effect of being absolutely fagged out by the day's work, he had gone to bed with the resilient assurance of youth that he would awake refreshed and fit in the morning. Instead, he woke up feeling aged beyond the power of the mind to grasp: a mere crumbling ruin, compared to which the pyramid of Cheops was a parvenu and the Druidic altars of Stonehenge the mushroom growth of a paltry yesterday. Worse than this, there was a dregsy, bitter taste in his soul. It grew and spread; and presently as he lay miserably wondering at it, developed into a gall-and-worm-wood loathing of the circumstanding world's activities, but particularly of his work, the purposeless, futile, inexorable toil of The Guardian, daily re-galvanized into the appearance of life, but in reality doomed to swift and hopeless dissolution.

For a moment his thoughts turned from hatred to Marcia. A receding vision, "the lands of Dream among," hopelessly beyond the reach of a Failure. Inexpressibly old, Mr. Jeremy Robson wrote "Finis" upon the scroll of his fate and sat up in bed the better to contemplate the wreckage which had been himself. Immediately things began to revolve in his head. Wheels. Andrew Galpin's wheels. Wheels of all sizes and brutally distorted shapes whirling in counter-directions with an imbecile and nauseous suavity, weaving into unendurable patterns the warp and woof of his comprehensive hatred.

"Bosh!" said Jeremy Robson. He stood up and promptly fell down.

"Too much pressure," pronounced Doc Summerfield, arriving at speed. "You stop, young man, or you'll be stopped."

"Give me something to steady me up," begged Jeremy. "I've got to go to the office today!"

"Have you?" returned the physician grimly. "Drink this."

Sleep descended powerfully upon Jeremy, blotting out hatreds and worries and all other considerations for the time. It held him in its toils for successive days and nights; how many he could not have told. Once he woke up, quite clear in his head, and looked out across a broad piazza, through elms and shrubbery upon the crested lake, and was about to congratulate himself upon his recovery (though he could not quite figure out to what pleasant spot he had been translated) when Mrs. Montrose Clark came into the room—which was, of course, delirium—and asked him how he felt and whether he was hungry. Later Doc Summerfield arrived, declined to explain, said, "Drink this" (he was always and forever saying, "Drink this") "and I'll tell you all about it tomorrow."

So, on the morrow—or it might have been the following century for all Jeremy knew—Doc Summerfield came back and delivered a syncopated monologue:

"Yes. You are at Mr. Montrose Clark's cottage . . . No; you certainly can't go home. Don't be a jackass! . . . No; the paper hasn't gone up. It's doing very well without you . . . No; of course you're not going down to the office. Don't be a fool! . . . Heart? No; it isn't your heart. It's nerves. Overwork. That's all. Don't be a ninny . . . Certainly you'll be all right. In a few days, if you'll behave yourself and not act like a blithering simpleton . . . Drink this."

What seemed to Jeremy so long and uncertain a period was, in reality, only a little over a week. Came a day when the Montrose Clarks sent him out for a ride with their chauffeur, otherwise unattended, and he prevailed upon that guileless youth to take him to the office.

"Don't wait. I'll telephone," said he, and made for his den.

At first, as he entered, he felt a qualm of nausea. This passed, to be succeeded by a dull languor. He shook this off and, finding that wheels no longer revolved within his head when he tried to think, he decided that he was fit for work. Pursuing this theory, he settled to his work-table when the door burst open and Andrew Galpin rushed in.

"Where the devil—" he began and started back as from an apparition. "For the love of *Mike!*" he shouted. "Where did you come from?"

"The Montrose Clark cottage."

"Go back! Get out! You ought to be in bed."

"I have been. I'm tired of it."

"What would Doc Summerfield say?"

"The usual thing: 'Drink this.' What do you suppose he'd say to you?"

The general manager was red, perspiring, and disheveled, and there was a vague, wild, and incomprehensible gleam in his eye.

"Me? What's he got to do with me?"

"How do I know? You don't look—well, normal."

"Don't I!" retorted his subordinate with some heat. "Then just lemme tell you that I'm the only normal gink left in the business. I'm sane; *that's* what's the matter with *me!* That's what makes me look so queer and feel so lonely."

"You'd have to prove it to me," retorted his chief. "That's because you've got it, too. Only yours takes a different form from the rest. Go back to bed, Boss. But first, where's that file of special contracts?"

"Try the cabinet there. What do you want of 'em?"

Galpin found the documents, and turned upon Jeremy.

"Boss, this man's town had gone batty. Plumb bugs! Hopeless case."

"You know what happens to a man who discovers that everybody else is crazy, Andy."

"It's gone completely nuts over The Guardian," pursued the other, ignoring the intimation. "We're a hobby. An obsession. A fad! A fashion! A killing! A—"

"What's got you, Andy?" asked the editor anxiously. "Come down to earth."

"Can't! I'm a balloon. Watch me soar!" The usually stolid manager performed a bacchanalian fling. "Contracts!" he panted. "Reams of 'em! Money! Gobs of it! Circulation! Going uh-uh-up! Whee!"

"Andy, I'm not feeling very husky; but in a moment I shall throw you down and sit on your neck."

"Can't be done! I could lick the Kaiser and all his Botches single-handed. Boss, the luck has broke! The town is coming our way."

"How? Why? What's happened?"

"I'd like to tell you, but I haven't got time. They're waiting for me downstairs."

"Who?"

"Advertisers. Waiting to break into The Guardian. They're lined up in the hallways. I'll have to issue rain-checks."

"Stop talking like a lunatic, Andy, and explain."

The demented manager perched upon the corner of the editorial table, with an effect of being poised for instant flight.

"Don't ask me to explain, because I can't. I tell you the advertisers of this town have suddenly got a mania—and we're the mania. It began two days ago and it's been growing worse right along. I didn't think I'd ever be able to break through to the office this morning. They waylaid me on the way down. I don't know who began it. I think it was Stormont, of Stormont & Lehn. He fell out of a doorway on me, and when I got loose there was a thousand-dollar advertising contract stuck down my collar. Then old Pussy-foot Ellison came sobbing up the street—"

"What the devil—"

"Don't interrupt me or I'll bust! And never mind my metaphors. It comes easier that way. Well, he blubbered out his sweet message of intending to double his space in the paper instead of cutting us out; and before I'd got his tears fairly brushed off my shoulder, Vogt, the Botch, rushed in, threw his arms round my neck and tried to kiss me, and handed me an eight-hundred-dollar-space order in lieu of damages; and asked whether we wouldn't like flowers sent round mornings, gratis! Boss, I can just see you writing an editorial with one of Vogt's tea-roses stuck coyly behind your ear—"

"Never mind my ear. Go on!"

"How can I remember who mobbed me! I do recall that Arndt, of the furniture shop, knocked me down and dragged me into an alley; and when I came to there was a signed agreement to restore all the space they lifted from us, and twenty-five per cent over and above. And, by the way, I saw the Governor hiking into Bausch's office and looking about as cheerful as a banshee with a bellyache. Oh, there's big doings of some kind, you bet! All the morning the 'phone has been buzzing and—Who's that having hysterics in the hall?"

He threw open the door, and Mr. Adolph Ahrens, of The Great Northwestern Stores, bounded in, uttering a wild, low wail, the burden of which seemed to be something about a "misunderstanding." He also mentioned the word "blackmail," and hastily retracted it. He had always, he asserted passionately, been friendly to The Guardian. He admired it for its lofty courage, its unfailing fair-mindedness, its patriotism; and as an advertising medium he considered it without parallel or equal.

In token of which he had brought his copy for a full page in that day's issue. And would Mr. Robson kindly note that he had taken a box for the Loyalty Rally on Saturday, being as good an American as anybody, even if he did bear a German name? And so, exit Mr. Ahrens, stringing out deprecatory statements about a misunderstanding as he went.

"For Heaven's sake, Andy, what does it all mean?"

The general manager shook his disheveled head.

"Search me!" he said gravely. "Except for this: It means that The Guardian wins."

"Have you reckoned it up?"

"Don't need to. Outside a few of the Old Prussian Guard in the Deutscher Club we've got everything back that we lost, and a heap more on top of it."

"But who's been doing it? And what have they been doing?" cried the bewildered Jeremy.

"Not guilty on either count. Somebody's been impressing our friends, the enemy, that there's just one way to be saved, and that the only A1, guaranteed salvation is via The Guardian. Watch 'em crowd to the mourners' seat."

"What's the paper been doing since I—"

"Not a thing. Not a blooming thing, Boss, but just sawing wood. This game wasn't started from inside. I'll swear to that. Whoever's been doing the trick—and it looks to me as if there'd been some expert and ree-fined blackmail going on—has been keeping clear of us."

"Judge Dana!" exclaimed Jeremy, struck with a thought.

"Well, I've been sort of wondering about him myself," admitted the other. "Met him on the street yesterday and he wanted me to call him up as soon as you got back."

"All right. Here I am."

"Ay-ah? You've got to show me. You're not back till Doc Summerfield says you're back."

The door opened and the amazed physiognomy of Buddy Higman appeared. "The Boss!" he exclaimed. "Holy Moses! I'm a liar."

"What's up, Buddy?"

"I've been stallin' off Doc Summerfield and a crazy show-foor downstairs. They're waitin' now. They said would you come peaceable or be took. I told 'em you'd never been near here."

"Tell 'em I'll come peaceably, Buddy," said the editor wearily. He turned to Andrew Galpin. "Andy."

"Ay-ah?"

"You're sure this is straight? You're sure you're not the one that's crazy? Or I?"

"Am I sure! Go out the front way, Boss, and see the line waiting. That'll convince you. I tell you, unless something busts, we'll win out sure."

Hardly could the editor and owner of The Guardian, led away by Doc Summerfield in deep disgrace, assimilate the hope of ultimate victory for his paper and himself. He dared not let himself believe in it yet, because of the intruding thought of Marcia and of what triumph might mean to him.

## 41

CLICK-CLICK! CLICK-CLICK! CLICKETY-CLICK! One hundred pairs of knitting needles furnished a subdued castanet accompaniment to the voice of a long, lean lady-droner who stood upon the platform of the Fenchester Club Auditorium, and read from a typed list. At times she referred to various issues of The Guardian ranged on a flag-bedecked table. And at times the clickers paused to make notes in small books wherewith they had provided themselves for that very purpose. The gathering was the every morning meeting of the Fenchester Ladies War Reading Club.

Socially it was a comprehensively representative gathering, and something more. Pretty much every family whose comings and goings were wont to be entered (by Buddy Higman or some other arbiter of the elegancies) in The Guardian's Society Notes had at least one member present. Sprinkled among the women who made up the active list of membership were a few associate members, mere males, and in the presiding officer's chair sat Mr. Montrose Clark; for, after the regular proceedings of the day, special business was in order.

Miss Rappelje, the secretary, read from her list:

"Nicholas Engel, grocer. Last year, two columns a week, average. Since The Fair Dealer announcement, half a column."

The castanet chorus diminished while the knitters and crocheters entered a note against Herr Engel's grocery.

"The Fliess Brewing Company," continued the reader. "Last year five columns; now, none."

"Hurray for Prohibition! Beer's a German drink anyway," cried a voice, and there was a wave of laughter as the clicking resumed.

"The Great Northwestern Stores. Last year three full pages, regularly, and on special sales as high as five—"

"Pardon me." A member rose in the center of the house. "Mr. Ahrens sent a representative to tell me that, in spite of unsettled conditions, they have contracted to use more space in The Guardian than ever before, and to ask me to report it here."

"Let 'em!" commented a determined and ominous voice. "*I* shall wait and see."

From the murmur of assent which greeted this, it was evident that many would wait and see. So the reading went on, through dairies, laundries, undertakers, soft drinks, ice dealers, stationers, milliners, garages, all the lines of industry which bid in print for trade, while the knitters alternately toiled and made their notes.

Outside, in a small anteroom off the stage, Mr. Jeremy Robson put his obstinate head down and balked. Ten days' enforced rest, except for his one escape, had gone far to restore him to fitness. Now he fended off Judge Selden Dana and demanded enlightenment.

"Not a step farther till I know what I'm up against," he declared.

"All you have to do," returned the lawyer soothingly, "is to trust to me and do as I tell you."

"Is that all!" retorted Jeremy, with intent. "Who are these people outside and what are they doing?"

"They're your well-earned enemies, and they're saving the paper for you."

"Somebody's certainly done a job in that direction. But how? These sound like mostly women."

"So they are. As to how they're pulling your paper through, that's the simplest thing in the world. We got up a War Reading Club."

"Reading Club," repeated Jeremy. "Perfectly simple! Of course! Andy Galpin *said* the whole town had gone crazy since I was laid up. Andy was right."

"A great authority once proposed a classic question: 'Who's loony now?' Wait until you hear the rest of this. The club meets here every morning to do knitting and other war-work while certain extracts from the local papers are read to them."

"Good idea," remarked Jeremy, weary but polite. "Shall I have something put in the paper about it?"

"My Lord, no!" almost shouted Dana.

Jeremy leaped in his chair. "I wish you wouldn't do that sort of thing," he protested.

"Still a bit jumpy? Well, I'll explain in words of one syllable. But first apply your eye to this peep-hole and tell me what you think of our membership."

Doing as he was directed, the editor looked out over what, in earlier days, he would have identified as a mass-meeting of The Guardian's enemies.

"How much purchasing power per year in the local stores would you suppose they represent?" asked Dana.

"A big lot. Quarter of a million, maybe."

"Nearer twice that. Now, we've got a little committee called the Committee on Selective Reading. I happen to be chairman of it. Our committee chooses what advertisements—you get that, Jem?—what advertisements shall be read each day. That's our White List. Our members deal only with merchants whose loyalty is above suspicion. What would you think of the loyalty of an advertiser who quit The Guardian to go into The Fair Dealer?"

"Don't ask me. I'm prejudiced."

"So is the War Reading Club. It's my committee's business to keep 'em prejudiced—against any merchant who advertises in the wrong place. Now, our theory is that our members read no advertisements, themselves, and don't intend to; certainly not after The Fair Dealer appears. Therefore they know of the local advertising only as the Committee on Selective Reading chooses it for them. That's the *theory*."

"What's the fact?"

"The fact is that ninety-nine per cent of those women will see any merchant in town doubly damned before they spend a cent in his shop unless he sticks by The Guardian as long as The Guardian sticks by the country. Do you get it now?"

"Boycott!"

"And blackmail. You should have seen the weak-kneed among the store-people when we let our programme leak out! You heard part of it from Galpin."

"Dana," said the editor, "if you'd told me this before, you'd have saved me some mighty tough days."

"Couldn't risk it. Can't you see that we've been skirting the ragged edge of the law? If you'd been in on it, The Fair Dealer could have charged conspiracy."

"Then why tell me now?"

"We-ell, we can't work under cover much longer. Besides, I doubt if there's much of any fight left in Embree and his crowd." He peered out through the peep-hole. "They've turned it into an experience meeting now," he remarked. "Then you come on. They're expecting you. Will you come peaceably or be escorted?"

"Let me keep out of sight until it's my turn, anyway," pleaded Jeremy.

So the lawyer, leading him in, established him behind a wing where he was half-hidden, and placed himself as a screen. As he settled himself down, a plump and luxuriously dressed woman at the rear of the hall rose and said austerely:

"I disapprove The Guardian's local policy. I consider it unfair and prejudiced against—er—ah—against our kind of people. But while we are at war I agree to support it loyally and to deal only with those who support it."

"Are my eyes playing tricks?" whispered Jeremy in Dana's ear. "Or is that Mrs. Ambrose Galsworth, who tried to have me blackballed at the Canoe Club?"

"She's a new member. Wait! There's worse to come," chuckled the lawyer.

A little, lean, brisk, twinkling old maid projected herself out of her seat with a jumping-jack effect.

"I never expected to live to see the day I'd speak for The Guardian after they printed that awful political attack on my dear uncle," she declared. "But the country first! Put down Celia Jenney on your list. And"—her black bright eyes snapped out sparks—"if there's a store in town that don't want my trade while this war is on, all it has to do is to take its advertising out of The Guardian and put it into The Fair Dealer—if that's its silly name."

"She spends only about fifteen thousand a year in this town," observed Dana aside to Jeremy.

"No wonder the advertisers have been falling over themselves to get back into the paper!" murmured the editor.

After further informal pledges the chairman called for reports from the "Missionary Workers." Up rose Alderman Crobin—Crooked Crobin, as The Guardian had dubbed him for years.

"T'ree of my constitchoonts assured me this mahrnin'—voluntarily, ye ondherstand; quite voluntarily—that they are cancelin' their contract wid th' noo paper."

A tall, pale young woman rose in the center of the house, and as she moistened her nervous lips a murmur and a rustle swept over the audience; for this was Mrs. Dennis Robbins, Governor Embree's sister.

"I bring five pledges of advertisers to stand by The Guardian—and America," she said in a low voice; and a quick ripple of sympathetic applause answered her.

Before it had died away, old Madam Taylor rustled silkily to her feet.

"I'm the tax-dodger," she cackled. "See The Guardian if you don't believe it. But I never dodged a good fight. Two stores that I trade with cut down their advertising in The Guardian. So I cut down my trade with them. I cut it down to nothing. Now I understand they feel differently about the paper," she concluded malevolently.

Up popped pursy little Mrs. Stockmuller. "Me, I quit Ahrens anyway," she announced, and sat down flushed with the resultant applause of the multitude and suddenly conscious of latent and hitherto unsuspected capabilities as a public speaker.

Then little Anne Serviss pledged the support of three hundred University girls, and following her, the Reverend Mr. Merserole reared himself impressively into sight and hearing.

"Inter arma, rixæ minores silent," he proclaimed oracularly, "if my friend Judge Dana, whom I observe upon the stage, will permit me to alter a legal proverb to fit the occasion. 'In time of war, lesser quarrels are stilled.' Many of us have had our—er—trials with The Guardian. But all that is forgotten in the larger cause. I beg to report, Mr. Chairman, that eighteen members of my church—leading members, I may add—have signed an agreement to advertise in no local morning paper during the war."

"But that's boycott and against the law, isn't it?" queried some cautious member.

Dana jumped to his feet.

"Let 'em take it up!" he cried, his face lighted by a joyous snarl. "Just let us get 'em into court on it!"

A shout answered him. There was no mistaking the temper of that crowd. Friends or enemies of The Guardian's lesser policies, they were shoulder to shoulder now in the common cause. A conservative old judge was just resuming his seat, after reporting, when the door was jerked open and there burst into the aisle Andrew Galpin, livid with the excitement of great tidings.

"They've quit!" he shouted. Then, recalling himself to the proprieties, he added: "I beg pardon, Mr. Chairman. But they've quit!"

Mr. Montrose Clark rose. "Mr. Andrew Galpin, of The Guardian," he announced. "Mr. Galpin has, perhaps, matter of interest to present before this meeting."

"They've quit. That's all," said the excited Galpin. His wild and roving glance fell upon Jeremy Robson who had incautiously moved forward at sight of his associate, and the last vestige of parliamentary decorum departed from him. "Do you get that, Boss?" he bellowed. "The Botches have quit. We win."

"Who's quit?" "What's a Botch?" "Platform!" "Tell us about it."

"What's a Botch?" repeated the general manager. "Bausch is a Botch. Wanser's a Botch. The Deutscher Club's a batch of Botches. 'Smiling Mart' Embree's a Botch, The Fair Dealer would have been a Botch, but there isn't going to be any Fair Dealer. They couldn't stand the gaff you folks put to 'em. Publication day's indefinitely postponed."

Hardly had he finished when Jeremy Robson found himself being hustled by Judge Dana and the chairman, who had possessed themselves of an arm apiece, to the front of the platform. The house rose to him in a burst of acclaim. He looked out, with nerves aquiver, across that waiting audience of one-time enemies, opponents bitter and implacable, bitterly and implacably fought in many an unforgotten campaign;

now his allies, rallying to a service greater than all past hatreds, higher than all past loyalties.

Judge Dana's words echoed back to him: "In the same cause—with the last drop of blood—to the finish!" What terms could he find wherein to speak to these, his enemies of old, looking up at him with such befriending eyes?

Montrose Clark had delivered himself of a hurried and unheeded introduction, and now Jeremy stood, with shaking knees, gazing down at them. Opportunely and suddenly the parable of Nick Milliken came into his mind.

"My friends," he said unsteadily, "I can't make you a speech. There aren't thanks made for this sort of thing. But I can tell you the parable of Milliken. You know Milliken, the Socialist—one of us. He was talking to a bunch that were ripe for a strike, arguing against it because it would hinder one little corner of our war. This is what he told them: 'All my life,' he said, 'I've been fighting Wall Street and the firm of J. P. Morgan & Company. I'm against everything they represent. I expect to go on fighting them the rest of my life. But if I were walking down the street with Mr. Morgan and we met a mad wolf in the road I'd say to him: "Pierpont, let's get together and kill that wolf. Our little scrap can wait."

"That's what Milliken told them, my friends. That's all I can say to you now. We've had our differences, you and I. We'll have them again. They seemed big and bitter at the time. How little they seem now! For now we're facing the mad wolf of Germany right here in Centralia. He's in the heart of our State. "Let's get him out! Our little scrap can wait!"

They rose to him again.

"But, God bless your dear hearts," cried young Jeremy Robson with shining eyes and outstretched hands, "how can we ever fight each other after this!"

Up in a far corner of the gallery a pair of strong, little, sun-tanned, eager, tremulous hands went forth involuntarily as if to meet Jeremy's, unseen.

While that very unliterary and decidedly militant organization, the Fenchester War Reading Club, was pouring forward to overwhelm the editor of The Guardian, there gathered in the little side room a hasty and earnest conference of three. Andrew Galpin and Montrose Clark having left it, the lone survivor, Judge Selden Dana, remained to catch Jeremy as he came out.

"Jem," he said, "you've won."

"Thanks to you people!"

"Thanks to a good fight. Galpin tells me The Fair Dealer backers are through. We've scared the local advertisers out of their contracts and the paper can't hold 'em because of the change of publication date. Verrall made a fatal break when he put a date in that contract. They're through. But The Fair Dealer is going on."

"No! Who's going to back it?"

"Montrose Clark. He's going to take it over."

"For his corporation campaign. I see. Then this means another fight of another kind on my hands."

"He's going to use it to beat out Martin Embree with his own candidate."

Jeremy's eyes narrowed. "You know The Guardian can't and won't stand for you fellows' kind of candidate."

"You'll stand for this one."

"Who is it?"

"Jeremy Robson."

"Jer—Andy was right, *sure!*" gasped the other. "The town has gone crazy and I've gone with it."

"On a platform of Centralia for the War," continued the other. "Now put your lower jaw back on its hinges and I'll explain how this isn't as crazy from our point of view as you'd think. You'll be elected—for we'll lick 'Smiling Mart'—only for the unfinished term. The war will last that long, and while the war lasts internal policies don't matter. After the war—why, we'll have a newspaper of our own to lick you with when you come up for reelection."

"I'll give you a good run both ways," promised Jeremy. And the two men soberly shook hands upon it.

"What a scheme; the woman's boycott!" said Jeremy presently. "I might have known that was your fine Italian hand."

"It wasn't."

"No? Who did work it out?"

"A much cleverer politician than I ever thought of being."

"There ain't no sich animule," denied Jeremy. "Show it to me."

"I have been sitting at the feet of Wisdom, Wile, and Woman. Her other name," said Judge Dana, "is Marcia Ames. And my professional advice to you is to be on your way."

"In dreams she grows not older
The lands of Dream among—"

THE DEEP, SOFT THRILL of the contralto voice floated through the war air on invisible wings. The listener, coming softly up the pathway of the old garden, paused to hearken, to drink it in, with the fragrance of the late roses, the wine of the sun-drenched air, the peace of the shaded ways, all the other lovelinesses of a world suddenly blessed to his soul.

"Though all the world wax colder
Though all the songs be sung
In dreams doth he—"

The voice faltered and sank, at the sound of his foot upon the steps. The singer's hands strayed like suddenly affrighted things among the keys of the piano. She stood to face him as he entered, and of all the tremulous, tender beauty of her, only her eyes meeting and merging with his, were unwavering.

"Jem!" she said, very low.

"Marcia!"

She lifted her arms as he crossed swiftly to her, and clung to him, and gave him her lips in glad and complete surrender, while he held her close and murmured to her the words that he had been so hungry to speak, she so hungry to hear.

"Jem," she whispered presently, "you cannot give me up now, Jem."

"I never did, dear love," he said.

"Ah, but you did. You tried. How could you even try!"

"I never did. Not really. Not for a moment. Not even when I thought you had married someone else."

She moved in his arms to hide her eyes against his face.

"You must have known that I never could," she murmured.

"Don't you see," he pursued eagerly, "that if I had really given you up, I should have given up the paper, the fight, everything? Don't you see that, love?"

"Yes; that is true," she assented sweetly. "That must be true. Though perhaps you did not know it . . . Ah, Jem, but I have wearied for you!"

"When's the very earliest you can marry me, dearest?" he asked.

She looked up at him with her level and fearless eyes. "Any time, Jem."

"I'm asking a lot of you," he said, his eager face clouding for the moment. "It isn't all plain sailing yet; and there won't be so much to live on even here. If we go to Washington you'll find it doubly hard, I'm afraid."

"But I have my own money, Jem. And what is this about Washington?"

"Oh!" said he casually; "they want to nominate me for the Senate, against Mart Embree."

"Jem! You will take it?"

"If my liege lady approves."

"Of course she approves. It is wonderful. How could you keep it to yourself! Why did you not tell me the instant you came?"

"Well, you see, I was intent on other matters," said Jem, looking down into the flushed and adorable face, which flushed the more adorably at his words. He bent to her. "Dearest of my heart," he said passionately, "what does it all matter in comparison with you!"

Stepping gloriously from rose-tipped cloud to rose-tipped cloud as youth may do when winged with happiness and love, Jeremy, on his way office-ward, presently found himself at the Inter-Urban terminal being accosted by a man who said:

"If you are deaf, I can make signs."

"I beg your pardon," apologized Jeremy hastily. "Were you speaking to me?"

"Only three times," said the stranger. "So far," he added.

Thus recalled from his castle-building the editor contemplated his interceptor. The man was a stranger in town. He carried a small, nondescript bag. He looked like a country minister on a week-day, or a prosperous plumber off the job, or a middle-aged clerk on an errand, or any one of a hundred other everyday individuals. In fact he was in face, figure, dress, and manner, the most commonplace, humdrum, unremarkable, completely average individual that Jeremy had ever encountered. He might have posed as the composite photograph of a convention of ten thousand Average Citizens.

"I was asking you: do you know this city," he was saying patiently.

Now Jeremy possessed a singularly retentive visual memory. This memory had suddenly started working with a jar. "I do," he said. "Do I know you?"

"You do not," said the man.

"I'm not so sure," retorted Jeremy. "I seem to remember a talk at the Owl's Nest in Philadelphia, six years ago or so, by a distinguished globe-trotter and war correspondent.[1] Now if you hadn't told me that I did not know you, I would have said—"

"You would have thought," corrected the stranger, without the flicker of an eyelid.

"I would have thought you were that lecturer."

"Likenesses are deceptive," observed the other.

"And, in spite of your new mustache, remembering a meeting at the Lion d'Or just off the Place Clichy a year later, I would have said—"

"You would have thought," interpolated the other, imperturbably.

"I would have thought that you were still the same, and I would have said—that is, I would have thought that your name was Jerome Tillinghast."

"But you wouldn't say it."

"Not on any account, if there is good reason against it in the opinion of Jerome Tillinghast—who, by the way, didn't have that furrow over his temple when I knew him."

"Shrapnel," explained the other. "Russian campaign. Got me in the leg, too. So they packed me home, and Uncle Sam set me to work. My official name is James Tilley. And yours?"

Jeremy explained himself.

"The Guardian, eh? You're the last man in town I'd have looked up. But now that I've met you, I'll just mention that Washington thinks pretty well of The Guardian. Keep it up, my boy. And now, where would I be likely to find a bold and dashing patriot, by name, Emil Bausch?"

Jeremy gave the directions. James Tilley thanked him. "Nobody ever recognizes me," he observed, "or notices me, or remembers me. I'm such a common article. That's all that makes me valuable. So kindly forget all this. And good-bye."

Five minutes later he was sitting in Emil Bausch's private office explaining to that perturbed gentleman certain supposedly very private matters in connection with a chemical project in one phase of which Bausch had acted for a certain otherwise unidentified "Mr. Stern." Bausch was loftily contemptuous, though nervous.

"The other details," said the caller pleasantly, "are entered in Ledger M, under the cipher of x-32, formerly kept at 60 Wall Street."

Bausch gulped twice and said he had never heard of it.

"Fortunate for you," returned the other. "Take my advice and don't hear of it. Don't have any part in it. Don't do business with people who have. Trouble lies that way."

Thereafter Mr. Bausch repaired to the Deutscher Club where he had several more beers than was his wont, and subsequently delivered himself of touching appreciations of free speech and the privileges of American citizenship. He wound up, after dinner, by declaring to a puzzled assemblage that he knew his rights and wasn't afraid of anybody, even if he did come from Washington and wear a tin shield.

Meantime a supremely ordinary appearing person contrived to get himself admitted to the President's room of the Fenchester Trust Company, and introduced himself to Robert Wanser, who found his bearing, mild though it was, distinctly antipathetic. In a voice so quiet as to give the effect of being meek, the intruder ventured to advise Mr. Wanser to shun the Deutscher Club.

"Go to the devil!" retorted Mr. Wanser, whose nerves had been recently frazzled by local as well as national events.

"I'm giving you the opposite advice," returned the other equably. "Keep away from the Deutscher Club."

"Save your advice for those who want it. Who are you, anyway?"

"James Tilley, at your service. Sent here from Washington to help you avoid trouble."

The word "Washington" fell chill upon the banker's ear. Nevertheless, he blustered "The Deutscher Club is my club. The Government cannot tell a private citizen to keep away from a private club."

"But a well-wisher—such as myself—may suggest that he find his amusements elsewhere."

"Well-wisher! A(c)h! Spy. Is this a free country? In Germany one would not be so oppressed."

"This is not Germany. Bear that in mind. The Deutscher Club *is*—or something like it."

"But—"

"And, by the way, tell your wife—Bertha Wanser is your wife, isn't she? Exactly! She talks too much. Propaganda. Tell her to—"

"Vimmen, too!" snarled the other. "You can't even keep your hands off vimmen. Tell her yourself."

James Tilley sighed. "I will," he said, and departed, leaving an irritant, disconcerting and healthily prudent impress upon the mind of the grandson of '48.

As for Mrs. Wanser, she was profoundly displeased with the face, apparel, carriage, and particularly the manner of her unknown caller, which was abrupt and brusque.

"You go to the motion pictures, madam," he stated.

"Yes," she said, wondering.

"On the 11th you were at the Gayety. A Four-Minute-Man[2] spoke. You protested to the management."

"I did. I told the manager he'd lose my custom if they let such nonsense go on."

"The speaker was Professor Brender, of the University—"

"A German," she broke in. "And he gets up in public and makes shame of Germany."

"As a Four-Minute-Man he speaks with the authority of the Government. On the 14th you protested to the Orpheum."

"You been spying on me," said the lady, wrathfully.

"Certainly. You're a suspicious person. Take my advice. Stop talking, or if you must talk, talk like an American. Propaganda is a dangerous game. Go to those two movie managers and withdraw—"

"I won't," she declared, pale with fury.

"I think you will. Ask your husband. And do as he tells you. He'll tell you just what I have—if he's wise."

For all his modest disavowals of being able to make an impression upon people, there were now at least three individuals in Fenchester who would hold in tenacious and painful memory to the last day of their lives the smallest detail of James Tilley's unremarkable personality. He now proceeded to enlarge the list. Whether by chance or by design, he encountered Pastor Klink, who was doing some quiet research work in connection with back files of the newspapers, in the City Library, and Pastor Klink took the next train for home and a reflective silence. He met with the Reverend Theo Gunst and that fervid theologian retired to draft an editorial for the leading German religious weekly, reeking with protestations of loyalty, which almost tore his agonized heart out by its Teutonic roots. He ran across Gordon Fliess and earnestly counseled him against the strain of frequent railway journeys between Bellair and Fenchester. On the other hand, and as indicating a certain amiable flexibility of view on his part, he dropped in upon A. M. Wymett to extol the broadening influence of travel. A. M. Wymett traveled.

He called upon Vogt and Niebuhr, and Henry Dolge, the educational expert, leaving behind him devastated areas of alarm, caution, and at least temporary silence.

Within two days after his arrival, though he had said no word nor even given any hint upon either point, the Deutscher Club burst into a riot of American flags,[3] and Martin Embree made a speech so full of patriotic pathos that it brought tears to the eyes of his hearers, particularly the Germans.

Bausch, and Niebuhr, and Dolge, and a few others of the old school, however, took to meeting in a respectable saloon kept by one Muller down in "the Ward." To them came Gordon Fliess, and influential men from the Northern Tier, for conference. What passed there was asserted to be perfectly loyal, and supposed to be quite private . . .

But within a fortnight, James Tilley, more unobtrusive than ever, stepped off another Inter-Urban trolley, and stayed over one train. Thence he went to Bellair, and so passes into his chosen obscurity. He gave no advice this time. Not, at least, to Bausch, or Dolge, Niebuhr, or the respectable saloon-keeper, Muller; neither to Gordon Fliess. But the respectable saloon unostentatiously ceased to exist. And its more than respectable patrons named above quietly vanished, and the places that had known them knew them no more. Observing which, the more cautious Robert Wanser trembled, and congratulated himself.

Deutschtum, hitherto hardly bent, was now broken[4] in the State of Centralia.

PATRIOTISM HAD WAXED AND politics waned with the ebbing of the year 1917, in Centralia. Through the murk and fume of alien treachery, enemy propaganda, and the reckless self-seeking of petty partisanship had burst a clear, high, consuming flame of Americanism. Lesser matters were forgotten in the maintenance of that beacon-fire. Men of all types of political belief, of all classes, of all economic and social creeds, had abandoned their private feuds and bitternesses in the fervor against the common enemy. To them had rallied the finer and more courageous element of the German-Americans, some impulsively from emotion and sentiment like Stockmuller and Blasius, others, in the pain and travail of old ties broken and from the profound conviction of loyalty and right, like Professor Brender. Centralia, thirty years before marked by Deutschtum to be the Little Germany of the New World, was slowly, doggedly establishing its birthright of Americanism.

Poison still lurked in its system. There were whisperings in dark corners. The German-language press still gave heart-service to the Kaiser's cause in hint and suggestion and innuendo, while giving lip-service to the cause of the United States in artificial and machine-made editorials. The German pulpit, preaching an ineradicable Germanism by the very use of the German tongue, was lack-loyal where it dared not be disloyal. Over many a Verein and Bund and Gesellschaft the Stars and Stripes waved above seething revolt of spirit. Workers in all patriotic causes felt the dead-weight of a sullen, unworded, untraceable opposition clogging their efforts. But all this was negative. Deutschtum, a few short months before so arrogant and confident of its power over Centralia, was on its defense. More; it was in hiding. No other one force had done so much to drive it thither as that once yellow mongrel of journalism, The Fenchester Guardian.

The Guardian's den was brightly lighted on this December evening of 1917. It was brightly lighted on most evenings. Yet Doc Summerfield, aforetime of a pessimistic view regarding the effect of night-labor upon Jeremy Robson, was obliged to admit that he showed a steady improvement in spite of apparent overwork. Perhaps this was because he had provided himself with a highly valued assistant. The assistant was seated opposite the chief, reading proof on an editorial, when the door opened, and in stalked Andrew Galpin, traveling-bag in hand.

"Hello, Bosses!" he said.

"Hello, Andy," said his chief; and "Welcome back, Andy," said the assistant getting up to perch upon the arm of the chief editorial chair, thus leaving a seat for the general manager, who took it with a nod.

"I saw Cassius Kimball," he stated. "He's just back from Washington."

"Any news?" asked Jeremy.

"We've located Emil Bausch. But not for publication."

"Where is he?"

"Behind two rows of barbed wire, one of 'em charged with electricity, in a pleasant Southern camp. He's a member of the Millionaires' Club, there. They caught him on that chemical deal. Supposed to be wholesale drugs; really high explosives."

"Any other of our extinguished local lights heard from?"

"Muller, the saloon-keeper, is down there, too. But not in the Millionaires' Club. He's gardening. One dollar per diem. Martin Dolge is in Mexico."

"What about Gunst and Klink and the church outfit?"

"They've promised to be good. Three of their religious weeklies are scheduled to quit. Gordon Fliess has dropped his financial support of the German-American dailies. We're going to go stale for lack of opposition if this keeps on," prophesied Andy sadly.

"Cassius didn't run across Mart Embree down there, did he?" queried Jeremy.

"Ay-ah. He did. Says 'Smiling Mart' was running around like a little, worried dog, wagging his tail anxiously and trying to make his peace."

"Peace is still Governor Embree's specialty, then?" put in the assistant, from her perch.

"Why, I guess it always will be, so long as there's a German vote in Centralia," returned the general manager. "But what does 'Smiling Mart' amount to, now? We've got the whole bunch licked to a frazzle, and licked for keeps."

"Do you think so. So easily?"

Andy Galpin looked intently at Mrs. Jeremy Robson. "Maybe I'm wrong," he said meekly. "You think it isn't over?"

The little, tawny head was shaken emphatically.

"I think that we shall have it all to fight again," she said, in her unchanged, precise, and subtly caressing manner of speech.

"When?" The chief and the general manager challenged her with one voice.

"When Germany's peace offer is made. Then you will see Governor Embree and all that is left of Germany here making their fight for a peace which will be worse than war. That is why I will not listen to Jem's giving up the paper."

"What do you think of that, Andy?" asked Jem.

The general manager smiled his slow, homely, friendly smile at Marcia Robson. "I think what I've thought since the first minute I set eyes on her," he said: "that she's a wise guy. Boss, we haven't won this war over here until we've won this war over there, and don't you forget it! By the way, there's quite a little talk in Washington, Kimball tells me, about the new Senator-elect from Centralia."

"I blush, modestly and prettily," retorted Jem. "Or—Marcia, you do it for me. I'd rather stay here and run the old Guardian."

"I'd rather have you," returned Andy, with rueful emphasis.

"We shall be back for the fight that is coming," promised Marcia.

Galpin's eyes wandered slowly about the room and returned upon Marcia. "It gives me the shivers," he said, "to think how near we were to losing out on the whole fight when Buddy Higman went and got you. I'd like to have heard Buddy's argument."

"It was effective," laughed Marcia. "Buddy was honestly convinced that without The Guardian to guide it, the Nation would go to immediate destruction."

"Buddy's little plan turned out well for him," observed Jem. "Marcia is sending him to Old Central in the fall. Sort of a fairy godmother, aren't you?" he added, looking up at his wife. "Pull the paper through with one hand, save us all, and make a man of Buddy with the other."

"Do not give me too much credit," said Marcia, more gravely. "It was Andy who really held you here when you wished to go into the army."

"Oh, well, I had my stake in the paper, too," disclaimed the general manager, picking up his valise and hat. "Good-night, Bosses," he added. "Don't overwork and spoil your beauty, you two."

"Marcia," said Jem, after their aide had gone. "That night when you came back—don't go away while I'm talking seriously, please!—would you really have married me, right away, then and there?"

"Certainly, I would. I meant to. You were very cruel. You spoiled my plans."

He regarded her with suspicion. Was there a note of raillery in the sweet, even voice?

"What plans?"

"Why, to marry you then."

"And then what?"

"To put my money into the paper and keep you from selling it, of course."

"But if I wouldn't have taken it? And I wouldn't, you know."

"That would not have made the slightest difference," she said calmly. "You could not have sold the paper, in any case, if you had married me when—when I proposed to you."

"Couldn't I! I'd have had to, if matters had gone on as they were going."

"No. For you could not have sold the paper without the plant, and the plant being real estate, could not be transferred without the wife's consent."

"So it couldn't! You wretched little plotter! Who put you up to that?"

"I consulted a lawyer," she replied demurely. "On a hypothetical case."

"I'm jealous," declared Jem. "You were trying to marry me for my property and not for my winning self. Was that the only reason?"

Her face changed adorably as she bent over him. "What do you think?" she said.

"But I wanted to have—what is it Andy called it?—a stake in the paper, too," she continued, after a moment. "You have never let me. Do you think that is fair?"

"It's the only fair way. We're not out of the woods yet, with The Guardian. Newspaper property is going to be mighty uncertain before this war is over, and I don't want you involved in it. The Guardian has taken you in, little wife, but it won't take your money."

"Not even if you should need it? To save the paper?"

"Not even then."

"Jem, I—I want a—a stake in the paper."

"Why, Marcia! What is it, dearest? You're not crying, are you?"

"No, I *think* not. If I am, it is for happiness, Jem. I—I have a—a special stake now in the paper. I want to keep The Guardian to hand it down to—to—"

"Marcia!" He turned in the circle of her arms, but for once the frank eyes were hidden from him.

"—to our son," said the soft voice with a little catch in it. "I am sure it will be a son, Jem. If we name him Jeremy Andrew Robson"—the voice was muffled now against Jem's cheek—"he will be almost The Guardian's child—next to being ours, Jem."

Jem drew a long, deep breath of happiness. "There'll always be a good fight for a hundred per cent American paper like The Guardian to get into. That's the real best of the business, I guess." He bent over the little, proud, bowed head. "I hope he'll be as good an American as his mother," he said.

# NOTES

Chapter 1

1. Germans constituted the largest immigrant group in the United States. In 1914, nearly one in five Americans—twenty million people—were of German descent. More than eight million had been born in Germany or had a parent who was. At the beginning of the war, the majority of Wisconsin's population was of German origin.

These German-Americans were generally hardworking, well educated, and proud of their heritage. They tended to be pillars of their community, as the group assembled in the Fenchester Auditorium suggests.

"The fury that broke upon the German-Americans in 1915," historian John Higham observes, "represented the most spectacular reversal of judgment in the history of American nativism. . . . In 1908 a group of professional people, in rating the traits of various immigrant nationalities, ranked the Germans above the English and in some respects judged them superior to the native whites." Higham, *Strangers in the Land* (New York: Atheneum, 1978), 196. German immigrants, wrote sociologist Edward Ross in 1914, had "proved, on the whole, easy to Americanize." Edward Alsworth Ross, *The Old World in the New* (New York: Century, 1914), 51.

2. This patriotic German song originated out of conflicts with France in the nineteenth century. It was written by Max Schneckenburger as a call to defend the left bank of the Rhine River against French annexation. Germans often sang it during the Great War.

3. The word *Deutschtum* here refers to the sense of Germanness—its language, culture, and the like—held by ethnic Germans residing in foreign countries.

4. The Germans were extensively organized in local and national societies. According to Robert E. Park's monumental study, the *German-American Address Book* carried entries for 6,586 organizations. These included social and athletic clubs, veterans groups, philanthropic bodies, singing societies, and other cultural clubs. Robert E. Park, *The Immigrant Press and Its Control* (New York: Harper, 1922), 128.

The National German-American Alliance claimed two million members and argued strenuously against the United States going into war. At a January 1915 meeting in Washington, its leaders exhorted members to "bring their adopted country, misled and misrepresented by its newspapers, back to authentic Americanism." Local German-American organizations were urged to recruit speakers to "counteract the influence of the English press."

5. Originally Adams named the character Borst, but Ferris Greenslet at Houghton Mifflin asked him to change it because one of their authors, Sara Cone Bryant, was

married to a German-American by that name. Adams replied, "Sure, I'll change Borst, though with reluctance, as I knew a prize S.O.B. of that name and I wanted to follow him to hell (whither he went last year) with a record of his character. However, that's another sweet dream gone wrong. How would Bausch do for the name, or Balsch? I'm giving you an alternative, as God knows how many other German friends you are cherishing to your official bosom." Greenslet to Adams, September 3, 1918, and Adams to Greenslet, September 7, 1918, Houghton Mifflin Papers (hereafter HMP), Houghton Library, Harvard University.

### Chapter 2

1. In journalistic parlance at the time, a *pippin* was a scoop.

### Chapter 4

1. Adams introduced Socialists into the story to round out the picture of anti-war sentiments. When the American government declared war, many members of the Socialist party balked. Pro-war Socialists bolted from the party. Many volunteered with the CPI. Eugene Debs, a Socialist, ran for president in 1912 and was jailed for speaking out against the war in June 1918.

2. This is a reference to the novel *Kim* by Rudyard Kipling. The hero joins a Tibetan lama who seeks to liberate himself from "the Wheel of Things." The book was popular at the time. It was originally serialized in *McClure's* in 1900 and 1901.

### Chapter 5

1. Journalism instruction was new to universities. The University of Wisconsin, which established a department of journalism in 1910, was one of the first to offer courses.

### Chapter 7

1. Fenchester bears a strong similarity to Madison, Wisconsin. It is the state capital, has an analog to the University of Wisconsin (Kent College), and borders on four attractive lakes, of which Lake Mendota is the largest.

### Chapter 8

1. To many, journalism seemed an unsavory occupation thanks to the sensation-mongering of yellow journals such as those owned by William Randolph Hearst and Joseph Pulitzer.

### Chapter 10

1. Two of the chief targets of muckrakers were utilities and railroads, both of which are portrayed in this novel as taking unfair advantage of citizens.

2. Robert La Follette was short, not tall like Embree. But Adams may have imparted La Follette's confidence and oratorical skills to his Embree.

Chapter 11

1. German language instruction emerged as a contentious issue once the war broke out, as it was viewed as an engine for promoting German culture. In the summer of 1917, the *Wisconsin State Journal* called for the University of Wisconsin to be "Americanized" and questioned the large number of German language instructors. Enrollment in German language classes declined sharply that fall. Elsewhere others sought to legislate against the use of foreign languages. Iowa's governor issued a proclamation requiring that only English be used in schools, church services, on the telephone, and in public spaces. Louisiana went further, passing a law that forbid the use of German in any school. Senator Henry Cabot Lodge wanted to outlaw German language newspapers. Meanwhile books written in German were burned. The New York State Board of Education banned textbooks that contained anything favorable about the German Kaiser. "We are quite sure that the German language now is a hated language, and long will remain so," said the American Defense League.

Chapter 12

1. Department stores then, as now, were among the most important advertisers in daily newspapers.

Chapter 14

1. The children of German settlers in rural Wisconsin were instructed in German in the 1800s. This practice died out by the early twentieth century and ended with the clamp down on German culture during the war.

2. The war years brought an acceleration of efforts to Americanize immigrant groups. One slogan was "100 percent Americanism."

Chapter 16

1. The Germans were ardent, albeit extraordinarily clumsy, propagandists in the United States.

Propaganda efforts were conducted through the German language press, which the Germans subsidized. In 1916 the Germans bought the *New York Evening Mail* through a third party, and also purchased the *International Monthly* and a Jewish newspaper, and maintained an Irish news service. (Irish-Americans were a prime target due to their antipathy of the British.) Behind the scenes they financially sponsored two national movements, the American Embargo Conference and the Organization of American Women for Strict Neutrality.

The impact of German propaganda is disputed. The popular press, much like Robson's *Guardian*, and Congress, in hearings opened toward the end of the war, portrayed German propaganda as well-funded and crafty; revisionist historians claimed German expertise and funding were overstated. What is clear is that Germany shrewdly targeted audiences, including legislators with large German constituencies. In the early months of the war, German propagandists raised public consciousness that war guilt was shared by both sides, and they fed the Anglophobia and distaste for Russian despotism that resided in sectors of the American population.

The Germans were greatly handicapped, however, by the sway the United Kingdom held over the world's communications systems. In the first hours of the war, the British cut Germany's five most important Atlantic cables. This hampered the Germans' ability to send news to the United States. As the war dragged on, the Germans improved their wireless communication, facilitating the transmission of news, which made its way into both German language newspapers and mainstream American ones.

The British, however, continued to enjoy a great advantage. They had had a much easier time getting their message into the American press. They were aided greatly by the insensitive statements made by German officials in the United States. At the same time, they worked quietly to expose much of the German propaganda machinery. The impression in the end was that only the Germans were engaged in such activity.

Chapter 17

1. The reference here is to liberal revolutions that swept across Europe in the mid-nineteenth century. German revolutionaries argued for a pan-German government—instead of the fractured German Confederation—one that would be more democratic and respectful of human rights. When conservative aristocratic elements prevailed, the liberal revolutionaries fled the country. Many of the so-called "Forty-Eighters," who included liberal Czechs and Hungarians who failed in their countries as well, fled to the United States, particularly to Wisconsin. The liberal German Forty-Eighters readily sided with the Union Army in the Civil War, enlisting in such large numbers they constituted almost ten percent of the total force. Forty-Eighter Carl Schurz, a general in the Civil War, was the first German-American elected to the U.S. Senate.

2. This is obviously an editorial stance dear to Adams. His reporting of false advertising at the *New York Tribune* prompted lawsuits similar to those brought against Robson's paper by the Turnbull Brothers. When the Greenhut department store in Manhattan obtained an injunction to block a story by Adams on its merchandizing practices, the *Tribune* ran ads supporting him. One said: "Do you think he writes like a man who could be urged, cajoled, threatened or wheedled into printing, or not printing anything against his desires?"

Chapter 18

1. The German-American press was large and widespread. In 1914, there were 564 such newspapers; French language newspapers, in contrast, numbered only 43. In 1918, only sixteen states did not have a German language paper. The largest concentrations were in Ohio, Illinois, and Wisconsin. At one time Milwaukee had eleven.

Chapter 21

1. The reference here is to the June 28 assassination of the heir to the Austro-Hungarian throne. The Archduke Franz Ferdinand was making a short visit to Sarajevo, Bosnia,

which his country had formally annexed six years before. The assassin, Serb national-ist Gavrilo Princip, stepped out of the crowd and shot twice, hitting the Archduke in the jugular vein and his wife in the abdomen. Within minutes both were dead. With the arch-duke's death, the Dual Monarchy lost one of its strongest proponents for settling interna-tional disputes by diplomacy instead of guns.

## Chapter 22

1. In the first weeks of the war, the Germans enjoyed enormous success, sweeping through Belgium and putting the Anglo-French forces in retreat. "Yesterday was a day of bad news," *The Times of London* reported on August 25, "and we fear that more must follow." At the Battle of Tannenberg, five days later, more than thirty thousand Russian troops were killed.

2. Germany's actions in Belgium were particularly damaging to its image. The German government claimed its invasion of neutral Belgium was an act of self-defense. In October 1915 they needlessly executed a British nurse by firing squad, named Edith Cavell, who had helped Allied prisoners of war escape Belgium. The greatest source of outrage came from the German treatment of civilians, which Allied propagandists magnified. A boost to this propaganda came from an inquiry led by the respected jurist and former ambassa-dor to the United States, Viscount James Bryce. The Bryce report contained lurid, uncor-roborated testimony of German sadism that, as historians note, "exceeded any possible reality." John Horne and Alan Kramer, *German Atrocities, 1914: A History of Denial* (New Haven CT: Yale University Press, 2001), 234.

3. At the outbreak of the war President Woodrow Wilson called for Americans to be "impartial in thought as well as in action." By November 6, 1914, he had issued ten pro-nouncements that outlined measures to promote American neutrality. American sentiment was to stay out the war even if, on balance, it favored the Entente over the Central Powers. A *Literary Digest* survey of newspaper editors shortly after the fighting began found 105 editors sided with the Allies and 20 sided with the Germans, while 242 remained neutral.

## Chapter 23

1. The reference here is to newspaper publisher William Randolph Hearst. In addi-tion to giving attention to the German point of view during the war, Hearst had argued for United States intervention in Mexico.

2. Without warning, a German submarine sank the British passenger liner *Lusita-nia* in May 1915, killing 1,198 passengers, 128 of whom were Americans. The majority of Americans wanted President Wilson to express indignation, but not go to war over the incident. But factions of the country, such as those aligned with former President The-odore Roosevelt, advocated ending neutrality. The incident highlighted how traditional rules of war did not work well in this unprecedented conflict.

The Germans offered several justifications for their actions. First, its embassy in Wash-ington had placed an advertisement in fifty American newspapers warning that the ship could be sunk. Second, the Germans claimed the ship was not simply a passenger liner, but was carrying munitions. The British denied this, but the German charge was correct. Third, the Germans said it was no longer possible (as conventional cruiser rules called for) to give warning that it was launching torpedoes. To make such an announcement the submarine would have to surface and make itself vulnerable to guns, which were being installed on passenger ships.

Another factor that came in play was the British blockade of the North Sea. This was a legally dubious measure because the area was so large and not a site of actual fighting. The cordon stopped food as well as military supplies. After the sinking of the *Lusitania*, Wilson's Secretary of State, William Jennings Bryan, argued both Britain and Germany should be admonished, because the British blockade prevented food from reaching German civilians. He resigned when Wilson addressed only the German action.

Chapter 24

1. This refers to the 1912 election. Wilson's 1912 victory came about in an unusual four-way race among Wilson, the incumbent; William Howard Taft; Theodore Roosevelt, who created the splinter Progressive Party to oust Taft, his handpicked successor in the 1908 race; and Socialist Eugene Debs, whose showing was the largest ever recorded for his party. Wilson won with less than 42 percent of the popular vote, and received one hundred thousand fewer votes than Democratic candidate William Jennings Bryan had in 1908.

2. This is a reference to a resolution introduced by Congressman Jeff McLemore, a Democrat from Texas. The measure would have prohibited Americans from traveling on armed merchant ships in waters German submarines occupied. The goal was to avoid events that could draw the United States into war. Not wanting his hands tied, Wilson pressured Democrats to vote against it. The measure had support from House Republicans who represented Midwestern states with large immigrant populations. It did not pass, but largely thanks to the Republicans, it won 142 votes in the House (276 voted no).

Chapter 26

1. In September 1915, the Germans altered their submarine policy to end attacks on passenger liners. This policy stayed in place until early 1917.

Chapter 27

1. German-Americans were not the only immigrant group to side with the Central Powers: this also included the Irish who opposed British rule; Swedes and Poles who disliked Russia; and Jews who were anti-Russian, pro-German, or both. In addition there were immigrants with Austrian and Hungarian pedigrees who supported the Central Powers.

Chapter 28

1. In such a franchise, a business entity is allowed to, say, build a municipal transport line or utility gas line over which it has exclusive rights to provide service.

2. Masters (1868–1950) was an American lawyer and poet. He was a member of Clarence Darrow's law firm and published *Spoon River Anthology in 1915*, based on his experience in Western Illinois.

3. Charles Evans Hughes ran for president against Woodrow Wilson in 1916. The Wall Street lawyer was catapulted to fame when he headed an investigation of the inflated rates set by the gas and electricity trust in New York in 1905. He subsequently investigated insurance companies whose executives enriched themselves at the expense of policyholders and used policyholders' money to support politicians. Hughes was elected governor of New York in 1906, where he championed progressive legislation that benefited the labor movement, and created public service commissions that became national models. In 1910, President Taft nominated him to the Supreme Court. Following his defeat in 1916, he became Secretary of State under President Warren G. Harding and later Chief Justice of the Supreme Court.

As a presidential candidate in 1916, Hughes failed to adequately manage the war issue. In trying to satisfy disparate factions of the electorate—Republicans who favored war and immigrants who did not—he came across as wishy-washy. In contrast, Wilson benefited for firmly stating he would not be browbeaten by immigrant groups but at the same time wanted to avoid war at all costs.

Chapter 29

1. R. Constantin Theodor Dumba, Austrian Ambassador to the United States, was expelled from the country in 1915. British agents discovered papers that showed he secretly funded propaganda in the United States and sought to incite labor unrest. These papers were passed to the United States government.

Count Bernstorff, the son of a one-time Royal Prussian Foreign Minister, was the German ambassador to the United States. He returned to Germany when Wilson severed diplomatic relations with his government on February 3, 1917. Several of his staff had already been expelled when their ill-conceived plots came to light, as Dumba's had.

Among other things, German spies secretly provoked strikes, crafted financial deals to corner the market on strategic materials, and planted bombs. They also viewed the United States as a launching pad for disrupting the British as far afield as India, Egypt, and Ireland. One of the more fantastic plots was to invade Canada at three or four spots with a force recruited from German-American associations.

2. Such an advertising agency was run by Wolf von Igel, who had ties to German espionage. His office at 60 Wall Street was raided by two Secret Service officers in April 1916. The papers taken from von Igel's safe were given to Adams when he joined the CPI staff in late 1917. As noted in the introduction, Adams used them to write an article that was widely published.

3. Congress created the Council of National Defense in late 1916. It was founded to coordinate industries and resources for national security. The council saw itself performing "a well-nigh priceless function in acting as a sort of official incubator for new ideas

necessary to win a war under modern conditions." After the war began, the Council organized individual state councils that promoted patriotism and patriotic activity.

## Chapter 30

1. German propaganda became an obsession. Any anti-war sentiment was attributed to German influence. Every day newspapers and magazines carried headlines like these: "America Infested with German Spies"; "Spies are Everywhere." The United States government urged citizens to "report the man who spreads pessimistic stories, divulges—or seeks—confidential military information, cries for peace, or belittles our efforts to win the war." By fueling this obsession, the Committee on Public Information was able to dismiss inconvenient facts and opinions as lies planted by Germans, thus making dissent appear traitorous.

## Chapter 31

1. President Wilson called for war against Germany on April 2, 1917 before a joint session of Congress. On April 6, Congress passed the war declaration by votes of 82–6 in the Senate and 373–50 in the House. Wilson signed it that day upon receipt at the White House usher's desk.

## Chapter 37

1. "Timeo Danaos et dona ferentes," literally, "I fear the Greeks even when they bring gifts"—or, colloquially, "Beware of Greeks bearing gifts." The Latin phrase is from Virgil's *Aeneid*.

## Chapter 42

1. Perhaps this "globe-trotter and war correspondent" sprung from Adams's friendship with Will Irwin. Irwin covered the Great War early on. He later worked for the Committee on Public Information. Among other things, he helped organize programs, some through front organizations, to bring immigrant opinion in line with the Administration's.

2. As noted in the introduction, Adams worked with the Four Minute Men unit at the CPI. The advice given to Mrs. Wanser is similar to a statement made by Wilson's Attorney General, Thomas Gregory. A German alien had nothing to fear, he said, "so long as he observes the following warning: 'Obey the law. Keep your mouth shut.'"

3. Many German organizations, as well as newspapers, went out of their way to demonstrate patriotism. The Deutscher Club in Milwaukee renamed itself the Wisconsin Club.

This was necessary for self-preservation. The government clamped down on anti-war speech it considered subversive. Community leaders across the country were supportive of such measures and eager to help enforce them. In an editorial accompanying a Four Minute Man publication, the *Evansville Journal News* said it was the "duty of every American to hold himself ready to fire ammunition at any person who tells any story or repeats any rumor which smacks of German origin."

Samuel Hopkins Adams argued it was acceptable to ignore laws in order to stop unpatriotic speech. In one of his *Everybody's* articles, he cheered Council of National Defense representatives for secretly monitoring German-American saloons and threatening to revoke liquor licenses if patrons derided government policy. "It is by no means certain that this would stand in law," he conceded, "but the Council is more concerned with getting things done."

Of course, not all displays of German-American patriotism were self-serving. Many German-Americans *were* genuinely patriotic, and sent their sons to fight and die in the war. The foreign-born constituted about eighteen percent of the U.S. Army during World War I.

4. The number of German-language newspapers in the United States decreased during the war by about fifty percent. German language instruction in universities diminished, as few students wanted or dared to take it. In 1919, fifteen states barred all instruction in German through the eighth grade. This policy was overturned by the Supreme Court in 1923, but by that time, historian Frederick C. Luebke noted, "Mostly the German-Americans wanted to forget what had happened." Luebke, *Bonds of Loyalty* (DeKalb: Northern Illinois University Press, 1974), 329.